Getting

In Salem

2024

Event Anthology

TL Reeve and Michele Ryan

Catherine Stine

Cedar Rose

L.E. Martin

S.G. Blinn

Anya Bayne

T.A. - GothicMoms

Katie Richard

Kotah Jean

Jennifer Allis Provost

Sarah Zane

Natelie Bartley

Charli Rahe

Colleen Tews

By Bri Eberhart

Ashlyn Chase

Lori DiAnni

Nicole Zoltack

Micca Michaels

Copyright

Anthology Sponsors

Ames Mills

Catherine Stine

Magical Means

S.G. Blinn

Table of Contents

Loving Their Mate

By TL Reeve and Michele Ryan

Blurb

In the three years since Jamie Bishop has returned home, several things have changed. Now, mated to her wolves and safe, after the brutal attack by Mat and the Master, Jamie has other things to worry about—like if her twins will sleep through the night. However, tonight, nothing else matters, especially when she walks into her room to find her mates ready and waiting for her.

For three years, calm has reigned over Salem, but when a new arrival takes a seat in Mass Hysteria, their time for peace might be at an end. They say in Salem everything comes in threes, especially where matings are concerned. But will this recent addition to the community bring prosperity for the pack or will the peace Jamie, Zane, and Cian have created for themselves and those around them crumble at their feet?

Jamie Bishop Kane-Adock stared down at her twin boys as their eyelids lowered, drifting off to sleep. She couldn't believe they were already two years old. Didn't seem possible. She wished she could slow down time, relive all their firsts, again. Even though she realized there would be more, the ache in her chest still longed for those first few months of their lives. If someone would have told her ten years ago moving to Salem would change her life forever, she'd have laughed.

Ten years ago, she'd lost all hope of ever finding her place in life.

Now, she stood in the nursery Cian and Zane built for their sons. Life came at her fast. After one last kiss on their foreheads, she exited the room, closing the door behind her on the way out.

Things in Salem had calmed down since that fateful day when her life turned upside down. She'd started training with Matilda, her aunt, the energy already flowing through her veins like mana from the spirits. Jamie also learned about her ancestors. Being a Bishop came with tremendous responsibilities and even bigger expectations.

Even with a cloud of uncertainty hanging over her, things had settled into a dull roar. Since her battle with Mat, and subsequently, meeting the Master briefly, no other witches had gone missing, nor were there any rifts in the ley lines under Salem. It was as if whatever portal Mat had opened when he attacked Jamie closed the second he died.

Three years later, it still boggled Jamie's mind. She didn't understand all the intricacies of how witchcraft and portals worked. Nor did she understand the Master, but she prepared. Matilda told her the fight wasn't over yet and Jamie believed her.

Still, living with the truth hanging over her head every day was too big of a burden for anyone, so she lived her life to the fullest. Whatever came next, Jamie and her mates would be ready. Which, speaking of her mates...

She quietly padded down the hall to their room and cracked the door. There, on the edge of the bed, sat Zane. His legs spread wide in invitation, and his head thrown back in pleasure. The masculine groan that fell from his lips as Cian played with Zane's balls and sucked the tip of his cock had arousal pulling low in Jamie's belly. Rooted in her spot, she enjoyed the view. Watching her mates take their pleasure together never got old.

In the beginning, she wasn't sure if having bi-lovers would work for her. Then she'd been sandwiched between them as they kissed, and all her worries evaporated. Jamie couldn't properly explain the excitement pouring through her body in that moment. She trembled with need. Her breath hitched as a greedy little whimper filled her throat. Then when the moment came, and they were together, instant combustion. She wasn't embarrassed to say she got off on seeing her mates together or knowing Zane fucked Cian while he fucked her.

Simply put, it was magical.

Since their mating, Cian had grown his hair out. The shoulder-length, dark red, almost auburn, loose curls framed his handsomely rugged features. The couple day scruff he'd kept had become a full beard, enticing her even more. Even the fine dusting of hair on his chest and abs had thickened, and the only explanation she had for his new appearance was the strength of their bond.

Cian reminded her of a lumberjack in his prime and Zane... Fuck, that man had a stranglehold on her libido. Though he kept up a clean-cut appearance for his job as Sheriff of Essex County, when he was home with them, it was as if his wolf pushed forward, turning him into a beast of a man. In the most sexy, delicious way, of course.

"We have company. A little imp who'd rather watch than join us, mate," Zane growled. His left eye popped open, the grey of his iris sparkled with intent while his wolf lurked just under the surface.

Her heart fluttered and her body hummed with electricity. Even the mark on her wrist burned with interest. She wanted her men with a desperation nothing else could rival. She slipped into the room, closing the door behind her, knowing if the twins needed anything, they'd hear the boys through the monitor. Each step she took, closing the distance between them, felt as if she floated on a cloud of desire.

"Her nipples are hard." Cian glanced at her with a small smirk. "Bet her pussy is dripping too."

Her panties were ruined the second she peeked into the room and spotted them. Even now, her clit and pussy ached to be touched. To be filled and fucked until she couldn't walk straight. She exhaled a shaky breath. "You're both overdressed."

Zane still had his sheriff's pants on, and Cian's jeans hanged low on his hips. Their muscular chests and upper bodies were on display for her eyes only. She licked her lips. There was nothing like seeing her mates in their prime.

"So are you, little witch," Zane muttered. "Get that nightgown off and show us what is ours."

A shiver of dominance ran down her spine as she slowly removed the garment, never looking away from her Alpha. His gaze darkened and the wolf lurking within him pushed forward, showing himself to her. The wolf enjoyed their time together, pressing his luck. Occasionally, she wondered if the wolf would take over, changing the dynamic of their mating forever.

Zane's head tilted as his nostrils flared. "What were you thinking about, little witch? What made your pussy go sweet and hot for us?"

Heat filled her cheeks. "Nothing important." She went to her knees in front of Cian and shoved his jeans a little lower before laying across their plush floor rug. The soft fibers tickled her naked flesh, arousing her more. "Your cock is so wet, Cian." She licked his tip then cleaned his shaft, moaning as the spice of his precum hit her tastebuds.

Cian hissed, fisting her hair. "Because we can smell you, little witch." He directed her over his cock, pushing her limits with each bob of her head. His tip touched the soft pallet of her throat, and she swallowed around him. "Fuck, yes. Good girl." Bliss tingled across her skin. She was such a little praise slut. She loved it whenever they called her a good girl or worshipped her body.

"C'mere." Zane tugged at her hair, lifting her off Cian's cock. A thin translucent string of spit followed her until he crushed his mouth to hers in a desperate kiss. The absolute love and desire, spilling from him, turned her burning arousal into a raging inferno. His vicious claiming swallowed her cry of need.

Behind her, Cian gripped her hips, tipping her body to the right angle before pushing deep inside her. "Couldn't wait. Your little cunt was dripping on me."

Jamie was so wet even the insides of her thighs were damp with her juices. Heat suffused her. All her neediness came from watching her mates. The way they played with each other. The way they fucked. Even the sounds they made left her a little simpering bitch in heat. She shivered, desperate for her orgasm to coat Cian's cock in her cum. She wanted to watch Zane clean him, then fuck him hard, like the wolf always demanded of them.

"That's it, girl," Zane moaned. "Fuck him. Get off on his dick. Make him sticky and sweet."

Cian pinched and tugged at her nipples. The burning pain added to the pleasure building within her, coiling her insides. She reveled in their attention. Anticipation for what else they had planned left her breathless and ready for them. With Zane and Cian, she wanted them all the time and ever since having the boys, that craving deepened until she'd been frantic. "Suck his cock, mate."

Cian situated them, so Jamie faced Zane. His long, thick cock bobbed in front of her face, spilling precum from the tip in large drops that rolled down his impressive length, glistening the ruddy, tight skin. Jamie licked her lips. Her mind spun with ideas of what sort of debauched things they could do together before the night was over. Zane guided her mouth over him, pushing every inch he could into her mouth and over the soft pallet of her throat, only stopping when she gagged. He growled, flexing his hips.

Dizziness swamped her as the heady scent of her mate surrounded her. Jamie brushed her nose across the short hairs at his groin. She sucked in air as he pulled back, drawing his cock along her tongue while Cian fucked her in demanding strokes. They were both unhinged, spinning her out of control.

This was what she needed. What she craved from them. Time to turn off her thoughts and focus on them. Jamie floated on the pleasure cascading through her, giving over to both of her mates until the tight coil of bliss within her snapped and she was coming, hard. Behind her, Cian shouted. His pace increased until he was slamming in and out of her at such a pace. He elongated her climax, causing her clit to be sensitive to the point she pleaded for mercy. Above her, Zane hissed. He held her mouth on him while he fucked her throat in short, hurried strokes. The second he orgasmed; she found her release again while swallowing down Zane's cum.

"Fuck," Zane murmured. "We're not done."

She knew that. They wouldn't stop until they collapsed in exhaustion, or the boys needed them. Hopefully, the twins would sleep through the night giving them time to reconnect, which was always hard between their jobs and life getting in the way.

"We're only getting started, mate," Cian said. "I hope you took a nap today."

Jamie stifled a giggle as she climbed up Zane's body and sat on his lap. "Cian has a point. You are getting older, Sheriff. Wouldn't want to hurt you."

Zane growled, snapping at her. "Watch it, little witch." His eyes glowed that eerie shade of yellow and his lip curled, revealing the curved canine of his wolf.

"My, what big teeth you have," she whispered, nipping at his chin.

"The better to eat you with." Zane tossed her on the bed, then removed his uniform pants before prowling toward her. "I'm going to eat you up."

"Promises, promises," she sighed, allowing her legs to fall open, so he got the best view of her pussy still full of Cian's cum.

Jamie ran her finger along her slit, teasing him as much as she did the same to herself. The way his nostrils flared, and his eyes widened before becoming heavy-lidded, made her insides squirm with anticipation. Her heart quickened and her breath came in soft pants, waiting for the moment he'd attack her and make her scream.

When he did pounce, he bit her mark. Jamie screamed, writhing below him as he lined his cock up to her entrance and shoved deep within her. Unlike Cian, who took his time, Zane was unhinged. His thrusts were desperate. Craven. The small sounds he made at the back of his throat, while digging his fingers into her hips, set her on fire. She loved this version of her Alpha. Jamie arched to him, scratching her nails down his back.

Zane hissed. The growl that built in the back of his throat seconds before he bit her again left her a quivering mess. She hooked her ankles over his hips, holding him deep inside her as he fucked her in hard, frantic thrusts. Beside her, Cian caressed her flesh. The lazy grin of satisfaction on his face made her laugh, then groan when Zane thickened within her.

"You look like the cat who got the cream," Cian whispered.

"I've got something," she replied, running her fingernails down Zane's spine.

He hissed. "If you can talk, I'm not fucking you hard enough." He took Cian's mouth in a brutal kiss, nipping at their mate's bottom lip until Zane drew blood.

So hot.

The sob that fell from Jamie drew their attention back to her as she twisted below Zane, taking everything he gave her until she thought she'd shatter into a million pieces. "Please..." Seeing the way Zane dominated, Cian always turned her on. They were sex on a stick together. The pure masculine heat they created set her on fire.

Zane chuckled. "Soon, my little witch." He nuzzled her chin. "You pussy is creaming for us right now. That's so damn hot." His lips brushed across her cheek and the shell of her ear. "Tell me how much you enjoy watching us."

"So much," she whimpered. "Seeing you together makes me come so hard."

Zane groaned. "Are you going to play with our pussy while I fuck Cian?"

"Yes," she answered. "Always."

"Good girl. Now, get off on this dick so I can fill you up." Zane nipped the lobe of her ear before grinding against her in quick thrusts.

Jamie's eyes rolled up. Tension filled her. When Zane ran his thumb over her clit, or maybe it was Cian, she came apart. Jamie shook in her mate's arms as she rode out her climax. There was nothing like being fucked by Cian and Zane when they were in a mood like they were tonight. The second he groaned her name, Zane throbbed inside of her, sending her spiraling as mini sparks of a secondary orgasm snapped across her senses.

"Damn," Cian murmured. "That was sexy as fuck."

Jamie sank into the bedding, gathering her tattered wits as she came down from the best natural high. Zane tucked her into his side as he cuddled her to him. Sandwiched between her mates was the best place to be. A lazy little grin formed on her lips as her eyes drifted closed. When they were ready to start again, they'd rouse her.

Until then, she was content to rest.

****

Shit, they fell asleep.

Zane couldn't believe he left Cian hanging like that. He always made sure both of his mates were satisfied and last night, he neglected his beta. As he stared out the windshield of his cruiser, he thought of a million ways he could make up for the minor indiscretion. He had an idea or several ideas, but one seemed to be the best at the moment.

He pulled up outside Mass Hysteria and parked. As the Sheriff, if he wanted to go off duty for an hour, he could. He called in to dispatch, then exited his vehicle. Since the incident with Mat, things had settled back down in Salem and the quiet was welcomed.

It meant taking a bit more time for himself and his mates. Kind of like he was doing now.

With the parking lot mostly empty, he could sneak in and find his mate. Make up for falling asleep on both Jamie and Cian. Instead of going through the front door, he entered the bar through the delivery entrance. The darkened hallway with red and green neon beer signs greeted him along with the silence. It was still early enough the lunch rush hadn't begun, but he had a feeling once he left Cian, the place would come alive with the midday traffic.

As he came around the corner into the backroom of the establishment, he found Cian on the phone. In his hand was a shipping manifest. Zane frowned. He looked stressed and, if the hurried, harsh tone of his mate was any sign, pissed off. Cian stalked to a darkened corner of the room and Zane followed, keeping his presence unseen.

The bar was supposed to be their non-job. The one place they could have fun. By the scent of annoyance wafting off his mate, there was no fun to be had. Zane couldn't have that. He came up behind Cian, looming over him as hold Muzak filtered from his phone. His mate's shoulders stiffened momentarily before he relaxed, leaning his head back against Zane's shoulder.

He'd been neglectful again.

Seemed like they'd had this conversation before. Between them, they'd concentrated so much on Jamie and the twins. Sometimes they forgot to take moments for themselves. Without saying a word, Zane undid the tab on Cian's pants, then slowly lowered the zipper. He nuzzled his mate's neck, pressing kisses to the mark he'd left there, years ago, reminding Cian not only was he the best damn beta an Alpha could have, but the mate of his soul too.

A grunt fell from Cian's lips when Zane fisted his cock and his hips flexed, pushing deeper into Zane's palm. "This is unexpected."

"Pay attention to your call," Zane said. "Don't want them to know what we're doing."

A soft whimper fell from Cian's lips before he let loose with a shuddered breath. "This is such bullshit."

"I know," Zane murmured. "Just relax and let your Alpha take care of you."

"That's fucking hot."

Zane stroked his mate in long sensual pulls of his fist, using the precum dribbling from Cian's tip to slicken his palm. Behind the zipper of his trousers, his dick pulsed with need and his balls throbbed with arousal. With each stroke, the lust pounding through his veins drove him closer to the brink. The idea of getting caught fucking his mate excited him. Anticipation rolled through his veins. Zane wanted to bend Cian forward and fuck him until neither could walk properly afterward. He shuddered. His heart hammered. The wolf inside of him pushed forward, demanding he take what's his.

"Sorry about the delay, Mr. Kane," the assistant said, cutting off the monotonous music. "It seems the loaders didn't complete your order. We can have the rest to you by late tonight or first thing in the morning. We're sorry for the inconvenience."

Cain swallowed hard as Zane ran the pad of his thumb through the slit of his glans and spread the precum around his mate's tip. "That..." He blew out a breath. "That'll be fine. Thanks."

"Is there anything else I can help you with, Mr. Kane?"

"No... Not at all." Cain didn't even wait for the agent to end the call. He hung up and swung around on Zane. He dropped the paperwork on the floor while shoving the phone back into his pocket. His green eyes turned a shade of golden-hued, just like his wolf. He stalked Zane until he cornered his Alpha. "You."

Zane smirked, fisting Cain's dick once more. "Me?"

"You're proud of yourself." As much as Cian was his beta, they were a perfect match of dominance and brawn.

"Very much so," Zane said with a small chuckle. "You're not angry anymore. Aroused, yes. Desperate for a good fucking? Most assuredly."

"Cocky bastard." He took Zane's mouth in a bruising kiss, growling as he forced his way into his mate's mouth. This was what they both needed. What he should have given Cian last night before he fell asleep. "Take your cock out, Zane."

God damn, he loved when Cian became possessive and unhinged. Their give and take dynamic had only grown since mating Jamie, and in some ways, they both fought to dominate each other. It was almost as if their designation of Alpha and beta didn't matter as much as their mating. Their connection couldn't be denied. "And do what?"

"Fuck me. Now." Cian's gaze darkened. Yearning spilled from his heavy-lidded eyes. "Hard. Fast."

He didn't have to be told twice.

Zane pulled the lube packet from his pocket and placed it between his teeth as he spun Cian around. Before he could tug his mate's jeans down, Cian was rubbing his ass against Zane's crotch. His eyes rolled up and a growl of pure lust filled his chest. Damn him. This was supposed to be his chance to take care of his mate, while Cian seemed content to be Zane's undoing.

He exposed Cian's ass to his pursual before ripping the lube open with his teeth. "Show me your hole. Show me what's mine."

Cain bent forward, spreading his cheeks. The puckered hole twitched under Zane's stare, and he lost more of his control. He squeezed the clear, thick fluid on that tight ring, then used the rest on his cock. Though they were short on time—they could get caught at any second—Zane took his time prepping his mate so that he wouldn't hurt him. Even if they were wolves, it didn't mean he'd tear up Cian's ass.

The second he pulled his fingers from his mate's tight, fluttering hole, Zane pressed his cock there and pushed forward. He bit back, the wild sound filling his throat as the heat of his mate's clenching ass seared Zane's cock. Arousal swamped him. His mind spun and his legs went weak. The tingle at the base of his spine tempted him to give over to the pleasure on the first stroke.

Cain's ass throbbed, sucking Zane deeper, milking him. He pressed his forehead between his mate's shoulders and held steady, taking several deep breaths to center himself. Shoving into his mate's ass was like the first time all over again. The connection between them would never get old. Would never tarnish. If anything, their bond continued to grow and deepen with each passing day.

"Fuck," Zane muttered. "You've got me on edge already."

"Same," Cian huffed. "You got me leaking." He wrapped Zane's hand around his cock. "See."

He was wet, warm, and so fucking hard. Zane flexed his hips before retreating. A groan was ripped from his chest while Cian gasped, pumping Zane's fist faster. The unhinged need to drop his mate and mount him there like his wolf rode him hard. The instinct pounded at the back of his head, demanding he give over to the wolf's demands.

He sucked air between his teeth and closed his eyes. "Hang on." He guided Cian to his knees before taking up the dominant position behind his mate, giving over to the animalistic urge pounding through his veins. This was the way he was supposed to fuck Cian. To remind each of them of their place in their relationship. The minute he re-entered his mate, the wolf yipped at him, commanding him to give over to instinct and rut. The heady sensation overwhelmed Zane, reminding him just how long it'd been since they took this time for themselves. "This is going to be fast."

"Do it!" Cian yelped. "Now."

Zane bent over Cian's back, fucking him with powerful thrusts, forcing animalistic sounds from his throat. He didn't care if they got caught. He and Cain owned the place, and it wasn't like anyone should be in there as it was. Plus, most of their employees were shifters, witches, or some kind of fae creature. The frantic edge creeping in at the corners of his consciousness drove his lust along with his need to prove his mating.

Below him, Cian trembled and babbled while stroking his cock. His ass twitched with each pump of his fist, begging Zane to give him what he wanted. Later, he'd take his time. Suck Cian's dick and eat his ass. Right now, they both needed to come. They needed to satiate the animals inside of them. To rut and fuck until both were limp and well sated.

"Zane... Please," Cian whimpered.

The muscles in Cian's shoulders stood out against his taut flesh, tensed by expectation. Zane wanted to lick each one of them. Bite them. Mark them. Cain's body was his. His to fuck. To love. To cherish. He couldn't stop his impending climax, nor did he want to. Zane latched onto the mark he left there on Cain's neck and when the tingle of his release spread through him like an inferno, he bit down, sending both crashing over the edge.

Cian's ass cinched up on Zane's erection, causing him to see stars. The splat of Cian's release hitting the floor was just as arousing as feeling him milk Zane's cock, encouraging the flow of his release. He didn't know how long they stayed in that position, or how long he continued to throb within his mate, nor did it matter. He'd stay right there until he physically had to move.

"Boss? You in there?" *Gideon*. Zane closed his eyes and let out a huffed silent curse. "There's a situation up front."

Cain grunted as Zane pulled out. "Give me five. I've been on the phone." He stared straight into Zane's eyes and a sparkle of mischief and relief filled those glorious green eyes of his.

"Right. Can do."

They'd been so caught up in each other, Zane hadn't even heard the other wolf approach. And Jamie's brother, to boot. Slowly they gathered themselves, righting their clothing. Cain grabbed a rag from somewhere and cleaned up the mess he made on the floor. A part of Zane hated that. He wanted everyone to know it was him that made his mate lose control.

To leave his mark behind.

Staring at his mate, a bubble of laughter filled his chest. They had to be the most ridiculous mates ever. Always taking chances.

Always pushing the envelope. He kissed Cian, then nipped his bearded chin. "I'll see you tonight."

Cian growled. "Damn right. You owe me a dick sucking and ass eating."

Zane tilted his head. Hadn't he said those things to himself? Not out loud?

"You said it," Cian teased. "My dick's already twitching at the idea."

"Insatiable," Zane muttered before kissing him again. "See you tonight, mate."

"Tonight, it is," Cian said. "I'll let Jamie know the plan so she can watch."

Zane grunted. Damn, he loved his mates. Especially when they were being cheeky with their Alpha. "Then you better be spread and ready when I get home."

As he stepped out into the early afternoon sun, the weight on his shoulders eased. Yet, even as he inhaled the warm summer air, there was still this undercurrent of something coming. He couldn't put his finger on what it could be nor erase the idea of the Master watching them, even though they hadn't seen hide nor hair of the ghastly being. Still it was as if the unnatural being waited for the right moment to strike. They knew three years ago he would return. All Zane hoped was that they'd be prepared for whatever the Master had in store for them.

Until then, he slipped into his patrol car and grinned. He had the one thing the Master didn't. Love and family. Nothing could destroy that. Because love was the strongest magic in the world.

****

Samuel Porter stepped into Mass Hysteria and took a seat at the bar. This was his first day of freedom. The first time he'd been alone in, well, he couldn't remember. He glanced around the bar, taking in all the little details. From the fire salamanders in the wood stoves to the brownies cleaning the smallest corners of the business. There were many types of creatures lurking within those four walls.

Glancing over his shoulder, he spotted two men at the pool tables, laughing about something while drinking a beer. He wondered what it was like to be so free without a care in the world. Though he might not appear abused and defiled, the magic cast around him hid those unsightly scars that never seemed to heal fully and always seemed to fester. He wasn't a wolf like those he'd been sent to infiltrate. He wasn't even sure he was a witch. If he was one, why didn't he have the power to stop the Master from torturing him hour after hour. Day after day?

Samuel glanced down at his wrist. The star and crescent moon. He'd had it for as long as he could remember, though he never understood why it made him special in the eyes of the Master. If he expected the magical being to explain, he didn't. Only telling Samuel he'd be the one. The chosen. What for or why, Samuel supposed he had to figure that out yet.

"What can I get you?" A man with shaggy brown hair and the greenest eyes he'd ever seen, asked.

Samuel couldn't speak. He swallowed the dry lump in his throat trying to comport himself, so he didn't look like a fool or raise suspicions. "I-I don't know. What's good here?"

The man grinned. "House special. It's an IPA called *Witchy Woman.* Cian and Zane, the owners, came up with it. I think you're going to like it."

Samuel nodded. "Sure. Sounds great." He licked his bottom lip, fearing he'd never fit in with those around him. If only they knew his true assignment and why he was there. Then again, if he blurted the truth, would it end his suffering quicker? The thought had merit. After all, if he went back to the Master empty handed, he was dead. If he took his life or gave himself to the pack of wolves governing the area, they'd make his death a quick and relatively painless one.

"Enjoy." The bartender said, placing the pint in front of him. "If you need anything else, I'm Gideon."

Samuel nodded, staring at the orange and yellow beer with glittery froth. "I'm Samuel. I just moved to town."

"Well, Samuel," Gideon said, flashing him with a brilliant smile. "Welcome to Salem. I hope you enjoy your time here."

If only Gideon knew the truth, he wouldn't be so friendly to Samuel. He took a sip of the beer and grinned. Gideon was right. It tasted pretty good. There was a hint of fall in the drink, like pumpkin or clove and something citrus. There was also a trace of sweetness on the back of his tongue along with heat. None of the flavors should have worked together, but they did.

Maybe the beer was a sign. Perhaps he was supposed to be in Salem for a reason other than for the Master. *Wouldn't that be something?* He snorted to himself at his fanciful thoughts while finishing the pint. No, Samuel was never that lucky.

If he had been, he'd already be dead.

About the Authors

TL Reeve, a bestselling, multi-published author, was born out of a love of family and a bond that became unbreakable. Living in Alabama, TL misses Los Angeles, and will one-day return to the beaches of Southern California to ride the waves at Huntington Beach. When not writing something hot and sexy, TL can be found curled up with a good book or spending quality time with her college-bound daughter.

Michele Ryan is a multi-published author. She embraced her creative passion and co-authored several books with fellow author TL Reeve. Michele has also published two solo novellas. Michele is a lifelong resident of the state of New Jersey, along with her husband and three children, whom she refers to as her hobbits. When Michele is not plotting or writing, she can be found either volunteering at her children's school or reading.

Read More from TL Reeve and Michele Ryan

http://www.apachecountyshifters.com/

Until Ireland (Aurora Reynold's Until series)

Until Waverly (Aurora Reynold's Until series)

Until Posey (Aurora Reynold's Until series)

Welcome to our Window Rock Universe

<u>Apache County Shifters</u>

Kalkin

Caden

Rapier

Osirus

<u>Becoming Alpha – An Apache County Shifters sub-series</u>

Salvation – Apache County Mates/Rejected Mates #1

<u>TSU Series</u>

Unrequited Mate

Alpha's Mates – formally Sorority Row

Bearing It All

Let It Ride

Silence Isn't Golden

<u>TSU After Dark</u>

On The Air

Revelations (BTS Halloween)

Lupercalia (BTS Valentine's Day)

Martyrs (BTS Ruined)

<u>Psychic Retrieval Agency</u>

Midnight (BAD Bad Alpha Dad)

Fallen Protector (BAD Bad Alpha Dad/Fallen Angels)

Misfits

<u>Leaving the Past Behind</u>

Unbreakable

Entrapped

Lost and Secrets

Shattered

Blackmailed

<u>Black Ops: Project R.O.O.T (Running Out of Time)</u>

Rule Breaker

Extracting Mateo

Jaqueline's Quest

Exploiting AJ

Betraying Bex

Blind Justice

Counter Strike: Schoell's Contract

Silver Bullet

Soldier, Tailor, Spy

Black Ops: Project R.O.O.T. Second Chances

Finding Fawn

Salem Wolves

Mating Their Witch

Loving Their Witch – super short

Simon Hadley Files

Twisted Solstice #0.5

Haunting Salem #1

Susan Stokers Special Forces Police and Fire Badge of Honor Tarpley VFD series

Fighting for Brittney

Fighting for Amanda

Warrior's Passion – Gods of Thunder MC

Apollo-G Not Necessary – Gods of Thunder MC

Gentleman Sadist – Suspenseful Seduction World

Amnesia: Shift Happens Anthology

Bred: A Charity Anthology

In the Heat of The Moment: Charity Anthology

<u>FILO – First in Last Out</u>

Tainted Blood

Tainted Christmas

<u>Coming Soon</u>

Jace – Apache County Shifters #5

Until Always (Aurora Reynold's Until Series)

The Magic Foxes

Catherine Stine

Kai ran and ran and ran, crashing deeper into the southern pine thicket. The crackling of twigs and thrashing in the underbrush right behind had her heart pounding in her throat. Why was this Dr. Laura woman forcing her at gunpoint into a remote pine forest? No towns around for miles. Kai didn't dare ask. Why had Laura taken a leashed fox with her? Was its damn tame behavior a surface ruse? Would the genetically altered animal tear her apart? Bolts of hard panic thundered through Kai. Laura had seemed so vanilla, so logical, with her orderly kennel of foxes all documented and labeled. How had the visit to Laura's research farm spun so fast to hellish? What did she want with Kai? Was Dr. Laura jealous of her yet-unpublished research? Did she intend to kill her and steal it?

Kai raced through the forest, and prayed her visit wasn't a lethal mistake. The genetically altered fox at her heels might be mild-mannered, but Laura was surely a sociopath. Kai made a sudden dodge to the right.

"Hey! Keep straight," Laura barked as the fox yipped excitedly. "March, don't run."

Kai followed orders and slowed to a steady march, Laura's gun a visceral heat on her back. Stumbling over rocks and exposed roots had Kai cursing under her breath for offering Laura a ride. Fitfully, she reviewed earlier events. As if it might reveal a way out.

They'd been driving on Route 47 to Echo Falls past this forest with no one for miles when Laura abruptly grabbed the wheel and forced it to the right, sending the car into a tailspin. It careened onto the rocky shoulder, just missing an orange post with one of the small historical markers she'd seen along the way. "Hey! What the fuck do you think you're doing?" Kai had shouted, trying to regain control.

"Stop the car. Now!" Laura pried Kai's hands off the wheel. The fox in the back screeched like a siren.

When Kai tried to grab the wheel again Laura pulled out a pistol and leveled it at Kai's head. "Take your pack with your research notes and get out now!"

Kai stumbled over fallen pine trees and clawing pricker bushes and tried to make sense of what made no sense. Tried to figure out who this Laura was and what she could possibly want without actually asking her. A gun was aimed at Kai's skull. If she angered this bitch or distracted her, Laura could fire the bullet.

"Go!" Laura kept yelling at Kai. "Go!" This followed by the fox's piercing yips.

If Kai could unravel the events that had transpired even before the scary car ride she might see more hidden clues. Earlier that afternoon she'd visited the farm where people bred foxes for continuous domestication studies. Kai, as a veterinary researcher, was familiar with such studies. She and Brien, her former partner had conducted bioengineering and selective genetic breeding experiments. After this tour, she said she was headed to Echo Falls for the night, and Laura, one of the breeders asked if she could hitch a ride.

Laura had a slim fox on a leash with a pointed snout and eerie blue eyes that seemed to study Kai in the car mirror. Laura had tied the leash to Kai's headrest in the back. Kai thought it was strange to see a fox wag its cottony tail like a dog and lick a human's hand. It was one of the ones bred over and over for friendliness to humans. She had peered with curiosity but also trepidation in the rear-view mirror at the thing as she drove, bracing for needle sharp canines to sink into her neck. Though the fox had stayed mellow enough as it sniffed the air through the slice of opened window.

***

Now, after marching twenty more minutes deeper into the pine thicket, and with no clues gleaned from her memories Kai went icy with panic. Escape was futile.

"Keep walking!" Laura pushed her with the muzzle of the gun.

Bravery was born of fear that Kai would die in here and her body would never be found. "What do you want with me?" She stopped to twist around and peer at a scowling Laura, who raised the pistol between Kai's eyes. "Where are you taking me and why?" Kai persisted.

"Get going. *Backwards.*" Laura wagged the firearm impatiently.

Kai's last memory before she was shoved into a deep pit was of the fox's wet nose snuffling while its cold, sentient eyes regarded her.

***

Kai's back was killing her. Her eyes were swollen shut and the breath knocked out of her. She groaned as she tried to shift position, stretch her legs. One leg wasn't working right and hurt like hell. Broken?

When she opened her eyes, she feared her brain had been bashed so hard she'd become delusional. The sight in front of her was too nonsensical— a comical horror show—to be real life. A hunchback, facing away from her was stirring a pot of foul-smelling liquid. Male or female, she couldn't tell. Facing her in a line on the other side of the trench were five red foxes. No regular beasts, these were elongated and standing tall on their hind legs. Stranger still, they wore embroidered purple capes and held rods in their elongated paws. They glowered at her, not with foxes' snarls, more like disdainful judges.

"What the hell?" she roared. The hunchback, ignoring her, wore a likeness of Laura's yellow sweater and black yoga pants. "Laura? Is that you? What the goddam hell! I'm talking to you!"

The hunchback turned. Indeed, it looked like Laura but a Laura who had aged terribly and swiftly into some sort of bark-skinned hag. No gun in her hand at least. There was that. If Kai could walk on this broken leg… if she could slink away, she could struggle out of this sinister forest.

"Shut up," warned Old Laura. "You think you're so high and mighty. Well, the time has come to be judged." Her lips curled into a rotten grin. "But first, a drink of the Black Sighted Tea." She scooped up a ladleful of dark, sour-scented liquid and handed the cup to Kai. Kai's hand went up, ready to bat it away. "Don't even think about smashing things." Old Laura's brows crossed over her hooded eyes. "If you do, you'll be judged quite harshly." Her tone warmed slightly. "Girly, this tea will make you feel special." With that, the foxes actually started to snicker, like hiccupping deviants.

This scared Kai more than anything. In her own fox experiments she had not achieved a cackling fox with a superior attitude. "Why should I follow your orders?" She tried one more time to resist. "You have no gun. You can't hold me here."

"Oh, don't I?" Old Laura pushed her hand in her pocket and pawed around with a menacing sneer.

One of the foxes stepped forward and wagged his carved wooden rod at Kai's legs. Chains manifested around her ankles and a padlock around each clasp snapped shut. He scowled, looking more like an irate man than any fox. Kai struggled against the chains, but her injured leg cramped with such horrid pain she fell back, wincing. Was this fox's rod a dark magic wand or what? "You criminals!" Kai hissed. "You'll pay!"

Old Laura came forth and pressed the cup to Kai's lips. "Open your trap and drink, girly." The hag forced Kai's jaw open and poured the tarry liquid down her throat.

Kai gagged and swallowed. This was no regular English Breakfast; this shit was gritty mud. She could only pray she might talk them into unlocking the damn chains. She imagined finding Laura's gun or stealing one of the fox's rods and beating them all to bloody pulp with it.

Except the Black Sighted Tea had its own plan.

Kai sank into a dizzying reverie of moving images. She was back on her own farm, with her husband, Brien, a fellow researcher, and they were feeding the foxes. Happy, easy times, when the first litters of white foxes were born from their Siberian starter set. When she and Brien were still in love, before his affairs, before he grew sullen and spent more and more time in his DIY barn lab. Before they finalized their cutting-edge DIY agenda.

Kai's reverie was on the verge of turning sour like the foul black tea on her tongue. Her inner scene was as scary as the one outside, and she realized she'd closed her eyes, as if shutting it out could eliminate it like spot remover eliminated an oil stain from a shirt.

She opened her eyes and blinked at the weird scene now playing out. The caped foxes were seated at a judge's table, and each held a gavel. Old Laura presided as the prosecuting lawyer, pacing back and forth with the opening argument.

"This woman is guilty of torture, your honors. Guilty of multiple murders as well."

"You're out of your mind," Kai muttered. "Or am I?"

The long table of fox judges all paused to drink the Black Sighted Tea from dainty china cups set before them. Old Laura sipped hers too, from the adjacent table piled with papers.

Papers with familiar handwriting. Kai's papers from her backpack! With a wave of helpless outrage, she saw her opened pack slung over the prosecutor's chair. "Those are my research papers!" Kai shouted.

"My research now!" Old Laura launched into rude chuckles and the foxes joined in.

Lunatics! Thieves! Kai's spirits sank to her feet. But how could one reason with nightmares?

"Tell the jury what you did with the Siberian foxes." Old Laura glared at Kai.

Why should I, bitch? You kidnapped and drugged me!

"Tell the jury now!" Old Laura screamed, her haggard face reddening. She pulled out a thin wand, not a gun from her pocket and wagged it at Kai.

Kai's breath caught. She'd seen what the fox had done with his wand. "It was Brien's idea," she mumbled.

"Don't blame it all on him," Old Laura warned. "That will get you cursed."

Though Kai had been a woman of science, not magic this threat was terrifying. She'd never put stock in the supernatural, and yet dark magic was everywhere. Kai glanced down at her ankle chains, then back up at Old Laura. "We were curious about body modification through genetic engineering is all. Could a fox be a guard dog? Could a fox be an icon of…?"

"Of what?" queried one of the foxes in a sharp, reedy voice.

Jurists don't talk. What kind of trial is this? Oh, yes, a sham one. Somehow, this calmed Kai down. Perhaps as soon as this delirium tea left her system this whole dreadful mirage would dissolve into clouds. Maybe her leg wasn't even injured. Maybe she would magically spin back to the time before the backward fall into this pit, and before Laura took the wheel from her with a savage lunge.

"The jurist asked you a question," barked Old Laura. "Answer it!"

"An icon of fashion and beauty."

"By whose standards?" asked a different fox jurist.

Kai gave a sardonic huff then glanced down at her trendy pink boots. "Whose do you think?"

Old Laura reached out and slapped Kai. "No sass, lady."

Kai's head jerked back. Her cheek was already hot and swelling. "*My* standards. The fox was beautiful; pink fur, pink eyes, a pink tail as fluffy as a Hollywood boa."

The line of fox jurists *tsked tsked* loudly.

"Were there any bad side effects?" asked a third fox jurist.

Yes, Kai recalled some. But she was reluctant to admit any. As if these strange, humanized fox jurists would fling off their purple capes and attack her, canines bared.

"I didn't hear you!" Old Laura bellowed. "Speak up!"

"Okay, okay. They had trouble peeing. The tint somehow leeched into their bladders. We treated them and gave them medicines. It helped," she added with twinges of guilt and defensiveness. It hadn't actually cured them.

"And the foxes bred to be guard dogs?" asked Old Laura, twirling her wand. "Describe the gene editing. What did you add? How did it manifest?"

Kai was a little dizzy. From the weird tea or the slap? "We enhanced their eyes. Put scanners in. Enhanced their teeth. Engineered them to have canines and claws twice the normal length. Ones that burst out when they scented fear, home invaders, and the like." She was dizzy but also proud and spurred to righteous anger. This Old Laura freak wasn't perfect. Far from it. "What's wrong with that? How is your breeding any better? You breed for the foxes to be all cuddly and kissy with humans. But what if they don't want to be? Who the heck do you think you are, Old Laura?"

"Shut up! I'm the prosecutor and I ask the questions, not you!" Old Laura stirred the cauldron of Black Sighted Tea, its stench as sour as charred turnips.

She ladled out a second dose and gripped Kai's chin, forced her mouth open and poured the crap down her gullet. Kai choked, and spit out what she could, but the magic tea was already working a more profound spell.

The next time Kai opened her eyes the foxes had shucked off their jurist robes and stalked toward her, turning into the white Siberian foxes she had experimented on. But not the successful test cases. The shocking variations, accidents, tragedies. There were two pink fox aberrations with horribly distended bellies and swollen paws. With kidney and liver damage from impacted bowels. There were foxes with blackened snouts unable to close because infected stubs of canines and incisors had made the flesh rot and swell. Two more foxes engineered to attack approached, one with burst eyeballs and another eyeless, when the nano computer programs in them had crashed.

Abruptly, dozens of foxes padded out of the forest and toward her. One spoke: "You killed us when the experiments failed and—"

"I was angry at my cheating husband!" Kai exclaimed.

"So, your precious Brien cheated on you," one sneered. "You could have just left him. Instead, you set fire to the whole farm and did not have the heart to set us free first. What did we ever do to you? How dare you destroy us because your bioengineering experiments failed miserably."

"How dare you!" the foxes snarled.

I had to kill you all. I was ashamed of our DIY failures. But her pride kept her quiet.

Dozens of sentient eyes scowled at Kai, and dozens of wet muzzles snuffed at her. Then they switched focus to Old Laura, turning their growls to where she stood by the fire. "And you! Don't think you're so innocent! Who said we want to be loyal slaves to you? Led around by our necks on leashes? We are the natives here! The true indigenous beings."

"Malarky. You are beasts, not humans," Old Laura mumbled. She trembled as she took dry sticks and lit them, spreading flames to the table where Kai's papers were piled.

"What are you doing, you sociopath?" wailed Kai.

"You should talk!" Old Laura screeched back.

The blaze leapt toward Kai, carried on dead leaves, fallen branches. Kai struggled against the manacles, but they held firm. The foxes stayed behind the jurist table, inexplicably free of fire.

The irony was that Old Laura went up in flames first, followed by Kai, still flailing against her ankle chains.

No one was there to witness the foxes' escape.

Rising smoke could be seen billowing from the forest and anyone within earshot could have heard the raucous whoops of the magical foxes.

The historical marker at road's edge, where the car had crashed, grew clusters of odd black flowers around its base every spring. The text on the sign that Kai had not had time to read seemed to take on a glow as time went on.

The Black Sighted Tea Ceremony was held deep in these woods from 1600 to the mid-1700s. It was said to be the first of the Indigenous Tribal council remedies for injustice.

Not in Kansas Anymore

By Cedar Rose

Author Note

This is a dark why choose fairytale retelling. There are some triggers.

Non-con

Stalking

Guns

Drugs

And probably others

Verity

Years ago, a wicked witch entered my life and took everything from me.

She broke up my parents, took my dad, even took my beloved dog—all because she didn't like me, or so that's the rumor.

I don't remember much about my parents, though I do remember loving a little dog. Just like every other little girl, I just wanted to be loved. To have parents that would love her.

And I have been loved. Even when I acted out, or threw teenage temper tantrums; my aunt and uncle loved me as one of their own.

On one birthday, I went to a psychic, wanting to know what my life would become, or what could have been. It was a joke, but it always stuck with me—to be perfect for them. I didn't want them to give up on me like my parents did.

From that day forward, I took to farm life like I needed it.

And just like today, mornings always come early. I'm always up before my alarm.

Cracking open my eyes, I see that the sun isn't shining. A storm is coming. Not unusual, but around here, that means tornados. It's the season for destruction.

Sighing, I roll out of bed and shower, dressing in clothes to take care of the animals. Work is dirty around here. But I can't complain. My aunt and uncle took me in when I had nowhere else to go. I'm not even sure what really happened to my parents. No one has ever told me. But Aunt Mavis and Uncle Dean really love me like one of their own. My cousins live on the back of the property, along with the farmhands. Aunt Mavis hopes that one day they'll marry and make babies. Every time she brings it up, they scowl, and I have to laugh. And then it always gets turned around on me.

They want me to find a good man to take me away from all of this, but I can't see myself leaving. I love working on the farm, even though it's hard work. People depend on us. I like that. It's important to the community.

The smell of bacon hits my nose as I open my bedroom door, and in response, my stomach grumbles. Aunt Mavis is cooking up a storm, just like she does every morning.

She smiles as I walk in. "Sleep good?"

I give her a nod as I pull out a mug for coffee. "I did. My new mattress is comfortable."

She pats my arm. "I'm glad. The old one should have been thrown out years ago. You deserved a new one."

I had been sleeping on the same mattress since I moved in with them, and even though I like this one, I kind of miss the old one. Memories and all.

Right as I take a seat at the table, my oldest cousin, Teddy, comes in the side door. "Morning, Mama."

She looks up and points her spatula at him. "Wipe your boots."

I snort, because it's the same thing every morning, and his response is to always try to ruffle my hair as he passes me to get some coffee.

"Dad is mending the fence, but he'll be up in a minute. Jessup and Jordan will be a few minutes later." He pours his cup and then takes a seat at the table. Jessup and Jordan are twins, and have that weird twin power thing. It drives me crazy sometimes, but they are the best older cousins a girl could ask for. In high school, they got into a few fights on my behalf. They have always had my back.

Aunt Mavis sets the plates down on the table, piled high with sausage, eggs, bacon, biscuits with gravy, some toast, and grilled tomatoes. It all looks good, and before I even take a bite, Teddy is done.

I start laughing at him. "Slow down, man. You'll get indigestion."

He grins. "Can't help it. Mom cooks the best food."

Aunt Mavis laughs. "Stop buttering me up. I'll leave you some in the fridge."

He smiles at her and kisses her cheek on the way to wash his dishes. "You're the best. Verity, can you feed the cows and pigs?"

Picking up my plate, I make my way to the sink to wash my own dish. "Sure thing." I love hanging with the animals on the farm. The cows are for milk, and the pigs are almost like pets. We just have them to have them. Each year we end up with another random farm animal, and while Uncle Dean gets mad, he loves them. He won't admit that out loud, though.

Picking up a bucket of oats from the barn, I head out to the trough and pour it in. Once I've done that, I grab the alfalfa feed and shred it. None of the cows are in sight, but they'll find their breakfast in their own time. I grab another bucket of fruit that I picked up in town yesterday, and chop it up for the two cutest piggies in the state. I'm biased though.

It's like they hear me coming, and as soon as I'm at the gate, they're waiting, nudging my leg as I enter their enclosure.

"I'm here, I'm here. You won't starve."

They have their own bowls, and I put the oats and fruit in there. They go crazy, and I'm soon forgotten as I exit to put the bucket back in the barn.

"Oh, Verity, can you do me a favor?" Uncle Dean catches me on my way out. He must finally be getting to breakfast.

"Sure."

He smiles and pats my shoulder. "Can you take the delivery to Destin today? I know it's a four-hour drive, but I need the guys here to start preparations for the storm. You should be there and back before it hits, but if it does, just use the credit card and stay at a hotel."

"You look tired, Uncle. You need to eat before Auntie gets upset. I'll take the delivery. I'll go shower again and change and be on my way."

He kisses the top of my head. "Best niece ever."

I giggle. "I'm your only niece, but I'll take it." We walk in silence back to the house and I have to hold in my laughter as my aunt gets on him about taking care of himself. *Same stuff, different day.*

This time I shower quickly, knowing I need to get on the road. I'm glad it's still early. By my calculations, I'll get there around noon, and hopefully be back on the road by two, which means I'll be back in bed watching Netflix by six with a plate of dinner. Not too bad.

Pulling on some jeans with a black tank top, I wrap a white and black flannel around my waist and slide on some silver converse. After braiding my hair, I'm ready. As I bound down the stairs, Aunt Mavis hands me a bag which is probably filled with snacks. "For the road."

"You're the best!" I hug her and grab the keys to the small van I'll be using today. I'm only going to a small grocery store and then stopping at a roadside stand, which is why it should only take a couple hours to offload.

"Drive safe." Aunt Mavis waves and I return it.

Plugging in my phone, I make sure to put on my playlist. I'm thankful that Uncle Dean got a new van that comes with Bluetooth. I like to jam out on the road.

After a quick stop at the local gas station for a drink, I'm on my way.

Verity

After parking by the back door of Niel's Grocery Store, I stretch. I made good time, only speeding a couple of times.

A knock on my window startles me, and I turn to see Matt, the owner's son. "Sorry," he tells me.

I open the door and slide out. "It's okay. I was lost in thought."

He smiles and opens the back door to start hauling in the boxes I have for them as his father steps out.

"You're pretty brave to deliver today," Niel states.

I glance up at him. "Uncle says I'll beat the storm home."

He signs the paper, and with a nod, heads back inside. Niel doesn't talk much, but he's a good man. He's never been mean to me or my family. He's just a gruff guy, and I have gotten used to it.

"He worries about everyone," Matt comments, solidifying my thoughts.

"I know. You good?" I ask as he shuts the back door.

"Yep, drive safe."

I give him a two-finger salute and turn the van toward the highway. I already stopped at Mr. Lazzo's stand, so I will be home before I know it.

But that's not my luck today.

About an hour into my drive back, the skies darken, the rain starts, and the wind starts blowing. *The storm is coming.*

I pull over to the side of the road and climb into a ditch, trying to wait it out. I've been through these before, so this is nothing new. But I'm still scared.

The car is off, my phone doesn't have service due to the storm, so the only sound is the howling wind.

I stare out the window as a huge twister comes barreling down the road. I can only hope it will pass me by.

I close my eyes and pray.

Draven

I sit at the back of the club just watching. I don't get a hard-on for the flesh that crawls through this club. I like a different type of woman.

"Lap dance?" a girl asks, and I wave her off. I have more important things to be doing.

"Seventy-five, and that's the best I have to offer," the man across from me says, leaning back in his seat, taking a drink of his beer. I don't need his money. I just needed him to take a drink. But I'll take it.

"Seventy-five thousand is a deal. I'll have it delivered. Sign right here." I pass him a paper, and he signs it. After, I bid him good night and walk right out of the club. In a few minutes, he'll be having a heart attack that he won't survive. *Sometimes it's good to be me.*

Some would call me insane. I probably am. Blood and gore gets me all excited. I just like the color red. My mother called me Draven and it's fitting I think. It means hunter and I do hunt. It's not like I go around killing anyone and everyone, but when someone does me wrong, I love making them bleed. Maybe it's about hearing the screams or seeing the life drain from their eyes. And while I love making the floors run red, I love the chase, the hunt more. Maybe it's the excitement of what's to come after I've caught them.

I walk down the block back to my car and drive the loop back to my home. Out of the corner of my eye, I watch in wonder, yes wonder, as a tornado appears by Mount Charleston. And something is shot out of the tornado. *What the fuck?*

I guess home will have to wait.

Verity

Screeching metal and wind blowing has me wishing that I was dead already. There is no way I'm going to survive this.

As soon as I think that, the van falls to the ground. My head hits the steering wheel, and I'm out for a few minutes. When I come to, the wind is gone, and I realize that I'm alive.

"I'm alive," I squeal. *But where am I?*

The van starts back up like we were never in a tornado, and I point it in the direction of the road, or what I think is the road. I just need to find lights or something to help me get home. A working phone or something.

The road, when I do find it, is dark, no cars. I drive through the switchbacks until I reach a small store with lights on. When I exit the car, I head inside, hoping to find a phone. What I do find is a man like no other. He puts models to shame.

I grab a few things, like snacks and drinks. "Umm, do you have a phone I can borrow?"

He shakes his head. "Sorry, no phone. But if you keep heading east, you'll hit Vegas."

My heart drops. "Vegas?"

He nods. "Yep. A little lady like you will want to be careful, though. Lots of weirdos."

He said Vegas. Where my dad is. The one person I don't want to talk to.

I thank him and pay for my things and when I walk outside, I see another man too hot for words putting gas in my van.

"Umm, hello?"

He turns around. "Someone can't go without gas for too long. You heading to Vegas?" I nod.

"Might want to be careful."

Totally mystified by these interactions, I drive away. *Weirdos.*

But they did tell me that Vegas was close. I've never been to Sin City. I just know that's where my father lives with his new wife. I don't know what happened to my mother, but from little snippets I picked up from behind-the-door conversations, I found out that my father remarried, and she was jealous of everyone that threatened her way of life. She was threatened by me, by my uncle, and by my mother, who was my father's true love, supposedly. I do know that my dad wanted to reach out to me, but his new wife threw a fit.

Hopefully, I can find a phone, a room for the night, and then get out of Dodge. At least my van is still working.

The engine sputtering shakes me from my thoughts. I look down at the dash and try to start my van again.

"No, no, no, no."

Pounding the steering wheel in frustration does nothing to help. I guess I'm walking. Uncle Dean will be upset, but he'll understand.

I don't know how long it's going to take, but I have to do it.

It's dark, and I pull my flannel on to comfort me, not to keep me warm—it's warm here already. I just need the comfort. It feels like a hug, reminding me of home. Even if I'm just going down the road, I wear one to remind me of my aunt and uncle.

Okay, I can do this. Follow the road, and hopefully it leads me to somewhere.

It's so quiet, I can actually hear my own thoughts. I mean, there's a slight breeze and a rustle of bushes every once in a while.

A twig snapping has me stopping in my tracks until a small puppy wanders out.

"Oh, are you lost, too? You can come too. We'll find you something to eat as soon as we can."

The puppy follows me and I like having company. It makes this journey easier, even though the puppy can't hold an actual conversation. I kind of wished one of my cousins would have come along.

Just one foot in front of the other.

I don't know how long I've been walking, but soon the road comes to a fork. The lone street lamp is giving off ominous vibes, but it's what sitting on top that makes me do a double take.

On top of the street lamp, perched like he belongs, there is a man. A lone man in a dark hoodie. I can't see his face, and I don't know how he got there, but maybe he can give me directions.

"I'm so sorry, I don't mean to bother you, but which way to Vegas?" Looking down both roads, neither gives me a sense of relief, but again, I'm by myself.

"You could go that way," he says, and as I glance up at him, he drops to the ground like a crazy person. If I would have done that, I would have ended up in the hospital. *Maybe he's not human?*

I still can't see his face, but once he stands to full height, I realize he's tall, and very built. *How do I know he's built?*

His hoodie is open, unzipped, revealing a chiseled chest—a chest you would find on the cover of magazines.

Stop ogling the crazy guy. Focus!

"Or you could go that way." He points the other way. *Fucking assholes around here, I tell you.* The other ones told me I need to be careful, like I don't already know to do that.

And then this asshole can't even give me a simple direction. *I really hate tornadoes.*

"Never mind, I'll figure it out," I mumble.

"You're going to Vegas?" he asks, and I stop for a moment.

"Yes, I need to get home."

He starts walking. "Girls like you should be careful."

Sighing, I start walking again, but he falls in step with me. "I can show you around."

I don't need a tour, just a phone. "I just need to find a phone."

"Well, still be careful. Hope you find one." He smiles, and it's weird. In the darkness, his teeth are almost a supernatural white.

And I hope you find a brain.

No idea why that thought popped into my head. I'm just on edge, and people around here are weird. I'm used to friendly neighbors, people that pull over to help. Maybe I should have waited until the morning and then walked to the nearest phone.

And who the fuck doesn't have a phone when they run a little store?

Apparently, the hot model that runs a store. Or maybe he was just fucking with me? Or this is like that Hill movie, and I'm never going to make it to the city to find a phone because they're going to kill me.

Stop it!

Glancing down at the little dog that found its way with me, I just start walking. "Let's get going."

One foot in front of the other, keep to the road.

Draven

I want to laugh as I follow behind her. Eventually, I'll head back to my car.

Las Vegas never gets tornadoes. Well, I can't say never, but rarely. I think in like sixty years it's happened twice. Three, I guess now with this one bringing a woman. A pretty woman. The minute I laid eyes on her, I swear my heart jumped a little. She probably thinks I'm crazy, and she would be correct. But still, sometimes you need a little crazy in your life.

Plus, she's alone, so she needs someone to look after her.

Pretty girls like her will get swallowed up by the seedy side of Vegas. She'll come to a small town first, but the people that own that store are already asleep. She won't be getting any help there.

I can feel the anger and frustration rolling off of her in waves. From other people, I would relish in that, but for some reason, I hate that she feels that way.

She's kicking rocks on the road, cussing under her breath, mumbling about her aunt and uncle. I'm sure she's crying as well.

I'm about to tell her I have a car when fuckface comes into view. And by fuckface, I mean Carrick.

Some might say I'm insane, cold even, but others say he has no heart.

She stops short, realizing someone is there, leaning against the side of the dilapidated store. The couple that owns it really needs to update it, but they don't have the funds. *Maybe I'll give them a donation?* If they were open, our little walk would be cut short. Call it a thank you.

"Oh, hello. Am I going the right way to Las Vegas?"

He grins, and she steps back. "You're going the right way."

Cryptic asshole, I like it.

"Thanks," she says as she keeps walking, the little dog following her.

Carrick falls in step behind her. "It's a big city."

She nods. "Well, hopefully I'll find a phone then."

He glances over at me. "Why the rush? Don't you want to explore?"

She glances over at him. "Big cities are not my thing."

He laughs like the lunatic he is. "Maybe cities don't like you. Little girls who wear Converses, that are out of place, and lost in a foreign land."

I swear she mutters something like, 'Vegas giving him a heart'. If she only knew half of why Carrick was like that, she would run for the hills.

Verity

The little store with the crazy guy was closed, so the only option I have was to keep walking. In the distance I can see Las Vegas. I mean, the space station can probably see Las Vegas from way up there. So bright and colorful.

If this was another time and place, I would love to visit, see what there is to do in the city, but I'd rather get home. I'd also rather be alone, but I've managed to attract two stalkers.

They stick to the shadows, but I know they're there. I'd tell them to leave, but they'd probably just laugh in my face. They're that crazy.

I walk for another hour and round a bend when I see a van. Leaning against it is a figure, a man I assume from the way they are standing.

"Hi. I was wondering if you have a phone or could take me to one?" I ask the guy.

He's smoking, and after I ask my question, he drops his cigarette and then stomps it out with his boot.

"I can take you to Wild Bill's Casino. They'll have a phone."

I don't let any disappointment show, but I'll take it, though I'll have to find a way to Las Vegas. But if this Wild Bill's has a phone, then my family can send money. And I can avoid Vegas all together. I guess I'm just apprehensive around strangers and rightly so, but I need a ride and any help I can get right now.

He stares at something behind me, and I know he sees the other two.

"Coming?" he asks, opening the sliding door to his van. For a split second, I think I'll be kidnapped. Ever see those memes with the white van and tacos written on the side, or the ones with books written on it and the caption about this is how one gets kidnapped?

Well, that's me right now. Probably.

I know it's wrong to judge. Maybe I should just keep walking. But I've been walking for so long that I really need to sit.

I slide in and hit the far side of the van, just as my two stalkers jump in. The nice guy says nothing as he closes the door.

I'm one step closer to home.

Or am I?

Draven

We climb in with Kasar. Yeah, we know him, too. Carrick sits in the passenger seat, and I climb in the back with the girl.

I just grin at her as she keeps backing up from me. She's scared. She's not in familiar territory. Vegas is a whole new world from Kansas. I saw her tag on her car. She's definitely not in Kansas anymore.

Carrick turns to Kasar. "Take her to Oz."

Her eyes get big. "What's Oz? I thought you were taking me to Wild Bill's?" She's almost in a panic. Can't have that.

Something tells me she's going to be feisty, but I grab her anyway. She tries to pull away from me, and I do something so uncharacteristic of me, I kiss her.

She struggles and then relaxes, so I let her go. She cowers back in her corner. "Don't do that again."

Oh, we'll be doing that again. One wasn't enough. She likes it, and I'll show her she'll like it even more.

"Oz will have a phone."

She stares out the window. "So, Oz is a person?"

She sighs when we pass Wild Bill's. But see, she would still need to get a ride from here to the airport or bus station. If I even let her go, but I digress.

We pass the overpass where the M is, and the large Cabelo's when the tires blow.

Kasar fights to keep us upright, but loses control. We start to roll and to protect her, I grab her again. This time, she doesn't put up a fight.

The van rolls down the embankment, and when we hit the bottom, it's lights out.

Kasar

I open my eyes on a groan, not my own. I turn my head and see Carrick waking up. "You okay?"

"My head hurts, but I think I'm good. You? Draven?"

Glancing over our shoulders, we see Draven stirring. "What the fuck happened?"

Pulling out my knife, I cut my seatbelt before handing it to Carrick to do the same. Draven wasn't even in a seatbelt. We use this for deliveries. But he's okay, I think.

After cutting the seatbelt, I try to open my door, but it's kind of hard when you're upside down. I then try the window as Carrick does the same on his side. Once I get it busted, I crawl out and then Draven moves to the front seat. He passes me the girl. She's bruised, but breathing. Carrick joins us on the driver's side, and we survey the van.

Bending down, Carrick tells us what happened. "Someone shot at us."

We always know it's a possibility, but who the fuck shot at us? That's the question of the day.

Whoever it is will pay.

I lay the girl on the ground and find a tiny wallet in her back pocket. Pulling it out, I learn her name.

"Her name is Verity, and she's from Kansas."

Draven snorts. "I already knew she was from Kansas."

Flipping him off, I make sure she's out of harm's way, and covered with my jacket as Carrick makes a call.

"Get here now!"

Whoever is on the phone better come through, because he can go off the deep end when he's pissed.

"Who do we think did this?" Draven asks, pulling out his phone and typing out some messages.

I tune him out and study the girl. I know I'm being a creeper, but I can't help but think she looks like someone.

It dawns on me, and I jump, spinning around. "She's his!"

The other two slowly turn to face me. Carrick has some bruising on his neck and face that is now showing, making him look angrier than normal. "Who?"

Pointing at Verity, I shout, "She's Alessandro's daughter. Look at her!"

They both glance down as they assess what I'm saying.

"We have to be sure," Draven remarks, and I agree, but she looks just like him.

Carrick dials a number and relays some info to the other person. I'm assuming is the tech guy we have on speed dial. It's our job to know who comes in and out of Las Vegas, even if it's a girl that was dropped from the sky.

Carrick hangs up. "It's true. Which means…"

"She has to be protected," Draven finishes. Sometimes I think they're twins the way they finish each other's sentences.

"What did the guy say?" I ask, needing more than just that. I get that she needs to be protected. She's not from the area. She's definitely not of our world.

Carrick runs a hand down his face. "Alessandro's first wife died in childbirth. Verity was that child. After that, he found a new wife."

We all know who his new wife is—she's a fucking bitch. She thinks she runs things in this town, and we've proven time and time again that she's a small fry. But she wants the world. Alessandro tries to placate her by buying her expensive shit, but it's why he's broke, though not many people know that.

"Apparently, the bitch didn't want to share the father, so they left her with her aunt and uncle, who took her in, no questions asked. I'm guessing someone has been following us and told her that someone was in town. Verity being here might make her think she's here to upset her way of life, if you can even call it that," he continues.

I wish we could just kill the bitch. Draven is silent while Carrick explains everything about this situation that has fallen into our laps.

Before I can ask him anything, a car pulls up. *Our ride.*

Out jumps Toga, who just asks what we need him to do. I lift Verity up, motion for her little dog to follow and then instruct him to drive us to our doctor and he needs to put the pedal to the floor.

"After the doc, we'll go to Oz."

Oz is a strip bar. I know, cliché. But we make a lot of money—legit money—with it. It's a front, and while the cops think we're up to nefarious things, they have never been able to prove anything.

Our boss will be able to help us figure out how to use Verity to take down the fucking bitch and Alessandro before sending her home.

But I somehow feel like I don't want her to go home.

Verity

I wake up to some beeping, and as I stir, I feel a hand reach out for me. "You're pretty banged up."

Banged up? What happened?

"We were in an accident."

Prying my eyes open, I take in the man sitting next to me. He's beautiful, and the one that told me he would take me to Wild Bill's. But we passed Wild Bill's, and then I remember us spinning.

"You're safe. I promise."

"You kidnapped me," I croak out.

He shrugs. "It wasn't planned, and I was going to take you to a phone and safe place."

My guess is Vegas isn't a safe place. "I just want to go home."

He pats my hand. "I know. But right now, you have to rest. We can take you to Oz after the doctor clears you."

My eyes dart around the room, and while I'm hooked up to a machine, monitoring my heart, I realize I'm not in a hospital.

"We brought you to a friend who is a doctor. I'm truly sorry for the tires blowing. The van is old."

Like mine was. I kind of miss my van right now. I wish I had just stayed home and waited out the storm. I can't do anything about that now.

"Can I use a phone?"

He nods and brings me a cell phone. I almost cry.

Dialing my family's number, Aunt Mavis picks up. "Hello?" She sounds like she's been crying.

"Aunt Mavis?"

"Verity? Where are you? We've been so worried." She sucks in a sob and it just makes me want to cry.

"It's me. Somehow, I landed in Vegas."

She's quiet for a few minutes, and I have no idea what she is thinking.

"Vegas?" she whispers, and I nod, then remember she can't see me.

"The tornado picked me up and dropped me in Vegas. Can you get me home?"

"We're going to fly out as soon as we can. Are you safe?"

I look at the man in the room and he takes the phone from me. "Hello. I'm Kasar. I picked Verity up. She's safe, and I'll make sure she stays that way until you get here."

I can't hear the conversation, but he answers a few questions and then hangs up. "They'll be here soon. Maybe you should sleep?"

My family is coming, and on that note, I fall back asleep.

Draven

Kasar comes out of the room looking guilty.

"What did you do?"

He flops down in the recliner and Carrick hands him a beer. "I let her call her family. It will take them a couple of days."

Carrick breaks his glass. "What the fuck?"

I'm guessing we all feel the pull. We were all drawn to Verity, and she's the key to getting Alessandro out of here. And once he's gone, she's safer in this world.

And then she can leave. *Fuck that.*

After that one kiss, I'll follow her to Kansas if I have to. I can run my team from there, and my boss can't say shit.

I leave them to argue and I creep into her room. Taking a seat next to her, I take all of her in. She's gorgeous, and she doesn't even know it. I'm guessing she grew up sheltered in Kansas, but I'm only assuming that because if she wasn't, she would be married by now.

She's groaning in her sleep, so I place my hand on her thigh, and she sighs, calming down. Her skin is soft, and I run my hand up her thigh, touching more of her. I need to touch more.

Doctor Moore's assistant changed her and then took her clothes to be washed. She came back with new ones, but left them on the table. She's naked under the sheets. I practically cut off his fingers when he poked and prodded her, but he snarled that he was doing his job.

Mine.

Lifting the sheet, I take in her bruised body, and that angers me more. That bitch had something to do with this, and I'm going to make sure she pays. Torture is too good for that fucking witch. I'll have to come up with something creative.

I move my hand to her mound, her pussy is bare, just the way I like it. She cries out again, tossing around. She's having a nightmare. Leaning over the bed, I kiss her, and she calms down.

I'm sick in the head, but I need to touch her. I can't help it.

My fingers trail through her slit, finding her clit. As I trace circles over it, my cock hardens. She starts moving with my hand and then her eyes pop open.

"Verity."

She blinks at me, but doesn't stop me.

"You want me to make you come?" I ask her, and she whimpers.

She must be as crazy as I am if she's letting me do this to her. In my defense, I would have done it while she was still asleep, that's how great my need is to feel her.

I continue fingering her, pushing two fingers into her wet heat. "You're wet for me. Good girl."

She must like praise because she lets out a moan. "Oh, my good girl is a dirty girl. I like that. Are you going to come for me?"

She gasps, her back arching off the table in response, but I pull out just as she's about to fall over that edge and she cries out.

"You're going to come on my cock and nothing else."

She watches as I strip, showing her my face and body. I'm ripped, I know that. Sometimes I hide my face because of the scar.

When I'm conducting business, I let my freak sideshow because it's intimidating, but dating wise, girls don't like it.

She doesn't seem to care as I slide up her body, leaning down to kiss her. My dick is hard—so hard—and her pussy is like a homing beacon. I slide right in, stretching her. "So tight. Perfect."

She starts to meet my thrusts as I pick up speed. Reaching between us, I pinch her clit. "Come."

And she does. She gushes all over my cock, making me come so fucking hard I see stars.

I stay seated in her, getting my breathing under control, and I utter that one word that she might fight me on, but will come to understand.

"Mine."

Verity

I just had sex. I mean, I've had sex before, but this was on a whole new level.

He started before I was even awake. I have no idea what made me wake up, but once I did, I didn't protest. Maybe I'm not normal. It felt good.

And when it was all over, he said one word… *mine.*

What does that mean?

And then I watched him dress and leave, but not before kissing my forehead. *The guy is crazy.*

The door opens, and in walks the guy that let me use the phone. He's carrying a tray with him.

"Hey! You're awake. I brought some food. It's not much, just a tuna sandwich, some chips, and apple juice. By the way, I'm Kasar."

"Verity."

He sets the tray on my lap and takes the seat that the other guy just left.

In between bites of food, I study the man sitting next to my bed. He's tall like the others and lean. He has brown hair, it's shaggy, but not in an unkempt way, and amber eyes that almost look like lion eyes. He's quite handsome.

"Thank you for earlier," I say as he looks up from his phone. He shrugs like it's no big deal.

"It was the least I could do. Once you eat, we'll take you to OZ where it's safer for you."

Safer? This isn't safe?

"You're safe anywhere, but it's a precaution. Better safe than sorry."

He stays with me while I eat, but it's not an uncomfortable silence. He has a calming presence to him.

Once I'm done, he takes the tray and gestures to the clothes on the table along the wall. "And we saved your dog."

I glance up at him. "He's a stray I picked up, but thank you."

When we got into the van, the little dog jumped in. I don't know what happened to him when we crashed, but I'm glad he's okay.

He gives me a smile and leaves me to dress.

I get out of the bed and pull on the clothes left for me; I guess mine were destroyed. The jeans fit perfectly, and the shirt is a little snug, but it works. They did save my flannel, and I could almost cry about that. My shoes are on the floor and I slip them on.

By the time my shoes are on, the door is opening, and the other guy is giving me the once over. "Let's go."

I stopped him. "Can I know your names?"

He doesn't stop, but he answers. "I'm Carrick, the scarred one is Draven. You already know Kasar."

"Thank you."

I'm not sure if I'm thanking him for answering me or saving me?

I look down at the ground, embarrassed about what I did with a guy I don't even know, then I see Draven leaning against the car, and he stops me. "Don't do that."

I can only nod as he opens the door for me, then the three of them climb in. There's a new guy driving, but he never looks at me. He starts driving, and Carrick tells him to take the route through the Strip.

I'm glad he does, I take in the lights of all the casinos, and different varieties of people. It's bright and colorful.

A few minutes later, we're pulling into a parking lot in front of a glass building lit up in green and gold.

Draven helps me out of the car. "Welcome to OZ."

I was wrong, Oz isn't a person. It's a place, and from the sign out front. It's not a place I would normally go.

It's a strip club.

Carrick

Her eyes widen when she realizes what this place is. She probably doesn't have strip clubs where she's from. Or if she does, she's never been.

We shuffle her in through the side door and to the office. No need for her to see the skin showing in the other rooms, nor do we need to fight off the girls that try to sit on our dicks.

Not happening.

My heart might be black, but the minute I laid eyes on her, it did start beating. And that's why I want whoever shot at us dead—by my own hands.

Kasar opens the door and takes her to the couch, having her sit while he goes to grab a soda for her. "Are you hungry? I know the sandwich wasn't that filling. I can order something for you."

She shrugs. "I'm not picky."

He smiles at her. "Burgers and fries it is." He takes a seat on the couch next to her and starts typing out an order to one of our guys.

Draven and I leave them to it and go in search of Charon. He smirks when he sees us coming, while some girl grinds on his lap. *Fucker.*

When we slide into the booth, he pushes the girl away. "Go make someone else happy."

She glares at him, but doesn't fight him on it. *Smart.*

The girls here are always trying to get in our pants, knowing we have money, though we don't flaunt it. Charon doesn't care about sampling the girls that come through here.

I, on the other hand, would rather slit their throats than have them touch me. It's even worse when they try to tell me some sob story. They haven't figured out that I don't give a fuck.

"Where's the girl?" he asks as he signals a waitress to bring a round of shots.

Draven leans on the table. "She's with Kasar, ordering food. Do you know anything?"

He looks at me and then at Draven. "Word on the street is that Druscilla is her step-mother."

He figured that out pretty fast, though we kind of already knew it when Kasar made the connection to her father. Then my guy told me the rest.

"You think she shot at us?" I ask, downing the shot the girl sets on the table in front of me.

He leans back in his chair. "I do, but I don't think she knows the girl is in town."

It was a freak of nature that brought her here. She wouldn't know unless someone told her that she was seen with us. Why she has such a hard-on for her step-daughter is beyond me. The girl stays with her aunt and uncle and lives a happy life.

I wonder if Alessandro is leaving her? If he did, it wouldn't be a loss—he's broke. And he can do better than her. She's only after money. With the three of us out of the way, she would try to charm her way into Charon's good graces, but he's not stupid.

"I think you need to call Alessandro. But first, I want to use the girl to call the bitch out. Her task is to get a face to face with her." He pulls out a vial and sets it on the table. Draven picks it up with an evil grin.

"She can use that to put in her drink. Draven knows all about it. If she can do that, I'll make sure she and her family get back home with no issues."

I cock my head. "Are they here already?"

He shakes his head. "No, but Kasar texted that they're on their way. They don't like to fly, so they're driving. It will be a couple days. All I want is for her to see her step-mother, get a confession, and slip that into her drink."

Draven scowls. "And then she leaves."

Charon glances at him. "Shouldn't have gotten close."

Well, too late for that. Even I want to be around her.

"We need to talk to her first." I stand and head to the office, pushing women off of me the whole way. I don't need their slimy hands on me.

Back in the office, Verity is eating a huge burger, and there are onion rings on the table. She looks happy.

She glances up and our eyes meet. "Do you want some of my burger?"

I shake my head no, but sit on the couch next to her. "We know who you are."

She jumps a little. "I never wanted to come here. It was like something out of a supernatural movie that brought me here. It's like something controlled that tornado. My step-mother isn't nice, and my dad just lets her do whatever. I only want to go home."

I nod and take the burger from her, setting it down before holding her hand. "Can you do something for us? We will be right there with you. We know that she might mess up and confess that she caused our wreck. All you need to do is meet her face to face, get that confession, and by then, your family will be here to take you home."

She looks at Kasar, then to Draven, before turning her attention back to me. "Will that help you?"

I'm taken aback by her question. She's worried about us, you can see it in her eyes.

Draven jumps in and replies, "Yes. You probably know by now that we're not on the right side of the law. In this city, we dish out our own justice. She's been trying to hurt us for a while."

She looks back at me and reaches up to palm my cheek. "I've known you for a couple of days, and for some reason, I want to help."

It's in her nature to help. She cares about people, and she's showing she cares about me. If that fucking bitch lays a finger on her, I will rip her head from her body, and stake it for the whole world to see.

"We'll be with you." I place my hand over hers.

She must be crazy to just jump at the chance to help us. I like crazy though.

She returns to eating her burger, and I sit back to watch. She's a fascinating creature. Making eye contact with Draven, his face tells me everything I need to know. *She's ours.*

Verity

I finish my burger and onion rings and Draven helps me up. "How about we get some sleep?"

He leads me down a hallway to an elevator, punching the top floor which is floor twelve. There are twelve floors in this place. The doors open to an apartment. It's simple, and yet pretty at the same time. It's all windows. The kitchen has an island, and the living room has a big screen TV. It's covered in hardwood floors, and the couches are a light gray offset by black book cases. He gestures to follow him through a door, which leads to a bedroom. There's just a bed, a dresser, TV, and bedside table in it.

"There's a bathroom just through that door." He points to another door.

"Thank you for all of this. I thought you guys were just crazy stalkers, and maybe I'm right, but at least you've been nice to me."

His face softens. "Can you sit for a minute?"

I take a seat on the bed as the door opens and the other two file in, leaning against the wall as Draven starts talking. "We've known you for a long time."

Huh?

I look over at the other two, but their faces don't give me anything.

"I don't understand?"

Carrick comes and sits on the bed next to me. "Before your mother died, we worked on the farm. We left when your dad left you with your aunt and uncle. You might not remember us, as we're a few years older than you."

Kasar takes over. "We kept tabs on you. But you literally falling into our territory wasn't planned. Draven picked up on who you were before the accident. We're here to make sure you're safe and make it home."

"What? I knew you before? You knew my mother?"

Carrick runs a hand down his face. "Get some sleep, and we'll show you some pictures in the morning."

I do as he says, but they don't leave. Draven takes a seat on the chair by the window, while Carrick and Kasar get on the bed with me.

I'm so confused, and I dare say horny. *What has my life become?*

"She's turned on," Draven drawls.

How did he know?

Carrick turns to the side to look at me. "Is that so? Even after what we dropped on you?"

Kasar scolds him, "It was a lot. I think we should have waited, but she can't wait."

In seconds, my jeans are off, and Kasar is ripping my panties down my legs. *It's okay, I didn't need those.*

His tongue presses against my clit, and I come off the bed.

"She likes that." Carrick lifts me up and pulls my shirt and flannel off.

What am I doing?

Who the fuck cares right now?

Whatever Kasar is doing feels so good that I don't even care. I feel a burning need in me—the impending orgasm that I so desperately want.

"Don't let her come," Carrick barks, and Kasar stops.

Carrick rises from the bed and strips, and all I can do is watch.

When his cock hits his stomach, my mouth drops. Oh my, he is big! Just like Draven.

He climbs on the bed as Kasar holds my legs open. Carrick guides his dick in and thrusts into me as I cry out.

"Holy shit," he mutters as Draven grins.

"Good, right?" Draven asks Carrick, who isn't speaking. Nor can I. He thrusts in and out of me, hitting the right spot, because I feel myself getting closer and closer to the edge.

"Open," Kasar instructs as he kneels near my head.

I open my mouth as he slides his dick in.

"Shit," he groans as he uses my face to fuck his cock.

I let him use me. I like what he's doing. I love what Carrick is doing.

"Fuck!" Carrick's thrusts become erratic, and it's as if he's almost having a seizure as he comes. That makes me come. My orgasm rips through me like a freight train.

"Swallow," Kasar moans, and then he's coming in my mouth. And for some reason, I want to be a good girl for him, so I swallow everything he gives me.

“Good girl.” He leans down and kisses me, tasting himself on my tongue.

Carrick rolls off of me. “Now you're ours.”

I can’t even say anything, I’m too worn out. All I can do is cuddle into Kasar’s embrace and fall asleep.

Kasar

We wake up before her, and get ready. We have our own rooms but wanted to stay with her. The minute she wrapped her lips around my cock, I was a goner.

I want more. I want her.

Once I shower and dress, I head to the kitchen to start breakfast. This isn't our apartment, but we've made it ours.

"What are we going to do?" Draven asks.

Carrick looks up from his phone. "She wants to do this. We will support her."

Draven snaps, "If that woman tries to harm her, I will not be held accountable for my actions. But if I get to use explosives that might help."

I chuckle, the guy is crazy.

Her door opens, and she steps out hesitantly.

Instantly, Draven is on his feet. "Come eat. Kasar is cooking."

She gives him a smile as she blushes. "Thank you. Would you like me to call my step-mother?"

Carrick hands her a phone. "It's under bitch. Send her a text. Tell her you want it in public. I will not have you going into any place that she deems suitable. Ask her to meet you at the Strip somewhere."

She nods and texts the witch as I plate pancakes and sausage.

Draven and Carrick dig in, but she's staring at the phone. "She is asking for a specific place."

Dumb cunt. She's stupid. She's letting us control all of this. Too easy.

"Tell her the Chandelier, Cosmopolitan."

She types it out and then hands him the phone. "She says seven."

That works for me.

"We need to get you a dress," Carrick remarks.

Her eyes widen. "A dress?"

"Not like a real formal dress, but something dressier than jeans," I tell her, and she relaxes. She doesn't wear many dresses where she's from.

"Eat up, and we'll go." Carrick picks up a sausage link and feeds it to her. Her lips close around it, and she bites down, hardening my dick.

Hopefully, he gets her something loose where we have easy access, because my dick needs her.

I need her.

She can't go.

Verity

They take me to a dress shop that celebrities would shop at. I mean, most of the dresses start at a thousand dollars. I browse through the store as the woman talks to the guys. More like she's flirting with them, or trying to, at least.

Draven shoves off the counter he was leaning on, and turns his back to her, heading straight for me. "Find anything?" he asks, and I tell him no.

"I don't even know what to look for. Not formal, but still dressy. I hardly wear dresses."

He looks me up and down. "You look better naked."

Oh, lord.

He starts going through the racks, and soon he's snapping his fingers at the woman who looks at me like I stole her puppy.

"Put these in a dressing room for my girl, and if you are rude to her, I'll burn this place to the ground."

My jaw hits the floor. He's nuts. The woman's eyes widen, but she does what he asks.

Kasar and Carrick throw in a few they like. Then Kasar takes me to the dressing room. "Come and show us. Don't make us come in here."

I clench my thighs together because I kind of want them to come in here.

Oh, my. I've been in their presence for a few days and now I only think about sex. Great sex, though.

But that makes me sad. I'll be going home to my chickens and horses. They'll stay here, doing whatever they do. The guys in my hometown can't compare to these three. *Freak my life.*

I undress and take the first dress off the hangar. It's white, knee length, with kind of a puffy skirt, and lace on top. It's modest and something I would wear to a wedding if it was in a different color.

Stepping out, I let them assess me.

Draven just smirks. "Still better naked."

Carrick shakes his head. "Not the one."

The next one is red, short, tight, something they'll love, but they shake their heads no when I step out. That's good because I didn't like it.

The next dress is a short black dress with sheer sleeves with cuffs. The skirt is loose, with an overlay of rhinestones. The cuffs have rhinestones on them as well. It fits perfectly, and I instantly love it, even if it's shorter than I would normally wear. I just hope they like it.

When I step out, they sit up straighter.

Carrick jumps up and comes over to me, towering above me, but I'm not scared of him anymore. I wait to see what he's going to do.

His fingers trail up my leg, all the way to my panty line. "Easy access."

He continues his assault, his fingers pushing my panties to the side before pushing a finger inside me, causing me to moan.

"Stay quiet and I'll let you come," he murmurs. Draven snorts as he joins us. "Nope, I want that woman to know she's ours."

Carrick thrusts his finger in and out before adding another. Draven's hand trails down my body, tweaking my nipple through the fabric of the dress until his fingers find my clit.

"Oh, God," I moan and Draven tells me to say it louder.

"Make her scream," Carrick drawls, and Kasar is on his knees, his tongue licking me like an ice cream cone while Carrick adds another finger. Draven kisses my neck and I'm on sensory overload. I hear someone screaming, and I realize it's me as my orgasm takes over, and I convulse from the pleasure.

When I stop shaking, the guys stand and look down at me with lust and approval. "That's the dress."

I dip my head and step back in the dressing room to change, handing the dress to one of them so we can go. When I join them at the register, I see someone added silver heels.

"I can't pay for this," I remind them, but they stop me.

Kasar kisses my cheek. "Our treat."

Carrick pays, and we get back into the car, but instead of the strip club, they take me to another house.

"This is our home," Draven tells me as he takes my hand, holding it as he shows me to a room on the first level. They're in a rush, so he shows me the shower, and that underneath the counter are new hairstyling tools.

"We had someone stock it this morning."

They're new at least. He leaves me to shower and get ready. I shower quickly, wrapping a towel around my body while I dry my hair. I find curlers in the cabinet, so I decide to use them instead of a curling iron. I might be a country girl, but I do know how to style my hair.

While the curlers set, I slip the dress on and admire myself in a full-length mirror in the room. I feel pretty.

Once the curlers are cool, I pull them out and then run my hands through them to separate them, but still look good. I set it with hairspray. I brush my teeth and then pull out my lip gloss.

I'm about to slip on my heels when I hear barking, and then my door opens and the small dog that I picked up on my travels bounds in.

"Have you been good?" I ask him, petting his ears. Kasar told me the doctor took him for me when I was out of it.

"I thought you would like for him to be with you," Kasar says from the door.

I look up at him and smile. "Thank you."

I slip on my heels and pet the dog one more time as he settles in on the pillows on the bed. "I'm ready."

I take him in as I follow him to the front door. He's dressed in dark jeans, a button-up shirt, with a jacket even. The other two are dressed similarly as well, and I realize I might not make it through the night without needing their hands on me.

Their eyes heat up when they see me, and I know I'm blushing.

"Ready?"

I am, but I'm not. This is my step-mother. The woman that took everything from me.

"Let's get this over with," is all I can muster to say.

Draven

Carrick drives us to the Cosmopolitan and uses valet parking. Appearances are everything.

I'm keeping them up as well. Under my jacket is an arsenal of weapons, from my gun to grenades. I have a knife in my boot. And if that witch harms a hair on my girl's head, I will show her why people think I'm crazy.

Carrick holds her hand as we walk through the casino. Sometimes, we stop to let her look at something, and take in all the lights. She's never been in a casino, so this must be exciting for her.

Maybe we can do a day on the Strip before she leaves?

Nope, she's not leaving. Well, if she does, I'm going with her.

The entrance to the Chandelier Bar is on one of the upper levels, so we take the escalator to the floor, and tell the hostess how many are in our party.

Looking around, I can see we're early. Kasar checks his watch and holds up two fingers. Two minutes.

We order drinks as we wait. I know when she's here, it's like a feeling. Verity doesn't notice her, so I excuse myself and flop down in a seat at her table.

"Draven."

"Bitch."

She rolls her eyes as I just go on, "If you do anything to harm Verity, or make her cry, I'm not afraid to slit your throat right here."

"My, my. All this hostility over a girl? We're in a public place, I highly doubt you would do anything."

I open my jacket and show her what I'm strapped with. "Try me, bitch. I will not hesitate to end your life."

"Alessandro will not be happy if you hurt his precious wife," she coos, and I have to gag. *Who the fuck would want her wrinkly ass?*

"We both know that you are on the outs with him. I'm guessing it's him wanting out?"

Her face reddens. "You don't have any idea about my life."

I show her my jacket one more time. "I don't give a fuck about you. My promise still stands."

I leave the table and head back to mine, looking at Verity who only nods.

Pointing to the table, I see that Verity looks sick. Carrick frowns, and Kasar offers her some water.

"I'm fine," she says shakily, her voice barely above a whisper. She's not fine, but I know she will be after all of this.

She gets up, and we watch her walk over to her step-mother.

She showed up with no backup—no men—not that she has many. My guess is she thinks that Verity doesn't pose a threat to her. She probably didn't think we would be here. Or maybe she did, but just not in the open like this. She probably thought we'd be watching from across the bar.

I'm not letting Verity step into the snake's den without watching her back.

Verity declines a drink, but sits. Both say nothing for a few moments. I hail the waiter on the way to deliver Druscilla's drink, when he bends over, I order another drink and then slip the contents of the vial into hers.

It's time for this bitch to heel.

Verity

"You're a long way from Kansas," Druscilla drawls, picking at her nails instead of looking at me.

I huff out a sigh. "I didn't ask to come here. I'm not trying to see you or my dad, but here I am. I'm not even sure why you hate me so much?"

She looks up as the waiter sits drinks down at the table. I don't drink mine; I don't usually drink, anyway.

She takes a sip. "I didn't want to raise a child, nor did I even want them. I had to sever that tie between you and your father, so I could have all his attention."

"Sounds like you are an attention seeking whore."

She slaps me across the face. "Learn your place. If you haven't guessed by now, Las Vegas is my kingdom. Those men you've attached to yourself are thorns in my side. I learned of you coming into town from some watchers I have. They watch all the entrances to the city. I was told a girl from Kansas was here, and I got curious. Once I was showed a picture, and saw who you were with, I had to take precautions."

"Lady, you are delusional. I don't want your kingdom or anything you have. I just want to go home."

She glares at me. "Go home and don't come back."

"With pleasure. I got what I came for."

She goes to say something, but she gasps for air and grabs at her neck.

I yell for a waiter to call 911, and then I hightail it out of there. The guys are seething when they see what she did to me, but I don't care, I got what they wanted.

"She did it," I tell them as we practically run out of the casino. I'm trying to keep up, but I've never had to run in heels. Draven recognizing this, picks me up and practically carries me all the way to the car.

He sets me in the back seat as they climb in, and Carrick takes off, driving through all the Las Vegas traffic with ease, even though I'm shaking.

"Oz?" Kasar questions, and Carrick nods. I'm curious as to what the rest of the club looks like. This little trip has opened my eyes to a lot of things. I don't judge people for what they do—criminals included—because they have to make a living someway. Do I like violence? No. But so far these guys haven't shown any to me. Though Draven has threatened a few people, but that's it.

Carrick parks, and Kasar comes around to help me out of the car. This time we enter through the front door.

This place is not what I expected. The place is covered with plush green and black couches, and numerous sconces on the wall. There's a huge chandelier in the center of the room, and the stage wraps around the whole space. I watch as a topless dancer prances around the stage, making her rounds to all the patrons. I look away and let Kasar take me wherever.

We don't go to the office; we sit down at a booth in the back. A girl appears and takes our orders. Well, she takes the guys orders, I just wanted water.

A minute later, a man takes the last seat. "We haven't met. I'm Charon."

He's nice looking with his blue and black hair that's slicked back, and crisp clean suit. His eyes are a bright blue that are very alluring. All four of the guys at the table could be models. Why they seem to care about me is beyond me.

"Nice to meet you," I say softly, and he smiles—a perfect smile.

"She's charming. Good job, by the way. She's dead."

What?

I look at Carrick in confusion, who leans over to say, "Your step-mother."

"I killed her? I didn't mean to." I start to panic. I'm shaking so bad I can't breathe.

"It's okay. You didn't kill her," Draven whispers to me.

"I didn't mean to," I whisper to him, and he takes my chin in his hand.

"I did it. I had a vial in my pocket. I intercepted the waiter. I'm the one who killed her. You had nothing to do with it."

Does it make me a crazy person that I care and don't care? I didn't want her dead, but I also don't care that she is. I did care about being arrested.

"They will come for me," I tell him, and he shakes his head again.

"Footage was wiped," he replies, and I breathe a sigh of relief.

I kind of can't wait to get back to my boring life in Kansas.

"So, I can go home now?"

Charon looks at me with his bright blue eyes. "Yes. I'll tell you where your family is staying."

I sigh with relief.

He rattles off a hotel, and I look over at the guys, who look sad. “Thank you for looking out for me. I will remember this for the rest of my boring farm life.”

Draven’s arms circle around me, and he kisses me before saying, “I can’t let you go.”

“I have to go. I don’t belong here.”

I slide out of the booth, not wanting to linger, hating that they’re sad.

Basically, I flee out the door and into the night where I’m met by the one man I wanted to avoid. “Dad?”

He steps closer, and I can see he’s aged. “It’s been a while.”

“Yeah, it has. I’m leaving. Have a good life.”

I don’t see it coming, but someone hits me from behind, and it’s lights out.

Carrick

We follow her out, I didn't want her to go. I get why she has to, but for some reason I just can't let her go.

We were going to try to talk to her, ask her to stay a little longer, but Alessandro was out there.

Before we could get a chance to jump in, something hits her from behind, and she goes down.

I run out and cradle her, looking at Alessandro who looks shocked. "I didn't do it."

He's right, he didn't do it.

"Someone did. I'm taking her to her family." I nod to the others to get in the car.

"I just wanted to talk to her," Alessandro says, and I just glare at him as I set her in the back of the car.

"You had that chance many years ago, and you chose the fucking bitch," I snarl at him. He steps back a bit. *Smart.*

Alessandro runs a hand through his hair in frustration. "I know. I should never have left her. Is Mavis and Dean in town?"

"Yes. They came to get her when a freak tornado dropped her at Mount Charleston."

He doesn't say anything for a minute. "It was fate don't you think?"

"Fate?"

"She showed up here. It's fate. I want my daughter back."

I shove him up against the truck as Kasar jumps out, probably to keep me from killing this asshole. "You don't deserve her. You left her for that fucking dead cunt who got your ass in financial shit. If you want her back, talk to your family. But if I were her, I would never speak to you again."

He shakes his head up and down. "I don't deserve her. But I will grovel at her feet for the chance to be her dad again. I'm coming with you."

I shove him out of the way before telling him the hotel we're heading to. I climb in the back with Verity, and we take off to her family.

"What are we going to do?" Kasar asks.

I stare out the window as I hold her hand. "Let her go."

Draven slams his hands on the wheel. "Not good enough."

"What else can we do?"

Kasar turns around and levels me with his gaze. "Go home."

Home.

Verity

My head hurts. There's no beeping, so maybe I'm dead? *Would my head hurt if I was dead?*

I pry my eyes open, and I see I'm in my room. *What?*

Did I dream about everything that happened?

The door opens and Aunt Mavis carries a tray in. "I was so worried. I was hoping you would wake up. I made you some soup."

She sets the tray on the bed, and I just stare at her. "What happened?"

She stares out the window, but doesn't answer me right away.

"Aunt Mavis? Did I dream everything?"

The door opens before she can answer me, and Dad walks in. Aunt Mavis takes a seat on the chair near the window. Dad takes the other and so does Uncle Dean as three guys enter my room.

"I must be dreaming. All of you were in my dream." This was said to the three guys. Carrick, Kasar, and Draven.

"It wasn't a dream," Uncle Dean clarifies.

"Oh. What happened then?"

Carrick sits on the bed. "We took care of it." I don't want to know what he means.

"Aunt Mavis?" I catch her attention, and she smiles at me, and then at her brother.

"Everything is alright. You're home, thanks to these three."

Turning to the guys, I whisper, "My life was turned upside down meeting you guys, but you did try to keep me safe. And you seem to care about me."

Kasar kneels next to the bed. "We do care. It's why we came home."

Home?

"We moved to a farm up the road. We're growing hops for beer. It's a business venture with your dad, who wants to make amends," Draven says with a growl. Okay, he's not happy with Dad, but I'm not happy with him either.

"Why?" I ask Dad and his face falls. He's aged some, but he's always been handsome.

"I got caught up in trying to play with the big dogs," he says. It's an answer and a non-answer. I'll accept it for now.

"And I'm home. Vegas happened."

It's a lot. Those few days in Las Vegas were weird and exciting as well as scary.

"Eat your soup." Aunt Mavis points at the bowl, and I just snicker. She's always taking care of me—all of us.

My cousins walk in a few minutes later. "You're awake!" Teddy ruffles my hair, making Draven growl.

Kasar smacks Draven, and I laugh.

"I'm awake and home. There's no place like this—like home. I'm happy to be back."

Jessup and Jordan smile as they take a seat on the floor, and I feel a sense of calm wash over me.

This is the way it's supposed to be.

This is home.

Carrick

Epilogue

A year later

"Ready?" I ask Verity.

She hands me her suitcase as we head out the door.

We're going on a trip to Las Vegas, but just the Strip. She didn't get to see it, and we wanted to show her, but shit happened. Her cousins are coming along with us.

A lot has happened in the last year. We started a brewery with her dad, and it's taken off. We built a bigger house on our property with the first million we made. It's good to be in legit business.

I made a vow to find out who hit her, and take care of him. One of Druscilla's men that had been having an affair with her was upset, and since word on the street was we did it, he went after Verity. Needless to say, he's pushing up daisies now. He used a wine bottle that he stole from the bar in Oz. Charon fired his bartender for that. The girl is lucky all she got was fired.

So yeah, we still dabble in the dark underbelly, even making moves into Kansas City, but we keep our secrets to ourselves. Verity doesn't need to know because she would only worry.

I also bought a private jet so we don't have to fly commercial. Draven is on the no-fly list for his antics—no surprise.

Kasar went back to school to get a business degree to help with the brewery. Verity takes online classes, and she helps her aunt and uncle during the week.

We even brought Teddy on with us, giving him stock in our company. He's a great addition.

Verity and her dad have made amends, and he dotes on his daughter, as he should. Her family accepts us as one of the family even though Draven can get a little intense sometimes. Now it's usually over football games, though he did scare one of the guys at the feed store for looking at Verity. *Yeah, he's still crazy.*

She once told me that I didn't have a heart. Honestly, I didn't until her. I love her.

We all do.

It took her a while to come to terms with us sharing her. She had doubts, but I think that's passed. Every day we try to show her how much we truly love her. Not that I care.

Draven helps her into the car that will take us to the airfield where our jet is. Dean is driving us. Alessandro opted to stay here, he still hasn't paid off all his debts, but I'm going to make a side trip while the other two keep her occupied and pay his bookie what's still owed.

Teddy, Jessup, and Jordan take up the back, and Dean drives to the airfield. This is the same van that Verity was driving the day of that fateful tornado. I had it towed to Kansas and then fixed it up, making it even better. Dean even hugged me.

Anything for family.

The plane is waiting for us as we start hauling bags onto the plane, and Verity says goodbye to her uncle. When she's done, she joins us.

We strap in, and she snuggles against Draven while Kasar talks to the guys about some new game that came out.

Covering her with a blanket I wink at her, and she blushes as my fingers pry her legs apart, and I start fucking her with my finger.

"Don't be loud," Draven whispers for only us to hear. Verity can get quite loud.

"If you make a sound, you won't get to come," I tell her, and she tries her hardest to be quiet by biting her lip. It's cute.

I press my thumb to her clit as I thrust my finger in and out. I can feel her legs shake, and looking up at Kasar, he grins. He knows what's going on.

"Carrick," she whispers, and I wink at her, picking up the pace.

"Does my good girl want to come?" I ask her, and she nods.

"Come." Draven kisses her neck, and she comes on a silent cry, like the good girl she is.

I pull my finger out and suck on it while holding her gaze. "Yummy."

She blushes again, and soon Draven is giving her a repeat of what I just did.

So much fun.

She falls asleep after her third orgasm, and I lean my head back, content.

I love Verity, I love my family, and I was given back my heart.

There is no place I'd rather be.

This is home. Not just Kansas, but with these people.

There's no place on Earth I'd rather be.

Acknowledgements

Thank you to the ladies that read my story as I wrote the first half. I appreciate it.

Thank you to my family and friends that have supported me.

Thank you to everyone that told me not to give up in whatever venture I pursued.

Books By Cedar Rose

Ever's Last

Bayou Knights

Heathens

Psychos

Bayou Sunlight

Luck is For Losers

Upcoming Books

No Escake

Dear John

Laying it Bare

Mends the Heartache

By L.E. Martin

~December~

As I sat at my desk in my small office in *Trendy Threads for Him* staring at the computer screen trying to decide what detail to add to my latest social media advertisement proof, the harsh insults coming from the next office wandered over to me through my open door. Since I didn't have a window in my office, I hardly ever closed my door, not liking to feel as if I were working in a closet. Besides, it wasn't like I was working on some top-secret project. I was one of the company's graphic designers.

"I can't believe he's still here. I didn't think he'd last three days and it's been over three weeks." The nasal tone belonged to none other than Trudy, our company's biggest loud mouth. She didn't even have anything nice to say about those she called her friends.

"He's probably not even smart. He must know someone in the company to keep his job. Does he even bring in any sales?" The responding snippy voice belonged to Randi. The only other shrew who worked here.

I guess experiencing a bad marriage and then the ensuing ruthless divorce tended to be something people bonded over and then resulted in making them spiteful people. I'd never been married so I couldn't relate to their situations. Although it was still no excuse to be so malicious to someone who didn't deserve their viciousness.

"At least if he had any intelligence it would make up for his unattractiveness. His clothes are baggy so there can't be any type of appealing body underneath. We design eye-catching clothes here;

why doesn't he wear them the way he's supposed to? Not several sizes too large and so unflattering." Trudy's nonstop offensive slurs grated across my last nerve.

I had to have this graphic finalized and emailed to the marketing director before the end of the day, which was in two hours. I tugged my hand through my mass of auburn curls before shoving up from my chair.

Storming over to Trudy's office, I narrowed my hazel eyes on the two of them sitting at the small table in front of Trudy's desk, drinking lattes and spewing ridiculousness.

"Don't either of you have anything better to do than sitting around bad mouthing other employees?"

Trudy slowly pivoted her head to gaze at me and rolled her blue eyes. "Don't tell me you have a crush on Colten Lockhart? Gawd, he's not even a hot geek. His black thick rimmed glasses definitely don't scream sexy genius. Really, December. Are you that desperate? Or are you just one of those who always has to come to the rescue of the poor creature who can't defend himself?"

"What are you, eight? This is a work place not an elementary school playground." The three of us were in our late twenties. But maybe I was the only one who had matured since middle school.

"You're not in charge, December. Besides, I have my proposal turned in. Randi and I are busy going over other design ideas."

"She's not in charge, but I am." A deep rumble from behind me had me jerking around. Sam Blackton, who was the CEO of the men's clothing line, stood in the doorway. His brown hair never had a strand out of place and his shrewd brown eyes never ceased to make my pulse race with fear. I wasn't doing anything wrong, but his presence was that authoritative.

"Save your idle chit chat for the lunch hour, ladies." Mr. Blackton's steely gaze locked on Trudy and Randi for several tense moments. Then he shifted a less severe look my way. "And Ms. Adams, I would like you to stop down and speak with Mr. Lockhart when you get a moment today before you leave. His shift in the store ended thirty minutes ago, so he'll be in his office. He brought some impressive ideas to my attention for a new fall casual line up. He's already shared with the head of the design department so I'd like you to sit down with him to come up with some potential promotional ideas. Summer has already started so we need to get this rolling soon." Leaving me with his demands, he turned and headed down the hall toward the bank of elevators.

So many snarky remarks begged to come out of my mouth, but I refused to stoop to their childish level. Instead, I spun around and retreated to my office.

Once tucked back inside my space, I worked to slow my heart rate so I could focus on my job. But it wasn't trying to burst from my chest because of the brief tense interaction with the boss. It wasn't even from anxiety over getting my graphic finished and turned in, sooner rather than later. Now I was even more eager to get finished with the project so that I could head downstairs to the salesmen's offices. Never having an excuse to head down there before meant I'd only been able to talk to Colten once. And that was on the day he was hired, when Mr. Blackton had been walking him around to introduce him to everyone. So we only exchanged about ten words; not near enough for me to be satisfied.

I didn't share Trudy and Randi's opinion of Colten. Instead I was drawn to the mysterious and alluring guy who hid behind thick glasses and loose clothing. Although our interaction was brief, in those few memorable minutes, I detected there was so much more to him than what he allowed people to see. Did I have a crush on Colten? Well, no. I had only met him once. But was I attracted to him and want to get to know him and develop a crush? And then move on to so much more? Why, hell yes I did.

Dropping down into my chair, I directed my attention to the design displayed on my computer screen. It was time to focus. The sooner I finished, the sooner I could head down to talk to Colten. The salesmen's day ended two hours after mine, but I wanted all the time I could get with him.

Forty minutes later, I hit send on my email to Rick, attaching my final mock up for the advertisement. Then I shut down my computer before grabbing my purse from the bottom drawer of my desk. With my assignment completed and submitted, I could now see to the request from the CEO. As I headed out of my office, I briefly scanned the simple deep purple dress I was wearing. I hadn't given much thought to my outfit when I had slipped it on this morning. However at this moment, I hoped the clingy material gave my few curves some appeal and the simple black pumps highlighted my legs. I stood at barely over five feet so I often wore heels. And now I was boarding a crazy train. It was a meeting to discuss the new fall line, not set up a date. Besides, for all I knew he wasn't interested in dating.

On autopilot, my feet steered me toward the elevators since my office was on the fourth floor while the salesmen's offices were on the first. We had a small store on the first floor as well, since a pretty decent customer traffic flow graced our location in Mobile, Alabama. However, a large portion of our sales were generated online. Our inventory spanned from the most casual to sophisticated men's wear and traversed the trendy young adults as well as those who were well refined and in their early retirement years.

So lost in my thoughts, I almost missed the elevator doors opening onto the first floor. Thankfully, the background music streaming through the overhead speakers caught my attention since the song *Bigger Than Me* was one of my favorite songs. I stepped off of the elevator and strolled through the store, casually glancing at the merchandise. Sometimes I really wished I had someone to use my employee discount on. But the last guy I dated didn't deserve any gifts.

Then I headed in the direction of the dressing rooms which were situated right before the hallway that would lead me to the offices in the back. Taking a deep steadying breath, my heels clicked on the laminate flooring as I neared my destination. Six offices lined the hallway, three on each side, with an extra room used as storage being the last space at the end. I glanced at the name tags, searching for the one I needed. His door was the second one on the right.

I rapped lightly on his door, which was slightly ajar.

"Come in." His deep husky response sent shivers racing down my spine.

When I stepped inside, my eyes were immediately drawn to the tall figure sitting behind his desk, his concentration on his computer screen. His dark hair was slicked back and my fingers itched to run through the strands. *Easy girl.*

After a few taps to his keyboard, Colten shifted his attention to his guest. The boyish smile he shot me dampened my panties.

"Mr. Blackton told me to expect you today. I'm glad you were able to make time to meet with me. Come have a seat." He gestured to the plush chair positioned to the left of his desk.

Shaking off my body's unexpected yet gratifying reaction to his smile, I settled myself into the offered seat. This particular spot gave me an unobstructed view of the man and my eyes ate him up, from his light gray long sleeved shirt to his charcoal colored slacks. Neither article of clothing was overly huge on him, but he definitely didn't wear his clothes snug. The secrecy of what lie underneath was a mystery I craved to uncover.

"I'm excited to work together on some promos. I don't get to do that often. I usually have to work alone. I mean, I bounce ideas off of others when I get stuck, but it's always fun to team up. And Tawnie is usually the one who collaborates with others. She has more experience so she is the one who gets to do the promos on our new releases. Then I work on keeping the lines fresh with my graphics."

"Mr. Blackton thought you were the perfect choice to work with me and my ideas. He said he believed we would mesh well together." When he took off his glasses and set them on his desk, I almost swallowed my tongue. Damn was he handsome. And his bright green eyes were hypnotizing. Like I could seriously get lost in their depths and willingly do anything he commanded, merely because of the fact they put me in a trance.

"Do you want to go to dinner tonight?" I suddenly blurted. See! His eyes put me under a magical spell. And my traitorous mouth just spewed whatever the hell it liked. It wasn't that I didn't like the idea – oh quite the opposite; I actually loved the idea – but that didn't mean now was the perfect time to admit to my goals. My cheeks heated with my directness. "I'm sorry. That was so un – "

He lifted his hand to stall the rest of my apology. His boyish grin stretched across his face. "That was the best offer I've gotten all day."

"You mean others have asked you out before?"

"No." His smile dimmed slightly. "I was teasing you. I'd love to go to dinner. And no, no one else has asked me out from here."

"Well, I've been dying to go out with you. I've just been waiting for the perfect opportunity."

His eyes lost a bit of their sparkle. "You didn't want anyone to know you were interested in the awkward guy."

"No. That wasn't it at all. I was too nervous and shy to come down here without an excuse. Since I had to come down here today per the CEO's request; it made me take the chance I've been waiting for. I was worried you'd turn me down."

"Not a chance." He stretched his arm out to my chair and tugged it closer to him. "How about we get started so we can then talk about more interesting things; like where to go to eat." Slipping his glasses back onto his face, he shifted his attention back to his screen.

"So you don't have to wear glasses all of the time?"

"No. Only for reading, but sometimes it's easier to just leave them on my face. Then I don't forget them."

Staring at his profile, my mouth betrayed me again. "Easier for me too, cuz gah those eyes are hypnotically alluring." I slapped a hand to the traitor, but not quickly enough to muffle my confession.

Glancing over at me, he twisted his mouth in the most adorable way. "Everything about you is captivating. I don't think there is any way you could hide any aspect of it."

His words sent shivers all up in my belly and I was beginning to wonder if my panties were going to be salvageable by the end of the night. *Although maybe there'd be no need for my panties* ***before*** *the end of the night.* If I kept up with these thoughts I was going to be useless to him for getting any work done. *Focus. Work now; play later.* "Okay, show me what you got."

We spent the next two hours brainstorming and volleying ideas. Once we had a few solid promos designed, Colten sat back in his chair and folded his arms behind his head. The action hinting at some muscles underneath his shirt and distracting the hell out of me. I really wanted to unwrap him and investigate myself.

"I'll email these to Mr. Blackton and if he wants anything edited or more created; we can get together another day this week."

"Your work day ends after mine so I'm available any day after four. Although since this seems to be part of my assignment for now; I guess it wouldn't be a big deal if I came down here earlier."

"We'll see what he says about these and then I'll confirm with my schedule which days I don't work the store floor after four. Then we can plan to meet those days." He glanced at his Apple Watch. "Are you ready to get out of here?"

Move on to our date? Absolutely. "Yeah, I'm starving." And not just for food. "Any place in particular you'd like to go?"

"As a matter of fact, yes. It's a cozy Italian place about ten minutes from my place. My treat."

"But I'm the one who asked you out."

"True. But we're a team now and you came up with the idea to go out to eat tonight and I proposed the place. Besides, I'm traditional and the guy should pay."

"So a real date." Not just going to grab a bite to eat.

"Everything is real with you."

I wasn't sure what he meant by his response, but figured since we were dating I'd eventually get the chance to learn it all.

Colten powered off his computer and stood, offering me his hand. Once I slipped it inside his, he tugged me up to him, kissed me on the cheek, and led me out of his office. I knew he was tall, but he stood almost a foot taller than me. Normally I complained about being so short, but I loved feeling petite walking beside him.

Once outside we walked around to the side of the parking lot where the employees parked.

"I didn't think about the fact we drove in separate cars. Do you know where Bella Italia is? And are you okay following me to the restaurant?" He stopped at a black SUV.

My lips curled into a huge smile and I gestured to my gray Ford Escape. "This is my stop. And I can meet you there. I know where I'm going."

"Huh. For some reason I always park beside your car. I'll see you in about twenty minutes." Leaning down, he pressed a kiss to my forehead before ushering me into my car.

After I backed out of my spot and headed toward the exit of the lot, I glanced in my rear view mirror and caught a glimpse of him slipping into his own vehicle.

Nervous and excited butterflies flitted around in my stomach. I couldn't believe I was actually going on a date with Colten! What if he invited me home with him afterward? What if he didn't? And if he didn't; what if my mouth played traitor again and blurted out I wanted to go home with him? Gawd, that would be so embarrassing. I wasn't the type to sleep with someone on the first date, but with him I really wanted to change that.

When I pulled into the lot at the restaurant, Colten was waiting at the end of the sidewalk for me. While I strolled over to him, he stepped off of the curb and met me to take my hand, entwine our fingers, and lead me into the building.

Dinner was the most comfortable yet tantalizing date I had ever been on. We chatted, laughed, and touched throughout the meal. He shared about his younger years and his early interest in fashion, yet didn't say much about his middle and high school years. Although in all fairness, that was the awkward phase not many of us liked to talk about. Especially on a first date. Maybe once we knew one another better, he'd be more comfortable sharing about that time too. I told him about all of the mischief my younger sister and I would get into and how I loved to draw and create things. Especially by hand, but loved the more options I had now using computer programs.

After dinner was over and Colten paid the bill, he slipped his hand over mine and gave me a gentle squeeze. "I don't want our evening to end yet. Would you like to come over to my place so we can continue? If I'm being too forward, please don't feel like you'll hurt my feelings if you say we need to slow things down. We could just watch a movie or – "

Leaning toward him, I dropped my lips to his for a teasing kiss. "I was really hoping you'd offer first so my mouth wouldn't blurt out things again. I'm not ready for our evening to be over either. It's almost magical being here with you. I feel like we've know each other for months, but I've only talked to you one other time. And it was only a brief interaction. But I don't want you to think I do this a lot. Go home with someone on the first date. I don't."

"You don't strike me as that type of girl at all. Besides, I don't believe you are treating this as a casual fling. And I'm not either. I feel the same exact way. I feel some kind of connection between us. So are you ready to head out then?"

At my nod, Colten slid out of the booth, grabbed my hand, intertwined our fingers, and escorted me out to the parking lot. He walked me over to my car and gave me a lingering kiss, on my lips this time. His tongue licked at my lips and when I opened, he tangled his with my own briefly. "3124 Edson Lane in case you lose sight of my car. Watch for me to pull out and then follow."

I ducked into my car while he headed to his. After I backed out of the spot, I searched the lot for his vehicle. I spied him pulling out of a spot several rows down. He waited for me to get behind him and then led me out of the lot, into traffic, and toward his house.

About ten minutes later, he pulled into the driveway in front of a garage that was connected to a quaint crème colored two story house.

Pulling in beside him, I shut off my engine, retrieved my keys and stashed them in my purse before hopping out to join him. "This is a cute place."

Grabbing my hand, he walked me across the short pavement, up the few steps, and onto a cozy porch. A swing, small table, and four wicker chairs sat there tempting one to accept its open invitation.

After opening his front door, he tugged me inside. "Welcome to my home. Make yourself comfortable. Would you like a glass of wine, water, or iced tea?"

I kicked off my shoes at his entrance before strolling over to his dark gray plush couch, my eyes eating up my surroundings. His walls were painted dusty rose and his floors were dark hard wood. His couch, loveseat, and recliner were part of a set. The kitchen area sat off to the left; the walls light blue, the cupboards a deep walnut, and all steel appliances. "I'd love a glass of wine. Thank you." I plopped down on the couch. "Your place is beautiful."

"Thank you." He uncorked the bottle, poured two glasses, and then joined me on the couch. Handing one to me, he brought the other to his lips and took a small drink.

I did the same before setting my glass down on the coffee table in front of us.

He clicked on the flat screen that hung on the wall across from us. "What are you in the mood for?"

Probably the wrong question to ask; or maybe the right one. My body had been like a live wire since I had walked into his office. Hopefully we were on the same page. Scooting closer to him, I placed my hands at the hem of his shirt, and then ran them up the inside, relishing the feel of his taut muscles and smooth skin.

His eyes drifted closed and he let out a soft moan.

Perfect. We wanted the same thing.

Feeling bolder, I clasped the bottom of his shirt in my hands and brought it up and over his head before tossing it to the floor. Then I licked my lips at what I uncovered. "Why would you hide this gorgeous body? Is it so I don't drop into a swoon everyday while at work and then am rendered useless?" Shifting up onto my knees, I ran my lips along his collar bone and then down his left arm, loving how his muscles bunched under my touch. When my lips encountered white lines traced into his skin along his upper arm and on down his forearm, I traced the marks with my tongue. His skin was riddled with scars. But I was more interested in getting physically closer to him at the moment, not uncovering all of his deep-rooted mysteries. The more time we spent together; the more I knew he'd open up to me. Besides, we all had secrets and scars.

Releasing a deep sigh, Colten took my face in his hands and brought my gaze up to his puzzled one. "Everyone else who has seen these have cringed, showed me pity, or acted like they were more intriguing than me. Your reaction is so refreshing." He tilted his head to the side like he was analyzing me to figure out if I had an angle. Then he pressed his lips to mine. He gave me one second before his tongue pushed inside my mouth to wrap around my own and then hungrily devoured my mouth.

When he pulled back, he shot me a warm smile. "I cover up the scars because I don't like the prying questions. So many times it was so they would then have something to gossip about, but with you I'd like to share. I know it's because you want to get to know me. And the scars are a part of me."

"I'd really like you to tell me about them. Even though I'm sure it doesn't make great pillow talk, but we haven't made it to the bedroom *yet*." I shot him a mischievous smile.

"Fuck, you're perfect. If that's where you want to end up, I'll be more than happy to take you there. But first I'll tell you about my teenage years. That's when I suffered the injuries." He took in a shuddering breath.

"My parents died when I was thirteen and my brother had just turned eighteen. Some relative probably would have taken me in, but my brother insisted he would take care of me. That our parents would have wanted that. But that meant he had to put his life on hold, girlfriend and college, stuff like that. He grew to resent me pretty quickly. We fought a lot and many times it turned physical and I walked away with cuts and bruises. I'm not sure how he managed not to break any of my bones."

He blew out a rough exhale. "However, this went on for years until one time he got so mad he threw me through our glass patio door. The shattering glass cut up both of my arms. There was so much blood he thought I was going to bleed to death. It was his wake up call. He sent me to stay with my grandparents for a while and the two of us went to counseling. First to deal with the grief of losing our parents at a young age and then with how to bond again as brothers. It took us over two years, but we've never been closer. You can see why I don't like telling people about this. It paints my brother in a bad light. And it wasn't that he didn't love me. He didn't know what to do with all that pent up grief, frustration, and anger about not being able to care for me and still live for himself."

"I would never judge him. I couldn't imagine what he went through. What both of you went through. Thank you so much for trusting me enough to tell me. I want us to learn everything about one another." I cupped his face in my hands and gave him a tender kiss. Then I stood up from the couch and offered him my hand. "Would you take me to your room? I want to show you something."

His face still held a faint trace of sadness from diving into memories that still tore at him, but his eyes twinkled at the thought of what I would be revealing. Oh I'd definitely be showing him that, but there was something more important I needed to share first.

Rising from the couch, he took my hand.

As he led me down the hall, I was both nervous and excited. Excited to get to the sex part, but nervous about opening up to him about my past. He had been a young kid so didn't know what to do. I had been twenty three and old enough to know how to escape it.

Inside his bedroom, he led me over to a king sized bed that took up the far side. His walls were tan and the carpet a crème color. His dresser and nightstand were stained dark. After pulling back the navy blue comforter, he gently pushed me down onto the mattress. Then he slid in next to me and we faced each other.

"Are you doing a strip tease or do I get to unwrap my gift?" His boyish grin shot another flash of arousal down to my core.

"Not really a strip tease, but I want to show you something first. You shared something difficult with me; I want to reciprocate. Because I trust you and I want you to know about me too. My last boyfriend was abusive. I stayed with him for two years believing he would change. That he meant it every time he said he was sorry."

Colten cupped my cheeks in his hands and pressed a gentle kiss to my forehead. But said nothing. And I was so thankful. Just like him; I didn't want his pity.

Taking the hem of my dress in my hands, I slowly slid the material up my body and over my head before depositing it on the ground. I watched as his eyes hungrily ate up the skin I revealed. But I also noticed he wasn't searching for the scars he knew I was going to tell him about. They weren't important; I was.

"He slapped me around anytime he didn't get his way. I ended up with so many split lips, black eyes, and bruises everywhere from on my face, down my arms, my stomach and thighs. He didn't even care if people could see them. They embarrassed me, but not him. They were like trophies for him." Craning my neck back, I pointed to the bottom of my skull right at my left ear. "He threw me into an end table and split my head open. I needed stitches. It's one of my scars."

Colten leaned toward me to peer at the mark and placed a gentle kiss there. The action sent a shiver up my spine. A good shiver.

"One night I had a migraine and didn't want to have sex. He was so pissed off; he cut my clothes off of me and then dug his knife into the skin at the top of my thigh. He thought he'd help out and give me another pain to focus on." I pointed to another reminder of how I wasn't strong enough to get out of a toxic relationship.

Once again, Colten didn't say a word and I was glad he didn't ask the question I knew was on his mind. I could see it in his turbulent expression. Instead, he ran his lips along the scar.

"I did finally get to the point where I had had enough. We were fighting because I didn't want to go out to the bar with his obnoxious friends, but instead to my parents for the evening. In a fit of rage, he threw me into my full length mirror. That's how I got the scars along my right arm and a few along my side."

His fingers lightly traced the marks.

"While in the emergency room, I told them I wanted to talk to a police officer. I pressed charges, got a restraining order, and thankfully he stayed away after that." I blew out a shaky breath. Talking about my past always drudged up horrid memories for me. "I hope I didn't ruin the mood, but I wanted to share with you, not wait until you saw the scars for yourself. I want you to know I trust you."

"You didn't ruin anything. Right now I want to love your body all over. Show you just how precious you are and worship you the way you deserve to be. I want to make love to you. If you still want me to tonight."

"More than anything."

He shot me a wolfish grin before his lips whispered along my skin. As his mouth skimmed down my body, his hand slid down between my legs to my wet center. Pushing my thong aside, he dipped a finger inside of me and we both moaned in tandem.

He had only begun his explorations of my body, but I was so impatient for more.

"I do this to you?" His words were infused with awe and his gaze shot up to mine.

"Ever since you first smiled at me in your office. I can't wait to feel you inside of me."

"You won't get any argument from me. But I do have a confession." He reached over to his nightstand and pulled out a packet of condoms. "You had mentioned that you don't normally do this; well neither do I. I've never had a girl over at this apartment and before then when I was at my old place it was almost two years ago. So my condoms were expired. I bought this packet a week after meeting you in the hopes of us getting together." A blush crawled across his cheeks which I found incredibly adorable. "I hope that's not terrible of me."

"Well, it's not like you came up to my office and said 'hey I think you're cute, wanna go to my house and fuck." A giggle slipped out when his eyes widened at my candidness.

"But what if I was thinking it?" His blush deepened.

"I love that so much. So hot." I grabbed his face, pulled it to me, and pressed my lips to his.

But I didn't have control of the kiss for long. Tilting my head for better access, his tongue swooped in and he devoured my mouth again. When we finally separated, he quickly stripped out of his pants and boxers, and slid on the condom. Then after divesting me of my bra and panties, he settled his body in between my thighs.

"You are so beautiful; every part of you." Taking himself in hand, he lined up with my entrance and slowly pushed in. "Fuck that feels incredible."

Winding my legs around his waist, I pulled him in farther. My body spasmed as the intrusion shot bolts of electricity throughout me.

Slowly, he withdrew and then shoved back inside. Each consecutive time with a bit more force.

My eyes rolled into the back of my head as an unladylike moan ripped from my chest.

"So I take it that feels pretty damn good?" His voice held traces of cockiness.

With the way my body was thrumming; he was entitled. "Better than good. Please don't stop."

A rush of tingles sparked across my lower belly, igniting a fire deep in my core. When Colten's dick rubbed along my clit with his next several thrusts, the zaps morphed into an explosion of white heat and I screamed out his name as my orgasm tackled me; leaving me panting for breath.

Three thrusts later, Colten joined me in my bliss; my name a barely distinguishable word released in his feral growl. He dropped down beside me on his side and snuggled me into his arms, feathering kisses along my temple and down my cheek. "Stay with me tonight."

I only hesitated for a moment. He was who I had been waiting for. "Okay."

"I can drive you home to get stuff for tomorrow so you don't have to leave earlier for work. I'm really glad you agreed to stay. I want us to be an official couple, but we can slowly tell people at work. I don't want to rush you. I don't like to be – "

I cut off his rambling with a hot kiss. "I like that idea. I don't care who all you tell. I'm not embarrassed. I've actually wanted this since we first met too. And workplace relationships don't go against our policy as long as they don't interfere with our job. So I'm glad circumstances brought us together; made us take that first step. I'm really looking forward to staying the night."

He cuddled me closer to his chest. "Good. I want to wake up with you in my arms."

After we snuggled for a few minutes, we got up to clean ourselves off and get dressed. Then he ran me home, where I quickly packed a bag after taking a brief shower.

Back at his house, we crawled into bed. Wrapped up in his arms, I experienced the best night's sleep I'd had in a very long time.

The next morning, we got ready for work together like an actual couple. I had to be at work two hours before him, but he still ate breakfast with me and said he'd use the time to take care of some chores before heading into work.

I passed Trudy on my way to my office and she shot me a strange look. I shrugged it off. Maybe my face radiated the fact that I had had an amazing night last night. Good. I hoped I wore the expression all day long.

Two hours into my day I had to head upstairs to Tawnie's office to grab a packet I needed for my next project.

When I returned, I discovered a vase of flowers on my desk – tiger lilies, which were my absolute favorite. I wasn't a roses type of girl. I didn't remember telling Colten about my favorite flower, but we talked about so much and so easily; I could have easily forgotten. Wanting to see him in person instead of calling to tell him thank you, I headed downstairs to talk for just a minute.

He was organizing a section of ties when I got to the store, but he shot me a sexy smile when I stopped in front of him. "So you really don't care if people find out about us sooner rather than later."

"Well, no. I don't care who knows. But I wanted to thank you in person for the flowers. I don't remember talking about flowers last night, but we talked about so much."

"I didn't get you flowers. I didn't want to seem overzealous." He shot me a frown.

"Oh. That's okay. I didn't expect anything. There wasn't a card, so maybe my mom sent me them." I shrugged. While I worked today; I'd have to do some investigating.

"I hope you don't have a secret admirer." His scowl grew.

"Too bad if I do. I'll have to put a stop to that. I'm yours." I shot him a quick flirty smile. After all, we were in the work place and although I wasn't going to hide my relationship with him, I wasn't going to do anything to jeopardize it either.

"Shoot." He rummaged through the top box setting on a cart beside him. "I must have left one of the boxes of ties in the storage room."

"I can go grab it before I head back upstairs."

"Thank you. We really do make a great team." His lips curved into one of his devastating smiles.

My heels clicked as I made my way down the hallway. I'd only been in the storage room one other time, when I was helping unload an unusually large delivery. We didn't keep a lot of items in stock. Most of the time it was used when we were rotating seasonal apparel or if there was something that was incredibly popular and we wanted to make sure it was available in store.

As I headed past the last of the offices, the hairs on the back of my neck stood on end. But before I could put much stock in the sensation, I hard body slammed into me from behind and pinned me to the wall right beside the door at the very end of the hallway. The intruder twirled me around so fast, my head spun briefly. When angry blue eyes locked on mine, his hand clasped around my throat, ensuring I wouldn't let out a peep.

"Did you get my flowers?"

Yup, but they would be promptly thrown in the trash.

"A peace offering for us to get back together. I think it's been long enough. Retract the restraining order. I've been amply patient."

My eyes widened at his audacity, but I shouldn't have been surprised.

His grasp tightened and I prayed someone would venture down this way. With his body pressed up tight against mine, I couldn't move my leg to knee him in the crotch and my nails digging into his forearm had no effect on him.

So caught up in our standoff, I didn't notice my rescuer until an arm struck out like a cobra and fingers wrapped around my ex's forearm, the action instantly releasing the grip on my throat. In a flurry of action that only lasted a couple of minutes, Colten had Darin's arm pinned behind his back and had wrestled him to the ground.

"Call security." Colten grunted in my direction.

Darting into the storage room, I dialed the security desk and requested immediate assistance.

A few minutes later, an officer charged down the hallway; cuffed Darin; and handed him off to another officer who had joined us. Darin tossed out obscenities and threats as he was carted away.

I sagged into Colten's waiting arms and he hugged me close. "I'm guessing that was the ex."

"Yeah." My voice was raspy as I lay my head against his chest, my heart pounding at my ribcage like it was desperate to break through.

We took a few minutes to inform the officer about what had happened.

Then when it was only the two of us; I gazed up at him and gave him a small smile. "How were you able to do that? I'm not saying you aren't tough; I've seen your body, but wow. He's like three or four inches taller than you and probably weighs at least twenty pounds more than you do."

He kissed the top of my head. "While my brother and I were going to counseling, he insisted that I take self-defense classes as well. I want you to take them. I'll even go with you and I can refresh on some things."

"Okay. That's something we can do as a couple." And was a really good idea. I was sure Darin was going to be in a bit of trouble over today's incident, but I wasn't sure when he would finally just leave me alone. And self-defense was a good thing for anyone to learn.

"Are you okay? Other than being a little shaken up?" After leaning back slightly, his fingers lightly traced over my throat. "He left marks on your skin again." His growl was a bit terrifying. "Will you be okay to walk back up to your office by yourself? And I know you're a tough woman," he smirked down at me. "But I'm sure that was a bit terrifying."

"I'll be okay. I know you can't leave the floor. But I'll hang out in your office after I'm done for the day. We can leave together. And maybe you can follow me home to pack a bag again for tonight and then we can head to your house."

"I love the way your brain works." He gave me a squeeze before taking my hand and leading me back out to the store area.

Thankfully, there weren't any customers browsing at the moment. However, Mr. Blackton stood at the jumbled tie display, his expression unreadable.

"Sorry, Mr. Blackton. There was an incident." Colten didn't release my hand.

"I was just informed of the situation." He shifted his gaze to me, not sparing our connected hands a glance. "Please, stop by the security office on your way back upstairs to make sure they have everything accurate and nothing else needs included. I want to be sure this issue is taken care of promptly and appropriately. I don't tolerate attacks on my employees. I trust you are okay, other than a bit unsettled. You don't need medical attention?"

"No, sir. The marks will fade. And my throat is a little sore, but I'll grab some hot tea on my way back upstairs."

"Very good. And by the way, the graphics you two sent me are spot-on. I will be having the two of you work together on many things in the future. You make a great team. Keep up the impressive work." With that parting compliment, Mr. Blackton turned and strolled out of the store.

Careful not to push our luck, I ran my hand up Colten's chest briefly before locking my eyes on his. "We do make a wonderful team. And he doesn't know the half of it." I shot him a flirty wink. "I'll see you after work, partner."

After stopping in the security office, I headed up to the fourth floor with a little bounce to my step. Yes, the altercation with my ex had been a bit scary and my hands still held a slight tremble from the confrontation, but now I had someone in my corner I could count on for everything.

Right after stepping inside my office, I grabbed the vase of flowers and promptly stormed to the staff restroom and tossed them in the trash. I didn't want them anywhere near me. Then I got back to work, smiling to myself. I was so glad I took a chance on Colten because I couldn't imagine being any happier than when I was with him.

The End

Laying it Bare series:

Laying it Bare with a Friend Request

Laying it Bare with an Ex-Con

Laying it Bare with One of the Guys

Laying it Bare on the Run

Laying it Bare in Pre-Med

Laying it Bare After a Loss

Laying it Bare Through the Lies

Laying it Bare Biker Style ~ Ryder

Laying it Bare Biker Style ~ Grayson

Laying it Bare Backstage (February 2025)

Other Titles by L.E. Martin

The Renters

Blood Covenant Split (Blood Covenant Duet Book One)

Blood Covenant Restored (Blood Covenant Duet Book Two)

Blood Covenant Forever (A Blood Covenant World novel)

Phoenix

By S.G. Blinn

Bartholomew

I see you in a ring of fire, an array of orange and red dancing around your feet.

You wear a torn wool petticoat that barely grazes your bloodied feet and an apron dyed with luscious colors of the sun. Your moon-kissed skin is littered with dirt and ash. Small cuts and abrasions are grazed by the twilight breeze. Chained to a wooden platform, your bruised wrists bound tightly behind your back, you look towards the end with a fearless expression, your dark curls matted to your forehead and cheeks. It's covered in the trash they threw at you.

You should have been warm and protected in your bed, yet you are here, ready to die.

It is risky being here. If they find me, the consequences of my death would ripple unparalleled. But selfishly, I could not let you die alone.

In this life, I have only known you from a distance. You came to this little mountain village to escape prosecution. They saw someone new. You resided all alone in a house on top of a hill. They saw someone unique. Differences were not welcome. You were forthcoming and direct, you argued with anyone who tried to tell you what to do. That was dangerous to those set in their own ways.

You came at the wrong time: this world fears a strong woman.

"The Devil has cursed us!" a mother holding their child cries.

"She is the one that doomed us all!"

"You are the reason they are dead."

This village has been plagued with illness and drought. There was nothing anyone could do to prevent it. Without the rain, the crops died. Without medicine, the sick perished. They concluded you are the reason for their peril. Your differences caused them to chant for your destruction. Rather than learn your name, they called you a witch.

You were sitting in a rocking chair next to the forest-facing window, inhaling the sun as if it was the very air you breathed, when a dozen men viciously pulled you from your home, dragged you through the village square, to the spot you now stand.

The village gathered for your death sentence. Their words are sharper than any knife they could wield. Still, that fiery spirit burns within even as you stay quiet. How could you be so calm? Bodies huddle close to your platform; they all want to witness what will happen next, but you will not struggle, satisfy them with your pain.

You know what is coming and are ready to answer death's call.

And I stand among the crowd, waiting for you to notice me.

"Burn her!" a child yells.

"Kill her!" a man hollers.

Your silence infuriates them. Even as filth is unleashed, you never part your lips. Your eyes hold an undying rage that glistens with the yellow flames. Those eyes reflect the deep red of their hate.

How could the world wish the destruction of a person as beautiful as you?

The magistrate, dressed in his lavish robes, approaches the platform. The mark of fire was hanging from a golden chain around his neck. He spoke with such certainty of your crimes.

"You stand before us today as a servant of the Devil himself. Do you confess to your crimes of witchcraft?"

"Repent!" the crowd yells.

"Confess!" others chant.

You remain silent, your face still: you are the witch that accepts your fate. No amount of pain will give them the satisfaction of seeing you beg. This is going to be your end.

You are stronger than anyone I will ever know. I envy that strength.

Around the platform are sticks and brush from the surrounding forest to help feed the dancing flame. The magistrate comes forth holding a torch in his hand.

"In your silence, you have confessed your sins."

"Burn the witch!" a child hollers.

"Burn her!" others wail.

Their pain is carried throughout the night, and so the magistrate obeys their demands. An evil glint fills his bright, green eyes. He throws the torch into the pile below the platform, and he walks a few steps back. Within moments, the fire dances at your feet. Soft crackles ignite a larger flame that peeks through the wooden boards you stand upon.

The crowd celebrates. Their voices break through the night air.

"We will be free from her evil!"

"Scream for us!"

Your feet would have started to grow warm, but you do not seem bothered. You silently scan the masses, watch them scream their disdain for your existence and dance around the growing flames.

As you look through the crowd, your eyes find mine.

The first thing you will have noticed is we share the same eye color, golden like the summer sun, a trait of those blessed by this earth. The second, my face does not show the same distain for your existence. I am a witch such as yourself—yet something more.

The fire licks your ankle and you flinch. The flames grow mightier and it feeds off your agony. A moment of pain flashing across your face makes my heart ache. Your face scrunches up and you bare your teeth to prevent the scream from escaping your lips. They rejoice.

I blink. Your expression calms: you seem to know what I am.

"Burn!" they chant.

"Scream for us!" some wail.

Their voices grow yet you remain strong.

I have seen death in many forms; you've watched your sisters burn. Those who use the elements against our kind hurt us in the most volatile sense. We are here to preserve this world, use the elements for its protection. Our voices help the birds sing. Our hands assist the flowers' growth. Our bodies create the very wind that cools them on a hot summer day. Even with all we do, we are being destroyed by them.

I don't look away. I trap you in this moment. I will make this quick, a final gift to you in this short life otherwise full of hate and fear.

Maybe you thought your fate would be different. How wrong you were.

I never wanted you to feel this pain. As the fire strokes your skin, your body relaxes. The embers dance up your petticoat. The apron's bright colors turn to ash. It consumes you. The crowd grumbles about how you did not scream, about their lack of amusement, but I feel a tear escape down my cheek.

This isn't the final end, my lovely phoenix, I promise.

I do not want you to be afraid. I will always be with you, to guide you to your rebirth. We will have another chance to be together.

All you have to do is wait.

Aubryn

225 Years Later

For my entire life, I have had the same nightmare, a fear I cannot control. I'm bound by something heavy and cold, unable to move. Darkness surrounds me, but I'm engulfed in fire and pain.

Then, voices grow louder, the infinite dark space creating an echo of chanting. *Witch.* They know what I am. The voices scream as fire peeks through the floorboards at my feet. *Burn the witch.* Fire erupts around me, and I scream.

As a child, this dream terrified me. A coldness crept through me, making me cry. It felt like a warning, a foreshadowing of something to come. I would run into my grandmother's arms and beg for her to make those images go away. I still remember how she would touch my head, give me a smile, and tell me not to worry. That was all I ever needed.

She was my safe space.

My grandmother raised me. I never questioned why I didn't have any parents because she told me that I was loved. When I asked about the dream, she told me they were my ancestors telling me to be careful, and a heaviness would fill my heart. The dream showed a woman who died because she was different. All those blessed by the Mother that created us were doomed to the persecution of others.

Now, at the age of twenty-five, I stand in the house that once held the most beautiful woman. My grandmother had passed two years ago. I've tried not to be sad about it because I was told that they found her in her garden. A hunter had come into her space for directions and found her unresponsive. The hospital told me over the phone she had a heart attack. It was her time. I wish I could have been at her side, but that was not how fate allowed it to happen.

Being my grandmother's only living relative, I was left this house—a gift, the will explained, to help me better understand the person I'm meant to be. She always knew how to make the sadness and fear disappear, but still, I feel alone now.

Thirty minutes from the nearest town, this old, rustic, brick-walled farmhouse is perfectly isolated from those who may judge me. The single, open floor plan has many windows. I will never be trapped in this enclosure of memories, but every memory we had together fills this space.

She had taught me to read on the same wooden table that still stands in the kitchen. The books were old; its pages were brittle and had to be handled with care. They smelled of basil and mint. She explained it helped keep the moisture away and preserve the paper. She taught me about the Mother who created the earth and her gentle teachings. I longed for those stolen moments of her time.

I now stand in the living room facing the large, open, double glass doors. A warm summer breeze blesses this space. Looking at my bare feet, I think about the story my grandmother had told me:

"Those who lived before, who shared our blood, blessed this space. Within their final moments, their ashes fertilized the soil to encourage new growth for the future."

The story has clearer meaning in her death. To be lying on the earth that bore her, surrounded by the flowers she helped grow, was her way to return to Mother. She spent her entire life as caretaker of this place, but it was always meant to be mine. I feel its power.

"Meow."

My golden eyes shift to a long elegant black cat walking through the open doors. The first thing I always notice about that feline are his golden eyes. They are like mine, enchanting, but they also hold many wonders of his glorious adventures.

Many myths surrounded the true origin of a black cat. Some call them a bad omen, others use them for luck. I have no preference regarding the folktales. In my world, it is recommended to get a familiar, a connection to the earth that can help guide my magic, but he does not belong to me. I sadly never had that connection. Still, it is wrong to call him anything other than my equal—all creatures of this world deserve my utmost respect.

When he enters this space, I am captivated by his presence. Those golden eyes entrap my attention and he swallows all sense of time. He never gets closer than a few feet. That is all I am worthy of getting from this wonderful creature. I will not dare to touch his precious fur, not until he allows me to be in that space of trust.

I smile warmly. "Good morning to you, too, Bartholomew."

He sits on the wooden floor. His lean, well-groomed body is encased in black fur, with speckles of white littering his chin. If the sun hits him at the right spot, he looks like he's glowing. It's a wonderful sight to witness.

The coffee I hold slowly grows cold.

No; I shake my head. He is only a cat. I'm romanticizing the idea of something more. I have read too many novels about a brooding animal-shifter protecting what is *his.* Or, a brave hero saving the princess. I am not a damsel in distress; but it feels like Bartholomew was watching over me, and in this moment, he knew I did not want to be alone.

I laugh. "In case you have come to inspect this fine establishment, I cleaned the entire house. There were too many cobwebs and forest critters. No offense, but I am still not looking for a roommate."

My grandmother died two years ago. I had tried to get back sooner, but something was keeping me away. My mind kept being drawn to menial tasks of my personal life so I allowed this house to remain vacant. Never did anyone come near it. The forest made the trails impassable, and the weather never damaged the house. It was protected, waiting for me to reopen the warmth it once held.

"Not much of a talker, huh?" I joke to Bartholomew.

Those golden eyes watch me.

I remember the first time I met him. It was when I first came back to this house. I had stood in front of the door, unable to enter. I didn't think it would hurt as much as it did, but an uncontrollable sadness had overwhelmed me.

His single meow snapped me to the present and called me towards the house. He sounded like he was in trouble. I didn't think, I only reacted. Barreling through that door, the sadness was replaced by the image of him standing in the open doorway, basking in the sun.

I took it as a sign that he was meant to be here, with me. I didn't know if he was a familiar, but it felt right to include him in my life. So I named him Bartholomew, a fitting name for a wise, old soul.

I always smile when I think of that memory. He invited me into this space and stayed with me. He filled an ache in my heart that longs to be loved.

A sadness hits my heart. Today feels different. Why does it feel like this is the last time I will ever see him? A single tear threatens to fall from the corner of my eye. No, I refuse to allow this moment to be taken back by my emotions.

My computer dings a high pitch, drawing me out of my musings. In the age of technology, one way a witch can make a living with their craft is by having a flashy business model. The internet is an ideal place to put on a majestic performance. It has made it safer for people like me to pursue something different, and I have control in doing readings in this house. Some may call it risky, but it feels safe for me. And what is living without a little risk anyway?

I walk over to the kitchen table and look at the computer screen. Setting the coffee cup aside, I review my website's home page:

Behind the vale. To the ones you love.

The future you crave. The peace you seek.

All you have to do is believe, and I will guide you there.

I have the ability to reach people. It isn't a gimmick; everyone's eyes give an energy that leads to their desires—or more often, lead to their destruction. Sometimes the fear of someone knowing your deepest secrets prevents you from living your best life, so I want to create a safe space for anyone to feel at ease about what they seek.

The notification shows a booking scheduled for tonight.

"Let's see what they want," I mutter.

The website is simple enough to navigate: I can see all the bookings in the administration bar at the top and update my information easily.

The individual is requesting a reading of love.

"Alright, Bartholomew, it is time to prepare!" I announce.

The cat had fallen asleep near the open door, probably enjoying the sunrays pouring on his fur.

I turn and look towards the front of the house. Everything I will need is tucked away in the living space near the front door. It has a large sitting area with a stone fireplace and a variety of shelves filled with items from the forest—vases filled with valerian for readiness, a bowl of dried thyme for courage, and my grandmother's hand-woven basket for guidance. In that basket are stones we collected at the river and hand-carved to help guide me to where I am needed.

I check the clock. It won't take me long to set up the table. That means I can catch a quick nap before the reading. I want to be ready for whatever may happen.

"See you in a few, Bartholomew!" I laugh at my unintended rhyme as I walk into my bedroom and close the door behind me so the world would not disturb me.

The hours tick by, and darkness quickly follows. I emerge from my slumber and get to work. It doesn't take long to prepare the space. A large dark cloth over an oval table, a few foldable chairs, and my stones from the shelves. What takes the most time is deciding what to wear because my outfit holds a connection to who I'm truly meant to be. I don't need to hide anymore.

Knock. Knock.

It is time.

I change into a long beaded red-and-orange dress that hugs my body and dangles around my ankles. The vibrant color reminds me of the roaring flames in my nightmare. My thick curly hair is down and wild—my grandmother said my hair reminded her of raven feathers; there is no point in taming a mass of hair that is meant to be free.

Knock. Knock.

I forgo putting on my simple black shoes; they will take away from the presentation. I shift my body and walked towards the red front door. As I walk past a mirror on the wall, I take in my appearance. I am nothing special. I don't stand out with a full-face of makeup or lavish jewels. Maybe if—

Knock. Knock.

I need to stay focused. I sigh and fix my hair, the silver and gold rings on each finger glinting in the reflection. I slide bracelets of colorful gems onto my wrists. Then, I'm complete.

Turning and reaching forward, I touch the cool steel knob and turn it.

A wave of fear overtakes me. Images of a man holding a burning torch of dancing embers makes me want to run.

Thump. Thump. My heart won't stop racing in my chest.

"Meow." That small creature's voice breaks the fear creeping in.

My eyes strain against the darkness. Within moments, the candlelight illuminates Bartholomew sitting in the doorway. A creature I trust. He quickly stands and walks away, gone as quickly as he appeared.

I blink, and a man stands in his place. He wears a three-piece suit as dark as the shadows at his feet, and his eyes are hidden by the rim of his fedora. His existence instantly swallows me whole.

"Welcome." I don't know what else to say. I become breathless.

There is a long moment of silence. It doesn't feel awkward, though. I move to the side, sweeping my arms out in silent instruction.

He walks slowly forward. Once he crosses into my space, a cool breeze from the open window brings his scent to me. It is a cold, tender, woodsy smell. I close my eyes. A calmness overtakes me. I want to wrap my arms around that smell, to be engulfed in its safety. It brings a sense of happiness I never felt.

I watch as his silent steps bring him forward. His attention goes around the room, and he scans every shelf he can see. I want to begin but a part of me says *be patient*. This room is part of the experience I offer. He can take all the time he needs.

His gaze stops on the watercolor paintings on the wall. They are framed in old wooden rectangles that enchant the memories of my dreams. He draws closer to the fire of bright orange with a splatter of reds, the daunting darkness lingering on the sides.

"To never scream, not even in the face of death, could be seen either as courage or stubbornness." His voice is deep.

I take the man in. His words hit me hard. He saw the feeling within the images. The woman did not have a mouth: she could not scream, a small detail anyone could have missed.

I shake my head. My heart begins to beat rapidly in my chest. A gnawing ache grows.

His body is rigid and his shoulder flexes as he slowly turns around. Making no noise, he lifts his gaze, and those deep golden eyes meet mine. I cannot look away.

His face is flawless—sharp jaw line, fine nose, and a cold judgemental stare that grips me. The man doesn't blink as he shifts his body and sits down at the table.

"I need to find someone," he adds.

A silent song exists underneath the low drawl of an accent I cannot place. The air is taken from my lungs. My body starts to become fatigued. Only when he looks away do I regain control. Could he be looking for family—? No, it was a lover. The longing in those eyes is screaming out to her. He is in pain. His face is cold in expression yet soft in those golden orbs of wisdom.

I need to stay focused. I have a feeling if he asked me to do something, I will comply without a moment's hesitation.

This man could be dangerous.

I shake my head. This man is here for a service. I will not disappoint him. I need to regain control of this situation.

I take a few steps towards the table and clear my throat. "I am not a magician, or a detective. I cannot locate—"

The man's dark leather glove touches the table. His fingers splay across a pile of smooth stones that lie side by side, never stacked. They connect me to this world, their guidance leading me to a place that no one can see. These stones are charged with the energy I use to draw my visions. They are a vital piece to finding what he seeks.

"I seek the one that I am destined to love."

I wait a moment before I speak. "Tell me about them."

He gives me a sad smile. "The stars speak of an uncontrollable fire that I will never be able to grasp. A love so pure and always out of my reach. It will be smothered before I am able to hold what is mine."

The way he speaks holds knowledge and balance.

He pinches a red stone in his fingers. Raising it from the table, the man brings it near the candlelight. It glistens a soft rose-color hue. Red could have many meanings. Pair the stone with particular desires, and it could lead you to what is truly anticipated.

He looks at the color created from the candlelight, then says, "Are you waiting for me to say something?"

I need to know why he picked that stone. Each were hand crafted from the raw materials my grandmother had collected over her lifetime, but that specific red stone was mine. Among the dozen before him, he picks the only one I hand-carved with a whisper of love to the moon? Why that—

His gaze shifts to mine.

My cheeks flush. Did he know that stone was mine? Was he here to grant my wish? That was impossible. This world had lost its magic when it stopped believing in the Mother: my wish couldn't be fulfilled, there was no possible way he was here for me.

I clear my throat and sit down, visibly shaken by this handsome man. There is an aura about him that I do not trust.

It's dark. A shadow lingers around him. No emotion or purpose is felt, but it is watching me. I want to run but those eyes keep me in my seat.

I hold out my hand. "I use the stones to energize the visions. They need to be left undisturbed."

The man nods. When his fingers touch my palm, I see a spark. A golden light disappears within seconds. Rather than pull away, the man puts his hand in mine. A course of power rushes through my body. It feels like jolts of electricity aimed right for my heart. I hold my breath.

Looking to him, I become lost in those eyes. His lips do not move, but I only hear his voice in my head. "I need you to stay asleep, my phoenix. We will be together soon."

My heart stills for a beat and I blink. My entire vision shifts.

The man is gone.

I shoot up in my bed and realize I am no longer in that room. A cold sweat covers my face. What happened? I was— He— I need to ground my thoughts.

What time is it?

I reach for my phone and find where it always lies, at my bedside. When I touch the screen, it stays black. The cellphone is dead. A panic rises in me. Images of that beautiful man flash in my mind. It didn't feel like a dream.

I jump from my bed and my bare feet hit the cold wooden floorboards, and then I notice there is no noise. The birds, summer breeze, and even the trees are silent. Everything feels too still to be real.

My feet gain speed as I rush into the kitchen. My eyes dance to the clock on the wall. It had stopped, the time yet to be discovered. My breathing hastens. My chest becomes heavy. I look for another source of time.

The stove.

When I turn to face the appliance, the numbers are blinking.

What time is it?

What day is—

"Meow." The familiar call of my sweet Bartholomew takes me out of my panicked state.

"Bartholomew?"

Every window and door are closed: he couldn't get into the house. He is nowhere to be seen.

My feet slowly bring me to the front of the house. It looks undisturbed. How could this be? That man, the one in the suit, he was here last night. Yet the candlewicks are unburned, my stones are still in their basket on the shelf, and the presence of him is not in the air. Did last night really happen?

"What is going on?" I whisper.

My computer dings. I turn to look towards the kitchen table, a feeling of déjà vu hitting me. That is never a good sign. This is how they always started—the nightmares. I would be in a familiar place and then pulled into the darkness surrounded by fire.

No. I do not want to go there. It hurts. The fire burns, their voices scream for my death. I swallow hard. The computer dings again.

"Meow."

A warmth touches my legs, but when I look down, I don't see him. I can feel him—how can this be? Never has that cat allowed me to touch him. His soft, warm fur rubs once more between my legs, bringing a sudden comfort to the panic rising in my chest.

I blink, and there he stands.

Those golden eyes look up. He appears with a silent shift. I hesitantly pick him up and hold him tightly to my chest. The softness of his fur tickles my face. It grounds me. The purring soothes me. As I close my eyes, I feel the world once more shift around me.

"You are no longer safe."

It was *his* voice.

My eyes slowly open. Bartholomew is gone. I am now sitting back at the table across from the man with the golden eyes. The candlelight around me dances. It creates many shifts of light that cover his face, and I can't make out his features clearly.

My heart beats rapidly. I blink once more and I am now standing.

The room seems to wash away in an unseen summer breeze. All that remains is a flame in the distance. The longer I look, the more I realize that flame was growing bigger.

Taking a single step forward, I am drawn to its light. Like a moth trapped in its own demise, I follow it.

With a single breath, *he* appears before me in that same windless breeze. I can see him and those golden eyes. He slowly approaches me, and within those eyes, I dare say, I see an unbelievable sadness.

He takes another step towards me. "Listen to my warning, Aubryn. You are not safe."

I regain the ability to move. My body wants to run away but my mind makes me take steps forward. With every step, the fire dims. My red-and-orange sequined dress moves silently. A warmth engulfs my bare feet that slowly wraps around my legs.

The man reaches out his hand. "I do not want you to feel this pain."

"What is happening to me?" I whisper.

"You were born to die."

I suck in a breath. A single tear forms in the corner of my eye. I should be afraid of his words, but my mind accepts them. Is this true? I want to be scared, to run, but in his presence, I feel a calmness that keeps me right where I needed to be. I want to hear the sweet deliciousness of his deep voice.

"I do not understand."

He lets out a soft sigh. "It is a cycle that we can't seem to break. All I can do is take away the pain and shield your eyes from the horrors that you are about to face."

The warmth grows from my legs to my chest. Something itches at the back of my mind. Those golden eyes tell me he is one of my people—those blessed by the earth. Yet, he is something more. Something that isn't . . . human. He is a being beyond this reality, beyond my comprehension.

But he smells of the forest that I love. Morning dew and a cooling, woodsy taste that blankets your senses. I feel safe.

My body feels split. What I see does not equal what I feel. There is no source of the heat. My body gets hotter. I smell something—smoke?

A single panic is erased when I regain the smell of the forest, of him. When I finally touch his hand, he pulls me into his safe embrace. His head moves and I feel his soft lips at my ear.

"Do not wake up, my phoenix. I do not want you to feel this."

I do not know what he is doing.

My mind shifts from the man to the smell of a wood-burning stove. It reminds me of the dark nights spent with my grandmother. We would talk about our ancestors, along with our hopes of the future. All she ever said to me was she wanted me to live. I never understood what that meant until this moment.

I could still feel the warmth of the red woven blanket wrapped around my shoulders. I would sit at her feet, listening to the stories of the ancestors and the teachings they provided.

"Your nightmares tell a story of the golden sun surrounded by the infinite flames. Your name foresees the struggles you will face in this life, and the next. I never wanted this fate for you, my sweet child, but there is no escaping him.*"*

I never understood what she meant. The term *golden sun* had many meanings. It could symbolize strength or new life—but *him,* a man that I would never meet? My grandmother knew what was to come, that was her gift. Everything made sense now.

Smoke fills my senses. I cannot see the source of the fire.

Closing my eyes, I let my body relax.

"You are Death," I whisper into his chest.

His strong arms hold me close. He seems afraid to let me go. "Your life is on an endless cycle, a curse that started when you fell in love with me."

I chuckle. "It sounds nice, to love someone as beautiful as you."

He does not match my humor. "You will burn, my beautiful phoenix."

My hands grip his suit. The fabric is soft and tickles my skin. "You were there all those years ago. I saw you in my dreams."

"I will be there when your end has come, I will take away your pain, I will watch over you—now, and always."

Images flood my mind. Fire. Pain. Life after life I feel those two realities. I always die by fire at the age of twenty-five. Every time the flames kiss my skin, I see his golden eyes. Those eyes watch over me, protect me, and at this moment, I accept my fate.

"I am tired," I whisper.

He kisses the top of my head. "Sleep, my phoenix. I will hold you until you rise again."

His strong arms are familiar. Death. He has always been with me. Those golden eyes have watched over my soul since it first came into existence. In each life, I am in his arms. Not always as a lover, sometimes as a guardian, teacher, protector, or even a friend.

He has always found his way into my life before I die to give me what I need. In this life, it was a companion.

My body becomes light, and my mind is now clear. I love this man, and as he holds me tightly, I know that he will find me again.

Death can never be defeated.

Bartholomew

Fire will always come for you. It doesn't matter what kind of life you live, roaring flames will always be your end.

Ding. Ding.

I can always hear your clock, a life pulse that will slowly tick until it chimes at your final breath. A sound I dread.

In this life, you were a carefree witch who only wanted freedom. You had eyes of the sun and hair the color of shadow. You moved into your grandmother's house to try and live on your own, yet you weren't interested in learning all aspects of your gifts.

The connection to the earth was clouded by our curse. You never knew why you couldn't call upon a familiar. Your frustration made this form an easy choice: I came to you in this life as a feline.

But, I could not come to you while your grandmother was alive. She knew of your curse. The familial line of your first life whispers of a single female that will hold the love of Death, a story they would have never shared with you.

When you returned to this sacred ground, I could approach you and you accepted me without question. You named me Bartholomew because you needed a friend. You got to laugh and be free.

Because, since I chose to love a witch hundreds of years ago, your soul is cursed for all eternity to burn. It is always at this precise location, where we had our first kiss. An action that sealed our fate.

In this life, I made sure you were sleeping at the end.

All I could do was watch as the man appeared. He wore a dark green suit with a golden symbol of fire on his lapel. They saw you as the enemy that needed to be destroyed.

He approached your red door, which you never locked, the innocence of your heart unable to lock out the world. This man, he did not knock. As you slept, he walked into your space with a red gas canister in hand, ready to bless the world with the ashes of a witch.

All of this happened when you took a nap before your appointment. You never woke up. I couldn't bear to see the pain on your face. A selfish act, but one that would benefit that beautiful light.

Sitting in the grass, all I can do is watch, and wait. Help would never come in time.

The fire slowly creeps up the walls and peeks from the windows. I hear the forest warn others of the danger, yet I would never let the flames spread to hurt another.

But you can never escape.

Neither did he. I made sure he never left that house: those who dare harm what is mine burn too.

With great sadness, the humans will never know that you can never be saved. This house will be your coffin. Your body will burn and your ashes will once again bless this earth.

My little witch, how I love you. One day, we will get to be together. In another life, we will live as one. All I have to do is wait and pray that one day my actions will be forgiven.

Sleep until we meet again . . .

Under a Magick Moon

(A Beyond the Pale novel)

By Anya Bayne

Once separated by a magickal barrier, the human and the Fae worlds existed side by side. When that veil began to collapse, the worlds of Fae and humans as we knew them would never be the same. Now, both sides are forced to co-exist - Beyond the Pale, and these are their stories.

One

Walking out to his car, Rian Delaney tapped the fob to unlock and start his Porsche. *Fuck, it has been a long day,* he thought wearily. He was ready to return to his cabin, grab a glass of wine, and relax in front of the fire. Maybe turn on some television and go brain dead for a few hours before he crashed for the night. That was one of the good things about being single and living alone. He could do absolutely nothing if that was what he felt like doing.

Climbing into the driver's seat, Rian sighed and leaned his head back, pinching the bridge of his nose. He didn't want to think about their latest tech project and if his brother Liam called him about it. He might just turn him into a goldfish to stop his badgering, even if it would make their mother lose her mind. That was one thing about being witches. One always had to worry about fights with siblings because instead of having a black eye or bloody nose, one could end up as anything from a rat to a fucking toad. One never knew what an angry sibling might get pissed off and do. However, their mother had a keen sense of when they misbehaved, except when it came to their sister Emma. She tended to get away with the evilest things ever.

Emma had once turned him into a hamster for nearly a week, and it took Liam tattling to their mother for him to be turned back into a human. He owed Liam a massive debt for that because Emma had gotten revenge later for that tattle.

Rian decided to go to a takeout place and grab dinner. Thia food would be the only thing, he thought with a grin. He was the only one in his family who loved Thia food.

He quickly placed his order using his ordering app, then pulled out of his company's parking lot. Rian frowned at the haze that had taken over the evening as he felt the air laying heavy with magick. Damn it, the pale was active today. So, who knew what could happen? Rian knew he needed to get his food and get his ass home, where it couldn't affect him. He frowned as his phone rang.

"Hey, Mum, I am heading home now. I can feel it." Rian told her upon answering.

"Ye had best be makin' it quick, Rian. This one will be bad, and I don't want any of my children to end up on the other side of the Pale." Aine Delaney warned her son.

"I kern, Mum. I'm stoppin' to grab a bite of food, then I will settle into the cabin for the night." Rian promised her.

"Hurry yerself up, boy-o, I have a feelin', and ye kern I'm never wrong 'bout these things. Somethin' will happen tonight, and I dinna want ye caught up in it." His mother spoke firmly.

"I'll message you as soon as I am home," Rian assured her. "Now, I need to go in and grab my food. I love ye and will speak more later." Hanging up, he exited his car and hurried to grab his order.

By the time he returned to his car, the sky had turned an ominous shade of greenish-blue. The magick fairly swirled in the air around him. Swearing, Rian quickly climbed into his car and hurried home.

The rain began as a light sprinkle. As he turned on the long drive up the side of the mountain, Rian was sure he could make it home before the worst of the storm hit. Then the hail came pouring down, damn it, these were big enough to leave dents in his car, which meant getting the Porsche fixed. As one chunk of ice cracked his windshield, he swore and smacked the steering wheel.

Rian swore louder as the rain grew heavier, lightning ripping across the sky in a blinding flash. His mother had been right. This was no ordinary storm connected to the Pale. This was connected to a large opening in the Pale. He felt the massive surge of magick in the depths of his soul. He'd been alive long enough to know the difference. Suddenly, something large and pale-colored flew across the road in front of his Porsche, causing him to slam on his brakes and swerve.

TWO

"Holy shit!" Rian swore and ran a hand through his long, dark hair. Whatever that had been was huge. Sitting there, he took a deep breath. The thing that had flown across the road had crashed into the trees.

He stopped there for a few minutes and tried to decide whether to drive on or see what it was. Then, as suddenly as the storm had come on, it stopped. Scowling, Rian looked around and frowned at the steam rising off the pavement and the hail littering the roadway.

"I must be out of my feckin' mind!" Rian spoke to himself as he opened his car door, then stepped out into the humid night air.

Slowly, Rian made his way over to where he could see broken trees and limbs scattered across the area. Whatever had hit these trees had been huge and had struck them, making pieces of wood and leaves explode everywhere. Could it have been a small plane? Damn, if it was, someone could be seriously hurt. He thought with worry as he made his way over the downed trees and stepped over broken branches. Rian frowned in surprise at the ice that coated the trees and branches. The frosted grass under his shoes crunched. Raising his hand, he formed a sphere of magick to light up the area.

Whatever had crashed here was huge and powerful. Rian could feel the magick still hanging in the air as much as he could see his breath from the cold.

Suddenly, the clouds chose that moment to part, allowing the full snow moon to show itself and casting an eerie glow over the woods. Something a few feet away from him, nearly buried under broken branches, caught his attention. A person was lying there unmoving, their pale skin a stark contrast to the darkness of the trees and the moonlight filling the world around them.

Hurrying over, he quickly knelt beside the person to check and see if they were alive. Hell, he couldn't tell anything with all the branches covering them. Cursing softly, he used his magick to clear away all the debris. His breath caught at the sight of the small woman lying there unconscious. She wasn't just unconscious. She was completely naked. Rian quickly checked her pulse, then removed his jacket. *Gods above, she must be freezing*, he thought, but was surprised to find she was extremely warm to the touch. Carefully, he wrapped his jacket around her. "Hey, can ye hear me, *cailin*? Wake up." After several attempts, Rian knew he had no choice but to take her somewhere where he could look her over better. He wasn't a healer like his aunt, but he could at least do the basics for her until he could get his aunt to come take a look at her.

Carefully, he scooped her up and carried her to his car. Using his magick, he opened the passenger door and laid down the seat. Once he had her lying there, he quickly strapped her in, then prayed to the Gods that she wouldn't wake up and freak out about being in his car. Returning to the crash site, he looked around for anyone else and found no trace of other people. Frowning he decided he had taken long enough and hurried back to his car to check on the woman. She was still unconscious, so he quickly climbed into the car and drove the rest of the way to his cabin. Pulling into the garage, he sighed in relief that she had not awoken. Hurrying, he removed her from the vehicle, took her to the guest room, and tucked her into one of the spare beds.

After he had her settled, he immediately called his aunt Brenna and explained the situation.

"Does she have any injuries ye can see? Or any bumps on her head?" Setting down the phone, Rian checked but found nothing that could explain her unconscious state. Then he noticed her wrists. Red welts and cuts ringed them.

"I… I think she might have escaped from someplace or someone." Rian grew angry as he explained the marks on her wrists to his aunt. Quickly, he took pictures and sent them to her. *What kind of sick fuck would do something like this to such a tiny, beautiful woman*, he thought, furious on her behalf.

"Can ye come over tonight?" Rian hoped she would say yes. This woman would likely do better waking up in the company of another woman versus a strange man. He didn't want to scare her when, in all likelihood, she was probably already terrified.

"I can be there in an hour if she wakes. Keep her as calm as possible," Brenna instructed him. "Give her a bit of water or juice if ye have some."

Three

"Gods, I hope she does nae wake 'afore ye get here," Rian spoke with a sigh. He couldn't even imagine the kind of nightmare that could be. He certainly didn't want to frighten her more. Rian knew he wasn't exactly a small man, standing six feet, three inches in his bare feet. Though he wasn't the bodybuilder type, he was largely built with plenty of muscles.

Walking into the bathroom, he wet a washcloth with warm water and wrung it out. He would wash the dirt off her face, then wait for his aunt to get there and check her out. After a moment, Rian realized he should probably find her something to wear. He should have asked his aunt to bring her at least a nightgown or something. With a wry sigh, he left the bathroom and went to his bedroom. There, he pulled out one of his T-shirts and frowned at it. The woman was tiny compared to him. She would absolutely swim in the thing. He would need to call his mother or sister if she was here for more than a day and have them get her some clothing. But hopefully, there was someone safe she could call to come get her. Hell, he should have called the police now that he thought about it. All he had been thinking about at the time was to get her someplace safe and warm.

Her head was pounding. Slowly, she opened her eyes and winced at the light. Hesitantly, she looked around. *Where am I?* she wondered as fear filled her. Looking around the strange chamber, she saw an open door that appeared to lead somewhere deeper into the building she was in. Slowly, she sat up and realized she was completely naked. Throwing back the covers haltingly, she climbed for the bed and staggered toward the window. If she could open it, she could slip out into the dark and hide until she felt better. As she tried walking across the room, her vision grew blurry, and the room spun around her. She hit the odd bright candle that lit up the chamber, causing it to shatter as it hit the floor. Then she felt herself falling. Suddenly, she was scooped up into strong arms.

"Whoa there, ye should nae be up and 'bout cailin." The male said to her as he held her close, then moved back to the bed.

Panic filled her as she tried to struggle and get away from him. When he set her back on the bed, she grabbed the covers, pulling them up even as she scooted away from him, nearly falling off the other side. He spoke to her, but she didn't understand his words.

"Yer safe, ye kern?" Rian tried to reassure her in his deep, accented voice, but she didn't seem to hear him or understand. He wasn't sure which.

Gods, where am I? She thought frantically, looking around for a way to escape from this huge male.

Rian was afraid she would hurt herself, so the only thing he could think to do was use magick on her and make her go back to sleep. Raising his hand, he froze as he looked into the most beautiful violet-colored eyes he had ever seen. *Holy Hell, she's gorgeous*. Rian thought as he simply stared at her.

She looked at him and growled low. *I will not allow this male to hurt me*. She thought, even as pain pounded in her head like the hammers of the dwarves' forging weapons. Gods, the pain was so bad, but she pushed it aside as she fought to stay conscious. Her body was so tired and ached from the abuse it had taken from escaping.

"Well, what have we got here?" A woman's lilting voice came from the doorway.

Rian snapped out of the trance he was caught in and looked at his aunt. "Oh, thank the Gods ye are here, Aunt Brenna." He quickly pushed up off the bed. "She woke, and I think I have frightened her." He paced the room, running his hand through his long, pitch-black hair. "I dinna mean to."

"Let me look and try to get her to talk to me." Brenna entered the room and sat on the chair Rian had placed beside the bed. "Hello, there. I'm Brenna Delaney. My nephew Rian here found ye after yer accident. Can ye tell us yer name?"

The woman looked at the strange female and cocked her head. Nothing the female said made any sense to her. She had no clue what language the female was speaking. The words were unlike anything she had ever heard before. These two spoke to her in their strange tongue. "I don't understand you." She replied to the female.

Four

"What did she just say?" Rian asked his aunt with a frown.

"I dinna kern, but I might kern someone who does." Brenna pulled out her cell phone and made a call. "I need yer help. My nephew found an unconscious woman who had an accident, and I think she is either speaking Fae or Elvish. Can ye try speakin' to her?"

"Aye, but my Elvish 'tis a bit rusty." The man told her gruffly.

The woman looked around curiously to see where the other male's voice came from. When a man's harsh voice came out of the thing in the female's hand, she jumped, then stared at the little box in wonder. He spoke familiar words, asking her name. They were an older dialect of Fae. "My name is Lilja, of the ice clan." She replied in Elvish.

"Where did you come from, Lilja?" He asked her from within the box.

"How do you fit in that tiny box? Are you trapped in there?" Lilja asked curiously as she studied it, then looked at the woman who must be a sorceress.

"That thing she is holding is called a phone. It is a way for us to talk over great distances. I am not trapped inside of it. It's kind of a magick box that lets you hear my voice." He told her with a laugh.

"Where are you?" Lilja asked him, frowning and not believing this witch did not have him trapped and possibly enslaved somewhere.

"I am in a place called Maine. Who is the Ice Clan, Lilja?" He asked her carefully. If memory served him right, he knew who and, more importantly, what her people were.

"We are the last Ice Dragon shifters in the Realm," Lilja told him sadly.

"How did you get through the Pale and into the Human Realm?" The male asked her.

"I don't know. I was trying to escape from Viktor. And a storm happened, then I woke up here," Lilja explained to him, frowning deeply. She had heard stories of the human realm but had always thought they were mythical. Something to scare children. "This cannot be real."

"I am afraid this is very real, Lilja. Can you tell me who is Viktor?" The male asked her in concern.

"He is a sorcerer who has proclaimed himself king. He has captured and destroyed my people to steal our magick." She felt tears prick at the back of her eyes as she fought not to shed them. She could not show weakness to her new captors. "Who are you?"

"I am Aeon, I was once among the Fae Court. I was trapped here years ago. These humans will not harm you. You can trust them. They will keep you safe." Aeon assured her. "My mate and I will come there to meet you and help you understand what is happening," Aeon assured her gently. "Until then, please, Lilja, stay with them where you are safe. They will protect you. They have powerful magick."

"Brenna, are you still there?" Aeon asked her.

"Aye, what did ye find out 'bout the *Cailin*?" Brenna asked curiously.

Aeon quickly relayed what he had learned. "She doesn't know any human languages. The region she is from is in the heart of the Fae Realm, high in the mountains. They have very little contact outside of their area. They even have minimal contact with the Fae or Elves, but they trade with the dwarves, or they did, last I knew."

"Did you say she is a Dragon shifter?" Rian asked with a raised brow, not believing this. "Are you trying to say this tiny woman shifts into a dragon?"

"Aye, she is an Ice Dragon," Aeon told him, sure that Brenna's nephew was having difficulty believing it.

"She must be one tiny dragon." Rian laughed and shook his head in disbelief. "I think I could span her waist with my hands, and she barely comes to my breastbone."

"That might be, but don't let her human size fool you. She could be any size, and you won't know unless she is able to shift." Aeon explained to him.

"You think she lost her ability? Her magick?" Rian was horrified at the idea.

"That could be possible, or whatever this Viktor has done to her weakened her, and she is now drained." Aeon sighed wryly. "I think there is a good chance this bastard could come after her."

"I won't let him touch her," Rian replied venomously. "I won't allow anyone to hurt her ever again."

Brenna looked at her nephew in surprise. She had never heard sound so angry or protective. A small smile hovered over her lips. His mother Aine, would be thrilled when she called her later.

"I need to learn whatever language ye were speaking. I want a way to communicate with her." Rian informed Aeon. "I can pay you to help me."

"I don't need your money. I just need to know you will take care of her." Aeon assured him solemnly. "She may very well be the last of her kind. Mia and I will be there by tomorrow night."

"Thank you." Rian was grateful for the help.

He looked at the beautiful young woman with large violet-colored eyes again, and he felt drawn to her, a need to protect and care for her like he had never felt with any other woman before.

Five

Brenna hung up the phone and looked at the young woman. "What do ye plan to do with her, Ri?"

"What do ye mean?" Rian looked at his aunt as realization dawned. "Ye'll be staying the night, will ye nae? What if she needs something, aye?"

"Nae, I must get back to yer uncle," Brenna told him flatly. "Ye'll be fine with her, and Aeon will be arrivin' on the 'morrow. Until then, get her somethin' to eat and drink, show her where the *leithreas* 'tis, and ye both shall be fine. I'll try to check on ye 'fore I go meet up with Aeon and Mia."

Rian paced and mumbled. "All I wanted was a quiet night after the day I've had. Now, I have to babysit a Dragon shifter and hope she doesn't get upset and bar-b-que me."

"She's an Ice Dragon, so she can nae be breathing fire, ye git." Brenna shook her head at her nephew.

"Oh, that 'tis so much better. She could turn me into an ice sculpture." Rian ran a hand through his long, dark hair.

"Oh, don't be a git, I doubt she'll harm ye. She's scared and unsure. Ye heard what Aeon said 'bout her. She has lost her magick. I doubt she can shift right now if she'd be wantin' to." Brenna laughed at him. "Just be nice to her, and treat her with kindness, and ye'll be right as rain. Just keep Liam away from her because ye kern him and how he is with beautiful women."

"Oh, he'll nae be allowed within fifty miles of her unless he truly understands she is off *feckin'* limits to his lecherous hands. Nae one shall be allowed to touch her." Rian snarled and paced.

Nae one but you, Brenna thought with a small smile. The boy was attached to the tiny Dragon shifter. When Brenna's phone dinged, she looked down at her. "Aeon has sent me a few simple phrases. He thinks ye may need to help with her until he can get here, and he says to give ye his number just in case ye need it." Brenna quickly forwarded everything to Rian's phone.

Rian quickly scanned the list of phrases that Aeon had sent him, then paced and messaged Aeon for a few other vital phrases he felt would help him to quickly create an app that would allow them to communicate at least on a fundamental level. It should only take him a couple of hours to develop and make it work. Thank the Gods, he was a Tech genius and owned one of the largest technology companies in the world.

Lilja watched the large man pace and speak in the strange language. As he tapped on the little box in his hand. She could tell he was unhappy about something, but she wasn't sure what. However, she had the strangest urge to climb off this bed, go to him, and try to soothe him. Sitting there, she studied him. He was very handsome for a human male. Nothing like what she had thought a human would look like.

Suddenly, her stomach rumbled loudly in hunger. She had little access to food during her escape and very little in the days before she fled. She only had the strength to break free because her father and her brother Keija had smuggled her portions of their food. Viktor had been trying to break her through starvation to make her bow to his demands, but her father had used this against the sorcerer, allowing her to escape. Lilja was supposed to go find help for them, but as she flew trying to get away from Viktor's creatures, the storm appeared suddenly, and she had been sucked into it, then woken up here.

The sound of the male's voice pulled her out of her reverie. Frowning, she looked at him as he spoke to her in his strange tongue. Lilja cocked her head as she watched him mimic what looked like he was eating something. She couldn't help but smile at him as he pretended to chew. He acted like he took a bite of something and then said a strange word.

"Eat," Rian told her slowly, then gave her a hopeful look.

"Eat." Lilja mimicked him, smiled, and then frowned as the male jumped off the bed and hurried from the room. Her shoulders sagged. *What did I do wrong to make him leave*? She wondered, frustrated.

Rian hurried to the kitchen and looked around for something to feed her. Shit, what did a Dragon Shifter eat? He wondered, blowing out a breath. Seeing the takeout bag, he quickly grabbed it and got out a couple of plates, then dished out food for each of them. Gods, he hoped she wasn't allergic to anything.

Grabbing the plates and silverware, he hurried back to the bedroom. He found Lilja sitting on the bed, her knees drawn up and arms crossed over them. Her face was buried in her arms. *Fuck*, he thought frowning. *Did I hurt her feelings or scare her*?

"Lilja?" Rian said her name softly, not wanting to frighten her. When her head whipped up, he gave her a small smile and held up the plate. "Eat?" He asked her hesitantly.

Lilja lifted her face at the sound of his voice and looked at him. When he held the plate up and said the strange word, she sniffed the air, smelling the scent of food. Her stomach chose that moment to give another loud rumble, and he smiled at her. Lilja's breath caught at the sight of his smile. God's help her. This male was beautiful.

Rian sat down slowly on the chair by the bed and held out a plate to her. He frowned as she quickly tucked the blanket around her to keep her breasts covered, then reached for the plate.

Six

Lilja took the plate eagerly. She looked down at the strange offerings on the plate, unsure of what these things were, but some of it she was positive was meat. Feeling like she was starving, she quickly began picking up pieces of food, sniffing it, then devouring it. The taste was odd but not altogether bad. This was not roasted oxen, but she had not had the luxury of such food in months. Not since Viktor had captured her family after destroying her village.

Rian watched her shoving pieces of food into her mouth as if she were starved half to death. He smiled as she licked her fingers and her lips. Apparently, she liked Thia food as well. At least they had that in common. He would need to make an order for groceries to be delivered in the morning because he couldn't chance leaving her alone. He knew his refrigerator and cupboards were all but bare. Once they finished eating, he would put together a quick online order and hope they could get there early. Currently, all he had was coffee and not even any cream to put in it. Watching her, he noted that she preferred meat to vegetables. But ate everything that was on her plate before she was finished. When her plate was empty, he looked at her and smiled, then held up the plate he made for him.

"More?" He spoke the word slowly. When she nodded enthusiastically, he handed her his plate and watched her pick up pieces of meat at a more sedate pace. *Hopefully, the two plates will satisfy her hunger for now*. He watched her. That was nearly all the Thia food he had purchased.

"Lilja?" He spoke her name again and smiled at her.

"Drink?" Rian asked, mimicking the motion of taking a drink. She nodded enthusiastically, and this time, when he stood up, she just watched him intently as he walked out of the room.

As Rian returned to the room, he smiled, this time to see her sitting on the bed, still eating but humming a simple tune. Slowly, he held out a cup with water in it. He would need to put juice on the list of things to be delivered.

Lilja reached out to take the cup, and when their fingers brushed, she felt a sensation like she had never felt with a male before. When their fingers touched, she could have sworn lightning raced from his fingers to hers. Her breath caught, and her heart pounded. Her eyes widened as she looked up at him. What kind of magick does he possess? Lilja wondered. He could not be a human. Could he? She had been told that humans did not possess the magick like those in faery. But if it wasn't magick, what was this? Could he be her mate? That was impossible, as he was just a simple mortal human.

Rian had nearly dropped the cup as he felt something akin to lightning race through him from her touch. His aunt had been wrong. Lilja's magick was not gone. He had just gotten a sample of it, and her magick was powerful.

Taking the cup, Lilja sipped from it, then set it aside. She waited for him to sit down, then pointed to herself and said. "Lilja." Then she pointed to the male, hoping he would understand what she was asking.

Rian smiled and touched his chest. "Ry-an." He told her slowly.

"Ry-an," Lilja repeated, then smiled and touched her chest again. "Lilja." Then she reached toward him. "Ry-an."

Rian spent most of the night working on the new app to help Lilja communicate and learn English. The rest of it was spent in vivid dreams about her. After only three hours of restless sleep, he gave up and climbed from bed.

Since the groceries had already been delivered, he decided to cook them breakfast. Standing at the stove, cooking bacon and drinking coffee, Rian thought about his beautiful guest. A sound behind him made him turn around, and his mouth nearly hit the floor. Lilja stood before him, dressed in one of his white T-shirts. She looked tiny in the garment. However, the sun shining through the kitchen window made the garment nearly transparent.

Lilja smiled shyly at him, then said softly. "Ry-an."

Quickly, he set his cup of coffee aside, and without thinking, he stepped forward at the same time she did. He cupped her small face in his large hands, then captured her mouth in a fiery kiss. He was elated when she slipped her arms around his neck and kissed him back just as passionately. Rian was sure he had to be dreaming.

For more of this series (Beyond the Pale) and other stories like it, as well as to find some other amazing author's stories, plus follow us on social media, find out Website and REAM, visit the Magick Moon Ink Publishing Landing page at https://Linktr.ee/Magickmoonink or scan the QR code below.

Follow Anya Bayne on Kindle Vella for Series like this one and her epic RED: Hearts of Two Kingdoms! As well as many other great stories.

DEAD WITCH TALKING

T.A. - GothicMoms

COPYRIGHT

This book contains mature content and is intended for adults 18+ only. In addition, this story does have triggers and may be unsuitable for some audiences.

Underlayes

Underlayes is another dimension where all sorts of nocturnal creatures reside; witches, vampires, fae, shifters, werewolves… The dimension was created by all these creatures working side by side to escape the scrutiny and danger to their existence that stemmed from the human world. All throughout time humans have been known to fear anything they do not understand and have almost always tried to eliminate what they fear. Even though most of these mystical creatures appeared to be as humanoid as humans, though more enhanced, the powers they possessed struck a fear in humans like nothing else ever could.

When God created the earth, He had some help along the way. While there is only one true God, He has many underling goddesses and gods who help Him. Let's think of God as the CEO. Just as God created man in His image, He allowed His goddesses and gods to create certain races in their images as well, though they weren't allowed to create as many as He. Only their images had nothing to do with color, for their races come in every color, shape, and form there is. No, their images were more so based on…characteristics. Like, for instance, Hekate and her necromancers or Aphrodite and her beautiful sirens. They are more nocturnal than humans since most of these creatures are more powerful and not ruled by the moon. Also, some of these beings have a very deadly reaction to the sun, while others are equally as powerful by night or day.

Some of these creatures may indeed become quite deadly, although usually only when provoked. And, yes, there are some who tend to be more violent and sadistic, but regular humans can be, too. After all, most serial killers, though not all, are indeed human.

Originally, the intention was for these nocturnal creatures to have their time at night and keep to themselves, while regular, mundane humans were to rule the day, unawares. Well, as all good plans go…

For three hundred years, these nocturnal beings have lived peacefully amongst themselves, or have they? Has that peace been nothing more than superficial, a mere illusion? Let's face it, people do tend to see what they would like to see and ignore what is going on right before their eyes if and when it suits them. See, there has never been anyone, or any group, to truly rule all Underlayes. Though most factions have their own leaders, or kings and queens, no one race rules the entire realm. And with so much power rolling around unchecked and unbalanced, the so-called peace came to a brutal and bloody bitter end.

A battle that had been prophesized, the Witch Wars, finally came about, and Tialanna of the House of Sekhmet, an elemental witch/vampire hybrid, rose victorious, and became the Queen of all Underlayes. But nothing comes without a price, and for Queen Tialanna, the price was a great one indeed, one she and her sisters continue to pay even now. Including the loss of their mother.

The youngest of the three taking it harder than the twins, possibly because she suffered the loss of both of her parents. Having been forced to take her own father's life to claim her own throne as Queen of the House of Sekhmet. And sometimes grief can make people do things they otherwise wouldn't.

Chapter 1

"Elyssia, open up this Goddess damned door right now!"

"Come on Lyssy, this is getting beyond ridiculous now. Open up!"

"Not by the hair on my chinny chin chin!" I shouted right back at my sisters. They were not about to stop me from doing this. No way, no how.

Without bothering to look up from the spell I had read over and over at least a million times, I threw another layer of ice over the door when I heard a huge crack from all of their excessive banging. I knew with all of my heart that both Tialanna and Anya meant well, but they didn't have the slightest clue about what I was going through. Though in all honesty, how could they?

This was just yet another Mother's Day to them. Every year since our mother had died they hadn't been forced to spend it alone, like I had. Anya had Kierra and their son, Lucas, doting on her hand and foot, showering her with gifts. Tia, well, things had been a tad different for her. While she'd had a kid of her own too, she had secreted Jelissa away for the majority of her life, and one of her mates hadn't even known she'd existed until not too long ago. But, the two that did know made sure she knew how appreciated she was on every Mother's Day. And Tia and Anya did the same for their mates on Father's Day. To top it off, they also still had a father.

I didn't have any of that. And while I didn't begrudge them any of their happiness, I'd be lying if I said I didn't blaze green with envy whenever I looked at them these two holidays every year. And green was so not a good color with my ebony skin or shock of blue hair.

So, call whatever it was that I was going through at that particular point in my life; self-pity, depression, insanity, or just plain stupidity, but I was bound and determined to have at least one parent back in my life.

"You don't even have her body, Elyssia!" Tia shouted, again, "Just let us in and listen to reason. Even if you had the power to raise the dead, they never come back right, especially after this long."

"I do have a body! Courtesy of your very own blood cave!" I shouted right back. All the shouting back and forth almost made want to go ahead and let them in. Almost. "If that whackjob Nana came back, then why not Mom?" Even though the situation was totally different, seeing as how Nana hadn't completely died in the first place. I wasn't about to say any of that out loud, even if they knew it just as much as I did.

It sounded like one of them punched the other right before Anya said, "How was I supposed to know that's why she asked where we kept the leftovers? Geez, don't give me that look. I thought she may have had a hot date with a necromancer."

"She doesn't even go on dates. She has a mate, remember?"

"Oh, I remember. But someone apparently needs to remind the two of them of that. Her mate is one of the reasons we have so many bodies piling up lately. That vampire has developed a drinking problem."

"Can't you two just go away and leave me alone so I can concentrate?" I asked them as they went back and forth discussing me like I wasn't even there. They didn't even have the decency to attempt a whisper. "Go talk about me and all of my convoluted issues in another room, in your own friggin castle!"

"Elyssia, please, with all of the ice you've been hurling at this door, you've got to be dehydrated by now." Tia pleaded with me. She sounded like she was well on her own way to being exhausted. "Even if you do go ahead with this dumb ass plan of yours, we have a right to be in there. She was our mother, too."

"Just because you're making sense doesn't mean I need to listen to you!" that came out all wrong, maybe I *was* dehydrated. After a resigned sigh, I said to my two bull-headed older sisters, "If I let you in here, you had better not try and stop me! You have to promise me that you believe I have everything under control. You can just be spectators in awe as I bring Mom back to life."

Against my better judgement, I concentrated on all the ice I had over both sides of the door that kept them on the opposite side of it, *away* from me. What happened next put a smile on my face so big I didn't even bother to try and hide it. As chunks of ice fell down to the floor, my vampy-witch sisters did their bests to shove the door right off of its hinges. Then they both promptly stepped on some melting ice, slipped and landed right on their cute, fat butts. "Did I do that?" I asked in a mock nasally voice right before I laughed so hard I'm pretty sure I peed myself just a little bit.

Chapter 2

"Not funny you jerk!"

I don't even know which one of them said that, my own laughter had deafened my ears. They had tried and failed to get up at least five times at that point. Then to make matters worst I couldn't help but say, "How many hybrids does it take to walk through a door?" They looked like a tangled, hot mess down on the floor in a heap like they were. Tia and Anya weren't textbook identical, more like mirror images of each other; one with shocking crimson hair, the other a platinum blonde, one's complexion was more high yellow than the other, both had fangs. We were only half sisters, we shared the same mom, and more than once I had wished their dad was also mine. Then I wouldn't be an orphan. But then again, since their brother on their paternal side turned out to be my still unclaimed mate (he'd had a mate before me, but she died, leaving him with three girls to raise, I didn't want to make things awkward for anybody) … Did I mention my life was a hot mess?

If looks could kill I'd have been a dead witch with how they stared me down after my brilliant joke that they didn't even laugh at. Finally, I curtailed my laughter enough to say what they were too pissed at me to realize, "Tia, you do know you could just heat that ice up enough the melt, then to evaporate, right?" Anya had the nerve to scoff at that like Tia was the only one not thinking straight. So, I turned my undivided attention towards Tia's mirror image with a lopsided grin and said to her, "Anya, you could've just whipped up some wind and blew all of it out of y'all's way."

We were down in the basement of my castle, the base of all witch operations, in my water room. Though, right about then there wasn't much water to speak of. I had used almost all of it fruitlessly trying to keep my sisters out. What once looked like a miniature hot springs, with a small pond that surrounded the entire room, water cascading down like small intermittent waterfalls that led to said pond, and a blue, ceramic tiled floor for easy clean up resembled a dried-up disaster zone right then.

Once Tia and Anya got their wits about themselves and were able to stand on their own two feet, they made their way over to altar where I had everything all set up and ready to go. Well, almost everything. “Dang it,” I muttered to myself. I gazed up at my sisters then and noticed them gawking from my ‘display’ and back to me liked I’d grown a third head or something. “What?” I asked them, “Don’t stand there acting like you’ve never seen a dead body before. Y’all drink blood for Sekhmet’s sake.”

“Yeah,” Anya chimed in, the first to be able to verbalize her thoughts, “but we don’t lay they naked asses on display on a bed of roses, surrounded by all types of herbs and whatever else you’ve got going on up there.”

I just rolled my eyes at her, “I did not let you in here just to make fun of me. Look, I forgot something upstairs. Don’t touch anything while I’m gone.” Right before I flashed out I asked them one more thing, “How long do those humans stay alive when you forget to feed them?” All I got in response were the both of them staring at me slack-jawed again. “You know, y’all had a lot more to say when you were on the other side of that door.” I didn’t even bother waiting for them to say anything, just flashed myself upstairs to the kitchen and made my way to the walk-in refrigerator.

When I saw that the first one was a tad bit dead, I decided that putting them in the fridge hadn’t been such a brilliant idea. Good thing I’d grabbed more than one. I tossed Mr. Blue aside then grabbed the other one and tossed her over my shoulder like a rag doll, then flashed back down to the room.

I dropped the husky woman down on the floor the second my feet made purchase. Her incessant teeth chattering in my ear was irritating. I didn’t know what it was she had done to end up in the dungeons and didn’t really care. Just knew that whatever she had done in life made it so she deserved whatever she got. And since fresh blood was required for the ritual I was about to perform that made her perfect. The other guy would’ve been too, if he hadn’t up and died on me.

“Are you seriously humming right now?” Anya asked me with a huge amount of astonishment in her voice. “Tia, I’m really getting worried now.”

"Just now?" Tia muttered under her breath. "Elyssia, sweetie, can we please just sit down and talk about this?"

I just let them continue to talk amongst themselves while I gathered the athame, chalice, and basin from the alter. I bent down, then kneeled directly in front of the terrified looking human. Whatever she tried to say to me didn't register, but it *was* making my ears ring, maybe she was screaming. Anyway, it abruptly stopped when I slashed the athame across her throat. I put the chalice directly beneath the wound and let the warm crimson liquid pour inside until it was an inch or so away from the rim. Once I carefully placed the chalice carefully back on the alter, I knelt back down to fill the basin. There wasn't any need to be as delicate in the basin process. I just needed to get enough blood to wash my face and hands with.

I stood and placed the basin on the alter, then felt a hand placed on either shoulder, and decided to ignore them. I cupped my hands and dipped them into the blood then splashed the liquid up and down my face like it was some Noxema instead of the plasma it truly was.

Those two hands were still on my shoulders and becoming harder to ignore as they started applying more pressure. I didn't have time to acknowledge that, I was too busy trying to figure out how to light the candles with my blood-soaked hands, "Maybe I should have lit them before dipping my hands in the blood. Tia, could you-"

"Elyssia!" they both shouted directly in my ears, not only effectively cutting me off from what was bound to be a long rant but also made it impossible to ignore them any longer. Because right then when they shouted my name while they still held skin contact, they also punched it with power.

My sisters didn't hurt me, at least not physically, and definitely not maliciously, far from it. Instead they filled me with their own pain and grief. They showed me that regardless of the fact that they both had a child of their own, even though they both had mates, they still grieved our mother just as much as I did. In some ways they grieved over her even more than I did. But their emotions were even more complicated than my own.

Tialanna's emotions were truly all over the place. All of the anger, hurt, confusion, and pain that she felt towards our mother, she also felt it at herself. Our mother had let Tia go most of her life not knowing who her real father was, that she was part vampire, or that she had a twin sister. And she'd died before either of them had been able to properly show her that anger over that, even though they both knew the decision was made to protect them, it didn't change how they felt. And when Tia had her own daughter, Jelissa, she'd made the very same decision. Now her own daughter hated her guts since she'd recently learned the truth. Seemed history was doomed to repeat itself. And my big sis hadn't learned a thing from our mother's mistakes. So, when Mother's Day came around, she was reminded that she no longer had a mother, and that she had a daughter that may never come to love her.

Anya was also a jumble of emotions. Especially since our mother's final act was to give her own element of the wind to Anya, in order to save her life. As angry as Anya had been with her for forcing her to grow up without her, knowing the truth of it all but still having been forced to keep her distance, with that final act Anya couldn't deny the love our mother must've had for her. That more than anything pissed Anya off. Our mother had been taken from us too soon for her to go through all of the emotions with her. Too soon for her to be able to hate then forgive her, she never had the chance to have any sort of relationship with her, good or bad. And with her own child? She may have held onto him so tight and sheltered him to the point of pushing him away. This was the first Mother's Day she remembered spending without him.

To top off all of that grief, pain, hurt, anger and every other emotion they were battling? They were also worried that their baby sister, me, had finally flipped the script and lost my ever-loving mind.

I saw all of the events of the day from their point of view and was horrified by what I saw. I really did look like some type of human lunatic that had escaped the insane asylum. The looks of sheer desperation and madness that were in my expression when I tried to convince them I was doing the right thing, even though the necromancers refused their help, saying how foolish and dangerous it was. So bound and determined to not spend another Mother's Day without my mother I refused to listen to reason from anyone. What's worse? I was acting like a selfish, spoiled brat, as if I were her only child. The only one that had been left behind to grieve her.

"I'm sorry." Were the first words to part my lips once my brain began to lift from whatever trance it had been under. I could taste salt from the tears that fell from my eyes.

"Whoa." Was the next thing I said when I cracked my eyes open. Somehow or another we had levitated hand in hand. We were at least five feet off the floor, and wow, everything below us looked terrible. In our trance we all must have let loose our element in some way. The candles had burnt to practically nothing, items were disheveled in all types of ways, including the goblet of blood, like a huge gust of wind had hit. And almost everything on the alter was wet.

"What the fuck," this came from Anya, "Every time I touch the two of you at the same time some weird shit happens."

Before Tia had a chance to add in her two cents, we all fell into a heap on the floor. And just like that our tears and anguish turned into laughter. Right up until Tia said, "Uh, guys, where's the body?" After that, all we heard were screams.

Chapter 3

"You think there's a chance that might be Mom? Ow!"

Anya slapped me upside the back of my head for that lovely sentiment, "No, that thing is not Mom. I may not have grown up with her like y'all did, but I'm pretty sure she didn't look or act like that on her worst day."

The screams I'd heard had come from us. We'd all looked up to the ceiling in the middle of the room and seen the body, only that's no longer how it could be described. It was more like something from out of that movie *The Grudge*, only it still held some color. The way it kept contorting its body and eyeing us was way beyond eerie. "What the heck is it?" They both gazed at me like they wanted to throttle me.

"You've got the nerve to ask us what it is? It came from your spell!" Tia seethed at me through a set of clenched fangs. "You know, the spell everyone begged you to *not* use."

"Well, that's not the outcome I was going for." I said to her, gesturing towards my messed-up experiment. "Ok, we just flash out of here, find a necromancer to help us put this thing down and send it back to wherever it came from." There went that look again, "What?"

"You warded us from flashing in and out of here." Tia and Anya both said to me in unison with a huge scowl on their faces.

"Oh, yea. Forgot all about that. K, I'll flash out and come back with some help." They didn't seem to like that idea either. "I'm open to suggestions here." They both shushed me then, literally. "How rude!" I told them both, then went back to looking at…it. It had cocked its head to the side, studying us. But I didn't like the way it seemed to keep reverting its focus back to Tia. Her and Anya were completely silent, so I assumed they were communicating with their mates.

It seemed to take a deep inhale as it contorted its body, twisting the top half all the way around. It must have sensed the two demons that were about to flash in, since the wards only kept out other witches, not demons or angels.

Kierra was the first to flash in, and that seemed to set off all types of alarms in the creature. It started making some type of eerie clicking noises, then launched itself at Kierra, knocking them both to the floor with it on top. It threw back its head and shrieked so loudly I slightly wondered if it was part banshee. Only thing any of us could do was cover our ears, instinct to try and block out the debilitating noise. Just as it reached back it's arm to take a swipe at Kierra, Bran, one of Tia's husbands whom was full demon, flashed in.

And to everyone's utmost surprise, before the thing made purchase with Kierra's face, Bran said the one thing none of us expected, "Mom?", as he shed the guise of that of a normal, male witch and took on his full demon persona. As he walked towards that thing in all of his seven and a half feet glory, with midnight leather skin and multi-colored hair cascading down his back, the thing that Demon Bran called 'Mom' mirrored his every move.

She no longer crawled around on all fours looking like something straight from a horror movie, but far from it. She now stood tall, strong, and proud, every bit the female version of Demon Bran all the way down to the tail without a single flaw on her leathery, scaled skin. Even the glistening tears that fell from her eyes did nothing to distract from her beauty. "Tridamoreous?" she asked in utter astonishment in a husky, guttural tone as she reached up to graze her hand against his face. And even though they were both as naked as the day he was born they grabbed onto each other in a loving embrace. I could feel the love pouring off of them in waves and there wasn't anything sexual about it, just a mother being reunited with her son.

From her position on the floor, Kierra, who barely says a word groaned and said, "This would be a whole lot less awkward if you guys put some clothes on."

"You've been gone this long gallivanting with," she swallowed her disgust before she said the word with disdain, "Angels?"

"Actually…" Kierra rebutted, right before she shifted into a male with large, black, leathery wings with steel tips at the bottom, and two horns protruding from either side of her head. "I'm more than just an angel."

"Well," she stated as she donned a beautiful, gossamer red silk gown from out of nowhere, and Demon Bran suddenly had on a matching red leather suit, minus a shirt. "I stand corrected. Seems we have a lot to catch up on. By the way, rumor has it I can walk in my own skin here? Or must I don the meat sack I hitched a ride in?"

I just let them all continue to talk amongst themselves and walked over to start cleaning up the altar. Had a feeling there would be even more drama to deal with and I just wasn't up to any of it yet.

While I was busy scooting candle remnants into a bucket, I felt a familiar presence flash in beside me. Instead of saying anything, Darvyn just grabbed another bucket and helped me with the clean-up. Yes, the two of us most definitely needed to talk, but right then wasn't the time. Sometimes words aren't needed, just companionship, knowing that whatever you're facing you aren't facing it completely alone.

The rest of the motley crew left about halfway throughout our duties without saying anything. Which was probably for the best. Too much had gone on in that small amount of time, too many raw emotions that we all needed to deal with in our own way.

It wasn't until Darvyn walked up behind me and gently grabbed the back of my hand that I noticed I had been scrubbing the same spot for so long that I had almost put a hole in my altar table. His hand stayed there even after I'd finally stopped my obsessive motion in a silent question. In response I let go of the sponge, flipped over my hand and interlaced my fingers with his.

We walked to my chambers in the castle. Sure, we could have just flashed up there, but this was a night that required simplicity. We walked past several other witches, but they knew not to say anything, or even acknowledge who I was with. I think the entire court knew what a precarious situation it was for us, especially that day, a day that was at its end.

When we finally made it up there, I surprised myself by not having said a mumbling word. For once, I just let him focus on me. I didn't ask him anything about his daughters, if they knew where he was, and if they did were, they alright with it. Didn't ask how they had handled the day. If they weren't ok, then he would've been there with them, not with me. So, I just let that train of thought go while he ran a bath for me. This definitely wasn't how I imagined our first time being naked together, it was better than I could have imagined, and it had nothing to do with sex.

Darvyn took such gentle care with me as he washed away not only the gook, dried blood, and other crap I had all over my body and in my hair, he also washed away some of the pain. Now that was the true definition of love.

Once I was finally clean and he'd wrapped me in a plush blue towel that blended with my hair, he slipped a white gold, skull shaped locket encrusted with diamonds around my neck. Before I had a chance to pop it open, he lifted me up and carried me over to my extra king-sized bed.

When he tucked me in, under my black and silver satin sheets, Darvyn brushed back my wet hair (that would be a tangled heap of a mess come morning) and placed a chaste yet intimate kiss on my forehead. And in that crisp, delightfully hot accent of his said simply and sweetly, "Goodnight, my queen." Then flashed away.

In a testament of just how exhausted I was, I was out like a light the moment I closed my eyes.

Epilogue

At first I thought that I may have been dreaming, either that or I had really gone completely bonkers. But seeing as how the temperature had dropped down at least thirty degrees since I'd laid down I figured that maybe my mind *wasn't* playing tricks on me.

"Momma?" she stood in front of my fireplace in a dashiki and a pair of blue jean shorts, her cinnamon brown hair in a cornrow bun at the top of her head. Her arms crossed under her breasts with her hip cocked to the side in what used to be her "You sho nuff bout to get a whoopin" move.

Tears cascaded down my cheeks as I walked over to her, slowly, afraid that if I made any sudden moves she would disappear, and I would lose her all over again. I was about two feet away and ready to throw myself into her arms when she raised a hand to stop me. I could have sworn I felt a small gust of wind when she did so. That's when I noticed that I could actually *see* the fireplace directly through her body, almost like she wasn't there at all. She looked about as disappointed as I felt when she said in a voice that eerily echoed off the walls, "We can't touch, Baby Blue, just talk."

I opened my mouth to speak, probably to ask a million non-essential questions. She stopped me again, this time with a slight grin and a touch of laughter in her voice, "Before you start one of your long and drawn out tirades, I'm only here for a bit longer." Then in a more serious tone, "You have to let me go baby. The only way I can move on, is if you move on. I love you, and a piece of me will always be with you, you're my daughter. Nothing in this life or the next will ever change that." She placed her hands aside both of my cheeks and it almost felt like she was holding my face. "Now, go, live your life to the fullest. And go claim that mate of yours. He may be willing to wait around forever but stop making him."

“I love you Momma.” I told her through my tears.

“I love you too, all of you.” She began to disappear as she said, “Live your life. And if you ever try to resurrect me again, I’m kicking your ass.”

When she left me this time, I felt a bit lighter, more determined to build a future *with* my mate, and filled with purpose. I didn’t know what tomorrow would bring, but I was bound and determined to find some happiness in it. I looked down at my locket and opened it up. Inside were more than just the usual two compartments, there was a double-sided piece in the middle. In the first was a picture of my mother, the second me and my sisters, on the opposite side of that one was Darvyn and the triplets. It was the last that put a tear of happiness in my eye, an inscription that said, “For the Future” inside of a water drop.

The End

About the Author:

T. A. resides in Detroit, Michigan with her five children, and the rest of her dysfunctional family, where she was born and raised. She started her writing career in the midst of a very hard time in her life and is now a best-selling author. Her debut and award-winning novel, *Witch Wars,* and the world of Underlayes, was born from a mind that desperately needed an escape, so she created one.

The novel was inspired by her love of all things paranormal and how she wanted it seen. “We live in a diverse world, shouldn’t all of the characters in books, even paranormal also be diverse,” she says. “I saw so few paranormal books with a diverse cast until I read L. A. Banks. You know, with more than one or two diverse characters thrown in for good measure. Mine have it all, too.”

https://linktr.ee/gothicmoms

The Heart of a Graystone Witch

Katie Richard

Dumping the contents of the vial into the compound, I cross my fingers. I'm no good when it comes to alchemy, but Draven insists, I just need practice. Nothing happens for several seconds and then out of nowhere it starts to bubble. A cloud of smoke billows out the top, threatening to make a mess of the room. A hissing sound fills the air.

"Crap," I mumble.

I pull my gloves on tight, snatch the glass bottle with a pair of tongs, and head for the back door. Kicking the door open, I place the glass on the metal table filled with all my other failed experiments. Letting out a huff, I watch as the inky black liquid spills out the top of the beaker and coats the table like a volcanic eruption. The thick ebony mixture drips off the edge and scorches the grass below, leaving a dry shriveled up patch of brown. Why is this so hard for me? Draven and Janice make it look too easy. A drop of this, a dash of that and poof they have the perfect combination of ingredients.

Turning on my heel, my face slams into a hard chest and a yelp escapes my throat. My arms flail out to the sides to catch my balance before a set of hands snatches my waist in a firm grip. Heat shoots up my skin like an electric current. My body only responds like this to one individual in particular.

"Whoa, there. It's just me," Gabriel says. He tightens his grip on my sides before tugging me behind the shop's van.

"Are you trying to give me a heart attack?" I whisper, tilting my head to see behind him. "What are you doing here?"

Draven and Janice have raised me since I was a baby. They're not my biological parents and didn't want to be called by that, so instead it's Gramps, and Meemaw. Although they mean the world to me, they don't believe in mixed species relationships. The Ember's are old fashioned like that. When Gramps found out I was dating a guardian, he lost it. He said, "There's several warlocks in town I could've chosen and yet, I sully our family name to be seen dating an immortal."

We've kept our relationship hidden from the public and have to sneak around to be able to see each other. Draven knows pretty much everybody here, since the Alchemy Palace has been a staple in the heart of Graystone for over a century. It's completely absurd because Gramps is friends with so many immortals here. Gabriel's an immortal guardian, the same guardians who protect not only our homeland in Graystone, but they keep the balance between humans and the supernatural. Unfortunately, humans can't be trusted with the knowledge of all the things that go bump in the night. That's the main job of an immortal guardian, to protect the humans. How the heck is that sullying our family to be tied to one?

"I missed you." He nuzzles his face into my neck, his hot breath fanning against my skin.

My body relaxes into his as his cologne drifts around me like a cloud and calms my nerves. "I missed you too," I sigh.

Wary that any minute we could be caught, I look up into his chocolate brown eyes and tell him, "Eight o'clock down by the pier. Meet me there?"

A grin stretches across Gabriel's face. "I wouldn't miss it."

The pier on Sundial beach is our usual spot. There's a small alcove just under the wooden planks out of view from prying eyes. Surrounded by nothing but a sandy beach and waves crashing into shore, the area's usually eerily empty late at night. But it's perfect for the couple that can't be seen together.

I met Gabriel at the Guardian Academy a few years ago. That's the school that all immortal and wizard children attend. Watching him from a far for many years, I didn't think he ever noticed me. I was just a quiet, shy little witch who only had eyes for him. He'd meet my gaze on occasion but never spoke to me. That is until the ball, when he asked me to be his date. Standing on my tiptoes I place a soft kiss on his lips before I need to shoo him away. He can't be seen hanging around back here. Gramps will have a field day if he catches him.

Saying goodbye's always the hardest part. It's like he takes a piece of me with him when he goes. After he disappears around the corner of the bushes behind the store, I take one more glance at what was supposed to be a speed enhancing elixir to help our guardians be faster in battle. Unfortunately, it did not turn into the emerald, green liquid I've seen Gramps craft on several occasions. Give me almost any spell and I can execute it, but potion making is my nemesis. Turning away from the cemetery of failure, I waltz back inside the shop.

"Another one?" Gramps asks as I cross the threshold.

I flinch in response to his voice. Oh no. Did he see Gabriel? Could he have heard us? My pulse pounds a steady beat just below my skin. My palms turn sweaty, and I fight the urge to wipe them on my jeans.

"Yep. Why can't I just be a witch who does spell casting? You know, have you make all my potions for me." I laugh to cover the unease of wondering if I've been caught. It would be so much easier if we could just be a normal couple. Other immortals and witches in Graystone date without a problem.

"That's not how it works. This shop will be left to you one day, you'll have to learn to do it all." He shakes his head and tsks.

There's no indication that he's aware of what transpired out back. He's not acting strange. Well, more strange than usual in his formal button-down shirt, tie and slacks. For a man who owns his own shop, you'd think he'd dress a little more casual. Not him though, always dressed to the nines as if he belongs on the cover of a wealthy, silver fox magazine.

"Maybe that's why I was left on your doorstep as a baby. They knew then I wasn't going to cut it as a witch." The words fly out of my mouth before I realize it. Most of the time I keep that to myself, but lately it's been a struggle. I don't like secrets, and I have a hard time not blurting them out when it feels like the anxiety has a chokehold on me.

What happened to my biological parents anyway? Sometimes I swear I can remember being with them. Flashbacks of a past or images of a life I don't recognize seep through at random times. I feel a connection with somebody, I don't know if that makes me crazy or not. But I know I can feel them out there. It's like a sixth sense. Sometimes it feels as though they're close by, but I never recognize anybody around from the visions. Surely, I can't be the only orphan whose felt that. The Ember's were never able to have kids of their own, so I'm they're only one. I've been spoiled and sheltered, so I shouldn't complain. But I just want to know who my real family is and why they left me behind.

"None of that nonsense. You're a strong witch, but you're young. You'll get there, and as for finding an orphaned child on my porch? That was nothing short of a miracle. You were destined to be part of our family, Margaret Ember." Gesturing to the table, his bushy eyebrow raises. He chides, "Now back to work."

I grumble under my breath as I push the black curtain aside that separates the storefront from the backroom. The bell above the door chimes as a customer walks in. She looks to be about my age, but I've never seen her before. I watch her for several seconds as she peruses through the multitude of crystals lining the wall. Big or small, weak or powerful, we carry them all here. They number in the hundreds. After all, we must supply all of Graystone. There's thousands of immortals and witches living on the island, counting on us to have what they need.

Each crystal's examined by me before it goes up for sale. Their aging eyes aren't the greatest at checking for impurities in the gemstones. Only the finest stones will do. The customer's long auburn hair trails behind her and I only catch a glimpse of a side profile. She puts a few things into her basket and looks down at the list in her hand. She must be new to working with crystals as she seems hesitant on which ones to grab. I start making my way toward her, thankful for the opportunity to be distracted from the potions, but the old warlock steps into my line of sight.

A bony finger points to the back of the shop. "Practice."

I huff, knowing full well he knows my stalling tactics. Scuffing my sandals across the wooden floor, I disappear into the back to see what else I can mess up. What havoc can I wreak next? I wonder with a smirk. As I flip through the worn grimoire, I find my mind drifting to Gabriel and I bite my lip in anticipation of seeing him tonight. It's been almost a month since we've been able to steal more than a few precious moments alone.

Page by page, I look for something simple to craft. Scanning over the directions of a simple plant rescue potion, I decide that'll be a good one to try. Steeling myself for the possibility of another wrong outcome, I grab all the ingredients out of the large metal shelving system against the side wall. I line them up in the order they're written on the aged paper. A jar of compost tea, a small vial of dragon's blood, crushed amethyst, turtle shell, blackthorn and dandelion root extract.

Setting a new beaker in front of me, I double check every amount the recipe calls for and pour them slowly, wincing at every drop that falls in. Once all the ingredients are in, I take my long metal spoon and give the mixture a good stir. The colors mix and form a beautiful, dark purplish hue.

"Well, it's now or never," I say, holding the glass up to the light to see the shimmering ground crystals within. "Let's do this."

It's to help bring back an aloe plant I forgot to water for some time. The long green leaves are shriveled and dry. Tipping the glass, the thick potion seeps out and pools around the base of the plant. Ever so slowly, the soil begins to soak it up. Within a minute the leaves begin to turn from brown to green and swell to its original size. A thin stalk shoots up from the center of the plant and little bell-shaped flowers form.

Taking a few steps back, I cross my arms and stare at the aloe. I'm waiting for it to blow up, turn into a man-eating monster, or some other ungodly creation. The minutes seem to tick by at a snail's pace while I wait with bated breath. Nothing else happens. Gently poking a thick leaf with my finger, it remains unchanged. Letting my breath out in a whoosh, my shoulders relax. Maybe I'm not so hopeless after all.

After cleaning up the backroom, it's finally closing time. I dash out the front door, calling behind me, "I'll see you back at home, Gramps."

"Where are you off too so fast?" he asks.

Groaning internally, I turn back to face him. "Meeting up with some friends, don't wait up for me."

He eyes me warily as if he doesn't believe my white lie. "Okay, be safe Mags."

Rolling my eyes, I tell him, "It's Graystone. It's the safest place in the world."

"There's still bad folk out there," he warns.

"I'll be fine, bye." I wave at him as I take off in the opposite direction.

Checking the watch on my wrist, I sigh. I'm going to be late. My flip flops slap against the boardwalk as I near my destination. Glancing around to make sure nobody else is around, I hop over the rail and duck under the pier. Gabriel's sitting on a blanket, leaning against one of the large boulders and munching on a bag of pork rinds.

"Well, it's about time you show up. I was starting to think you ghosted me," he laughs as he tosses one of the fried snacks at me.

I kick off my sandals and plop down beside him, bumping his shoulder with my own. "As I recall you're the one with a habit of standing *me* up."

"That's not fair, I got called away for an assignment." He squeezes my sides until I let out a giggle.

"Assignment, or another girl friend?" I playfully poke at him. This is an ongoing joke between us. I know there's not another woman, I only say it for fun.

"I got all the woman I can handle with you," he snorts before his face turns serious. Lines form around his eyes and mouth.

Alarm bells sound in my brain, as dread settles in my stomach like a brick. "What's wrong?"

"I have to go away for a little while," he says quietly.

I sigh. "Another assignment?"

"Something like that," he states, looking down.

It's not like him not to be forthcoming. "What aren't you telling me, Gabe?" I ask.

His eyes hold mine prisoner and it feels like he's searching for something in my features. "Graystone's in danger." He reaches an arm behind him and scratches at his neck. "All I can tell you, is that I'm going to be out of the country for a while on a special mission."

"How long?" Wetness coats my eyes and I fight the urge to swipe at them. He just got back from another trip; I've barely seen him this past month.

His eyes soften as he cups my cheek in his warm palm. "I don't know yet, but I'll be completely unreachable."

I don't like the sounds of that, he's always been able to keep in contact. It's his duty to protect the people of Graystone. If missing him is a sacrifice I have to make for the greater good, than it's one I'm willing to pay. As much as I hate to be apart from him and am already dreading the constant worry, I'll have while he's away, I know it's for a good reason.

"When?" I close my eyes and lean into his hand.

"First thing in the morning," he rasps.

Tomorrow? My eyelids snap open, and I move my mouth to respond but quickly close it when I don't know what to say. I was expecting to have at least a few more days.

"I need you to promise me something," Gabriel says in a more serious tone than I've ever heard come from him.

"Anything," I whisper in the small space between us.

"Don't trust anybody." His throat works on a hard swallow. "No matter who they are."

My heart beats hard in my chest, slamming against the bone as if trying to break free. "You're scaring me."

"I'm sorry. I don't mean to, but the intel I was briefed on today is…" He rubs at the scruff of his beard. "Well, let's just say it blew my mind when I found out the truth. And it's making me question everything I've ever known."

He wraps his arms around me and tugs me into him as he leans back against the large boulder. Inhaling deeply, I snuggle closer to him. These slivers of stolen moments have meant the world to me, but it's never enough. I'm always left wanting more. Wanting a life together that we no longer have to hide. I'm done hiding, consequences be damned. I'm telling the Ember's this weekend about us. They can accept it or not, but I love who I love. There's no denying it and I shouldn't have to feel ashamed of that. They either accept all of me or none of me, there's no in between.

"Wait for me?" His hoarse voice draws me away from my thoughts.

"Always," I say without hesitating.

I knew there were risks dating an immortal guardian, and this is the biggest one of all. Their dangerous lifestyle is nothing short of terrifying when you're the one left behind, loving them from afar. Wondering if they're going to come back home to you, alive. I bite down on my bottom lip to distract myself from that possibility. I can't go there.

Gabe reaches into the small black bag beside him and pulls out a velvet box. The breath halts in my chest as my eyes zero in on the ring box in his hands. Flicking my gaze up to his, he's quick to answer the question swirling around in my head with a cocky grin. Oh my god! It is what I think it is.

He slowly opens it up to reveal a deep blue topaz stone wrapped in an elegant pattern resembling tree branches. The moon's light reflects off the water and shines on the polished surface of the gem. It's absolutely gorgeous. My eyes meet his again, and he takes a slow, deep breath.

"This is my promise to you. You'll never have to walk this world alone. I promise to be by your side through the good, the bad, and the worst of times. To hold your hand through it all and be the shoulder to carry all your burdens. To be the one to lift you when your spirits are down, and help you celebrate the victories. I vow to love you and only you until my last breath. This life we choose may not be easy, but there's nobody else I'd rather share it with."

Screw holding the tears back, they flow freely down my cheeks and dampen my shirt. I've dreamed of this moment a thousand times, and yet nothing compares to the real thing.

"Maggie… my little witch." His smile broadens conveying more confidence than his shaky timber does. "Will you do me the honor of marrying me?"

"Yes!" I launch myself at him and he tumbles backward on the sand wrapping his arms around me.

His lips find mine and for a moment everything in the universe is perfect. The perfect life laid out for us, is in our grasp. One with a little clapboard house, complete with a white picket fence. It doesn't matter that he's a guardian and I'm a witch. It doesn't matter that he's off to some unknown battle tomorrow. It doesn't even matter that our country's in danger.

Pulling my lips back slightly, I whisper against his mouth, "I love you, Gabe."

His mouth twists into a smile against mine. "I love you too, Mags."

Tomorrow can wait. Tonight, it's just us here in this moment. One witch, one immortal, two halves of a heart that make it whole.

This is a short story written by Katie Richard, based on her YA fantasy romance series: Destiny Of Graystone. Check out my website at www.katierichard.com to learn more!

Bleeding Wonderland

By: Kotah Jean

A Why-Choose Alice in Wonderland Retelling

Chapter One - Allie

The snick of the blade as I slid it over the sharpening stone mellowed my mood as I gazed out at the sun rising on the horizon, painting the sky in vibrant hues of purple and pink.

This was a morning ritual I did religiously every day. It calmed the storm that brewed every time I closed my eyes. No matter what I'd tried, every night was wrought with the same nightmare I had to endure.

It was bad enough when I'd experienced it live and in color, but reliving it every night for the past fourteen years twisted my mentality. I shook my head, trying to clear the fog from my mind, but like the pest the past was, it hovered subconsciously.

A shudder ran down my spine as I swiped the blade across the stone again, and I closed my eyes, reveling in the sound.

My life might have started out normal, but thanks to that damn witch, she tore everything and everyone that meant anything away from me all because she saw me as a threat. How can any mother see their eleven-year-old child as a threat to their throne? For fuck's sake, I was a child. Her own flesh and blood. Granted, I might have been the heir, but I didn't want that seat any time soon. Or ever, for that matter.

None of that mattered to her, though. If there was a chance for her to lose her reign, she was bound and determined to destroy the threat before it even had the opportunity to come to fruition.

My breathing grew harsh as the memory flashed through my mind, the pain still ever present as it was back then.

"Oh, Alice, it's time to come back inside for your next lesson of the day," my mother, the Queen of Hearts, said as she stood on the balcony

overlooking the garden I was currently in, playing hide and seek with my best friends.

"Do you have to go, Alice?" Chester whispered in my ear, making me jump and spin around with a squeal, clutching my chest in fright. This was why I always hated playing hide and seek with him. He could literally melt into the shadows and sneak up on anyone.

His lips spread in a wide grin, showcasing immaculate white teeth. He was pleased with himself that he had once again scared the crud out of me.

"You know Mom, Chester. If I don't, I would hate to think how she would punish me this time," I whispered as tears gathered in my eyes.

Mom wasn't the worst parent in the world, but she wasn't the best either. If I defied her, she found many creative ways to take it out on me. She had often threatened to hurt my friends if I didn't do as she told me to. I couldn't let anything happen to Chester, Hayden, or Mack. They were all I really had besides Mom, even though the residents of Wonderland treated me like I was one of their own. I could never tell if it was because of who I was as a person or because of where I stood in accordance with the throne.

Rustling in the bushes caught my attention right as Mom yelled again, "Alice, you have one minute to get up on this balcony. You know what will happen if you continue to disobey me!"

Mack and Hayden burst through the hedge bush into my little hiding spot, stopping in their tracks as a single tear leaked from my eye. I reached up and hastily wiped it away, not wanting to look like a baby in front of my three best friends, but the floodgates opened as more trailed down my cheeks.

Chester disappeared from my view as he melted back into the shadows. Then, his incorporeal arms wrapped around me in a comforting embrace and held me tight as Mack stepped up my front and cupped my face, wiping my tears away with his thumbs. Hayden molded himself to my back, wrapping his arms around my waist and nuzzling my neck as he breathed me in.

"Don't worry, Alice," Mack murmured as he dried my tears. "Only a couple more years, and we will take you away from here so we don't have to worry about the queen," he sneered her name, "again. It'll just be the four of us. Forever."

"Promise?" I choked out.

"Promise," all three boys said with conviction.

I took a shuddering breath, moved out of their embrace, straightened my back, and took off toward the castle. Before I was in my mother's sight, I looked back at the three boys who meant the world to me. I didn't want to leave them, but I wanted to protect them more. All three watched me with various expressions of adoration and love, making me blush under their gaze.

"Ten seconds, Alice." Mother's voice cut through the garden like a whip, sending a tremor down my spine. She sounded pissed.

With one last wave, I stepped out from the bushes and hurried across the lawn, taking the steps two at a time until I stood before her, shaking under her scrutiny. I knew I had pushed my luck when she called me, but hopefully, she would let it slide.

Her lips curled in a sneer, and she moved around me without a word, heading back inside the castle, sure I would follow. I sped up my walk until I was just slightly behind her on the right side and pushed my shoulders back, raising my chin high, just like I was taught in my daily lessons. After all, the Queen of Hearts couldn't have a slouch for a daughter.

My brows furrowed as we walked past where I usually had my lessons and continued further into the forbidden part of the castle, the one area Mom told me I was never allowed to go. What's going on, *I wondered to myself.*

The air chilled as the walls changed from white marble with gold accents to hard gray stone, and the beautiful hardwood floors disappeared, only to be replaced with what looked like packed dirt.

A sense of foreboding hit me hard, and my steps faltered, my breaths coming in short, sharp pants. Something bad was about to happen; I just knew it. Mom peered over her shoulder, and her expression soured as she saw me falling behind. Spinning on her heel, she marched up to me and grabbed my arm hard, her nails digging into my tender skin. She then continued in our original direction, practically dragging me behind her.

I choked down a whimper at the pain, knowing if I let out even a sound, she would make me hurt worse than I already was. My nose crinkled as a musty, moldy smell invaded my senses, but it didn't seem to bother her in the slightest. I still had no clue where she was taking me, but I would do anything just to be back in the garden with my best friends.

We passed through a wooden door that looked ready to fall off its hinges, entering into a room where her most trusted guards were gathered around, salivating and leering at me as Mom pulled me in front of her and threw me at their feet.

This time, I couldn't hold back the whimper as I slammed into the hard-packed dirt, my palms and knees taking the brunt of the fall. Hands from the numerous guards started grappling for me, pulling at my hair and clothes. My cry echoed in the chamber as they finally got me off the ground. Fear like no other slammed into me, and I screamed as I was thrown over an unknown man's shoulder.

"Mom!" I cried, my voice cracking.

"You know what to do, gentlemen. Get rid of the brat," my mother sneered, her lips curling up in a smug grin as I thrashed around but could not get free.

"Yes, your majesty," they all chorused as one.

The sound of groaning wood reached my ears, and then a cool breeze wafted through the air as the bright twin suns of Wonderland blinded me after being in such a dark space. I squeezed my eyes shut but continued fighting as hard as possible to get free. But being only eleven, there was no way I could take on all these men who were trained to defend the castle.

The guards marched around the back of our home, and then it disappeared from sight as they continued into the forest at the back of the property. All the adrenaline quickly fled me, and I finally slumped in exhaustion. I knew I had to do something, but honestly, what could I do?

Taking one last chance, I opened my mouth and screamed as loud as I could. "Chester! Hayden! Mack! Save me!"

My body was unceremoniously tossed onto the forest floor, this time my back and my head taking the impact. Bright lights danced in my vision and then blackness threatened to take me, but I shook my head as hard as I could, knowing I needed to stay awake. I couldn't sleep, no matter how badly I wanted to.

"Shut the fuck up, you little bitch," the guard, who threw me down, gritted out between clenched teeth. "Those little boys aren't coming to save you. They knew this was happening and were happy to know that they were getting away from your whiney ass."

Shock at his words rippled through me, and I opened my mouth to scream again, but it was cut off as something was shoved in my mouth. Then, before I could rip it out, my hands were tied behind my back, the rope so tight it cut off the circulation to my fingers.

"Fuck, she's annoying. Let's go, Monty. I want to get back in time to watch the Queen tell everyone her precious little brat is dead," another said, clapping Monty on his shoulder.

A whimper slipped past my lips, and I tried to use my legs to crawl away, but Monty grabbed me and tossed me back over his shoulder, resuming their trek through the woods.

Tears trailed down my face, and my heart broke as everything unfolded before me. My best friends, the boys I had been in love with, who promised me forever, lied to me. They never wanted me. They wanted to get rid of me. That hurt worse than knowing my mother didn't want me anymore.

A ripple of magic washed over me, and I just knew we were getting closer to the portal of Wonderland. If they were going to end my life, they might as well just do it now. Without my best friends, I had nothing left to live for. I clung to their promises every time my mom took out her anger on me, knowing that I just needed to wait a little longer till I could get away from her for good. Now, I had nothing.

The stomping of feet stopped, except Monty's, as he broke through the line of guards, and then he set me on my feet, my knees buckling as my head swam with dizziness from being over his shoulder for so long. Before I hit the floor, he steadied me, then pulled away like I had burnt him.

He knelt in front of me, and I flinched as he reached around and untied the rag he had put in my mouth, pulling it away.

"Why are you doing this to me?" I whispered as tears continued cascading down my cheeks.

"Why wouldn't we?" he asked as he returned to his feet. "You are a threat to the Queen, and we take those threats seriously. Goodbye, Alice."

Before I could say anything more, he shoved me with all of his strength, infusing it with an incantation to send me flying. Portal magic swallowed me whole, and the last thing I saw before it snapped shut were the guards sending me lecherous grins and patting themselves on the back for a job well done.

Darkness engulfed me, but I didn't cry out. There was no one to cry to. Everything was taken away from me, and there was no reason to even fight anymore.

I fell for what felt like hours. It was nothing but me and the darkness, and I welcomed the dark as my new best friend. At least not being able to see where I was going, I couldn't get my hopes up that this was just some new brand of punishment Mom was using to get me in line. If I fell forever, at least I knew the dark would never leave me like everyone else had.

The pitch blackness started lightening, turning to a charcoal gray, and I knew I was about to be spit out somewhere. I fought to return to the darkness, adrenaline flooding me once more. I wanted to stay here where I knew I couldn't be hurt again. The grayness continued to lighten, and sound started filtering through my ears, the first thing I'd been able to hear besides my harsh breathing.

I'd never been through the portal before, so I didn't know what to expect when it spit me out on the other side, wherever it was I was going. I squeezed my eyes shut, bracing for whatever was going to happen. The light behind my eyelids got brighter, the sounds got louder, and I felt like I was falling faster, my hair whipping around my face.

Taking the chance, I cracked my eyes open, tears leaking from my eyes as the ground rushed up at me quickly. I knew it would hurt when I hit, but I locked all my muscles right as—

I startled as a hand landed on my shoulder, and I jumped up, spinning around and thrusting my knife out as the sharpening stone clattered to the ground. Before I could connect with whoever scared me, a hand gripped my wrist, stopping my forward momentum. It was then that the memory fully cleared from my eyes, my blue orbs connecting with a pair of silver ones, concern marring his face.

I swallowed hard, and a shudder wracked my frame as my hand loosened around the hilt of my knife, slipping through my fingers and joining the stone on the floor.

"You don't have to do this, Allie. You can stay here with me, and we can forget all about this," my pseudo-father, Thomas, murmured as he pulled me into his barrel chest, holding me tight. I knew I didn't have to do this, but it's what he trained me for, what we both wanted since the day he found me on the streets—alone, broken, and so damn tired that I was ready to give up.

"I know," I croaked, then cleared my throat. "I know. But we deserve vengeance for what we have both endured. She took everything from us, and if I can do something to make her pay for her sins, I am going to. Then we can both go home," I said, conviction lacing my tone.

Thomas pulled back and cupped my face in his rough, calloused hands. "Home is wherever you are, Allie. Just come back to me so I don't have a heart attack, okay?" I snorted. He wasn't THAT old. "You know your old man worries, and I won't stop until you're in front of me again."

"Okay, Thomas." I sniffled, and he pulled me back in for another hug. This was the last morning we would spend together until I completed my mission. In a few short hours, I was leaving the safety of his home, where he had brought me fourteen years ago, and I was heading back into Wonderland to mete out punishment to all those who wronged us. Including the three boys who once had my heart, promised me the world, and then threw it all away.

The only ones who would be safe from my wraith were the people who formed the resistance. From what I knew, they formed not long after I disappeared and had been trying to stop the Queen and her guards at every turn. There were some successes, but their numbers were dwindling after every clash, partly from fear and partly from death. They had somehow been sending Thomas communications over the years of everything happening back home. I personally didn't know anyone who was a part of it, but they knew I was coming, and they knew why. I wouldn't even care if they killed me after completing what I set out to do.

My one objective was clear.

The Queen of Hearts would die, even if I had to bleed Wonderland dry.

Chapter Two - Allie

Nerves rattled my frame as Thomas and I sat side by side on our black suede couch, going over the latest correspondence that arrived from Wonderland right before he pulled me out of my memories.

My rucksack was already packed, leaning against the light gray wall near the front door. My knives were sharp, strapped to various parts of my body, and even though my mind should be clear, I couldn't help but worry that something was going to go wrong. Not the right mindset to be in when getting ready for something of this caliber.

"This isn't good," Thomas muttered, pinching the bridge of his nose as the paper crinkled in his hand. "From what the leaders say, they are starting public executions. What is the point? Are they trying to instill fear in everyone? I just… I don't get it." Emotion leaked from his voice, and I knew at that moment the death of his wife was at the forefront of his mind.

Thomas was one of the many Wonderland shifters that had inhabited the realm, and when his wife was taken from him, he felt their bond break. He never really talked about her much, but every time he did, you could tell how much he loved her and how her death affected him. They never had the chance to have kids, and I always wondered if that was why he took me in so easily. But sadly, he never found anyone else to fill the emptiness of his life except for me.

He was a handsome man, twenty years older than me, but he still looked like he was in his mid-twenties—my age. I could understand why starting a relationship with a mundane human would be hard. He aged a lot slower than people in this realm, so while he continued to look young, anyone he would have tried to get close to would age quicker than him. People of this realm wouldn't understand, and he would most likely end up in a lab somewhere. Not the life a shifter—or anyone for that matter—should have.

Thomas towered over my five-five height, standing tall at six-four, with a large barrel chest, an olive skin tone, deep brown eyes, black hair, and neatly trimmed facial hair. When I was little, people would think I took after my mother and not him, but as soon as I turned twenty, people started to think Thomas and I were in a relationship. *Gag.*

Every few years, we would move around to avoid suspicion, so I'd experienced much more of this realm than any Wonderlandian has been able to. Unless they left like Thomas did. But since we were at the pinnacle of bad shit happening in Wonderland, we returned back to where we started, the original home Thomas and I shared.

We first started discussing my mission when I was fifteen and full of so much teenage angst, anger, and resentment. I had bottled it up for those first four years, and finally, it all exploded out of me in rage, and I took it out on Thomas. The one person my ire shouldn't have been pointed at. But he was the only one around, and I got lucky he didn't kick me out for taking it all out on him.

"I don't get it either. But we'll put a stop to it. Do we know when the first one is set for?" I asked with no hesitation whatsoever. "Hopefully, it'll happen in a few days, and I can stop it before it even starts."

Thomas tossed the crumpled paper on the coffee table and sat back on the couch, running his fingers through his hair. "Two days. Do you think you'll be able to find the resistance by then and get to the castle in time?"

I mulled over his question. "I should be able to. It really depends on where the portal puts me. From what you've told me, they were shutting down portals, so who knows how many are still active and where they are. I could end up in the castle's backyard or on the opposite side of Wonderland. Hopefully, these resistance people have a way to traverse the land quicker, or there is a chance I won't make it." I shook my head. That would be the worst-case scenario if I missed the chance to save innocent people.

"Alright," Thomas clapped his hands. "Go make sure you have everything together, and let's get going. The sooner you get there and take care of this mess, the sooner we'll be together again."

I jumped up from the couch before I could change my mind and stay here where it was safe and made my way down the short hall to the bathroom. Flicking on the light, I shut the door behind me and stepped up to the mirror. Last week, I told Thomas I didn't want anyone to recognize me, that I knew my blonde hair and that I looked like the Queen would be a dead giveaway as to who I was. He agreed wholeheartedly and ran out to get me black hair dye.

Sometimes, I wondered how he could even look at me since I looked exactly like my mother. I would think I would be nothing more than a reminder as to what she took from him. But he never once held it against me, even though, at times, I thought he should have.

It was different looking at myself in the mirror now. Twenty-five years as a blonde, now I had deep black hair, the same shade as Thomas'. My bright blue eyes were a contrast to the darkness, and with my pale skin, I could easily pass as one of the vampires from human folklore. There were Wonderlandians who survived on blood, but they were blood mages, not this vampire idea the humans had. They could consume regular food but needed the blood to fuel their magic.

My hair had also grown out from what my mother kept it at. When I was little, I remember asking her numerous times if I could grow it out, but those conversations always ended with me getting yelled at. She wanted my hair to stay short, almost like a boy's. I knew now that it was just another thing she did to keep the attention on herself and not on her daughter. I almost wondered if she would have been happier if I had been born a boy. I snorted. Of course, she would have been. Wonderland has always been run by a queen. Not a king. So, if I was a boy, she would have another knight, not an heir to the throne. She would have been safe.

I gathered my waist-length hair and pulled it into a high ponytail, then spun it around, securing it with another hair tie, leaving my hair in a tight bun on the top of my head. If I could leave it down, I would, but not knowing who I might run into, I didn't need to give them something they could grab me with.

My black leather pants fit like a glove to my curves, and the black leather vest was a little tighter than it should be, pushing my ample chest up, but I needed something that was going to stay close to my skin. Thomas had these made and then sent over from Wonderland, imbued with magic to stop most elemental attacks, and they were internally layered with a lightweight mesh to stop daggers, swords, and bullets from penetrating through the fabric. The entire outfit weighed less than a pound, something humans would pay good money for if they had the chance to get their hands on it.

My packed rucksack contained more outfits like this, the resistance doing their part in keeping me safe while I did what they deemed impossible. I was sure they were wondering what made me different to where I could achieve the impossible, but not only did I have a score to settle with mommy-dearest, I was also the only one who could wield the Hearts sword. Besides my mother, of course, but she locked it away when I was five because I got too close to the only weapon that could kill her.

It wasn't my fault, though. The sword called to me, and even now, not even residing in Wonderland, I could swear it still whispered to me in my sleep to claim the power it held. I didn't want the power, though; I just wanted the bitch dead.

"I got this," I murmured to my reflection, staring deep into my own eyes, willing myself to believe it. "Meet the resistance, stop the public executions, get the sword, and kill my mother. Easy peasy." It would be easier if we didn't have public executions to contend with now. But I refused to allow more people to die at her hands. These were my people, and they needed me.

"We should get going, Allie," Thomas called from the living room.

I closed my eyes and took a deep breath, blowing it out slowly. When I reopened them, determination shone brightly in my blue orbs. This would be a cakewalk, or at least that was what I would keep telling myself, and I had an entire resistance to back me up. We were better together, and we would accomplish this mission.

Setting my shoulders back, I checked over myself one more time, and then I called, "Coming." I flicked the switch off, bathing myself in darkness, and spun on my heel, meeting Thomas back in the living room.

He stood by the door, my rucksack slung over his shoulder, pride lighting up his eyes. "Ready?"

"Let's do this."

***

The ride to the Wonderland portal wasn't long, so I didn't have any time to rethink my decisions. Not that I would.

I really wished Thomas was coming with me, but he had explained he still had a few things he needed to finish here before he could join us. There were last-minute things the resistance asked him to bring over, but they wouldn't be ready for another couple of days, but we just didn't have that time. I needed to go now.

"Alright, Allie," Thomas murmured, walking in step with me toward the portal entrance. "You are to meet a member of the White Roses in the flower forest. They will take you to the resistance camp, and from there, you will meet with the leaders and go over the full plan. Make sure you let them know that you plan to stop the executions. They might already have that idea in mind, but you'll just need to verify it with them."

I rolled my eyes. We literally just went over all of this in the car. "I know. Keep worrying the way you are, and you'll get gray hair."

Thomas stopped suddenly and turned me, mock-gasping as his hand flew to his chest. "I will never go gray! And if I do, it'll be because of you. I'm surprised we made it through your teen years without me getting grays."

"Ha! That makes two of us!" I snorted and took off running. Thomas chased after me as his booming laughter echoed around the open field.

From what Thomas told me, the portal area was at the edge of a field surrounded by a forest, the portal itself in a tree. This was my first time seeing it, so I didn't know exactly what I was looking for, but I could feel the magic pulsing around the expansive space. It felt just like I remembered from when I was eleven and ejected none too nicely from Wonderland.

Thomas caught up to me and veered to the left toward a tall pine, its trunk larger than any of the others in the vicinity. I couldn't see the actual portal itself, which was starting to worry me. Just because the magic was here didn't mean the portal was still active.

He stopped at the base of the tree and dropped my ruck, then knelt down and swiped at the ground, uncovering what looked suspiciously like a wooden manhole cover. Definitely the oddest thing I'd seen in the middle of a forest. He lifted the circular piece, and a blast of portal magic swept out, sending a shiver down my spine. The magic steadily pulsed, almost as hard as what my heart was beating.

This was it.

Thomas tossed the wooden cover to the ground and grabbed my ruck, then stepped back and turned his head toward me. He beckoned me forward, and I took sure steps till I stood next to him, my shoulder brushing his arm.

"I just wanted you to know that no matter what happens, I'm so damn proud of you," Thomas said, emotion leaking from every word.

Tears gathered in my eyes, but I blinked them back. I was a badass assassin now, and badasses didn't cry. I reached for my rucksack and put the straps over my shoulders, then clipped the chest and waist straps, tightening them so I didn't lose my ruck somewhere along the way.

Thomas and I both knew this could very well be the last time we ever saw each other, depending on the outcome of my mission. But I knew neither one of us wanted to say goodbye. He never once asked me to call him dad, even though that was the relationship we had. But he did make it clear that I could call him that if I wanted to. It never really felt right until now.

I wrapped my arm around his waist and hugged him tight. "Love you, Dad."

His breath hitched, and then he engulfed me in his big arms, kissing the top of my head. "Love you too, kid." His gruff voice was muffled in my hair, but it didn't hide the sniffle.

Backing away, I squared my shoulders and stepped up to the portal. I looked back over my shoulder and watched as a tear slid down Thomas' cheek, and he hastily wiped it away, not wanting me to see how much this affected him. I smiled and tossed him a wink.

Then I jumped into the darkness, returning once again to Wonderland.

A Raven in Queen Maeve's Court

By Jennifer Allis Provost

Bored, Maeve shifted on her throne. Once she was the Queen of Connacht, but now she ruled the Seelie Court. It seemed that when one was queen, whether it be in the mortal or fairy realm, one was also fated to sit through endless hours of nonsense.

This present nonsense involved… Well, Maeve didn't really know what it involved, since she hadn't been paying attention. Two of her subjects were ardently making their cases, voices raised and arms flailing as each described how the other was the villain of the piece. Maeve imagined that it was a dispute over property, or perhaps a quarrel over livestock. Then she sighed; nothing *that* interesting ever happened here.

What I wouldn't give for a cattle raid. Maeve leaned against the high back of her gilded throne, her eyes half-closed as she recalled her time as the Queen of Connacht. She'd been a right terror, she had, with the surrounding kings so afeared of her attacks they'd slept with one eye open. Not that Maeve had ever been a terror to her own people; no, to them she was always fair and just, and always sought to do right by them.

Then there had been the white bull of Cooley, rumored to be the finest bull ever to walk upon Irish soil, and Maeve had to have it. Sneaking behind the old king's back and absconding with his prized possession would be her greatest victory. And abscond with the bull she had, with nary a loss on her side.

However, her eyes had gotten bigger than her stomach, so to speak, and the theft of the bull proved to be the straw that broke the camel's—bull's—back. Her enemies, heretofore easy to handle, had had enough of her thieving ways and banded together against her. They'd even had the gall to send an assassin, a young pup who'd barely reached his manhood, to end the menace that was Maeve once and for all. The assassin wasn't so much a threat, but the army at his back, who were threatening to kill every last member of Connacht if Maeve wasn't readily brought forth, well, they were a force to be reckoned with. Maeve, ever one to weigh her options, took the matter under advisement, and decided that the best course of action was to flee and live to fight another day.

Of course, the question then became: to where should she flee? The surrounding lands were full of her enemies, and Maeve was loath to leave her native Ireland for a haven across the sea. So her trusted commanders spread the word of her untimely death, and she went under the hill. Or rather, to Underhill.

A fairy hill, or *brugh* as the countryfolk called them, was the equivalent of a mortal city. One of the main differences between the two was that, whereas humans had sky above their heads, the fairies had dirt, roots, and the occasional burrowing creature over theirs. And, of course, the *brugh* was full of fairies, magical folk who spent their days feasting, drinking, and playing tricks on their hapless mortal neighbors.

In many respects, Maeve and the fairies weren't all that different.

It was easy enough for Maeve to gain entry into the brugh. She merely lay on the grassy hillock, and waited to hear the sounds of revelry within. Mortals were often welcome at fairy banquets, either as servants or sources of amusement, and it was no trouble at all for Maeve to slip inside and join the merriment; after all, she'd done it often enough in her youth, before the demands of queenship had left her little time for such joys. Only this time, she didn't withdraw as soon as the sun rose.

Instead, she found herself a snug corner, and when the revelry began at next evening's dusk she joined anew. After a score of nights spent this way, Maeve came to the attention of Eleanore, the Seelie Queen.

Eleanore was not at all pleased at having a mortal woman setting up house in her *brugh* and demanded that she take her leave. Well, Maeve was a queen herself, and wasn't about to take orders from anyone, least of all a fairy. The ensuing battle was short, yet bloody, and ended with Maeve upon the Seelie Queen's throne, her golden hair stained crimson with Eleanore's blood.

There had been other opponents over the years, but they dwindled as Maeve's time on the throne increased. After a time, no one challenged her at all, and her life had become an endless cycle of merriment and sleep, interrupted by the occasional, boring, dispute.

Who would have guessed that immortality would serve as its own punishment?

A commotion at the far end of the hall roused Maeve from her boredom; it seemed that an interloper was scrapping away with her guards. She waved away the two bickering banshees, still oblivious as to the nature of their dispute, and gestured for the person in question be brought before her.

"He forced his way under the hill," stated the captain of Maeve's guard, a gruff man called Fergus. "When we told him we would toss him out on his arse, he said he'd like to see us try!"

"I'm all for you trying," said the prisoner, who now had Maeve's full attention. He was young, all wide eyes and gangly limbs, and covered in scrapes and bruises as well as filth. But his coppery hair flashed in the dim light, and his eyes were the greenest she'd ever seen.

"What's your name, boyo?" Maeve demanded. Most men bristled when called by such juvenile terms, but the prisoner only smiled.

"Baudoin Corbeau," he replied, bowing as much as he could while being held by the guards.

"And, Baudoin Corbeau, why have you found it necessary to infiltrate my home?"

"Legend says that the Seelie Queen is the most beautiful woman on earth," he replied. "I had to see you for myself."

"And?" Maeve prompted, raising an eyebrow.

"And," he continued, his gaze heavy, "those legends do you no justice."

At that, hot blood spilled up Maeve's neck. She was no stranger to flattery, and rolled her eyes at most of it. However, something about Baudoin, something in his deep voice and emerald eyes, resonated within her.

"It didn't occur to you to bathe before presenting yourself to this beauty?" Maeve quipped, struggling to regain her composure.

"Forgive me my slovenly appearance, but I was forced to dig my way into your hall," he replied. In that moment, Baudoin accomplished what no other man had ever done—he rendered Maeve speechless. Her eyes flew to Fergus, who nodded.

"Like a bald mole, he scratched his way down from the surface," Fergus explained. "Wasn't even bright enough to use a shovel."

"I didn't need a shovel." Baudoin cocked his head to the side, and Maeve saw a glossy black feather tucked behind his ear. Though it appeared thoroughly mundane at the moment, Maeve recognized an article of magic when she saw one.

"What…" Maeve cleared her throat, then continued, "Why would you dig your way, *by hand*, into a *brugh*?"

Baudoin shrugged. "I couldn't find a door."

Maeve threw her head back and laughed. "Well, it wouldn't be wise for us to advertise the way under the hill, now would it?" She gave the interloper another long look, then clapped her hands.

"First, you'll be needing to clean up," she said, "then you'll put on some proper attire. You'll join us for our revels."

"My lady," Fergus said, "he wears cold iron!"

Maeve looked at the knife strapped to Baudoin's forearm, then to her guards' bronze swords. Fergus, for all his posturing, was terrified of iron, and of how it could render him helpless. Maeve, however, held no such fears. "Of course he does," she admonished. "He's a mortal."

"He is too dangerous— " Fergus began, but Maeve silenced him with a gesture.

"If he's gone to all the bother of tunneling through the hill, the least we can do is feed him," Maeve replied, rising from her throne and descending the few steps to stand before Baudoin. Now that she was so close to him, she realized he was older than she'd first thought, his wide grin having given him the appearance of youth. Slowly, she slid Baudoin's iron knife free, smiling only slightly as Fergus cringed. "As my guest, I do expect you to be on your best behavior," she murmured, gliding a fingertip across the flat of the blade before sheathing it at her belt.

"Of course, my lady," Baudoin replied. "Anything for you."

As Fergus and Seamus led Baudoin away, Maeve couldn't help but wonder what "anything" encompassed.

***

After sundown the wine flowed freely in the Seelie Court, as it had last night, and the night before. Maeve sighed as she lifted her goblet; really, she had no one to blame but herself. She had known that for all their endless parties, fairies were a boring lot, content to perform the same tasks, over and over until the end of time… That is, unless a hapless mortal happened to interrupt them. Why, if Maeve hadn't stumbled into the *brugh*, they'd have let that old hag Eleanore lead them right to the bitter end.

And now, Baudoin was here.

Maeve set down her empty goblet, and the elf to her left immediately refilled it. She fought the urge to knock the vessel away, to fling the contents into the serving girl's eyes, and only just fought it. Angry and irritated, she snatched the goblet up, smiling when a bit of wine splashed onto the girl's dress, and walked among her people.

Before long, she found the *brugh's* newest resident, Baudoin, seated among her warriors. He was regaling them with stories of his past victories, likely all false, but he held his audience in the palm of his hand. He hardly missed a beat when Maeve sat beside him, only sparing the queen a sidelong glance.

"And that," Baudoin concluded, "was how my family came by its emblem." Awed murmurs rolled across the table; whatever story Baudoin had told obviously met with her people's approval. "What have we done to earn a visit from our gracious queen?"

"Oh, just curious as to the sort of manure you've been spreading," Maeve replied. Baudoin grinned, unoffended. "You look like you've bathed."

"That I have," he replied. "Allow me to thank you, my lady, for your most excellent hospitality." He clinked his goblet against hers, then they both drank deeply.

"You're not afraid of our food and drink?" Maeve questioned. "Haven't you heard that you could be trapped with us forever as the price of your indulgence?"

"Forever with you would pass in the blink of an eye," Baudoin murmured.

He smiled and ducked his head, and Maeve couldn't help but smile in return. Through the haze of wine she examined his features. She found Baudoin's strong jaw, marred by a tiny scar, quite appealing, as was his bright, unruly hair. Maeve sighed. He was nothing like the perfect fairy men she'd come to know, and that was the point. These fairies were so damn perfect that they were ugly; for all their magic, they'd never caught on that, sometimes, the flaws were what made one beautiful.

"Bow Dane," Maeve murmured, elongating the syllables of his name. "Such an odd, unwieldy name you've been saddled with."

"It's French," Baudoin informed her. "My surname means Raven."

"Mmm. Bow Dane Corbeau." Maeve shook her head. "Twice as unwieldy. I believe I'll give you a new name."

Baudoin raised an eyebrow. "Oh?"

"Oh." A hundred names flitted through Maeve's mind, all good, strong Irish names, and a fair few of them fairy in origin. None of them were right, though; none quite suited the man before her.

"Beau," Maeve said, laughing. "I shall call you Beau!"

Baudoin shook his head. "My mother won't be pleased. I'm named after my grandfather."

"She doesn't need to know," Maeve said. "It's only a name for me to call you while you're in my *brugh*."

Baudoin smiled. "I'd like that," he murmured, bringing his goblet to his lips. "I knew I was right in coming here, instead of visiting that other fairy queen."

Maeve blinked, her shoulders squaring. "Who? Oh, do you mean Nicnevin?"

"Is that her name?" Baudoin asked. "She's the one who claims she's lovelier than you."

At that, Maeve threw back her head and laughed. "The Unseelie Queen said that?" Calmed a bit from her outburst, Maeve wiped her eyes. "That one's got hair like a horse's tail and a smell like a barnyard, if I recall."

A commotion at the far end of the hall drew their attention; it was Fergus, winning at dice yet again. Arms raised high in victory (really, it was only dice) he locked eyes with Maeve and smiled. Out of habit she smiled back, though from Fergus's grimace she could tell that hers hadn't quite reached her eyes.

"Tell me, Beau, what are your plans for later this evening?" Maeve asked Baudoin, who nearly choked on his wine. "Not like that, you fool," Maeve added, thumping him on the back.

"Then, how do you mean?" Baudoin rasped.

Maeve indicated the far end of the hall with her eyes. "After the *brugh* goes quiet, meet me before the crimson tapestry." Baudoin nodded. Satisfied, Maeve rose, and added, "And Beau, don't keep me waiting."

The mortal stammered a reply, but Maeve was already walking away. She liked that her remarks had put the young man off-balance, almost as much as she liked the young man himself. Deep in thought about her coming time with Baudoin, Maeve didn't notice Fergus until he stood directly before her.

"May I escort you to your chambers, my lady?" Fergus asked, his gaze heavy.

"Not tonight," Maeve replied. She attempted to move past him, but he grabbed her arm above the elbow.

"And why not?" he hissed. "Found another, have you?"

Maeve looked coolly from Fergus's hand upon her to his eyes. "Who are you to lay hands upon me?" she asked, loudly enough for those nearby to hear. "Who are you to question me, your queen? If I desire my rest, it is my right."

Fergus, noting that they were now the object of several curious stares, abruptly released Maeve's arm and backed away. "As you wish," he grumbled, before stalking away to the far end of the hall. With her head held high, Maeve left the hall and entered her chamber, alone.

Perhaps it was because of the incident between the queen and Fergus, heretofore her favored companion, or perhaps the shorter summer nights were to blame, but that night the residents of the *brugh* went to their rest long before dawn. Maeve hadn't slept a wink, fearful that she would miss the opportune moment to slip out unseen.

She stifled a yawn as she entered the darkened hall, the corner of her mouth curling upward as she spied Baudoin waiting for her. He, too, looked like he'd forgone rest, but no matter. The early morning air would revive them both.

"So punctual," Maeve whispered, coming up behind Baudoin. "I worried you'd fall asleep with the rest."

"I was warned not to keep you waiting," Baudoin replied, extending his arm. "And what are my lady's plans for the morning?"

"I thought we'd pay Nicnevin a visit," Maeve replied, tucking her hand above Baudoin's elbow.

"Is she expecting you?"

"Why would she? She hates me nearly as much as I hate her." Baudoin raised his brow, but otherwise made no response. As they walked toward the *brugh's* exit, Maeve added, "Besides, I'd like to know if you find the old witch fairer than me."

"I can't imagine that I will," Baudoin replied. Maeve turned her head, hiding her darkened cheeks from her companion. Luckily, the hall was in shadows.

The walk across the rocky meadow was short, and the sun crested the hills as Maeve and Baudoin arrived at the Unseelie *brugh*. Maeve took a deep breath as she stared at the hillside; she'd only had one occasion to visit the Unseelie Court, and that hadn't exactly gone smoothly. Still, she knew that Nicnevin, for all her spouting, was no match for her. Her confidence increased tenfold when Baudoin slipped his hand into hers.

"Shall we?" he asked, indicating a chasm in the hillside. Maeve nodded, and together they descended into the darkness that was the Unseelie Court.

Unlike Maeve's hall, which was suffused with the warm smells of bread and mead, Nicnevin's home stank of brimstone and unswept floors. Maeve wrinkled her nose; it was as if these filthy fairies didn't have the sense to use some of their human pets as housekeepers. Clearly, her rival was a fool, as well as untidy.

Once they turned the last corner before the great hall, Maeve had to clamp her hand over Baudoin's mouth. He'd nearly cried out in shock at the sight of Nicnevin's warriors, all strewn about the hall like dropped pieces of kindling.

"They tend to drink something fierce, and sleep where they fall over," Maeve whispered in his ear. "Worry not, their heads are too heavy for them to stir."

Baudoin nodded and followed Maeve as she carefully picked her way among the unconscious folk. Spread across the head of the feasting table was Nicnevin herself, lying atop her cloak of thorns. Maeve had no idea what caused the Unseelie Queen to be positioned so, what with her legs splayed outward and dress unfastened to there, but she whispered a few likely scenarios to Baudoin.

"I'm sure nothing of that sort happens at your court," Baudoin replied.

"Never. We're quite respectable, for a disreputable lot, that is."

"Well?" Baudoin asked. "We've found her, and you were correct: she's not half as lovely as you. Now what will we do?"

Good question, that. Slowly, Maeve grinned; she could think of one thing that would thoroughly incense and humiliate the Unseelie Queen. Maeve squeezed Baudoin's hand, then bent over Nicnevin's face and kissed her square on the forehead, leaving behind a shimmering, silver impression of her lips.

Maeve and Baudoin ran, hand in hand, away from the Unseelie Queen and her court. Once they exited the *brugh* they fell to the grassy meadow, laughing like two children who'd stolen a pie.

"Will it wash off?" Baudoin asked.

"No," Maeve said, wiping away tears. "If I've worked it rightly, the mark will stay until the next full moon."

"Wasn't the moon full last night?"

"Aye," Maeve replied, succumbing to a new fit of laughter. Then Baudoin was caressing her cheek, and pressing his lips to hers.

"Well?" he asked once they parted. "Is my mouth shiny?"

"Careful, or I'll make it so." Baudoin grinned and helped Maeve to her feet.

"Will you ever tire of being a queen?" Baudoin asked.

Oh, if he only knew the decades of boredom she'd suffered. But then, all of that had ended when a green-eyed man had dug a hole into her court. "Why do you ask? Are you the answer to my life's question?"

"I don't know any answers," he replied. "But I'd like to look for them with you."

Maeve smiled, and kissed him again. She liked kissing him, this mortal man that made her feel more alive in a day than any magic ever had. "An excellent plan, Beau. Let's start on it right away."

***

And now you know how Maeve and Baudoin met. Catch up with their children—Max, Sara, and Sadie—in the Copper Legacy, available in print and ebook at the links below. Keep reading for a sneak peek from Copper Girl. Happy reading!

Copper Girl: https://books2read.com/CopperGirl

Copper Ravens: https://books2read.com/CopperRavens

Copper Veins: https://books2read.com/CopperVeins

Copper Princess: https://books2read.com/CopperPrincess

About the Author:

Jennifer Allis Provost is a native New Englander who lives in a sprawling colonial along with her beautiful and precocious twins, a dog that thinks she's a kangaroo, a parrot, a junkyard cat, and a wonderful husband who never forgets to buy ice cream. As a child, she read anything and everything she could get her hands on, including a set of encyclopedias, but fantasy was always her favorite. She spends her days drinking vast amounts of coffee, arguing with her computer, and avoiding any and all domestic behavior. Find Jenn on the web here: http://authorjenniferallisprovost.com/

Happy reading!

Spill the Tea, Witch

by Sarah Zane

Chapter 1

I was polishing a teacup when I heard the familiar peal of the bell. I turned around to face the customer. She was a tall scowling goddess of a woman, but I almost dropped the cup when I saw her tattoo.

The dragon crest of the Queendom that curled around her bicep was unmistakably the mark of the royal guard of Sherbrooke. My heart raced at the sight of it and my breath hitched when I saw the dragon's tail wrapped tightly around a crown. Only the personal guards of the royals had that honor.

I knew from the guard's appearance that she was too young to be the personal guard of either of the Queens, which left only one person she could be.

Inez Cyneward, the deadliest sword in the Queendom of Sherbrooke, hells, maybe even all of Zanaria. With her bronze skin and dark wavy hair, even her scowl did little to mask her beauty.

I saw movement over her shoulder and realized we weren't alone. My eyes moved to her companion and the rest of my already non-existent composure fled. I wasn't sure why I was surprised to see her in Inez's company, but it was startling nonetheless. I had never seen the princess up close before, but there was no denying it was her. Standing next to Inez was the heir to the Sherbrookian throne, Princess Serena.

The Queendom often spoke of her courage and her rebellious streak but seeing her now with her dark curls and warm brown eyes, it was a wonder they didn't talk about her beauty. I was struck by the thought that she and Inez looked like they could have been related. They had similar dark eyes and dark hair. Princess Serena was shorter than Inez and a good deal paler than her, but Inez could have passed for Princess Isabella, Serena's younger sister.

From what they said of Serena, she was as fierce and deadly as Inez. The pair of them made a striking sight, and would have stood out anywhere, but seeing them here in my grandmother's tea shop, of all places, I couldn't believe my eyes.

I only realized I must have been staring too long when Inez cleared her throat. I came back to myself, embarrassment rushing in, and immediately dropped into a low curtsy, grabbing for my skirts, unfortunately forgetting the teacup I was holding.

To my horror and utter embarrassment, the cup fell to the ground with a loud crash, cracking into tiny pieces. Thank the gods it wasn't one of my favorites. I looked up quickly at the women in front of me and rushed to say, "I'm so terribly sorry, Your Highness. I'm not normally this clumsy." I again thanked the gods that my grandmother wasn't around to disagree.

Grandmother. They had to be here looking for her expertise with herbs or teas. I paled. She would never forgive herself or me that the future Queen of Sherbrooke had come to our shop while she was away. I tried to remember exactly where she had gone and when she was expected back, but it was a futile exercise. She was always visiting this neighbor or that one; I could never keep her comings and goings straight.

I would have to do the best I could.

"Unfortunately, my grandmother isn't in at the moment, but let me get this cleaned up so you don't hurt yourself, Your Highness, and then we can see to whatever brought you in."

I gave a tentative smile before averting my eyes and dropping to my knees where I had dropped the cup. By the time I made it there, the princess was on her knees in front of me before I even noticed she had moved.

I paled when I saw her reaching for the pieces. "Your Highness, please allow me," I sputtered out quickly, horrified to see her on her knees in front of me cleaning up my own mess. By hand. The rumors weren't just rumors, then. She really didn't flaunt her magic.

For as long as I could remember, unnecessary magic use was frowned upon in Sherbrooke. The Queens believed that magic was a dividing force between people and to foster unity, those of us with the gift had to be mindful of not flaunting it. I had heard that the future Queen adhered to that but couldn't believe that she would stoop low enough to clean up a mess by hand.

Her hand brushed my still extended one, shaking me out of my stupor. I quickly grabbed some of the remaining pieces.

A moment later, Inez reached out for the princess. Whether to take the broken shards or help her up, I wasn't sure. She grabbed the princess's arm and pulled her up. It looked gentle enough, but Inez was scowling at her.

"Thank you so much, Your Highness," I said again, reaching out to take the shards from her.

Inez glared at me before the princess elbowed her in the stomach. Inez let out a disgruntled *oof*.

Satisfaction coloring her face, the princess turned back to me with an apologetic smile, handing over the shards.

"I'm so sorry, Your Highness," I said again, moving behind the counter and disposing of the broken shards.

"Please, there's no need for apologies. Contrary to what Inez here thinks," she said, gesturing in Inez's direction and rolling her eyes. "Accidents do happen."

Inez took a step closer to us, closing the gap between herself and the princess. "Apologies as well. The princess knows perfectly well that she's the one who has earned my scorn."

The princess huffed out a laugh. "Well then, apologies for both our behavior then, I suppose. I would introduce myself, but it seems you already know me." She gave me a soft smile before gesturing to Inez. "In case her reputation doesn't proceed her, this is Inez, my personal guard and closest friend."

Inez's scowl fell for just a minute at that.

Princess Serena didn't seem to notice and continued to explain. "We, well, I," she amended, "didn't come to cause trouble. I came here for your specific talents. I'm hoping you can help."

I gulped. I hoped I could help, too. My grandmother was the talented one, but I could do my best. I tried not to let my worry show and instead said, "Certainly, Your Highness. Though my grandmother isn't here, I'm sure I can help. We have many different blends for a large variety of concerns. Tell me what ails you or what you seek, and we'll see what we can find."

I felt myself internally beaming with pride that I delivered the welcome almost as well as grandmother would have. I hoped I was doing her proud.

"We actually weren't looking for your grandmother's talents." The confusion must have shown on my face, since she rushed to add, "Revered as they as are, I'm sure her tea and its quality is irreproachable, but I'm actually here for your talents, Callie."

The princess knew my name. The gods blessed future Queen of Sherbrooke knew my name. I latched onto the part of what she had just said that confused me even more and asked, "My talents?" I had no idea how she knew me or what talents she could be referring to. Confusion overtook the princess's face, and she looked at Inez, who just shrugged.

"You're Callie, are you not? I was told you could see things," she said, and when I didn't respond, she added, "in the tea leaves."

All the remaining color drained from my face. I had no idea how in the hells the future Queen of Sherbrooke had heard that. It wasn't incorrect per say, but I wasn’t a seer, not like the others in the Queendom. Even though my grandmother called me her little tea witch, no one except the village children came to me for readings. They found entertainment in my predictions. Although I tried to follow the royal family’s example and not use my abilities often, I couldn’t deny that I had an uncanny knack for being right about what I saw written in the tea leaves. But that didn’t make me a seer.

"Your Highness," I began tentatively, "I'm not sure what you've heard, but-"

She waved a hand, and I immediately stopped talking. She quickly said with a soft smile, "I'm well versed in the way of magic. I know it might not work or be accurate in the ways I expect. The gods only know how much my mother has reminded me of that," she said with a little laugh. "I'm not asking for a miracle, just for you to try to read the leaves and tell me what you see." She seemed to sense my hesitation because she asked, "What worries you?"

Her warm brown eyes radiated kindness that had me blurting out, "I'm positive my predictions and my skill pale compared to Her Majesty, the Fairy Queen."

Everyone in the Queendom knew that although the Fairy Queen had married into the royal family, she was the more powerful between herself and her wife. The Queen and the Fairy Queen had ruled over the Queendom for my entire life, and everyone spoke of the Fairy Queen's power. According to rumors, her magic knew no bounds, but since Sherbrookians were encouraged to practice magic responsibly, no one truly knew the extent of her powers. A simple reading would surely be child's play for her.

The princess smiled at that. "Sweetie, I don't need you to be better than my mother. I just need a reading from someone who isn't related to me," she said with a nervous giggle.

Well, that was curious. "What is it you would like to know, Your Highness?" I asked, hoping it would be something simple. I wasn't sure how she even knew about my skills, since I rarely used them.

"I'd like to know anything and everything you can tell me about my future."

I took a deep breath before saying, "I would love to help. Really, I would, but I'm not nearly as talented as many others who have the gift. For my readings, the topic needs to be more specific for me to make anything of the leaves. Is there something specific you need to know about?"

Her face fell, and she glanced at Inez for a moment.

"A waste of time," Inez said.

I bristled a little at that. They had come to me, basically asking for the impossible, and Inez was mocking me. I wasn't a seer, not really. I wanted to help the princess, but they should have known it was too big of a task. Thankfully, I was smart enough to keep my mouth shut.

After a moment of silent communication between the two, the princess turned back to me and said, "If I said all my problems come from my love life and I need to know more about that, would that be specific enough? I'm afraid that's as detailed as I can be."

Her anxiety was palpable as she waited for my answer. I didn't want to disappoint her, but her love life was still broad. Although, I thought in a burst of inspiration, if I did a full reading, it might be enough.

"I think we can make that work," I said, turning to get the tea canisters I would need. "It'll be longer than your average reading, but I think we can pull it off."

I grabbed the canister of black tea and the green tea next to it. I placed those on the counter and turned back around to grab the white tea canister, but it wasn't where it was supposed to be. I stood on my tiptoes and shuffled everything around. After a minute, I still didn't find it, but my eyes landed on the herbal tea. It wasn't white tea and wasn't ideal, but it would do in a pinch.

I grabbed it before I could change my mind and turned back to the waiting women, setting it on the counter beside the others.

"So how does this work?" the princess asked.

I looked around the empty shop and scooped the containers into my arms, saying, "Actually, let's go somewhere even more private. Just one moment."

I quickly made my way over to the shop door and sent out a small prayer to the gods that my grandmother wouldn't kill me as I flipped over the sign from open to closed.

I hurried back over to the princess and Inez and ushered them into the back.

I blushed seeing the disarray our kitchen was in with the remnants of our morning meal still on the counters, but we had already come this far. There was no turning back now. Besides, at least there were chairs and a table here. It wouldn't do to make the princess stand for her reading.

I placed the canisters on the table before pulling out a chair for the princess.

"Here," I said, gesturing to the chair. "Take a seat, Your Highness."

She smiled, taking the offered seat with a thank you. I waited for Inez to do the same, but she remained standing. I turned back to the princess and saw her eyes were on the cannisters. "So, how does this work? Do I pick the type of tea, or do you?"

I took a seat across from her and said, "Actually, we'll be using all three. Understanding the future can be quite complex, so we'll need to do a full reading. Three teas for the three times, past, present, and future."

Inez moved closer, and finally pulled out another chair, seating herself at the princess's side. "What do the past and present have to do with the future?"

"Well, if the question were a simpler one, we might not need the added context. For example, if you were asking about a specific someone, we could just look into the future, but to tell you about the future of your love life in general, I need the context provided by the past and the present."

"So why these teas?" Inez asked. I could see the skepticism in her eyes. It made sense. Princess Serena looked uneasy, and it was Inez's job to protect her, after all. I wasn't threatening her, but I could understand that as her guard, Inez wouldn't like me prying into the princess's life. But if they were here, the reason had to be important.

I didn't think Inez actually cared about the why's behind my tea choices, but I answered anyway.

"Black tea for the past. It's a morning tea, an energy provider, the best and only way to start a reading with the right energy. It never comes out right with other blends."

I pointed to the green tea cannister next to it. "Green tea for the present. The present isn't as finicky, so a green tea works, but an oolong would do the trick in a pinch too. More mellow than the black tea, it helps with digesting the hard truths of the present."

I didn't miss Inez's eye roll and wondered if I should keep going. I looked at the princess and saw I still had her attention, so I gestured to the last canister.

"And finally, white or herbal tea for the future. The future is always in flux, so a calming tea works best to facilitate the reading."

"So we drink the teas?" she asked.

I grimaced a little at that. I had heard some actual seers who used tea as their medium would have their patrons drink the tea, but for me, it wasn't about the tea, it was about the leaves.

"Actually, no."

"No?" the princess asked with a raised eyebrow.

"Well, I mean you can." I rushed to correct myself. "If you would like a cup of tea, I'm more than happy to oblige. It just isn't necessary for the reading."

She waved her hand. "That's quite all right. I'm sure your blends are lovely, but I'm rather anxious to get to the reading," she said carefully.

She and Inez shared a meaningful glance that I couldn't interpret. Inez put her hand on the princess's shoulder and Princess Serena turned back to me.

"So, if we don't drink it, what do we do with it?"

I picked up the black tea and opened the lid. "Hold out your hand, Princess."

She did, and I carefully sprinkled some of the black tea leaves into her waiting palm.

When she had a good handful, I closed the jar and put it aside, moving the jars from the center of the table, clearing space for her.

"Now close your other hand over the first, cupping them together, and shake them gently. When it feels like the right moment, put your hands over the center of the table and release, scattering the leaves there. How they fall is what I read."

Her eyebrows quirked and Inez looked even more skeptical, but the princess gently shook the teas between her hands. "Like this?" she asked hesitantly.

"Yes, that's perfect."

"And then I just release them?"

I nodded. "Yes, whenever you're ready, just release them. It doesn't matter how much or how little they scatter, I'll be able to read them."

She still looked unsure, but let the leaves fall in the middle of the table.

I took a deep breath and examined the shapes, paying particularly close attention to the concentration in certain areas, and asked again, "So, Princess, you would like to know about your love life?"

I didn't look away from the leaves, not breaking my concentration. I already knew the answer, but how she answered was important to the reading.

"Yes. I feel like I'm at a crossroads and I need to know if I'm making the right decision."

That was intriguing, but since she didn't offer more, I was smarter than to ask.

I examined the leaves. Their somewhat even groupings told me quite a lot. "The leaves are showing that your past has been a smooth one. There have been a few crushes, but nothing serious."

While most of the clusters were close to the center, there was one further away. "A girl from a foreign land?" I guessed. Part of it was guesswork, but getting an understanding of the past was imperative to being able to interpret her present and her future. I needed to get a sense for how the leaves interacted with her timeline.

This time, I looked up to see her blushing and nodding.

Inez was gaping at her. "Who?" she asked in a hushed tone, but Serena didn't respond.

"What else does it tell you?" the princess asked.

I examined the piles closer to the center. "Not much, to be honest, but it doesn't need to. The past acts as a bridge to the present and then the future."

I looked once more and saw a scattered line running away from the others.

I pointed to it and said, "This line here tells me that the present has introduced a complication."

Princess Serena's eyes widened, but Inez scoffed. "Clearly there's a complication. We wouldn't be here if there wasn't. Anyone could have guessed that. You're not actually buying this, are you?" she asked looking at the princess.

I felt myself shrink, concern weighing me down. If they didn't believe, I wasn't sure what they were doing here in the first place, but the princess gave me a comforting smile.

"It's okay. I'll take whatever information you can give me. Inez here is a bit of a skeptic, but I'm not."

That gave me some reassurance, but I was still quite nervous. "Well, I think that's all the past has to tell," I said after taking another quick glance at the leaves. After seeing nothing new, I scooped them up in my hands and placed them in a bowl on the side of the table.

"On to the present," I said, grabbing the green tea canister and opening the lid. I again asked for the princess's hand to drop some leaves into and she obliged.

As she shook the leaves, I let myself wonder what it was she was looking for, what I might see.

She let the leaves fall and right away I noticed a big difference from her past. The leaves were a lot more concentrated into one pile but more haphazard.

Something about the disarrayed, hectic nature of the arrangement made me sure she was in love, but that it was chaotic and something was wrong. Not within the relationship, but beyond it. Outside forces were causing turmoil. I hazarded a guess: "Your family doesn't approve?"

A soft frown crossed Princess Serena's features as she shook her head. "They don't know, but if they did, they wouldn't approve of him," she said, almost to herself, and I wasn't sure I had heard the last part correctly until I saw the scowl on Inez's face. I was starting to understand the princess's anxiety and desperation now.

The Queendom of Sherbrooke had been a Queendom for centuries. A man had never sat on the throne for as far back as we had records. Everyone, the Queens included, expected the princess to fall in love with and marry a woman.

No wonder she didn’t want her mother to do this reading, and no wonder Inez was so against her being here. If this were to get out, it would shake the very foundations of the Queendom. It wouldn’t, of course. I would never tell, but this was far more serious than I had thought.

I looked to the leaves again, searching for anything else noteworthy or anything I might have missed.

I looked closer and noticed a trail leading off from the main pile that I hadn't paid attention to before. I followed it and saw it trailed off into two paths, but I couldn't yet glean which path would be taken. This had to be what had brought her here today. "You're trying to come to a decision. This person, the one you love, wants a commitment."

She nodded again, and Inez looked shocked and then angry.

"He what?" she asked loudly.

"He worries about our future and wants security when it comes to me, wants a vow that I intend to make him mine."

Inez's face flashed through emotions too quickly for me to follow, but she seemed to land on disbelief.

"So, we're here to determine the best way for you to end things?"

Serena took a deep breath. "We're here for me to get some answers. I don't know what I intend to do."

Inez grasped her shoulder and turned her around so she was facing her, although the princess still didn't move her eyes to meet Inez's. Inez moved her hand under the princess's chin and tipped her face up, gently.

"You know you can't," she breathed.

"I shouldn't," the princess agreed.

"Shouldn't *and* can't. He's not worthy of you and he's not worth tearing apart the Queendom for."

I was inclined to agree that no matter who the man was, he wasn't worth the instability it would sow in the Queendom, but I kept my mouth shut.

"I haven't made any decisions yet. I just wanted a little guidance. With the Harvest Festival coming up, I know things are going to get crazy and I didn't want this weighing on my mind."

Inez continued to search her eyes.

I looked away, back down at the leaves for something else to focus on. Even though they were in my kitchen, I felt like I was intruding on a private moment.

I looked at the leaves again, and my eyes fell to where the paths diverged. It hadn't happened yet. It was possible it represented the festival, but I would need to do the future reading to find out more.

I scooped the leaves up and felt their eyes on me.

"That's all the present has to offer. It can't tell us any more about the decision," I said, depositing the leaves into another empty bowl and grabbing the herbal tea canister. "For that, we have to turn to the future." I was about to ask for the princess's hand, but she already had it laid out for me. I removed the lid and poured some of the leaves into it.

She shook them, but before she could drop them, I stopped her. "Wait, the future leaves are a little different. You have to spread them in a line, like you're planting seeds."

She just looked at me, unsure. I mentally berated myself for using a planting analogy with a princess as if she had ever planted her own crops. I moved my hands to hers and guided her in the motion I meant. I pulled back when I saw the glare from Inez, but the princess knew what I intended by then and spread the leaves.

I studied them closely, knowing this was the important part. This is what she was here for, and I had to be sure to be as accurate as possible. It seemed like the Queendom's future hung in the balance, but what I saw confused me.

It was clear she ended things with her current love, but it looked like she quickly became unhappily entangled with another, only to then have that break off as well. What didn't make sense to me was the dual nature of her end path. It wasn't saying that she ended up with two people, but that there was a second person closely entwined in her relationship line. I couldn't make sense of it.

"Well?" Inez asked, breaking my concentration for a moment.

"It's a little hazy," I said tentatively. I tried to be careful about how much I revealed about someone's future. Messing with the future was a tricky business, and I knew better than the mess with the gods and their plans. If I gave too much information, it might sway her and corrupt the future in some unknown way.

"I knew it. She's useless," Inez said accusingly.

"Relax and let her speak," the princess said.

"Well, you see this line here?" I pointed out the lines that I knew related to her decision. "These lines are showing that you stray from the path. You don't stay the course with your relationship."

The princess let her disappointment show a moment before nodding in resignation. "I was hoping you wouldn't say that, but I'm not delusional. I knew it was likely."

"It's not all bad news, though. I do see great love in your future, great trials, yes, but a great love that will endure them."

She seemed thoughtful before nodding.

Inez watched her carefully before turning to me. "Does it say anything of her great love? Is it someone she's already met or someone she's still destined to meet?"

If I was interpreting it correctly, she had yet to meet them, but if I was interpreting Inez's glances toward the princess correctly, that wasn't the answer she was looking for.

I glanced at the princess, who seemed to have retreated into herself, considering everything she had learned.

I wasn't sure she could take anymore, so instead I told Inez, "My apologies, it doesn't say."

She groaned. "Of course it doesn't. You're no help." She shoved her chair back from the table. In her anger, one of the bowls of tea leaves was overturned, spilling out onto the herbal leaves and scattering them into a new formation.

The princess looked at her. "Inez, please calm down. This isn't anything I didn't already know or suspect anyway. Please don't be angry with Callie for her help."

I moved to start cleaning up the mess when I noticed *which* leaves had been overturned. The green tea leaves, and the way they intertwined with the future leaves, had me staring. The spill had changed the story, and now that it was laid in front of me, spelled out like it was, I didn't know how I had missed the story's incompleteness before.

It was clear that Princess Serena and Inez's stories were intertwined, but it was even more clear that it wasn't in the way Inez wished. The leaves showed Inez was in the throes of heartbreak and made it very clear the object of her desire was the curly-haired, optimistic, lovesick princess in front of her. The story that unfolded in front of me confirmed they weren't soulmates, but that the princess finding her true love was the catalyst for Inez finding hers. Inez's happiness depended on Princess Serena, just not in the way she may have hoped.

The princess's hands reached out and scattered the tea, scooping it into her hands, and putting into the bowl. Once again, I joined her in cleaning up. Inez was nowhere to be found.

"Thank you, Your Highness," I said when the task was complete.

"No, thank you. I apologize for the mess and for Inez. You have to understand everyone is under a lot of stress with the Harvest Festival approaching."

"Of course, Your Highness. You've both been no trouble at all. I hope what little I could tell you was helpful."

She smiled, but it didn't touch the worry in her eyes. "Yes, quite." A moment later, she shook herself out of her reverie and added, "Thank you. Truly. You have given me more than you know."

"Anytime, Your Highness. I'm at your disposal. If I may say one thing though…" I paused, unsure if I should.

She nodded, and I continued before I lost my nerve. "The leaves say the road ahead won't be easy for you, but you will come out better for having traveled it. Be strong, be brave, and trust in the gods."

She smiled at that, the faraway look still in her eyes. "In the gods and the Queendom we trust," she answered back with an incline of her head.

"Long live the Queens," I responded, before adding, "and long live the princess. May her eventual reign be as brilliant as she is."

I saw a tear slip down her face before she quickly swiped it away and pushed back her chair. "I should be going. I need to find Inez. Thank you again for your help."

With that, she slipped back the way we came, and I waited to hear the door shut behind her, but I didn't. To my surprise, Inez came sauntering back into the kitchen.

"I don't know if what you said was true, but the Queendom owes you a debt, regardless." It looked like it pained her to say the words.

I was shocked. Of course, what I had said was true. Yes, I had held some things back, but nothing I had said was untrue.

"It was true," I insisted.

She nodded her head. "And we're all the better for it," she said, offering me a bag.

I took it and was surprised at the weight.

"For your troubles."

I tried not to show my surprise and instead dipped into a low curtsy. "Thank you so much."

"The Queendom thanks you," she responded, already moving to make her way out of the room.

Before she made it through the doorway, she turned around, uncertainty on her face, and asked, "Will she be okay?"

I considered the question, surprised not by the concern in her voice but by the fact that she had asked it in the first place.

"I believe she will be. The leaves show happiness in her future, a bit of a long road to get there, but happiness will find her."

She nodded at that, resolve on her face, and again turned to go.

"Inez," I called out before I could think better of it. "Happiness is in your future, too. Stay by the princess's side and happiness will find you."

She looked surprised at that before a small smile fell across her face. "Nothing could keep me away."

With that, she turned and was gone.

I wondered if this was the last I would see of them and selfishly hoped not. Armed with the knowledge that the welfare of our Queendom depended on the heart of a young lovesick woman, I was more anxious than I had been in a long while. If it weren't for what the leaves had shown me, I would be in a panic, but I trusted what I had seen. I may not know exactly what the future has in store for them or the Queendom, but I knew they would both find happiness. If the princess was happy, that had to mean happiness for the Queendom, too.

I sighed and started to make myself a cup of tea using the mixed green and herbal tea bowl. My nerves called for a tea blend that would ease my stomach and calm my nerves. The mixture of green and herbal leaves was the right blend to do the trick. If I hadn't needed it from the reading, I knew I would need it when my grandmother returned and found out I had hosted royalty without her.

Destiny's First Meeting

Natelie Bartley

Sunlight shone down at me through dark hair, and I smiled up at the man above me.

"Medea, you are the most beautiful woman in the world, I cannot wait until you are my wife," the man said. I leaned up and kissed him softly, my mind silent for all the warnings that Kidemonos had shouted at me for months.

"Soon, my love, soon. Once we return to Iolcus with the Fleece, and you take your rightful place as king." I felt the sea heave beneath us and used it to roll us over so that I sat astride my future husband.

"You are a goddess," he smiled as I rocked my body against his. His hands dug into my hips as he guided my body in the ways I already knew he loved.

I leaned forward and kissed him again. "And you," I groaned as I bounced hard on him, "are the world's most perfect man."

"Are you close, my queen?" he asked, his voice a husky whisper.

"With you, I am always ready," I moaned in response.

"Good," his voice grunted. "It may be presumptive, but since we are betrothed, I want to see our child within you as soon as possible."

I gasped as he rolled us back over and began driving into me.

"Yes!!" I screamed out, my voice carrying through the ship as my futures mixed in with mine. As the wave of my exultation crashed over me, cold water splashed over my face and I lost the moment I was in.

~~~~~

I sputtered awake as my mother's hand rested over my forehead. The cold water receded back into her palm and I sat up sharply.
~~~~~

"Mater!" I cried out angrily. She had not done that since I was a child.

"Get up, there is a ship on the horizon and your father needs you in the throne room. You are to receive these incomers." My mouth fell open as my mother stood back from the bed.

I could not believe her, but still got dressed quickly. A soft red chiton would do nicely, and my golden sandals to match but my hair was going to be the problem. It was an unruly mess, curly and knotted in the worst ways.

My mother looked at me and sighed.

"I will send your sister in to tend to *that*," she pointed at my face and then left the room. I sat down at the looking glass and attempted to brush my hair. A few moments later, my sister arrived.

"Good morning, sister," I commented cooly. I loved my sister, missed her dearly when I was off training with our aunt Kirke and Lady Hekate, but she was perfect. She looked like the rest of my family, golden hair with the most perfect sapphire blue eyes. Even our brother Absyrtus looked like the rest of my gilded family. But me? I looked at my reflection once more in the looking glass. I sighed. Dark brown hair cascaded down my back and over my shoulders. Even my eyes departed from the standard Heliadae amber or blue. I had green eyes, and I hated them.

"Oh, Medea," Chalkiope chided with a smile as she walked up behind me. We were only a few years apart, but now that we were in our twenties the difference in our looks stood out even more. She was the sunlight, and I was the night. But it is I out of the three of us who had inherited any of our family's power. As far as I knew neither Absyrtus nor Chalkiope had manifested any sense of power, our family legacy rested entirely on my shoulders. How this translated in my differing looks eluded me, but I hoped that one day I would understand.

Chalkiope began brushing my hair and ended up trying it into loose braids.

"I wish I had hair like yours," she whispered, running her hands over my shoulders, "maybe then he…" she gulped and I spun around in my chair.

"Did he lay his hands on you again?" I asked fiercely. Chalkiope bit her bottom lip and looked away. "Chal!" I shook her shoulders until she looked at me. She nodded to me shortly, and I stood up quickly, almost knocking her over. "I am going to kill him." I growled darkly.

"Medea, wait!" She grabbed my arm as I stormed past her. "You cannot, you know he is our father's heir."

"As if I care, I am tired of him hurting you and getting away with acting like the perfect son." The predator roared inside me and I wanted to rip the arm she held out of her hand and storm down the hall.

"Medea," her voice was a cry, a sad whimper that brought my eyes back to meet hers. "I am…"

My body froze, and Kidemonos appeared beside me. My hand rested on her abdomen and I closed my eyes. When our eyes met again, tears had welled in hers and Kidemonos stepped out of the room. Rage boiled behind my eyes and all I saw was red.

"This was not how I wanted to tell you," she said, her quiet voice only calming the beast within for a moment's respite. I knew that when I had the chance, the monster who plagued my sister would be no more.

"You cannot be happy about this, Chal," I whispered, taking her hands in mine.

"No, of course not," I pulled her into my arms, clasping her. "I am disgusted that I could never stand up to him, but, you know, father will never permit the ending of the child."

"I. Do. Not. Care." I growled out, clutching her tightly. "I will make it look like an accident. Have you told anyone else?" Chalkiope shook her head. "Good, leave it that way. Do you need to be in the throne room for this arrival?"

"No, but *he* will be there," I growled again and nodded.

"Go back to your room and stay there. I will come by after this foolishness is over." Chal turned to go. "And Chal?"

"Yes Medea?" She turned and looked at me.

"Thank you for fixing my hair," I smiled softly at her.

"You are welcome Medea. Now, do our family proud, such as that means." She disappeared out through my door. I followed her and stood beside Kidemonos as we watched her down the hallway.

"Keep her safe my friend, please, do not let him back in her room. I will fix this." I looked up at him and he smiled down at me.

"Your eyes, Medea," I stared up at him, unable to look away, "look like mine. A fire burns within your soul, young princess. Plus," he smirked down at me as he leaned down and whispered in my ear, "they are slitted, like mine." I let out a breath as my pulse quickened for a moment. "But I will keep her safe, as you request." The Colchian Dragon in human form strode down the hallway, following behind my younger sister, and stood outside her doorway.

I made my way down to the throne room and stood before my father's throne. My brother Absyrtus came in and stood beside me to my left. I wanted to punch him, or better yet, kill him, but I could not do that here. Later I would exact my revenge on him, but for now, I would be the eldest daughter of Aeëtes, Medea the Colchian Princess.

~~~~~

It felt like hours before a large group of men walked into the throne room, looking like they owned the place. Judging by the odor they carried with them, they had been at sea for weeks, and with the way most of them gazed around the room at the ladies of my father's court, they had not seen a woman in as long. Great. I hated it when raiders came, our women were strong, but we were no Amazon's.

A sharp piercing pain exploded between my shoulder blades and I almost lurched forward. Only the sense of power
~~~~~

coursing through my body as my father's representative kept me steady, but my brother noticed.

"Easy there, Medea, you would not want to look like a fool in front of the Argonauts." He whispered conspiratorially at me.

"The *who*?" I asked, but before he could respond the leader stepped forward and our eyes met. A jolt of electricity spread through my body and I took a step forward. It was him, the man from my dream this morning.

"My name is Iason, I am the rightful ruler of Iolcus, and the leader of the Argonauts." His voice was smooth as silk with eyes as blue as the Aegean. His dark brown hair was braided back in loose braids similar to mine with beads at the end. He wore a short beard, but it helped the rugged features of his face shine through instead of covering them up. His chest bore dark brown curly hair, and I almost groaned at how chiseled he was. Iason looked hewn from marble. I watched as his eyes scanned my body and I suddenly felt self-conscious about my figure. I had never thought I was beautiful before, and still did not feel that way under his gaze, but there was an appraising look to him I had seen in men eyeing a prime cut of meat. I did not like being compared to a side of beef, even if I was the one doing the comparison.

"Iason, it is a pleasure to meet you, I am Medea, eldest daughter of King Aeëtes. Welcome to Colchis."

We stepped forward and Iason bowed before he took my hand and kissed it softly.

~~~~~

"No, absolutely not!" My father objected as I laid Iason's request out to him.

"We do not need it, father! Our family carries the blessing with us, we do not need the Fleece." I argued back. "Iason needs it to better his kingdom and his people, you cannot fault him for that!" My hands balled up into fists and I fought desperately to keep my fire in check. It would do no good to attack the king of Colchis.
~~~~~

King Aeëtes looked down at me and I tried not to wither under his glare, I really did. But when my knees hit the marble flooring, I knew I had lost our battle.

"What is he to you, Medea?" My father asked, uncharacteristically soothing.

"Nothing," I lied quickly, turning my head, "I just think we are being greedy, hoarding the bounty of the Fleece, when much of the world is rotting without its power." A hand wrapped around my throat in a blur, and I gasped for air. "Pater!" I cried as much as I could through the pain.

"Never lie to me again Medea," he growled, a menacing sound erupting from his throat.

"I am not, Pater!" Stars spun in my eyes and I could not even lash out with my weak power with him constricting my air as tightly as he was. Aeëtes lifted me off the ground with ease and threw me the entire width of the throne room. I was simply a rag-doll to him.

My back slammed against a pillar, cracking it in two. There were times I was grateful to have inherited my father's power, now was one of them. I rose to my knees slowly before wobbling up to my feet. I swayed as the world spun beneath my feet and my senses fled from me.

"I love him Pater," I murmured, fully aware that he could hear me even at this great distance.

"You do not *know* him, Medea. Forget him and focus on your studies. Hyperion will not–"

"What do I care what he thinks?!" I roared, fire erupting from my hands in untamed tendrils of my power.

Aeëtes appeared before me in a flash of bright yellow light. "You *will* care, and you will *have* a care of your tone, about what the patriarch decides for your future." I opened my mouth to speak but Aeëtes backhanded me so hard I spun back into the column I had already cracked. "I will hear no more of this Medea. I forbid you from speaking to the travelers again. *I* will speak with them from now on. Now, go."

The dismissal was final, and I fled from the room.

~~~~~

As much as I wanted to curl up in a ball and scream in my room, I could not. My priority was and always would be, my sister. So, instead of venting my pain through destruction, I chose something else. My potions cabinet whipped open in a furor and I began the draught that would help ease my sister's pain. Spells flew around me, begging to be cast, whispering their secrets in my and demanding my attention, but I could not, not right now. I had to finish this.

"Willow bark and mugwort," I muttered to myself, "and a touch of chamomile. But what was that last ingredient?" I drummed my thumb against the stout wooden doors, feeling their magic tingle against my skin. Only I could open them, my touch or Kidemonos' if we were separate, would unlock the secrets within, and it was not until the dragon's head popped into my room while remaining in the hall that I remembered.

"Black Cohosh root!" I snapped my fingers and felt the dragon smile before his human form sauntered back down the hall. I do not know why Kidemonos' head popping into the room helped me remember the root, it was from the other side of the world and most mortals did not know the "over there". I only knew because there were people over there my Lady wanted me to meet, and deities whom I might encounter as I grew older.

I poured the ingredients into my cauldron and began brewing, resisting the urge to cackle as some of my sister witches were doing. I had to be quick. Normally, I would let this sit overnight, but with the mugwort and black cohosh, the tonic should be ready sooner. I added the chamomile last, giving it a slightly sweeter flavor. I only added it because this would take like absolute garbage, and I did not Chalkiope to spit any of it up.

Once the mixture turned a bright green, I bottled it up, ignited the rest in flames to destroy the evidence and locked up my cabinet once more. I rushed down the hallway to my sister's room and opened the door pushing past my dragon consort.
~~~~~

“Chal, I need you to drink this, and do not ask questions,” I said quickly, pushing the vial into her hand.

“What is it?” She asked softly, taking it and uncorking the bottle. Her nose crinkled at the scent and I waved at her to continue.

“You said you did not want this pregnancy?” My voice dropped to a low whisper. Unless someone stood outside the door, they would not hear us. Chal nodded. “Then drink.” I ordered her. I hated to use any of my inherited power of command on my sister, but I needed her to do this. I needed it for her benefit, not for mine. She tipped the vial to her lips and swallowed all of it. Her face grimaced as she passed the bottle back to me.

“Gods above Medea, what was that?” She asked, wiping her lips on her chiton.

I shook my head and kissed her forehead. “Nothing, my sweet sunbeam. If you have pains tonight, come to my room, and I will help ease it. But please, tell no one else about this.” Chalkiope nodded again, and I left her room. Kidemonos followed behind me and as we walked into my room, I shut the door and screamed, falling to my knees.

“Medea,” the dragon held me as I cried for my sister, my broken family, and the pain that coursed through every fiber of my being. I looked up at him and he just kissed my forehead. “I will monitor her until we can decide what to do about Absyrtus.” I nodded and began weeping again.

~~~~~

I checked on Chal the next morning, as she had not come to my room. Her sheets were stained with blood and I burned them as soon as she rolled out of bed. Even her sleep wear needed to go, and once she had changed and I put new sheets on the bed, she crawled back in and dozed off. I worried about her, but I had to explain to our father that she would be in bed for a while with a cold. My feet took me in the opposite direction of the throne room, and into the atrium. Where Iason stood. His *xiphos* was out, and he moved through motions I had seen our warriors take on the battlefield. I stood transfixed by his beauty, his strength, the slight glow of his tanned skin as sweat beaded down his arms in the sunlight.
~~~~~

As he turned, our eyes met, and I gasped as the pain that had originated in my back yesterday blossomed into my chest today.

"Iason, right?" I asked him softly as he lowered his *xiphos* and took a step towards me. I could not move, my legs had turned to stone under his gaze.

"Yes, my lady, and you are the princess Medea, am I correct?" I nodded, not trusting myself to speak again. "You are the most beautiful woman in the world." Iason stood within arm's distance and I struggled not to reach out and stroke his chest. I needed to stroke it, to run my hands along every muscle and trace every line of his body no matter where they led.

"Thank you," I scraped out as I looked up at his eyes again. The exact shade of blue as the Aegean in sunlight, I remained a statue in his gaze until his eyes closed again. "My apologies, your highness, for not receiving you this morning."

Iason coughed a little, and I titled my head. "Oh, I am sorry. No one has referred to me as royalty in many years, I had forgotten what it sounded like."

"I am sorry again, for causing you distress," I could not help it, I rested my hand on his forearm and electricity shot through my body. I fell forward, my body crashing into him. I expected him to drop me, but when his arms wrapped around my back, and he pulled me close I swore I heard a voice in my head warning me away. I had to silence it though, Iason was perfect. More than that, he could be my ticket out of here, if I played my cards right.

"You did not, but are you alright my lady?" he asked as he helped me stand again, cupping a hand under my chin.

"Fine, I am fine. What did my father have to say?" Iason growled softly, and I felt the reverberation through my body. My knees threatened to go weak again, so I simply leaned a little more on him. "That bad?"

He shook his head and took a deep breath. I was immediately grateful that he had time to bathe and refresh before this.

"Yes, and no. He has agreed to give me the Golden Fleece," I gasped and Iason's mouth quirked into a sly smile, "as long as I can complete three tasks. The first two, he has already told me of."

I wanted to step back, but Iason's arms held me fast, and I simply gazed up at him.

"What are these tasks?" I asked him, inhaling the musk of his body. The scent of ocean air and leather and stout wooden beams clung to him as much as I was.

"First, I must yoke the oxen of fire, and then I will need to plant the Skeleton Seeds, whatever they are," my face blanched and Iason stopped, "what is it, my lady?"

"That will surely kill you! My father does not intend to give you the Fleece, even if you were to succeed. He will simply give you a harder task if you accomplish this." I buried my face in his chest without even thinking about it, and Iason's hand cupped the back of my head.

"Shh, my lady, it is ok. How can I fail when I have such a woman cheering me on? You will cheer me on, will you not?" I nodded slightly, and he caressed my hair again. "Then there is nothing to worry about. Every hero needs their heroine, and you, my lady, shall be mine."

Heat blossomed in my chest where the pain had resided, and I looked up at him.

"There is a way, but…" my voice trailed off and I looked up at the bright blue sky above us.

"But what?" He asked me softly, his voice barely above a whisper.

"If I help you, I will be betraying my family, my heritage, everything." I whispered back, afraid of anyone overhearing us.

"Then I cannot ask you to do this. Family is everything, *means* everything to me. I could not ask you to betray yours, even if it means my death." Iason responded, brushing a finger along my cheek.

The thought of Iason dying tore holes in my heart and I shook my head, burying my face once more in his chest.

"If I tell you the secrets, you must swear to me that no one will know of my involvement. Not your crew, not the palace attendants and certainly not my father." I looked up at him again, a fire burning in my eyes.

Iason looked down at me and nodded solemnly. "This I swear, Medea, Princess of Colchis."

I nodded quickly and brought him over to a secluded corner of the atrium. "I will bring you an ointment to your ship tonight. Put it on immediately before you head for the barns where the oxen are. It is made from the blood of Prometheus and will protect you against their fire." Iason nodded as he pulled me back into his arms. I breathed him in deeply and sighed. "As for the Skeleton Seeds, once you plant them, fully formed skeleton warriors will spring forth and attack you. If you stay back and throw a rock amid their circle, they will become confused and will attack each other. That is the only way to destroy them. I am sure you could make quick work of them, but their blades are the only things that can put them back in the ground, so to speak."

Iason looked down at me and smiled. "You are so cunning and wise to know all this, my lady," my heart swooned, and I forced myself to look around us.

"Thank you, Iason, my lord," I whispered, but I felt the cords of his arm muscles tighten around me. "The third task, we shall have to see once you have completed the others. Now, go, father will want these done sooner rather than later, and I need to get the ointment for you."

I slipped out of his arms, regretting the warmth and security they brought, but before I could hurry away, Iason caught my hand, spun me back to him and pulled me into a kiss. A kiss! I had never…my mind faded into oblivion as his presence all but consumed me.

"Go," I breathed, as we finished. I dared not open my eyes for fear of seeing it as a waking dream.

"Find me on the *Argo*, my Medea," Iason murmured before letting me go and rushing out of the palace complex. I hurried back to my room, found the ointment and placed my personal blessing on it before racing down to the docks. I could not face Iason again, not looking as flustered as I was, but one of his crew, a man named Odysseus, offered to bring the ointment to him and I thanked him, already breaking my rule.

~~~~~

The trials went off smoothly, but I could not watch. I had to stay away from the travelers as my father put it, so I watched from my window. Iason was amazing, and he listened to my advice, which was a first for me. Except for Chal, no one paid attention to what I said while I was home. Chal, she had been sick, and I worried I had overdone the tonic I gave her, so I sent some healing herbs to help settle her body. That night at the banquet, of which I had to attend, my father commended Iason on his masterful skill in completing the tasks.

"Your last task will be the hardest, Iason of Iolcus." Aeëtes' voice boomed through the throne room. "You must kill the Colchian Dragon." I froze and stared up at my father, who glowered down at me. "Do you accept?"

"I accept, your majesty," Iason replied without knowing exactly what that would entail. But my father did, of course he did. I got up and sprinted from the hall ignoring the shocked cries and angry bellows from the crowd and Aeëtes.

I pulled Kidemonos into Chalkiope's room.

"We have to leave, Kidemonos, now." I said quickly as Chal sat up in bed. She was chalk white, and I sat down on her bed. "Oh, sweet sister. What have I done to you?" Her golden hair lacked its usual luster, and I sighed.

"You helped me," she replied softly, "I passed the blood last night, and now my body is simply taking a while to replenish it. I will be fine. But you, why do you need to leave?" I stared between her and Kidemonos.
~~~~~

"How much do you know?" I asked him. "And how much have you told her?"

"Everything." He did not meet my eyes, and I knew he was displeased with something.

"Ok, well, we need to go. Father has set the next task and I cannot let you die." I replied smoothly, straightening my chiton.

"Either me or Iason will die tomorrow, and you know it." Kidemonos stated. His matter-of-fact tone infuriated me.

"Not precisely…" I whispered.

"No Medea, I dislike that plan," he warned me.

"It is the only plan I have, my friend," our eyes met and understanding of what we must do passed through them. He nodded, and I sighed wearily.

"Will someone please tell *me* what is going on?" Chalkiope asked.

I kissed her forehead softly and hugged her. "No, sorry Chal, the less you know the better. At least, for now."

Kidemonos and I rushed out of her room and when I looked at him before my door I held his arm fast.

"You know what you must do?" He nodded, and I let go of his arm. "Then I will see you tomorrow, when it is all over." He kissed my forehead in the same way that I had just done to Chalkiope, but there was a promise of *more* to it that left me confused. He vanished in the blink of an eye, and I raced out to the *Argo*.

"Iason!" I cried out, hoping that he had already returned from dinner, and when I saw him on deck, I practically flew into his arms.

"Medea, what is wrong? You flew out of dinner as if the hounds of Tartarus were on your heels." He held me in his powerful arms and I felt safe again.

"You cannot kill him," I said, spilling over my words.

"Kill who?" He asked, trying to look me in the eye, but I kept my face in his chest.

"The dragon, the Colchian Dragon. You cannot physically kill him. If you do, I will…" I bit my lip, wondering just how far I could trust him.

"You will what?" He growled and moved me into his line of sight.

"I will no longer be what I am. We are bound, Kidemonos and I. If he dies, I shall surely die too. And if I help you," I had to speak quickly, "I will have to leave Colchis."

I bit my lip again, and he placed his hand on my cheek, his thumb resting on my lips.

"Of course you can come with us, we would be glad to have the revered Princess of Colchis with us on our journey." Iason said softly. "In fact," he let me go and jumped on to the rail of the ship before addressing his crew, "Argonauts, hear me! Hera, goddess of marriage and holy unions, hear me! Zeus, lord of the skies and king of Olympus, hear me! I swear by all that is good and holy, that if we succeed tomorrow, I will make Medea, Princess of Colchis, my bride!"

The crew clapped as thunder boomed across the heavens. Iason jumped back down and kissed me in front of all watching. I melted, absolutely went limp in his arms.

"Are you sure?" I asked, breathless from the emotions coursing through me.

"I would not have said it, if I did not mean it, my dear Medea," he replied, stroking my cheek. I flushed deeply and smiled. I wanted nothing more than to fall into bed with him, but we needed to plan out tomorrow's task, and the escape afterward.

~~~~~

The plan went perfectly. I snuck into the garden before anyone else arrived in the morning and hid in the bushes. Kidemonos knew where I was so he would not charbroil me, and even if he tried, I am not so easily burned. We could not just have Kidemonos pretend to fall asleep, my father would know. Iason had
~~~~~

to make it convincing, so I taught him a lullaby to put Kidemonos to sleep and when that "did not work", I gave him the sleeping draft I perfected a decade ago.

With Kidemonos asleep, Iason pretended to stab him, and then seized the Golden Fleece. As he did, the Colchian Dragon "withered away" into dust, leaving no trace behind, and Kidemonos resettled into my body where he normally resided. Iason did not know of that part, that Kidemonos and I were one. I would tell him soon, I kept telling myself that.

I raced into town and made my way to the docks, but an all too familiar sight loomed before.

"Absyrtus," I growled and raced for him.

No, Medea, we do not have time for this! Kidemonos screamed in my head, but I did not care.

My brother cackled at me. "Do you think you can leave, dear sister?" He said as I skidded to a halt in front of him. "And even if you make it out of the Black Sea, and through the straits, do you think you will be free of this place, of us?"

"Yes, I will, now get out of my way before I do something you will regret later," my voice was dark, edged with a venom I had never heard from myself before.

"No." He said simply, but before I could say anything he leaned forward. "Just think of what your leaving will do for poor Chalkiope. Why, who will protect her when you are gone?"

My vision went red, and I grabbed his left arm, tearing it from his body with no more force than I would swat a fly. Blood sprayed everywhere and the shriek of pain, or surprise, that pierced the morning air from my brother was nothing to the howl of rage that erupted from my throat. I tore the other arm off and threw them in the sea behind me.

Cries of terror sounded from the dock surrounding me, but I could not care less. I plunged my hand into his chest and wrapped it around his heart.

"You will never hurt anyone ever again," my words vibrated in my chest and I squeezed the life out of the monster who looked like my younger brother, Chalkiope's twin. When his body collapsed around me, I ripped his heart out and tossed it too in the sea behind me. The dock was deathly quiet around me, but I simply walked over to the *Argo*. The entire crew including Iason had witnessed what I had done, but amidst the horror, there was also a grim satisfaction on some of their faces. Iason's was the most surprising: joy.

"Medea, come on," Iason called out to me, a dark hand extended out. I reached for it, my heart beating painfully in my chest.

"I cannot believe I am doing this, my father will kill me when he discovers what we have done Iason," I replied. The man ahead of me looked at me and all my worry and pain faded to the back of my mind.

"We will simply kill anyone who gets in our way, as you have just proved. You are the most powerful and beautiful woman in the world," he stated emphatically, and I exploded into a ball of radiant light. I filled the morning air with my radiance, and a figure crouched behind some rocks barely escaping my notice. I was so enthralled with Iason, with our upcoming adventure, and becoming his wife, that nothing else mattered.

The only other being to bar my path was the dock hand who passed us onto the *Argo*.

"Beautiful sorceress, you truly are magnificent," he whispered as he assisted me and I looked at him. He was long in face, but not disproportionately so, with pale skin and blood-red eyes. He was well built physically, and I smiled down at him, thanking him for the help and the compliment. He clung to the shadows, still deep in this area of the docks, as if afraid to touch the sun.

"Thank you good sir, should we meet again, you may continue to give me such praise," I kissed his cheek in farewell, thinking nothing of it, believing he was simply a servant of my house.

"I will treasure this moment, my Princess, and I await the moment of your triumphant return as *my* Queen."

Iason and the crew were casting off, and I waved goodbye to the dockhand, missing what he had said, but he was gone. I made my way below decks and waited for the ship to make its way out into the Black Sea and away from Colchis before I returned above decks. I would need to clean myself before I could be seen again.

My lover wrapped his arms around me before I had the chance and dragged me back up to the top deck. He smiled brightly at me.

"We did it, Medea, we retrieved the Golden Fleece. Now I can return home with it, and you will be my wife and queen," Iason said as he kissed me.

"All hail Medea the Sorceress of Colchis!" Iason called out to the cheers of the *Argo*.

The Waters Hold Secrets

By Charli Rahe

Chapter 1

I heard the squeal of my front door open and I lifted my head as my belly filled with lead. My mom looked down at me standing bare foot in last night's clothes before the stairs. She shook her head and folded her arms while she walked away, leaving my dad to sigh alone.

"Have a good birthday?" he asked as I dragged myself up the concrete steps.

As I passed into the house, he cupped the side of my head and planted a kiss. He held out a manilla envelope with the other hand. I took it and straightened while he shut the door.

STOCKWELL

C/O THE D'SOUSAS

5621 N. Elmdale

Chicago, IL 60604

"Birthday card?" I asked.

"Open and find out. I had to sign for it. It must be important." He wrapped an arm around my back and led me to the kitchen at the back of the bungalow. "How was Adelina?"

"Law Offices of Hardwick & Son?" I murmured and raised my head. "She misses Charice. I think she's regretting choosing to live apart this year."

He nodded along as we crossed the wood floors to the kitchen at the back of the house. The windows gave us a view of the backyard, the garage, and the alley. I chose a chair at the oval table and ran my hand through my tangled hair. I groaned and rested my head on my arm. My stomach gurgled at the smell of my mom's French toast and bacon.

"I really don't want Adelina to go any further," my mom said as she shifted about the kitchen.

My dad sat beside me and rubbed my back. "She'll do what she's got to do for her marriage. She should've gone this year. The first one after you get married is important."

"They're all important," Mom muttered as she clanked pans and dishes.

My eyes burned. I inhaled sharply with a snort and lifted my head. "I've got to get some sleep."

"Eat first, Dylla," my dad kept his hand on my shoulder. "Soak some of it up." I saw the deep concern for my wellbeing in his dark eyes. He smiled when I settled and withdrew his hand. "Take today and we'll start that job hunt tomorrow."

Internally, I sighed. My live virtual tarot readings and being a brand ambassador weren't actual jobs to my parents. It wasn't enough to make a living *yet,* but it'd catch on soon. Dealing with my parents' well-intentioned, unsolicited advice became commonplace when my latest and greatest boyfriend of the season dumped me and kicked me out.

And yet, I persist.

**

I ate, as requested, and dragged myself upstairs after a lot of bright eyed and bushy tailed encouragement. Then, I promptly passed out in my childhood bedroom.

Sleep didn't last.

"Dylla." Adelina gave my shoulder a hard shove. "Is this your letter?"

I groaned loudly and attempted to peel open my eyes. One opened successfully. "It's probably a subpoena. Who do I owe and how much?"

"Your biological grandmother passed, and she left you a quote unquote 'estate' and 'undisclosed sum'."

That opened my eyes. I pushed up in my twin sized bed and scooted until we were side by side with our heads touching.

"Poppy Stockwell?" I muttered in a sleep thick voice. "Descendent…" My brows jumped to my hairline as I read on. "Riverton, Rhode Island?"

Adelina sounded as sure as I did when she said, "I thought you were adopted in Connecticut."

"You were adopted here," I said, sliding my eyes to the side of her face. "Right?"

Her dark, round eyes ringed with lashes darted to mine. Her full lips grimaced with a shrug. "That's what they told me. Could just be where she died."

That made sense.

"Mom!" I shouted and took my sheet with me. I jerked to a halt and turned to glare at Adelina, who smirked.

"Yes?" Mom shouted back.

I passed the full-length mirror angled against the wall. My thick chestnut hair looked like birds had taken up residence. My blue almond eyes were bloodshot, and I looked more gaunt than usual, with my favorite lacy floral dress hanging off my bony shoulders.

Brunette hair and slender builds were all Adelina and I had in common. She'd done an ancestry test years ago on her twenty-first birthday, a gift from her wife, and discovered her ancestors came from Portugal and England. So did I. She'd clearly come the generation after my family. I liked to think our parents chose us because they knew we all came from the same place… even if I looked like my bio family got out sooner, judging by my fairer complexion.

We told ourselves that *most* adopted kids wanted to learn about where they came from, if not *who*. With our parents, it never occured to me that something might be missing.

I opened my bedroom door and leaned on the frame as my stomach lurched. I drank too much, and it looked like I lost my favorite sweater.

"Did you adopt me in Rhode Island or —"

"Oh my God." Adelina marched from the bed and took the envelope with her. "Is Stockwell Dylla's bio last name? This is from a Poppy Stockwell out of Riverton, RI."

"Come down for dinner. We'll explain everything," Dad answered for Mom.

**

Thirty-six hours later, Adelina took a week off to fly to Providence, RI from Chicago with me to see what was left of my grandmother's estate after a lot of encouraging and apologizing from our parents. We were far from upset.

We sat around the dining room table digging into a past I never imagined. Riverton barely left a carbon footprint. All we found were a lot of Stockwells in the area and Poppy looked to have been the mayor and a small shopkeeper. We couldn't figure out who her offspring were and if I was a grandniece or second cousin twice removed *or* some other distant relative.

The second thing we found was an annual boat race in the bay nearest the town. A lot of tragedy struck there, and yet their thirtieth anniversary was that weekend.

Our parents essentially sponsored our trip because I was dirt poor, and it wouldn't be fair to ask Adelina, who was doing me a favor, to fork over cash for it. I had enough for five days to see if Riverton, RI would be my fresh start or if I was dividing it up to sell. I could go either way.

Adelina put her shoulder length curls into two tight braids and wore her sunglasses low on her celestial nose as she scanned the overgrown landscape. They let things grow. Chicago had a lot of green for a major city but the way the trees nearly reached the highway would not have happened in the Midwest.

Adelina pulled our rented coupe into the gravel parking lot beside the building with a sign that read, *Law Offices of Hardwick & Son.*

"Can you smell the water?" Adelina asked as she stepped outside of the car.

I breathed deep before shutting the door. "It must be close. I wasn't paying attention."

I could ask real people about Poppy; people who actually knew her and spoke with her.

I *still* wasn't paying attention.

We walked to the glass doors and entered. Someone tried to update the offices. The desks were still from the 90's but the wood floor and walls were on trend. Someone had changed the planters but the plants were 90's plants. You could almost see the struggle between father and son as they got into business together.

"Tilly?" A man reached us before we could take for five steps to the receptionist's desk. His nostrils flared as he lifted his nose to the air like someone passed him with a piping hot pumpkin pie.

I blushed and pointed to myself. "Dylla."

He blinked light blue eyes at me and scrunched his short thick brows. "My mistake. You…" He lifted his nose to the air again and he trailed off. "How can I help you?" He pulled his pouty mouth into a soft smile as he held out his hand.

He had to be around my age. His golden brown hair was stylishly tousled and his anvil jaw was clean shaven so you could spot the cleft in his chin. He was pretty cute, if you asked me. Adelina clocked him for me and I knew she spotted a bare ring finger.

"I'm Poppy Stockwell's descendent?"

His tan cheeks paled. "Uh — how did you know Mrs. Stockwell passed?" he asked. "We just put it in the local paper… today, in fact."

My eyes darted to the receptionist. Maybe that's who he was having a décor war with. The woman was hanging on tight to teased hair. Probably because it looked good on her.

"We got a certified letter." I took the envelope from under my arm and gave it to him.

He took a moment to scan it then read the letter.

"Can I get you ladies some water or tea? A soda?" the woman asked.

"Water," we both answered.

He sighed and scratched the side of his nose. "I'm sorry. I'm Alfie Hardwick. I'm the son on the sign. My dad has taken over as interim mayor after Mrs. Stockwell's passing." He offered his hand to Adelina and shook it. "Come into my office. Jennifer? Could you bring those into my office. Thank you."

We followed into his gold and white minimalist room. Alfie took a seat at the desk and gestured for us to sit, too.

"I have all the paperwork right here. I've only gone through it two days ago. It's good. Everything is okay now. You can be here. I'm sorry if I scared you," He opened a black folder and began setting sheet after sheet on his desk into little piles.

"Surprised. Not Scared," I corrected.

Alfie's eyes lifted again, looking deeper. "Sign these and I'll take you to the shop first."

**

The "shop" turned out to be much more than I anticipated. He warned us that it'd been closed since Poppy's passing and she employed three retired ladies to help her run things. I didn't get a chance to meet them as we wandered the crisp clean aisles of jars and bottles of ointments and other concoctions. It smelled of mint and lemons across the sage and white shop. Shelves stopped at shoulder height so we could see one another as we took in what had to be Poppy's pride and joy. Windows wrapped around three sides of the shop letting the prisms dangling along the beveled glass to cast rainbows over the wood floors. Everything led to this feeling of warmth and comfort upon entering, as if you healed by existing in its space.

Alfie smiled softly as he watched Adelina and I read the small baskets of goods behind the glass counter.

"Lotions, soaps, perfumes, ointments, candles, crystals, herbs, natural remedies, and spells." Our eyes slid to him. "Mrs. Stockwell had a lucrative shop. The town gave up on the idea that someone might come to fill her space. Not that anyone could," he conceded. I opened my mouth to respond. "Riverton's election is in a couple of months. My dad doesn't want to be mayor."

I chuckled softly with Adelina. Alfie didn't blink. "Uh, cool?"

"It's been held by your family for generations. I won't try to sell you on it. I've said what they'd want me to. I'll take you to the house," he said kindly.

**

"No freaking way," Adelina whispered as we finished winding up the rocky hill to the single Victorian house atop it.

It towered into the overcast sky with a steeple that held a window that looked far beyond the bay below. A widow's walk must've come from the primary bedroom from the French doors. It boasted a wraparound porch and yellow trim and shingling that reminded me of a gingerbread house.

The garden surrounding the house held more than flowers. Alfie carefully took us cover the cobblestone path where moss and creeping thyme grew to the natural spring that trickled between the giant hydrangea and herb garden. I discovered where Poppy had gotten all the supplies for her shop. The garden beds overflowed with blooms for the season.

"Good thing Dylla is a green thumb," Adelina joked.

"Do you?" Alfie asked.

Adelina pulled out her phone. "It's Charice."

She walked ahead so I fell back to walk beside Alfie.

"My adopted parents let me take charge of their garden beds. We don't have anything like this in Chicago." I gestured to the roses growing over the arch and breathed deep.

"Beautiful."

My eyes snapped open and I found Alfie looking at me.

"This place is truly beautiful. Are you staying or was your plan to sell?" he asked.

Telling him I recently got dumped and lost my job would not help my first impressions.

"It's more of a wait and see type deal. I didn't come here with expectations. Convince me." I grinned and saw the corners of his lips quirk. "Show me inside and talk my ear off. Riverton is off the proverbial grid and everything I found concerning Stockwells in this area was glib."

He masked a sigh as he took the keys out of his suit pants pocket. "This place isn't like Chicago. If you're looking for similarities you won't find them. Most of us don't use social media and go into whatever careers our family already established. There's a lot of fishing, swimming, sailing, tourists, and wedding planners. A lot of people come this way because it's an easy drive to Salem but not nearly so busy. Plus, the town goes all out for witches, werewolves, and ghouls." His brilliant smile returned as we came to the front of the house. Adelina waved to us as she stood near the white picket gate and turned her back as she talked into the phone.

I fell in love with the house and it's stained glass windows all over again. The detail in every inch moved me to tears. Alfie opened the door with a wider grin than I'd seen all day. The inside was much like the outside. I bet every piece of furniture was inherited, handmade, and one of a kind.

"The Stockwells have only had bad luck the last few generations. No one knew about you." I felt his eyes on the side of my face as I took in the farm sink and attached mud room. "The three youngest Stockwells passed… it'll be twenty-five years on Saturday."

I opened the cabinets and admired the elegantly designed plates. The entire house was a family heirloom. Through the window over the sink, I could see more of the back gardens.

"All at once?" I asked.

"Tilly, the youngest, won first place in her age bracket in the catamaran regatta. Canyon, the middle child and only son, won in his bracket."

"You knew him," I interrupted.

He nodded in my periphery and walked us down the hall to the stairway. "We were close. We were in the same grade and I took sailing lessons from Mr. Stockwell and he coached our swim lessons. He had the most sought after classes in the area. I only got in because of Canyon." He shook his head dismissively. "Skye was the oldest. She came in second. A major achievement for anyone." He frowned. "They say he made them go back out on the water that night and made them race again to see who was the best."

"I'm sorry I asked you. I didn't mean to make you relive it."

Alfie's face cleared and he gave me another small smile. "I've been thinking on it anyway with Mrs. Stockwell's death and the regatta coming up." His eyes ran over my face again. "We don't do much online but our local paper chronicles events fairly well. You can find them at the library. Tell Mrs. Gökcan I sent you. She talks a lot but she knows her way around the library and the history of Riverton." He held out the folders and set the keys on top of the shiny black cardboard. "This is all your now."

**

I shifted my head as I remade the bed. Adelina walked into the primary bedroom. There were five bedrooms in the giant house. Before I made Alfie relive the worst days of his life, he mentioned a remodel where servant bedrooms were rendered obsolete and became bedrooms for the growing family.

"Good idea. It looks like the old lady took great care of this place." Adelina looked around the rosy floral room trimmed in ivory lace. "Suits you already. What's this thing?" She sat at the foot of the bed.

It really did.

She pointed to the suitcase I found under the bed. I didn't mean to find it. It pulsed and forced me to find it. I looked normal enough but I knew there was something in it. Whatever it was, it called to me.

"I'm not sure. Don't —" I reached out to stop her as she unlocked it and knocked back the lid.

"I think we found her ceremonial garb. She'd shove some crystals up her ass and dance around in this thing."

"Come on. That's my great grandmother." I ran my hand over the rectangular piece of woven material. Dried flowers, grass, strips of fabric, and lace all threaded it together. It had to be handled with the utmost care. "It's a flag. I'm going to hang it."

"It's going to fall apart in the wind," she muttered.

"How is Charice?" I asked as I delicately carried the flag.

"Excited for you. Hoping there's room here for us after she gets out." She paused. "If she gets out." She shrugged. "There's a base in Natwick. It's not far."

Charice and Adelina were high school sweethearts and got engaged right out of high school when Charice enlisted and Adelina went to culinary school. They married as soon as Adelina graduated. We knew right away that Charice fit Adelina like a glove. They'd been inseparable from the start.

"How are you feeling?" she asked hesitantly.

I shrugged and she tossed a pillow in place. "Good, all things considered. I think I'm ready to dig a little deeper." We stared at one another for a long moment. "I think it might be good for me."

She nodded along. "I think so too. I snapped a pic and sent it to mom and dad. They can't believe there's no catch. Actually, they want you to send everything over just to make sure. I'm supposed to scan it all and email it as soon as we get settled."

I waved at the folder on the antique dresser. "Have at it. I'm not good at all that but it's pretty cut and dry. I get everything. If not me, any other living descendent. I'm worried that it isn't me. It just says, *'to the next oldest Stockwell daughter'*."

"Mom and dad will know," Adelina said. "Alfie seemed like a stand-up guy."

"I agree." I straightened. "Want to grab a snack and head to the library?"

Her mood visibly lifted. She got sad after calls to Charice. They missed one another and sometimes they let that emptiness morph into an argument.

"Let's go find out what I've known my whole life," she chuckled.

I arched a brow as I led the way into the narrow hall that cut through the bedrooms and second bathroom. "What's that?"

"That you're a witch bitch."

I laughed with her. "My tarot readings are going to slay in the shop or the back garden. I could put a table out there… hang some lights. Did you see the sculptures?"

"I love that you didn't debate me," she said as we reached the flagpole on the column.

*

*

Chapter 2

My eyes kept catching on townsfolk who slowed to watch us. Banners hung from the lamp posts advertising the weekend's final regatta and noted the anniversary. Thirty years of boat racing brought in the tourists. All of us out of towners looked fairly obvious; our heads searching either the area around us or our phones for directions.

The library had a playground on one side and a picnic area on the other on the same street as the elementary school.

A woman with round brown glasses and a head of wavy salt and pepper hair lifted her blue-eyed gaze and stared. She was slender with too much blush on her high cheekbones. Her brows kept their brunette shade but the gray suited her fair complexion.

"How may I help you?" she asked as she snapped out of it. She noticed Adelina and grew slack-jawed again.

"Dylla. This is my sister, Adelina," I began. "I am related to Mayor Stockwell somehow and I'd like to know. Mr. Hardwick mentioned that you might be able to assist."

Her expression softened. "Yes. Of course. You shook me for a second there. You look just like Poppy when she was your age."

The pictures of the skinny wild woman with white hair down to her knees came to mind. She'd had to wear glasses as she got older but there'd been something about her smile that held its youth. I took it as a compliment.

"Thank you. I noticed we had similar frames," I said with a blush.

"You hold yourselves the same. Isn't that funny?" she smiled wryly as she looked me over. Her eyes slid back to us. "My apologies. I'm Azure Gökcan, the head librarian. Call me Azure. I can lead you to the microfiche reader." She came around the desk and waved for us to follow her.

I noticed that we dressed the same. Sloppy librarian was my niche. Azure kept all the tidiness of her bestowed upon station.

"I know some of the dates off the top of my head. I'll write them down. You'll have to hunt for anything else." I plunked into the plastic chair as she leaned to write on the desk beside me. "We all loved Poppy so much. You won't find a soul who'd say a word against her. And after all her babies died in that storm. *Ugh.* I was a few years older than Skye. It was like yesterday. We woke up the next morning and our lives had all changed. Now the kids' dad drools on himself in his chair and can't mutter a single word."

She straightened and took in our shocked expressions.

"The sailing coach?" I asked. "He survived?"

"Barely." She gestured to the microfiche reader. "Do you know how to work this? He's just down the street in the psych ward. They thought about moving him to Boston or some other city but they think he'll get worse." She saw how we gaped at her and pointed to her head. "Brain damage. He nearly drowned. Well?"

"Well, what?" Adelina asked.

I gave myself a mental shake. "Yeah. I can run it. Could you write down the hospital's address?"

Azure smiled. "Sure thing." She bent over and added more to the printer paper. "Happy hunting, ladies."

"Thanks." Adelina eyed her as she walked away. "Everyone is too nice here. It's weirding me the fuck out."

"Chill. If it's too weird we'll leave when we planned. I owe it to myself to at least see if he's worth talking to."

"Yeah. You've got to. That's not how I meant it. Just… we'll stay together at all times. This feels like body snatchers type shit."

I gestured to a second chair at an empty table and she dragged it over. One other person sat in the library and stared at us.

They didn't even bother hiding it until Azure cleared her throat. The woman glanced away and lifted her book in front of her face.

I turned my attention back to the microfiche and stood with the paper in my hands to find the dates I needed.

**

It had been a long sad search. Poppy's husband, my great grandmother's, husband died right in their garden. A heart attack, the coroner said. Only after I looked ahead a bit did I find a small editorial claiming someone didn't like the way he'd treated Poppy at the regatta when it was supposed to be reader submissions concerning the race. That the paper put it in meant they wanted Poppy out of a bad situation… or maybe I was projecting.

After his death, she lost her younger daughter to a bad fall. The girl had been told so many times that she shouldn't play soccer so close to the edge. Witnesses said they saw her reverse right off the rocks and that was that.

Her surviving daughter didn't inherit Poppy's confidence. She shrank beside her strapping husband in their wedding announcement. There were three birth announcements after that; Skye, Canyon, and Tilly. All three died in the storm. Only Canyon's body was recovered.

I leaned back and stretched my arms over my head. Adelina twisted her torso to get blood flow back.

"I could really use a drink," I said hopefully.

She nodded. "Maybe Poppy needed all the voodoo who do to keep the curse away. That shit is depressing."

"Drinks," I agreed.

"All done? Did you find everything?" Azure asked.

"We'll be back. It's a lot of tragedy." I grimaced.

"Well, the suffering is over now," Azure nodded. "If you're looking to wet your whistle, there's a bar in the middle of Main Street that serves decent burgers."

"That's perfect. Thanks, Azure." Adelina pressed her hands together and looked to the sky. "I'm starving."

**

The Whispering Tower Pub looked like a dozen other bars I'd walked into that had pool games one side and the bar on the other and somewhere against the wall are tables for people looking for a place to eat.

Adelina and I sat there absorbing the information we received. We both ignored all the eyes on us. I ignored the thrumming in my chest, making me want to leave, race back to the house atop the hill, and… and what? I didn't know.

I had a healthy carnal appetite for a woman my age. The sensations I was feeling weren't normal. I would've humped the nearest man's leg if it wouldn't get me arrested. And as much as I'd joke about my sudden extreme libido, I only wanted one man.

As soon as we sat at the table, our eyes met. He sat too far away for me to see exactly what he looked like, but I got the gist. He had a full pink mouth and pearly whites he flashed in abundance. Blonde shaggy hair brushed his shoulders where tattoos peeked from under the tank top he wore with his flannel shirt. He had breathtaking bone structure and looked to be built like a tank.

"Talk to him. Those other guys aren't faking it. They like him. Maybe he's decent."

I laughed as she nudged me. "Decent is what I should settle for?" I set my hand to my stomach as my gaze slid back to him. "I overate. I feel like trash."

He stood. *Oh no.* He stared back at me as he carried his beer across the room. Cowboy boots stopped beside the stool. I was ever so grateful for fitted jeans that day as he began to grow along the left side of his leg.

"Want to dance?" he asked and held out his much larger hand than mine.

"Yes," I agreed, sounding winded, and he visibly shivered.

In my periphery, Adelina laughed and sat back to watch. The top of my head reached his shoulder.

I loved the way his hips moved when he talked. I followed this hips right of the dance floor and I dragged him behind me to the backdoor.

He had light blue eyes. I saw them for a moment in the bright outdoor light before I jumped into his arms. I noticed piercings along his ears and was totally clean shaven, yet heavily tattooed.

He braced my weight against the gritty brick wall of the bar and tore through my underwear faster than a blink. I was five drinks into my depression fiesta and my thinking impaired. Although I attacked him and didn't protest our mutual mauling.

But then he slid inside of me and I lost all common sense. I ground on him as he gripped my ass and thrust into me. If he fucked me any harder I was going to marry him.

My fingers curled at the back of his neck and I had to break our kiss to breathe. He moaned loudly with me with a woodsy cologne wafting from his skin.

He didn't ask when he slowly set me on my feet and gently turned me around. My body felt heavy and eager at the same time, just before his body heat reached mine.

I had one hand above my forehead and the other held the wall as he took my hips. If we went any longer someone was bound to come out and see us. I didn't care but it was a small town. He might.

"Are you seeing someone?" he panted in a smooth voice.

My skin tightened. "It's a little late for that. No?" I asked as I brought my arm down.

He reversed from me and shuffled back. I turned, eyeing him as he covered up. He frowned at me and looked oddly hurt before he stormed from the bathroom. I reached under my shirt and used my ripped up undies to clean myself before I threw them out.

Adelina would never stop giving me shit for this.

**

"We need groceries." Adelina closed the yellow fridge.

Poppy incorporated every color of the rainbow in some way around the house. I wanted to find each way and cherish it. I wanted to find more things in common with her.

I nodded and ran my fingertips through my freshly washed hair. "Find a diner?"

Adelina nodded. I turned and headed to the front door where a green velvet bench against the wall provided the perfect place to sit while you put on your shoes or, in my case, white sneakers to go with my very autumn friendly rust sweatsuit.

I combed my hair into a low bun and waited as Adelina stomped into combat boots and grabbed the keys to the rental car.

I'd inherited a van. We explored it when we got in late that night. Poppy used it as a delivery van for her shop. Flowers had wilted inside the back and I felt an unexpected pang of loss. Even Adelina felt it.

The first restaurant we came across was a retro greasy spoon with a classic counter and booths. Old photographs of the area were framed above the paneling. It might not be gluten-free but it would feel homemade.

I spotted my hostile one night stand sitting at the counter with a coffee and holding court like the young stud of Riverton. I darted behind a man leaving and slid into the booth while Adelina gave me an amused but curious look.

"The guy from last night," I whispered as I leaned to look.

His manner was so *easy* and relaxed. He smiled the whole time and the older men around him just ate it up. While he was sitting with his legs spread, all leaned back I noticed a star on his belt and I wrinkled my nose. That was one way for me to get over a crush fast. The law and I didn't mix well.

A sunny haired woman about Adelina's age wandered over with an apron and a beaming smile. "Welcome to Breakfast by the

Bay, but don't let the name fool you. We're open for dinner, too. Is this your first time here?"

"It is," I said. "What do you recommend?" I asked and covertly watched the handsome stranger.

"Any of the skillets. They have the best bacon."

"Cheese and bacon skillets," Adelina smiled and nabbed my menu to give them to her, "and two teas. Thank you."

"You're welcome." Her eyes ran over us before she walked away.

I ducked back and sighed. "I think he's even better looking in daylight." I frowned. Why hadn't I put makeup on? Not even lip balm.

Adelina scowled and turned away.

"What? You didn't even turn around to look at him."

She leaned closer. "Is it just me or are these people staring at us?"

A chill crept up my spine as I carefully shifted my eyes. Sure enough. It wouldn't have been obvious except that they were *all* doing it, or at least the people at the front of the restaurant and the people at the counter.

"Ah crap," I muttered.

"What?"

Tall, blonde, and beautiful stepped off his mighty throne to navigate his way around the tables to me.

Bright and Shiny looked up at Tall, Blonde, and Beautiful with a stunning blush. He nodded to her and her cheeks grew redder. Then his eyes slid to me but I hadn't stopped staring at the poor waitress whose smile crashed as she looked to me.

"Let me know if you need anything else," she said tightly and walked towards the kitchen.

"Good morning."

I clenched my teeth as my nipples got hard enough to cut through the poor table. "'Morning."

"I wanted to apologize for last night." He smiled and drew in a deep breath. "I staggered out to my car and while I sat behind the wheel, I realized two things. You were joking, and I was way too drunk to be driving. I fell asleep while I had this internal debate and slept until about an hour ago. Now I'm here. I'm Eddie." He offered Adelina his hand.

"Adelina. That's my sister." Adelina gave me a smirk.

"Dylla," I answered, and I saw his lips part as I offered him my hand.

I stood, and he turned. We held hands as I followed behind him to the hall. There was a back parking lot and the doors to the bathrooms.

I shoved him into the Men's and after a swift glance locked the door behind me. He didn't give me a chance to turn around. Eddie shoved my pants and underwear down around my thighs and came in hot.

My head fell back to his chest as he held me tight and pumped into me. His hand covered my mouth while the other played between my legs. His lips panted just beside my face, and I couldn't see straight.

It wasn't the alcohol, and I hadn't imagined it. The dick was just that good.

I bit down on his finger instead of moaning and he hissed and squeezed me tight as he came.

We jolted as one when the lock of the stall squeaked and the door opened.

Eddie spun from me, giving me a chance to pull up my pants before a stranger saw my bare ass. Not to be confused with the stranger that *did* see my ass and more.

Alfie gave Eddie a flat look and then met my eyes with disappointment through the mirror. "I suggest you take Miss

D'Sousa to a private area, Eddie. Don't you?" He washed his hands and took a paper towel to dry them.

"Won't happen again."

Alfie ran his eyes over me before unlocking the door and leaving. Again, I clocked his nostrils flaring, perhaps in restrained anger.

Eddie went to the sink and splashed water on his face. I shifted as I waited for him to speak.

"You're going to be trouble for me," he said hollowly. "I think I have to stay away from you," he whispered.

"Good luck with that," I muttered.

Eddie scoffed lightly with a smile he fought to keep away. I liked that his smiles came easy.

He took a paper towel and dried his hands. He glanced at me from the corner of his eye and left the bathroom.

I cleaned myself up and shuffled out of the bathroom. The restaurant goers faced Adelina, and Eddie had fled.

Adelina saw me and nodded to the people. "They want to know which one of us is a Stockwell witch." I knew she meant it with sarcasm but didn't want the townsfolk who were visibly invested to be offended.

"That'd be me. I'm going to be hanging around for a while at least, so if you all have any stories or memories…

They spoke over one another with smiles — real, genuine smiles that were scaring the shit out of me.

The pretty waitress turned to the people and gestured for them to quiet down. "We all loved Poppy so much."

"What about her daughter?" Adelina asked. "Or the drownings?"

"We tried finding things online," I confessed and spotted her nametag.

Kari sighed. "We're not a big internet town. Reception this way is terrible. You might want to keep everything you need for a flat tire handy because service is spotty."

"Those drownings never should've happened," someone muttered.

I swallowed hard. "I've heard it was their dad's fault."

People grumbled. "He was a difficult man but he loved his kids. When that exchange student died that family never got back on its feet."

"Not even Poppy could right them," another person offered.

Kari saw how lost I looked. "Armando Coasta and Skye Stockwell were pretty hot and heavy. She's the only one old enough to have had a kid back then."

"Skye broke when he fell off the boat and they lost him. Hugh had to knock her out to get them back to shore or they'd all die. She never forgave him for that."

"They had to have her committed."

"She hurt herself because she believed she didn't deserve to live."

"So sad."

Adelina and I sat in rapt silence as the people interjected commentary and corrections. If my mother was Skye, then I'd been born in a psych ward and given away instead of to my family. Or worse yet, Skye signed me away herself because I was a reminder of the dead love of her life. She was only sixteen!

"She was never the same. She came back a year later after a lot of therapy but she became combative and angry," the man stated with his eyes far away. "The hospital would have records. You are her next of kin and they're all gone now."

Other chirped in. I looked to Adelina. We were ready to go.

Chapter 3

Adelina turned on the front door of the hospital and flipped the cameras the bird. I grabbed her arms and pushed them down.

"This is probably the only hospital around. I don't want to break something and have to be treated here now."

They denied me everything even though Skye's signature was on my birth certificate.

"Hey." A woman in blue scrubs hid behind the wall of the hospital. Her eyes nervously scanned from side to side before waving us over. "I can't get files for you but I can tell you what I know."

I gripped Adelina's hand. "Please. Anything. I just wat to know them."

She smiled sadly. "It's not great news. Your mom was sent there for suicide. She tried three times in the first six months after Armando's death. Suddenly things changed and she tried to get better. They let her out. I heard it was her idea to race in that storm. They said it was the dad. He could be a jerk at times but he wouldn't have hurt them. That's why she was leaving him. Lots of people wish she'd left him sooner and then the whole thing wouldn't have happened. I think Skye knew just what buttons to push with Hugh to make him want to race. Those stupid catamarans." She shook her head. "Thirty years since it started and twenty-five years since their deaths." Her eyes scanned my face. "You look just like Tilly would've."

"I'd be a lot older."

The nurse shrugged. "Tilly was ten years younger than Skye. Skye was seventeen, Canyon was thirteen and big for his age. You look like them all." Her eyes darted. "I've got to go."

**

We headed back into the library for details about Armando, and suddenly Azure wanted to help. She wrote the dates she knew and hovered as we scrolled. I explained the scene at the diner and she brought up the drowning article with Skye and Armando's smiling faces from earlier on the day that he died.

"They were reunited in death," Azure murmured.

Digging my past didn't hold the thrill it once did.

"Have you met the cranberry farmers? Emma Raleigh was Tilly's best friend. You've met Alfie. Him and Canyon were going to run this town one day. Skye only had Armando." Her eyes grew distant. "You should go to the farm tomorrow. They'll know more."

**

We knew as soon as we pulled up that something was off. My stomach knotted and my cheeks tingled. Adelina's brow beaded with sweat as we rushed out of the car. I would've said it was in the air but I'd started feeling off as soon as we got to the hill.

The door was open, and a breeze blew papers over the porch.

"Don't go in." I grabbed her shoulder. I fished my phone out of my pocket to call the police.

We waited five minutes in the car, holding our breath. A white pick-up zoomed up the driveway with their lights on.

The lights temporarily blinded me.

"Dylla? Adelina? Are you ladies good?"

Was that Eddie?

"Yeah. We stayed in the car like your dispatcher said." Adelina got out of the car, so I followed suit.

"Please stay here until I clear the house." Eddie didn't pull the gun at his hip, but he hovered his hand over it.

I nodded and Adelina hugged my shoulders as he went to the house. Fifteen minutes later, Eddie came outside.

"It's clear, but for peace of mind, how about a hotel room on the Riverton Sheriff's Office?"

"What do you think?" Adelina asked.

If she didn't want to go she wouldn't have asked. Adelina got squirrelly when it came to her soft side. It was okay to be scared. I was scared shitless.

"Yeah." I nodded.

"Hop in my truck. I'll pick you up in the morning and we'll double check the house before you go back in. Sound good?" he asked as he held the door open for me.

His eyes locked on mine. Oh no. Not again.

I blinked and it was enough time to force myself to nod and look away. "Good."

**

An hour later we found ourselves on a cranberry farm. The hotel was being fumigated and it was the only one in town. Eddie really didn't like the idea of us in the house so he brought us home.

The farmhouse wasn't as old as some of the town and it hadn't been completely modernized. It maintained its rustic charm with modern function. From the little feminine touches I also knew a woman lived there and began to dread the next twelve hours.

"Emma?" Eddie called as he entered. "I brought guests! They're staying the night. Someone broke into their house and the hotel's being fumigated."

"Why are you shouting?" A woman rolled into the room and gaped at me.

She blinked blue eyes at me through glasses that rested on her porcelain nose. Her hair was highlighted to a luxurious caramel and her nails were painted pink.

"Tilly," she breathed.

"They think she's Skye's daughter. That she must've had her while she was away," Eddie explained.

Emma scrunched her face and looked at Eddie. "Are you blind? That's Tilly!" She looked at Adelina. "That's Skye's baby!" She reversed and turned. Before I knew it, she was out of the room. "I'll prove it."

"I'm sorry. Tilly was her best friend." His eyes looked sympathetically to me.

I didn't dare say anything because my body had completely locked up. I wracked my mind for images of Emma and couldn't find them. It was all gut and no brains. A part of me healed looking at Emma. I didn't know I was broken.

My memories were bad when I was little. The first thing I could recall was Adelina being brought home.

Emma returned and held out a yearbook. "I don't know what happened but I'm glad you're back."

I accepted the yearbook and it felt familiar.

"Emma. I want you to listen to yourself." Eddie wasn't rude or condescending to her. He sounded calm and concerned.

I knew to look for Stockwell. I found Tilly's picture and my breath came short. She wore my favorite shirt. I wore holes in that shirt until my mom had to throw it away. That was my second memory. It was just a stupid shirt. I couldn't explain my attachment to it.

In the next picture I'm in little Emma's lap with a goofy looking Eddie standing behind the wheelchair and the stupidest toothless grins you'd ever seen.

"She knows it."

"How about some sleep? We can work it out in the morning." Eddie waved his way. "There's chili you can heat up before bed."

"I'll get the other yearbooks and you can look at them before you go to asleep," Emma said in a rush before following. "Do you play video games? We can do some mindless multiple player games to clear our heads. It's better than therapy."

**

The chili and cornbread was delicious. The video games we played while ignoring how openly Emma seemed to be willing me into Tilly gave way to yearbooks spread over the guest room bed where Adelina fell asleep while on the phone with Charice. Any doubt that we weren't Stockwells and related by blood just not sisters but aunt and niece was gone. Adelina favored Armando. I didn't get how our parents wound up with us and it was too late to call. Adelina vented to Charice but I kept it bottled inside.

There was a soft knock at the bedroom door and I quietly answered it wearing my tank top and shorts. Eddie wore soft pants and his hair hung loose over his bare shoulders.

"I wanted to make sure you're okay. Emma and Tilly were closer than sisters."

"I'm sorry I don't remember you," I whispered.

His cheek twitched. "That hurt more than I expected. Please don't say that to Emma. It'll break her heart. She's doing well. She has these romance books people go crazy for. She's probably the only one of us on social media." He chuckled as his eyes welled with tears. "Agh." He laughed and shook his head.

I wrapped my arms around his neck and held him. "I'm going to stay in Riverton. Seeing Emma shook something loose. Or it's all this stuff with my family. I want them to have a happy ending. For my family." He withdrew and my brow knit.

He brought his hands up and cupped my face. "I am so happy you're alive."

**

"EDDIE!"

He gasped awake beside me. I heard him fall out of bed.

"I'm up! Don't come in here!" he uttered from the floor.

I stood naked as I scanned the floor for clothes. The door began to open and I grabbed the flannel to my chest.

Emma's eyes bugged when she saw us. "I — never mind. Adelina is gone. The door was open, Eddie."

She held out a sheet of paper to him.

It ends at the Regatta Race.

"What does that mean? I asked as panic crept in.

"Stay in here with her." Eddie ran to the bed and pulled a safe for underneath. He gave Emma a handgun and ran bare foot from the bedroom, closing the door behind him.

"You know how to use that?" I asked in a tremble.

Emma nodded. "You don't remember how to cast anymore. Do you?"

"Cast?" I asked carefully.

She pressed her lips together. "I'll sound crazy no matter how I tell it." She sighed and met my eyes. "Your family inherits certain abilities — witches, if you will. While we have a lot of humans here in Riverton, we also have families who arrived here first that are also werewolves. We're a special kind that came over with the witches as protection. It's not all classism. You protect us too. You keep the humans from seeing us and we make sure the Salem Witch Trials remains the patriarchal misogyny murder spree we all knew it was."

"That does explain why everyone around town acts like I soaked in pheromones," I mumbled. "I don't have the first clue what you're talking about but if you're trying to distract me to cheer me up its working."

Her lips quirked. "I promise, it's true. I'm also sorry. You're in a tight position right now and we're all hoping you step up without scaring you off. I'm also sorry if we've all come across extra creepy. We're so happy you're back."

Eddie rushed back into the room. "I've called the station. They're bringing a forensics teams here." My cheeks heated when he wrapped his arms around me.

"If this is someone's idea of a practical joke, it's not fucking funny," Emma spat and we heard her go to the chair lift.

"I think you should stay with me until we find her."

"She might've meant that note as when she'd be back by. Her and Charice have been fighting," I whispered.

"You can feel that someone cast," he whispered. "Does it scare you… knowing what I am?"

"I'm not sure I believe it," I whispered as I withdrew and searched his face.

"Believe it. That flag you flew was an enchantment." He licked his lower lip. "To find your mate. I took it down. I don't want to beat my ego up too hard but did you not feel it?"

I drew in a shaky breath. "Too strong." I swallowed. "I need to digest this."

**

More law enforcement. More questions. No answers.

I brought Emma with me or rather, Emma took me to see Hugh Stockwell after a huge brunch. Her van was specially built for her to drive. She loved her independence.

The staff at the hospital knew her. She visited Hugh Stockwell every so often to see if things changed. We walked into the game room were patients quietly spoke or played table games.

I recognized the man from the newspaper. He hunched a little but he was still a big man and they kept his appearance neat. He looked old and sometimes that was bad enough.

Our eyes locked and I watched his face contort. He went from a dribbling mess to registering shock on his face.

"Tilly?" he rasped.

The staff member with him jolted and stood rod straight. Hugh shuffled away.

"Tilly!"

I reversed and bumped Emma's chair. "Mr. Stockwell. This Is Dylla. Tilly was adopted and they changed her name," Emma stated.

He stopped too close to me as he wept silently and stared at me. "It was Skye," he sobbed. "She struck me dumb with one of her casts," he spat. "She attacked all of us. Canyon slipped right into the water, but you held on somehow. She missed you and you hung on," he whispered. "You're alive!" he shouted.

The nurses and staff members came into the room trying to calm the patients and soothe Hugh.

"No. No. It was Skye," he murmured as they sedated him. His blue eyes slid back to me. "I'm sorry I wasn't better." His eyes widened. "Skye comes to taunt me. She's Mrs. Gökcan! Mrs. Gökcan!"

"We have to see what happened here," a nurse explained before racing off.

We were escorted out and told us they'd call with an update. We got back in the van and I took deep cleansing breaths.

"The librarian?" My stomach lurched.

"Eddie? Can you check on Azure? Hugh Stockwell came through his… thing and said…" she sighed, "Azure might be Skye with a lot of cosmetic surgery to make herself look older." Her eyes widened and she looked to me. "She didn't come into work and you did a wellness check. Yes. She's here. Okay. Shook." The corner of her mouth curled before she sobered and looked ahead. "I'll take her to Poppy's." She ended the call. "Now that your fertility flag is no longer flying in the literal sense —"

"Huh?"

"You can try casting. How hard could it be?" She glanced to me and drew down her brows. "That flag you flew? The one that hasn't been raised in twenty-eight years? I'm not surprised you matched with Eddie. He's my twin brother. Three peas in the pod."

"I think you just told me I'm having a baby because I let my freak flag fly," she snorted, "and that I'm a witch while my sister who is really my niece has been abducted by my sister who pretended to be my librarian so she can finish what she started."

Emma pursed her lips in thought. "I mean, I didn't say all of those things but that sums up the day." Her fingers gripped the steering wheel. "Use those feelings. Channel them into the cast."

Chapter Four

Casting must've skipped a generation. I could barely cause a breeze and I wasn't sure it wasn't me waving around like a fish out of water. And on the topic of water, the bay made me nauseous. If I wasn't casting I was sailing, or rather sitting on a boat while Emma and Eddie quizzed me.

Eddie gleaned that it was Skye who broke into the house to see how close we were to the truth. I thought Skye wanted to know how much I remembered.

"Do you think she'd kill her own daughter?" I asked as Eddie's fingertip traced between my breasts to my belly button and back again. "He's all that's left of Armando."

"Could be she hates Adelina for reminding her of Armando."

I sighed. "What now? We stop Skye and she goes to prison?"

"She murdered Canyon. Georgia, your mom, had a heart attack when they told her. She died on the spot. You and Sky are witches but it was Canyon who was really destined for something more than Riverton. Hugh was somewhat of a bully even to Canyon, whom he was jealous of.

"I feel such a bond with Emma and you that it almost feels like I'm betraying Adelina by being closer to someone else. I'm scared for her but I feel safe with you."

"We're going to save her."

I scoffed lightly. "I can't cast or sail. I forgot all of it." My throat grew tight.

"I'll be on the boat with you."

**

All the tourists were out. Flags, banners, and sails whipped in the crisp autumn breeze. Eddie took care of getting a boat and entering the race. He had to use his position, but we'd be on the water for Adelina. He told his people what was happening and there was a heavy police presence.

"Take this." Emma gave me the walkie talkie and hugged me tight. "Wear the life vest. I want to get to know you again and I can't wait to be an aunt."

My heart did a little skip at that. A life vest settled on my shoulders and Eddie came around to hug Emma.

"We'll be safe. Skye wants to hear Tilly apologize for Armando though it was no one's fault unless it was everyone's fault."

"Unless her plan is to die too," Emma corrected. "Just be less stupid."

"I will," he promised and met the eyes of the officers watching over her. "Pinch my ass if you see her. That'll be our signal."

"What if she throws some kind of killer cast. My shield is weak. It's bendy," I squeaked.

"Deep breaths," he soothed. "I knew Azure. She has a cat. Adelina is her daughter. They could get to know one another. We'll say what we need to say to talk them back to shore."

**

It was windy and everyone had on hats or hoods. I couldn't make out anyone's face and the water grew choppy. I could see the organizers weighing their options before one of them shrugged. It was very scientific.

The water tossed us as the organizers readied. A gunshot blast fired into the gray sky and we raised our sails with our hearts racing, just as Eddie showed me.

A crackle of static barely caught my attention over the snap of our sail when it grew taut from the wind.

"Eddie!" Emma shouted on the walkie. *"Adelina is here! She just wants Tilly!"*

Strength trickled from my limbs and settled in my feet. My head turned to Eddie with a look of horror. He launched himself from a crouch to push me away. On reflex, I cast my blubber shield of air and was rocked off my feet as it hit what was essentially a bouncy air ball.

Eddie fell just after me, into the rolling depths of waves.

I fought to the surface with my life vest to help me. I took Eddie's arm and brought him beside a large mass. Our boat went o without us. We clung to a chunk of wood that suspiciously looked like it belonged to a boat that'd been blown to pieces,

Eddie took my face in his hands and stopped me before I could look for Skye. "You're okay. Don't look. We're alright." His eyes slid shut and he held me as we clung to the boat and waited for rescue.

**

Skye dropped Adelina in a field, hours away in a car, two days by foot. She said the whole town's reception was trash and went into a rage reliving her frustration. She wept a lot knowing that that would be the only interaction they'd ever share in her life.

Our parents picked her up from Poppy's and they were with Charice for now. My parents came clean about how I wound up in their care. I forgave them all — even Skye and Hugh, my biological father. It turns out I was found a day later by Mr. Hardwick, who Poppy cared a great deal about. He covered it up and Poppy found my parents and asked if they'd take me too because she now believed her family was cursed.

As I sat in the rocking chair awaiting the parade of costumed children with a pointy hat on my head, I couldn't help but think her worries were unfounded. The snake of flashlights as kids ran their way around the residential streets would eventually make their way to us on top of the hill.

"Ready all ready?" Eddie came out of the house and took the chair beside me. His big hand settled on my stomach and he winked at me.

"Ready?" I asked.

"Just have to put on my costume." Eddie kept my gaze as he slid on a wolf mask.

I chuckled as I leaned into his shoulder and soaked up his warmth. I'd see the animal in him one day.

A Perfect Storm

Dream Prophet Prequel

Colleen Tews

The blizzard wreaked havoc on the small diner in Bay City. As the winter days grew shorter so did my window of opportunity. This was my last chance to seek out that one person for redemption. Finding my way into the warmth of the diner, I smelled the patron's regret. Its salty goodness nestled its way down my throat. The lament they felt tasted sweeter than the day-old pumpkin pie in the display case. As The Keeper, my job wasn't an easy task, but it sure was a fun one.

I circled them all till I found just the right appetizer. There was the bedraggled alcoholic at the counter sipping coffee. Though he was sober the distinct taint of whiskey wafted from his dingy coat. Tempting.

The waitress with her black eyeliner smeared over puffy eyes offered to refill his drink. She was sweet and rejected. What was even more tantalizing was her pain. It was recent and clear in her mind. I hovered over her as she made her way to a table full of miscreants. I salivated when I sensed the blood flow between her thighs. This was not Mother Nature's doing.

"So, can I get you all anything else?" She brushed away a stray blonde strand of hair, then poised a pen over her order pad. Her nametag read 'Bonnie'. She shifted her feet twice while awaiting a response.

"No, just a check please." The young man said. His spiky brown hair wilted in the late hour.

"Jeremy," his girlfriend tugged his sleeve, "I want a piece of pie."

Jeremy draped his arm across her shoulders. "You sure?"

"Yeah. Besides I don't want to go out into that storm yet. Maybe after the pie comes it will slow down." She flipped her chestnut hair and batted her big doe eyes up at him.

"Sure thing, baby." Jeremy turned back to Bonnie. "Can we get one piece of apple pie first?"

"Of course, I'll be right back with your piece." Bonnie twisted her hips, causing the joint to crack, and went to retrieve the dessert. She mumbled under her breath, "When will this night end."

"Soon my dear, I promise." There was a sense of freedom in being able to say whatever I pleased. It wasn't like any of them heard me, unless I wanted them to.

I stayed behind with the lovebirds. Young love was almost as intoxicating as the whiskey on the alcoholic's coat or the blood between Bonnie's legs. There was more to their tale though. Their past spoke to me as if I were there when their journey to my dinner party began.

Jeremy stroked her arm. "What do you want to do after this?"

"Could we go back to your place? I really don't want to be home alone." She snuggled into him.

"We can do that. Baby, you shiverin'? It isn't that cold in here."

"I'm not cold. I'm just." She pulled away from him. "I'm just a little scared."

"Elizabeth Phillips, what's got you so scared that you shake that hard?"

She stared out away from him, across the table. A glossy expression marred her beautiful face. Our eyes met for an instant. Which was not impossible, but improbable. Being nothing more than a spirit had its advantages when eavesdropping on conversations. Nonetheless she looked right at me.

When she spoke next her words did not change her expression, only her lips moved. She was a blank slate. "I've got a funny feeling tonight that I haven't had in awhile. Not since my dad died."

Did my luck change? Had I found what I've desired for decades? I leaned across the table. This was my chance, my first contact ripened to perfection. She was open to me. Was Elizabeth the willing vessel that would aid me in my charge? All I needed was that one touch.

"Lizzie," Jeremy turned her away from me. "You don't need to be scared of anything with me here. I've got you. And that was a long time ago."

She blinked and gave him a half-hearted smile. "You're right. I don't know what I was thinking."

The gateway between us shut. An ache churned my stomach. *"Damn."*

Lights flickered. The cook yelled out a string of profanities.

"Sorry about that everybody." Bonnie rounded the corner. "It's just the storm picking up, but we should be okay. I'm heading out back to kick the generator."

Within minutes the hum of the generator firing up was heard over some random pop song. Bonnie walked in a brisk stride to the counter. She cut a slice of pie. They exchanged polite words as she served Elizabeth.

Tweets from a bird that popped out of a wall clock reminded me of my limited time. The hour was growing near. I had to make my move, but I needed more energy.

I followed Bonnie back to the alcoholic. "Are you sure I can't freshen your drink?"

"I'm fine." He scratched his dirty face. Flakes of skin fell into his cup.

"Bernie, you're in here every night. You sit there staring at the classifieds as if your life depended on it, sippin' on a single cup of coffee till the morning rush. If you want my opinion you need to be home, in bed, so you can get up refreshed."

"Last I checked, Bonnie, I didn't ask for yer opinion." He never looked up from his newspaper.

"Whatever." She snatched the coffee pot from the burner. Before he could protest, she poured the hot sludge in his cup. "By the way, refills are free."

"Bonnie!"

"Don't give me no lip. You're gonna drink it and be happy with what you've got. Understand." She beamed at him. With that she went back into the kitchen.

One would think that being offered anything for free would have made his day. It wasn't coffee he craved. His frustration came off him in waves. I massaged away the heavy burdens that lay upon him and whispered in his ear. *"You could really use a drink. No one will know. All you need is one little sip to take away the sting."*

His shoulders sighed under my strength. I stabbed a pressure point in his back. Bernie winced. He rubbed his eyes and groaned. "God, I can't. I just can't." Even as he spoke to himself, he reached for the bottle hidden in his inner coat pocket.

He glanced once around the room. No one was watching. Bernie poured the amber liquid down his gullet. With a jerk, he twisted the lid back on. Then thrust the bottle into the pocket hard enough that he could have shoved it through the material. "Three years down the fucking drain. Fuck."

He went back to sipping the coffee as if nothing had happened. His eyes watered. Bernie rubbed his face and brushed the unshed tears aside.

I loved denial. While he wiped away his sorrow I stepped into him. Every part of me became one with him. All of his memories were mine. I sifted through those hazy regrets from a lifelong addiction to booze. I hungered for the sweet spot. That moment where he lost who he was and how he came to be a cheap suit for an old haunt such as myself.

"#"

Three years ago, Bernard Langenthal was your average drunk. He was tossed out of bars at closing time, though loved by bartenders from Bay City to Detroit. Back then he was a car salesman, a thankless job where customers automatically thought he was out to cheat them. After a hard day's work Bernie did what Bernie always did. He went to the bar.

"Bernie, sweetie, I've got to close up and you need to get on home. I'm sure that pretty wife of yours is wondering where you are." Sherry, his favorite bartender, said as she escorted him to the door.

"I need ta go home." He slurred. "Do you 'member where I parked my car?"

"Where you always park it. Right next to mine. Walk me out?"

They walked, arm in arm, and kept each other from slipping in the snow-covered parking lot. Sherry helped Bernie get into his red pickup truck. "Drive safe, sweetie. I'll see you tomorrow."

"You, too." Bernie started his truck. He squinted at the dashboard as he made out the gears. Once he figured out where 'drive' was located he put the truck into gear and tore out of the parking lot.

"Dang it." He said when he noticed a sign for Midland. He moaned and steered the wheel to make an illegal U-turn. It was then that he saw the headlights coming for him.

The truck fishtailed. He turned the steering wheel into the turn, or was it against the turn? Black ice maintained his momentum. In a moment of clarity, of sudden sobriety, Bernie's truck smashed into Sherry's sedan. The side of his head ricocheted off the doorframe. The impact knocked him out.

The ringing in his ears mingled with the sound of Sherry's blaring horn. Blood coated half of his face. It shut his left eye. He rubbed it free, and saw Sherry's crunched sedan. "What have I done?"

He staggered from his truck. "Sherry? Sherry, you okay?"

She slumped over the steering wheel. Bernie pushed her back against the seat. Blood gushed from a head laceration. An arm was entangled in the wheel. The other was missing. The gear shaft was lodged into her chest. She was not breathing.

"Shit." Thoughts raced as he tried to come up with what to do next. Unsure as to what to do he leaned against the car. Through tears of horror and grief he saw the river that ran beside the highway.

He ran to the river's edge. It was frozen, but not solid. There were plenty of dark patches where the ice was weak. He wiped the adrenaline inspired perspiration from his upper lip, and knew what he had to do.

"#"

Bernie finished wiping away his tears and blinked. Sherry stood behind the diner's counter. Her skin has a bluish tint to it. She was bloated and her tender eyes bulged. She was dressed the same as she had the night Bernie killed her. She slammed her hand on the counter. *"How could you?"*

"Sherry?" He whispered.

She reached over the counter, grabbed the back of his head, and pulled him down onto his steamy coffee mug. The porcelain shattered. The drink scolded his skin, searing away bits of flesh.

He shrieked. "Help! Oh god!"

Bonnie rushed out of the kitchen. When she saw the damage to Bernie's face she said, "On my. Hold on." She ransacked the cupboard under the cash register for a first aid kit.

"Did you really think you wouldn't have to pay for what you did to me?" Sherry was inches from his face.

"I'm sorry." He cried.

"You dumped my body in the river and all you can say is you're sorry. You don't know the meaning of the word because if you did you wouldn't have had that last shot. But you will." Sherry slipped through the counter as if it weren't there. She straddled Bernie's legs. *"Eye for an eye."* She kissed him.

The steam from the coffee on Bernie's face stopped. The liquid cooled as it froze his skin. The blue tint in Sherry's skin brightened to that of a more normal shade as Bernie's paled. Under the dirt and the grime his coloring changed as hypothermia set in.

"Let me take a look at you." Bonnie said as she came to attend to Bernie's wounds. The first aid kit fell from her hands. Bernie's head dropped backward, frozen and lifeless.

Unbeknown to anyone in the room, other than me, Sherry climbed off her murderer. With newfound pep in her step, she came to me. *"I couldn't have done this without you."*

"No need to thank me. I'll get my payment."

"Do you really eat the leftovers?"

"The soul's heart. Yes."

Her eagerness radiated off her life a heat wave. Her desire for justice was a charming side dish. The main course lay before me.

I stuck my hand into Bernie's chest. I hungered for his sorrow. It was like mother's milk to me. To my dismay he was nothing but an empty shell.

The lights flickered. The florescent bulb over the table beside the lovebirds burst. Elizabeth shrieked. They ran from the table to the counter in the main hall.

I glared at Sherry. Had she stolen my soul? Was it she I needed to punish? I couldn't finish my mission without feeding. Fulfilling my pledge by aiding vengeful ghosts weakened me. The further back the incident the harder the memories were to obtain. Thus, the more difficult it was to cross ghosts to this side. There was more at stake than petty acts of vengeance tonight of all nights.

"What the hell happened?" Jeremy asked Bonnie, who stared at him wide eyed. I asked Sherry the same question.

She shrugged. *"Don't look at me. I just killed the bastard. That was it."*

Elizabeth stepped away from Jeremy. She inched her way not to Bernie, but closer to me. "What do you think you're doing?"

I jerked my hand from Bernie's empty chest cavity. All I could do was stare at her. This young woman saw me. She had to have been a clairvoyant or witch of some kind. This knowledge solidified my previous assumption. She was my vessel.

Bonnie walked between us. "I tried to save him, but I was too late."

"Save him from what?", Jeremy asked. "Why the fuck is he blue? Did he just come in from outside? Is the storm that bad?"

Sherry barked out a laugh. *"Are all humans this stupid?"*

"You were once."

Elizabeth walked around Bonnie to me. "If you're not human, then what are you?"

"Baby, who ya talkin' to?" Jeremy maneuvered to intercept.

"Him." She pointed at me.

"He's dead. We've been through this before. Remember, when your dad died. You can't talk to dead people."

"Not him." She shoved Jeremy. "Him."

"There's no one else there."

"But,"

"Boo!" Sherry jumped at her.

She shrieked.

I backhanded Sherry. She flew into the front door. The glass cracked. Lacking any reason for the door to crack caused all those mortals to jump. I really hated the living and sometimes the dead pissed me off, too.

"Leave spirit. I'm tired of your games. You achieved what you came for." Lying on the floor, Sherry laughed as she faded across the divide.

"I'm calling the police." Bonnie announced and stormed into the kitchen area. I refused to allow officers in blue to steal my last opportunity. I had strength for one last grab at a soul. Judging the smell of the blood that flowed from her there was a ghost bound to her pain.

Elizabeth cried with her face snuggled into Jeremy's sweater. She mumbled about how impossible this all was. "I want to go home."

"We can't, at least not until the cops get here." Jeremy stroked her back.

Swift as the wind I raced after Bonnie. She ran past the fat cook smoking a cigar. I followed her out the back door. The motion sensor light was already on due to the heavy snowfall. The brisk night air hit her hard. She ran her hands up and down her shivering arms. Her breath came out in a fog. After she lit a cigarette there was no telling where the smoke she exhaled ended and her breath began.

Bonnie dug out her cell phone from her back pocket. She trembled as she tried to dial out. On the third attempt she gave up. She kicked the wall. "I can't do anything right."

She plopped down on a snow mound. Bonnie took another drag from the cigarette. "Come on God, give me a break. I realize he's the one that died, but is all this supposed to be some kind of lesson. All life is sacred. Is that what you're trying to tell me? You tryin' to prove to me that I made a bad choice? Well, guess what? I already knew that."

Blaming God was always an easy scapegoat. If I had a soul for every time I heard that one then I would have completed my mission long ago.

Off in the distance church bells rang loud and clear. The reverent sound echoed off the nearby building. Sunrise was fast approaching.

She inhaled again before doubling over. "Fuckin' cramps."

I knelt in front of her. The pain her body was putting her through generated one lonesome tear. I smeared the salty drop across her cheek. *"You can make it all stop; the pain, the regret, even death itself. Relax."*

She rested back against the diner and shut her eyes. I accepted her invitation and merged with her as I had Bernie. Within seconds I was transported to two weeks ago.

"#"

"Ms. Kipling, the doctor is ready to see you now." The nurse told her as she pushed a wheelchair into the room.

Bonnie lay prone on the examination table dressed in a hospital gown. She sighed and prayed she made the right choice. The nurse helped her off the table and into the chair. Her fear must have been written across her face because the nurse said, "Don't worry. This is a quick and painless procedure."

"You're gonna knock me out, right?"

"As you requested." She nodded.

"Good. I don't want any memory of this."

The nurse transported Bonnie down a chilly, oxygen-enriched hallway. She yawned long before she reached the operating room. Bonnie tried to put on a brave face when she saw Dr. Tanner waiting for her.

"Good morning, Ms. Kipling. How are we going today?"

"As well as can be expected," she shrugged. What was the right answer to that question before this type of procedure?

He nodded with a solemn look in his eyes. Dr. Tanner laid a gentle hand on her shoulder. "Before we go in there, I want to ask you one last time if you're sure this is the choice you want to make."

"Absolutely." Bonnie confirmed without hesitation. She had spent many sleepless nights pondering over this dilemma. In the end she had come up with three options. One was obvious, but there was no way she could take care of a baby. She couldn't even take care of herself. The second was to carry the baby to term and give it up for adoption. That plan was snuffed out by her selfish nature. Bonnie knew she would have grown attached to the child in nine months and wouldn't want to give it away. This was the only other choice she was left to pick.

She settled onto the operating table and the nurse hooked up her IV. As the icy numbing agent coursed through her body, she reassured herself that this was the best thing she could do for both the child and herself. No, not a child, she scolded herself. It was an it, not a child or a baby. To think any other way was too painful.

An hour later Bonnie woke with a start. She rubbed her abdomen and cried.

"#"

Bonnie threw her cigarette across the alley. The snowfall slowed. Shadows ate away the light on the ground. A giggle chimed from the darkness.

"Who's there?" Bonnie snapped to her feet. The only response she got was another giggle.

Shadows pooled in the ambiance of the light. It was as if something blocked out the light, but there was nothing in front of the lamp and nothing above her. A heart shaped shadow flowed over the snow toward Bonnie.

She backed away from it. With her back to the wall, she attempted to scale the flat surface. The giggle grew louder and more joyful.

I watched with her in astonishment at the creativity of this premature haunt. It bubbled up as if the cells were still formulating what it was meant to become. It spoke to me without words. Since it was unable to communicate, I had to translate.

"No." Her mouth gaped open.

"Yes."

"It can't be."

"You are correct. 'It' cannot be. So, what is 'It'?"

"No." She whispered. She shut her eyes and prayed. Then reopened her eyes. She whimpered.

"What is 'It'?"

"It's a baby."

"Who's baby?"

"Mine." She dropped to her knees. Bonnie opened her arms out to the shadowy infant. "I am so sorry. Come to mommy."

The infant wobbled a bit, but was a fast learner. The baby took its first step. Then charged at its mother at full speed. The ghost encased its mother in shadow. Then the spirit smashed them against the diner's wall. Her skull cracked upon impact. The child giggled as it one faded through the gate to the other side.

"You are most welcome."

I did not have to search Bonnie's body for her soul. It stood before me. I cocked my head to the side. She was not just a soul, but was now a ghost. *"My baby said you're The Keeper? You right wrongs for ghosts?"*

"I facilitate such matters for a price."

"I need your help."

I grew tired of this. I was always the one they came to for aid. I was always the one with the helping hand. Did no one care that I might have needs, too?

"I do not have time to track down the person you hold responsible for your troubles. You made your choice. You got what you deserve." I walked away.

"What if I told you he is in that diner?"

"Who?"

"Guess."

I rushed upon her with such furious momentum that it made the baby look like a tortoise by comparison. I hauled her into the air by her throat. *"Speak now haunt or I shall hurl you into oblivion myself."*

"Jeremy. He was the father." That got her attention. I set her down. *"He refused to help me with the kid."*

"Because of Elizabeth."

"Yeah. He cheated on her with me and when I got pregnant, he told me to take care of it."

This worked to my advantage. *"Deal."* We exchanged the details and shook hands. Together we walked through the wall into the diner. I held Bonnie back in the shadows of a support pillar. We needed to remain undetected by Elizabeth for my plan to work.

She and Jeremy cuddled at their table. It was a disgusting sight. She was half asleep curled in his warmth. Soon my cold touch she would warm her.

"Ready?" I asked my partner in crime.

"As I'll ever be."

With a flick of my fingers the lights went out. The white and orange emergency lights went on. The cook cursed in the kitchen. Elizabeth bolted up. Jeremy stood up quick as a whip. The bird chime clock tweeted.

"What was that?" Elizabeth asked. She reached for Jeremy.

"Just the clock. Chill. The generator must have blown. I'm going to find Bonnie." Though she pleaded for him to stay at her side he left Elizabeth all alone.

I whispered into Bonnie's ear, *"Don't let him leave the room. I want Elizabeth to hear his crime."*

Bonnie circled behind the pillar to cut off Jeremy. Instead of stopping before him she walked through him. *"Jeremy."*

He stopped dead in his tracks. A shiver ran through him. A fog of breath escaped between his lips.

"Jeremy, tell her what you did." Bonnie let her words blow across the back of his neck. *"Tell her about me."*

"Bonnie?"

"Did she come back?" Elizabeth crawled out from the booth.

"Confess." Bonnie stepped through him again. Then turned and draped her arms over his shoulders.

"How'd you do that?" Fear muffled Jeremy's speech. It was the sweetest taunt I had tasted in a long time. "We need to get you warmed up."

"Its amazing the freedom that death brings. You have our child to thank for this by the way. He wanted mommy to pay a price. Frankly, with the way child support is divided up nowadays I figured daddy has to pay up, too." She fiddled with the small hairs at the back of his neck. *"But if you confess what you did with me to Elizabeth, I think I may actually let you live."*

Elizabeth walked up to them tying up the loose end of their haunting love triangle. "Bonnie, you remind me of…" When she stopped, I hoped she had done so to analyze what was before her. I wanted her to figure it out. Elizabeth reached out to Bonnie. Her hand went straight through her. "You're a ghost."

"Brava." I clapped my hands once as I stepped out from my hiding place.

"Who the fuck are you?" Jeremy asked over Bonnie's shoulder.

"I think you have more pressing matters to attend to. I'll just be over here." I leaned against the pillar.

Bonnie yanked his attention away from me to her by pulling down his chin. *"Tell her, Jeremy."*

"Tell me what?"

"Uhm, you're dead. I think the present is a bit more important than the past."

"You think wrong." Bonnie punched her fist into his chest. *"Tell her or I squeeze."*

He screamed. "Let go. My heart."

I held back my laughter. I hadn't realized Bonnie was that poetic.

"I won't ask again."

Jeremy's knees buckled. I figured the constricted blood flow to his limbs, particularly his brain, left him with a small window to confess to Elizabeth.

"Stop it. You're killing him." Elizabeth tried to pull Bonnie off Jeremy with no success. She slipped through Bonnie's body as if she were nothing more than a puff of smoke. Elizabeth fumbled into the wall. "Just tell me what she wants you to say. No secret can be worth your life."

"Fine," he choked out. "I knocked up Bonnie, and told her she needed to get an abortion. Satisfied?"

Elizabeth's covered her mouth with her hands. Her eyes were wide.

"Not yet." Bonnie applied the last amount of pressure required to crush his heart.

Jeremy's eyes rolled back into his head. He slumped the rest of the way to the floor as Bonnie's hand came free. Much to my surprise she was not empty handed.

She clenched Jeremy's soul as if she was afraid it would slip away with the slightest of breezes. Finally, a haunt learned how to pay back a promise. *"A deal's a deal."*

"That it is." I took the offered soul. I enveloped him. The process was similar to how I tormented mortals only reversed. He was forced into my essence. I savored the pain he felt for cheating on the woman he loved. The anguish he had for forcing the mother of his child to end the pregnancy. He wanted to be a daddy. The icing on the cake was the fear of the last few seconds of his life. The pain he caused Elizabeth tied to the tearing of his arteries. Priceless. The cries of all those before him that I carried within me bellowed into the dining hall, greeting him with their own suffering.

"What are you?" Elizabeth crept along the wall.

"What I am does not matter. Who I am is the answer to your prayers" I circled the room as I spoke, *"You see when one does his job right a crack in the world appears. The very fabric of reality splinters and the unusual happens. For some they get the chance to shine brighter than before, prove their worth as it were. Like you, Elizabeth you've proven to be*

quite more than you first appeared to be. You are a creature of tremendous gifts. However, for beings such as myself, well, the consequences are more tangible. I have a rather gluttonous occupation. And I was famished."

I cut off her means of escape. *"Now I am not hungry any longer. I am full and enriched by every life I have ever touched. There is just one thing I need."*

"What's that?"

"Your light." I slipped into her, not unlike any smitten man, but with my whole body, mind, and soul. Our psyches linked. My memories became her memories. She knew the meaning behind my mission. She accepted me with an open mind, a kind prayer and love.

"#"

The sun glinted off snow into the front window. Elizabeth woke to a man in a white grease-covered shirt shaking her. "Hey, you okay? With everything that happened last night I was worried you weren't going to wake up."

"I'm fine. You can stop shaking me now."

"Oh, yeah, sorry." He offered her a hand up. "My name's Chuck. Do you have any idea what happened?"

"No." As she stood up the memories came back to her in bits and pieces. "Bonnie and Jeremy are dead."

"Yeah, Bernie too."

"Who's Bernie? Never mind." She rubbed her stomach. She felt nauseous and hungry at the same time.

"Are you going to be okay? The police and paramedics are on the way." Chuck guided Elizabeth to a bench near the front door.

"I'll be fine. It's just that in all the excitement I should have been more careful." She brushed her hair back from her face, leaned back, and closed her eyes. "I'm pregnant."

Chuck took a step back. "Crap, was Jeremy the father?"

"Yeah." She lied, remembering the father of her baby. The mysterious ghost who visited last night. "I'm having a boy."

"Did you two decide on a name?"

Elizabeth smiled, lost in the thought of giving birth to a child with amazing gifts. She didn't need to think of a name. One came to her, "Nathaniel."

"The Thing About Ashridge"

By Bri Eberhart

Eva grips the messenger bag on her shoulder, her knuckles white from the pressure. She stands before three others who sit around a table, staring at her as if waiting for her to perform, while Fletcher—the guy introducing her—remains rooted next to her, beaming.

She glances around the high school gym; half of the fluorescent lights above them are busted out, casting the room in a darkish hue. There are no other chairs besides the three occupied ones, and the rest of the floor is entirely open, the stands pushed into the walls.

Eva can't put her finger on it, but it's *wrong.* All wrong. The way her heartbeat has doubled, the hair standing on her arms – a pit in her stomach warning her to *get out*. But she can't. She was sent there for a reason. If she can fix the PR nightmare in the middle of nowhere, surely, she can land a job anywhere after this, maybe in the city—where the traffic can drown out the noise in her head like all the unwanted thoughts that never seem to stop.

"Evangeline?" Fletcher asks, snapping her out of her spiral, his smile slipping.

"Eva," she blurts. "Just Eva is fine. Sorry. What were you saying?"

"That's Milo there on the left; he's been here the longest."

Milo's gaze never leaves hers, unblinking. His eyes are endless depths of black as he leans forward. "Evangeline means good news, right? Are you here to bring us some good news?"

She tries to offer a small reassuring smile, but it becomes more of a grimace.

Fletcher continues undisturbed, "In the middle is Lionel and, last but not least, Claire."

Lionel only nods, his sunken cheeks even hollower in the dim lighting. Claire's bright, unnaturally green eyes narrow as if deciding whether Eva can be trusted.

That makes two of us, lady.

The more Eva tries to focus on them, the more her mind plays tricks. None of their faces seem quite… right. It's almost like looking at a hologram, where the image might glitch if you stare too closely. And their skin—all different shades fade into a weird, unhuman gray, but it can't be; it's only in Eva's head. *Isn't it?*

"H-hi, it's nice to meet you all," Eva finally stutters, smoothing out her blazer with her free hand before giving a fake, trill laugh. "I noticed this place is kind of a ghost town on my way in. I'm hoping I can help with that."

Another light flickers out above, submerging everyone in shadows.

Fletcher's white teeth gleam in the darkness. "I'm sure you can."

"I think…" Eva starts, struggling to swallow as ice forms down her spine.

His voice seems oddly familiar, but how? That's impossible. They've only just met. But its deep, melodic tone tugs at a memory twisted inside her head. *Get out now,* the rational part of her brain hisses.

Of course, she doesn't listen. She has a job to do.

"I think I'd like to meet the others in town, check out the businesses, see where we're at, and then go from there. Will tomorrow work?"

"Sure, sure. I think we're all available tomorrow, right, gang?" asks Fletcher.

"I'm sorry." She blinks at the few bodies in front of her who sit as still as statues. "Is this *everyone?*"

Fletcher runs a hand through his mop of black hair before shrugging. "This is it."

Now, the panic bells are *definitely* ringing.

Why would the temp agency send her if only a handful of people lived here? Sure, she needed a challenge to prove she was worth it, but there's a difference between hard work and completely impossible.

"Do you mind…" Eva adjusts the strap on her shoulder again. "Sorry, excuse me. I just need to make a quick call," she calls over her shoulder as she rushes out of the gym.

Once outside, she gasps down the cold air, filling her lungs as a tremor runs through her. Her hands shake as she dials a number on her phone, pacing the empty parking lot lit by moonlight.

I can do this. Don't freak out now.

Images of living in a city flash in her mind, the never-ending lights, the bustle of the street; this is her only means of escape, her one chance at freedom… if she can just—

"Hello, you've reached Corporation Staffing. Leave a message, and an agent will return your call as soon as possible."

Her insides turn to liquid, her scalp tingling.

That voice… That can't be… No—

"Hi, this is Eva Jenkins." Her voice shakes on the way out. "I think there's been a mix-up with my assignment. Please call me back as soon as possible." She hits the end button, forcing herself not to throw her phone. It's not like she could afford another one.

But that man's voice on the machine. It really sounded like—

"Everything okay?"

Eva startles, clutching her phone to her chest as she spins around.

Fletcher throws up placating hands as he steps out from under the awning, the moon lighting up his unnaturally pale face. "Sorry, didn't mean to scare you."

"Oh, it's okay," she lies, shaking her head, her brown curls shifting with the motion. "Just jumpy from the long trip."

He lowers his arms, moving a step closer. "No doubt. I'm glad you're here, though. It's about time."

She licks her lips, her mouth suddenly dry, and does her best to force a smile, but her face seems frozen. The pit in her stomach expands until she's sure she's about to vomit.

The night around her is suffocating, and it's more than her anxiety talking. This is something *else.*

Eva knows what's real and what's not, what's safe and what isn't.

And this *isn't.*

It's Fletcher's voice on the voicemail, and judging by the knowing look he's giving her, he understands she's finally put it together.

Eva redials the last number without breaking eye contact, her vision blurred by tears when Fletcher's phone rings in his shirt pocket.

He smiles that sickening grin again, shaking a finger at her. "You're good. You've figured it out sooner than most. You do deserve a promotion." He takes another step closer as Eva steps back, her throat tightening, the bile scorching on the way up.

"The thing about Ashridge is… we're not just a *ghost town.* We're a town *full of ghosts*. And do you know what ghosts need to stick around?" He circles Eva like prey as her feet remain planted on the pavement. "Energy. New blood."

"Please let me go," Eva begs as a single tear falls.

He brushes it away with a cold thumb in a soft caress. "We can help you, you know. Fix those thoughts in your head that keep you up late at night. What you're trying to escape… *who* you're running from. Aw, come on now. Don't cry."

He circles again. His voice registers in such an understanding pitch that she wants nothing more than to believe him, but the goosebumps running along her arms remind her he's a monster.

Fletcher stops in front of her, tucking a piece of hair behind her ear. Her jaw locks, and though she screams inside her head, the words don't slip past her lips.

"But what happened to your dad wasn't your fault, was it? No, that's right. He had it coming."

He's in her *head*. He knows everything.

"I can fix you," Fletcher soothes.

Eva's knees weaken as his hypnotic voice lulls her into submission.

No. This isn't what she wants, but her body still doesn't respond.

"What's going to happen to me?" The words choke her on the way out when they finally come.

Is she going to become like him? The rest of them? Be stuck here in this town forever? Or will they use up her energy, and she'll simply cease to exist?

Eva's eyelids droop as fatigue worms its way through her bones. Her phone drops from her fingers, cracking on the pavement. Her bag slips from her shoulder, landing in a heap at her feet. Shadows creep into her vision, and though she fights it, she struggles to stay awake.

The thoughts in her head… they're winning.

Just rest now, they seem to say.

She always had a hard time sleeping. This could be nice. It might be…

"Shh," Fletcher consoles as Eva's knees buckle. She's lifted off the ground when the darkness surrounds her. Then, like an afterthought, he whispers, "I promise you'll like it here."

THE END

KARMA CLEANERS AGENCY

Ashlyn Chase

A shrill ring pierced the silence. I dropped my doodling pencil, grabbed the phone and chirped, "Karma Cleaners" into the receiver.

"Is dis da place dat fixes your fate an' shit?"

"Uh—yes." I had learned not to launch into a long-winded explanation of Karma, energy, or a 'what goes around, comes around' philosophy until asked. Most people who came to me knew they were in for it. "May I ask how you heard about us?"

"Bubba sent me."

"Ah, yes. Bubba. I remember him." *How could I forget my first assassin?*

"He said you could fix it sos I don't go to Hell."

"Actually, I'm not the one who needs to put in the effort. That's up to you. Are you ready to do whatever is necessary to clean your Karma?"

"Depends."

Wrong answer. "What do you mean?"

"Well, like I'm not gonna parade trew da streets in a pink tutu and tights."

"No one here would ask you to do that."

"Okay, den. What do I gotta do?"

"Well, the first step is to come in for an interview."

"Huh? Like a job interview?"

"No. It's more like an informational interview. We need to know exactly what we're dealing with."

"I don't gotta confess to anything in writing, do I?"

"No, our counselors are aware of the risks you take by talking to anyone. Many of them are former clients, and they would never have you write or sign anything. *Except the check.*

"Fine. Now what? Do I make an appointment an' shit?"

Oh, the things I could say…but won't. "Yes. When can you come in?"

"Da sooner da better. I got cancer an' I'm dyin' over here."

And so begins my day. This is not an unusual situation—in fact, it's fairly typical. Something happens—usually a life-threatening situation—to make some low-life open his or her eyes to the harm and chaos they've caused. It's usually at the eleventh hour, but we do as much as we can within their time frame.

You might wonder how they can possibly undo the damage. It's not so much a matter of undoing. It's more like counteracting—back-peddling and moving forward in a new direction, if you will. Sometimes I feel like we have to re-raise certain clients who were messed up from the get-go.

I assign the guy to Joe, one of my best success stories, and arrange an appointment for later that day. It's best to get them right in—before they can change their fickle, sociopathic, little minds.

Behind the storefront, which looks like a typical dry-cleaning operation, is the hub of the agency. I have a small office and all phone calls come through me. Sure, some people want to know if we can get ketchup out of a tux, but I send those calls up front.

Now to give Joe a heads-up. I dial his mobile phone.

"H--hello."

By the winded way he answers, I can tell I've interrupted something.

"Joe. Are you okay?"

"Yeah, I'm fine boss. I was just lifting weights."

Joe is one of my better counselors. He works as a bouncer now that he's stopped robbing banks, and he can handle the scariest ex-con or mobster.

"I have a client for you. He's coming in at three this afternoon. Can you be here by 2:30?" I hate to admit I'm chickenshit when it comes to hanging out alone with some of our scarier clients, but I'd be stupid if I wasn't.

"Sure, boss."

That's a good boy. "Great. Oh, and Joe?"

"Yeah?"

"Bring your brass knuckles—just in case. He sounds like a mean one."

"They usually are."

* * * *

That afternoon Joe walked in the back door, wearing his black leather jacket and black jeans. I smiled as he turned around to lock the door. Did I mention how great his butt looks in—well, anything? The rest of him was superb too. His dark brown hair just covered his collar. Thick eyelashes that didn't need guy-liner and full but not bushy eyebrows framed soulful brown eyes. I probably shouldn't ogle my employee, but hey—I'm human.

"How's it going, boss?"

I could ask him to call me by my first name, but I kind of like being *Boss*. It gives me an excuse to be bossy—which I am.

"Things are pretty status quo. We lost one, we gained one."

"Who did we lose?"

"The rock star. I guess he's too good for community service."

"Well, good riddance. He was an entitled, whiney, little brat anyway."

"Be careful. A bad attitude toward the clients will make your job even harder."

He chuckled. "And your attitude is so much better?"

"No. But I don't have to rehabilitate them. All I have to do is run the business, and I have an awesome attitude about the money we make."

Joe grinned, revealing a cute dimple, and my insides melted a little bit. I cleared my throat and tried to slap my 'Boss' persona back in place.

"There's something I've been meaning to ask you, Boss."

"Go ahead and ask. Raises will be given out at the yearly evaluation and bonuses are for brown-nosers. You're not in either situation."

He laughed. I like his laugh. More importantly, I like it when he laughs at my jokes.

The back door buzzed. *Damn.* I let him almost reach the door so I could see his luscious backside again, then stopped him. "He can wait a minute if your question isn't too complicated."

"It only requires a yes or no answer."

"Okay, that's simple enough. What is it?"

"Will you go out to dinner with me this weekend?"

My jaw dropped. Was this a date? A business meeting? "Depends. Who's paying?"

"I am, of course."

Yippeeee. It's a date. "I'll check my calendar."

* * * * *

So, Saturday night finally arrived. Joe pulled out my chair for me and everything. I tried to look casual. He didn't have to know I spent the day getting a facial, full body wax, and a new outfit. Speaking of which, the red satin teddy beneath my burgundy silk blouse felt positively sinful against my very bare skin.

"You look gorgeous," he said.

Give the man points for knowing how to open a conversation. "Thanks, you don't look half bad yourself. Is that Armani?"

He turned around and looked behind him. "Who?"

Oh well. Nobody's perfect.

He shrugged, then smiled at me. "I guess I didn't see him."

"That's okay."

"So, I've been meaning to ask…" he said quietly, "Why do you do it?"

"Do what? Karma Cleaners?"

"Yeah. I mean, I know why *I* have to do it. I'm cleaning up my own Karma, but I don't think you were ever arrested or anything, right?"

"Right. The thing is, I've never sacrificed anything in my life. It's the least I can do. Literally. The very least."

Joe laughed, then looked puzzled when I didn't crack a smile. "Wait. What?"

"I'm selfish. About as selfish as they come. It's not a sin, but it's not the nicest way to be."

"You're making up for being selfish?"

"Pretty much."

"By what? Not getting paid?"

I burst out laughing. "Oh, hell no. I get paid all right."

"Okay… I'm confused."

Color me not surprised. Look, there are no rules saying you must work. Even if you're born wealthy and never have to work a day in your life, most people would want to do something useful with their time, you know?"

"Uh… If you say so."

A smirk crossed my lips before I could squash it. I cleared my throat. "If you had all the money you needed and could do anything with your time, what would you do?"

Joe tipped back his head and gazed upward. "I don't know. I guess I never thought about it. I could see myself takin' a nice long vacation. Maybe enjoying the shade of a palm tree on a tropical island or something…"

"Okay. Well, up until recently I was doing less than that."

"Wow. Didn't you get bored?"

"Frequently."

"How did you hear about the agency?"

"Hear about it?"

"Yeah. I mean, you didn't invent it or anything, did you?"

"Actually, I did."

Joe's jaw dropped and he gaped at me for several seconds. "How?"

"Well, everyone knows about Karma, right? Not the Hindu Goddess. Just the concept she stands for."

"Yeah, pretty much."

"Well, one day I got flash of inspiration to start an agency to make bad people do good things."

His forehead wrinkled as he took that in. Finally, he scoffed. "Nah, I don't believe it."

"Believe it."

He leaned back in his chair and stared at me, agape.

"Look, it was one of those 'crazy things that just might work.'" I used air quotes and everything.

"I—I..."

He obviously needed a moment to recover. Mercifully, the waiter showed up and introduced himself. *Perfect timing*. He took our drink orders and scurried away.

Joe did look a little less pale after the waiter departed. He leaned in a whispered, "You made the whole thing up?"

I shrugged. "Are you expecting an apology?"

He shook his head. Not like a nonverbal, 'no', but more like he was clearing the cobwebs. "So, really...You really, really made the whole thing up?"

"Look, you enjoyed the feeling of helping kids at the community center, didn't you?"

"Yeah. It did me as much good as it did them. Maybe more."

"So, what's the problem? You gained some self-esteem, aren't robbing banks anymore, have a good job now, and a *great* boss…"

He leaned back and let out one of the loudest, booming, belly-laughs I've ever heard. As it went on and on, I wasn't sure if I should be insulted or embarrassed. People were staring at us. Normally, I don't give a rat's ass what other people think, but this was Joe. My friend. My crush.

"Shh… everyone's looking."

He struggled to get himself under control and wiped the tears leaking out of the corners of his eyes.

"And I thought the cons were on the other side of the desk."

The Ghostly Librarian

Lori DiAnni

I stood at the entrance of the annex to the old library, built a century ago. The stone walls were nearly hidden by ivy, its twisting vines crawling relentlessly up the weathered facade. Delicate leaves fluttered in the breeze, casting dancing shadows across the stone. The Gothic architecture cast long, eerie shadows in the fading twilight. It was odd to see such an ancient structure attached to the modern building. I hesitated, my breath catching in my throat. I was here for a story; a journalist chasing a tale of mystery and perhaps, if the rumors were true, the supernatural.

I entered the newer portion of the library and found Mrs. Thompson at the reception desk. We had met last week where I had decided to come tonight to start my research at the behest of my boss. She had worked there for decades, knew about the article I was writing and trusted me enough to lend me the key. She made me promise not to tell anyone about it.

She grinned. "Hello, Clara. You're here to do some research, am I correct?"

"Yes, I am. I can't wait to dive into the story of your resident ghost."

"You sound skeptical, Clara, but I tell you, the stories are true."

"Have you actually seen her?"

Mrs. Thompson winked. "Perhaps a couple of times, but only from a distance which is where I prefer my ghosts to be." She ended her sentence in a whisper as she leaned closer to me. "Do you have the keys?"

"Right here in my bag." I patted the side of my tote.

"Good. Remember, we close at nine. No one will come for you so if you lose track of time, you'll be spending the night with your ghost."

I shivered at the thought but returned her smile. "I'll make sure I'm out on time."

With that, I headed toward the back of the library where it connected to the old one. This older section of the library, now used primarily for storing artifacts and genealogy records, was off-limits to the patrons accept by appointment. Even the staff, who had seen glimpses of the ghost and heard whispers and cries, avoided it unless necessary.

I fished the key ring from my bag, the cool metal smooth against my fingers. I inserted the ancient key, and with a click, the heavy wooden door creaked open, its sound echoing through the silent halls. Dust motes danced in the slivers of light that pierced through the stained-glass windows, creating a mosaic of colors on the worn wooden floors. I stepped inside, the air cool and musty, filled with the weight of countless untold stories. Each step I took reverberated, breaking the stillness that seemed to have settled like a shroud over the entire building.

My boss, a lover of anything supernatural, had assigned me to write a story about the rumors of ghosts at the century-old library. It was supposed to be a captivating piece, blending history and mystery, but as I ventured deeper into the labyrinth of bookshelves, I realized it was much more than that. As I walked, I couldn't shake the feeling of being watched. The hair on the back of my neck prickled with unease.

As I ventured deeper down the hall, the shadows seemed to grow darker, the air heavier. I trailed my fingers along the spines of the books, feeling the rough texture beneath my fingertips. I imagined the stories these old books held and wondered about the people who had written them. A sudden chill ran down my spine, and I stopped, listening intently. There it was again—a soft whisper, like a breath of wind through the pages of a forgotten book.

"Hello, Clara."

The voice was barely audible, yet it sent a shiver down my spine. I spun around, my heart pounding in my chest, expecting to see someone standing nearby, but the library was empty, the silence oppressive. I swallowed hard; my mouth dry as I forced myself to move forward.

"Who's there?" I called out, my voice sounding small and uncertain in the vastness of the library. There was no response, only the echo of my own words. I took a deep breath, steeling myself against the rising tide of fear.

I continued down the aisle, the weight of the silence pressing down on me. As I rounded a corner, I caught a glimpse of movement out of the corner of my eye. A figure, pale and ethereal, stood at the far end of the aisle. I blinked, and it was gone. My heart raced as I approached the spot where I had seen the apparition, my footsteps tentative and slow. So, it was true. The library was haunted.

The air grew colder, the chill seeping into my bones. I felt her presence before I saw her—a young woman in her early twenties, with long, flowing auburn hair, wearing an outfit from a bygone era; her form translucent, standing with an air of melancholy. She floated a few inches above the floor.

"Who are you?" I asked, my voice trembling and barely above a whisper. I gripped the edge of a nearby shelf, steadying myself and preventing myself from running in the opposite direction.

She smiled, a sad, wistful expression. "I am Evelyn Whitaker. I've been waiting for someone like you."

Her voice was soft, almost musical, and it filled the air around us. I felt a strange sense of calm wash over me, despite the fear that gripped my heart. "How do you know my name?" I asked, taking a step closer.

"I heard you talking to Mrs. Thompson. You didn't see me, but perhaps you felt my presence. A chill, maybe?"

I nodded. I remembered the day last week when I had spoken to Mrs. Thompson about my assignment, and I distinctly recalled feeling a chill and a sense of being watched.

"You have a gift, Clara," she said, her green eyes intense. "You can see me, hear me…sense me."

I swallowed hard, trying to process what was happening. Evelyn's expression grew somber. "I believe you can help me."

"Help you? How?"

"I need you to uncover the truth of my past. I need someone to reunite me with my love, Jonathan Hart."

I certainly hadn't expected this when my boss handed me the assignment. Writing about a possible haunting was one thing, but coming face to face with one who wanted my help, was another story altogether. Her words hung in the air, heavy with the weight of years of silence. My journalistic instincts battled with a growing sense of empathy, but I relented. "I'll help you," I said, my voice firm despite the fear that still lingered. "But I need to know everything."

She nodded, her form flickering like a candle in the wind. "Follow me," she said, turning and gliding down the aisle. I walked behind her, my footsteps silent on the worn floor. She led me down a dark hallway and stopped at a door. A sign was attached to it: **Do Not Enter. Restricted Area! Only Authorized Staff Allowed.** Evelyn glided through the door.

I withdrew the old keyring once more and inserted the other key into the lock. With a satisfying click, the door creaked open. I hurried inside and halted, staring at the room before me. Cobwebs clung to every surface and hung like a shredded curtain from the ceiling. Decades of dust shrouded the leather armchair, sofa, and a small table with a Tiffany lamp, obliterating their colors, giving them a ghostly appearance as well. It had once been a place of comfort, a refuge from the outside world for Evelyn. I could envision her sitting there, lost in a book, oblivious to the passage of time.

"This was my sanctuary," Evelyn said, her voice barely above a whisper. "Where I found solace in the stories of others. And…where Jonathan and I met in secret." She turned to face me; her eyes filled with a sorrow that seemed to span decades. "I fell in love," she said simply. "But our love was forbidden. Jonathan was from a rival family, the Harts, and our romance was doomed from the start."

I felt a pang of sympathy for her. "Do you know what happened to him?" I asked, sensing there was more to the story.

She nodded. "He was taken from me, brutally," she said, her voice breaking. A tear rolled down her pale face. “We are unable to find peace until we are reunited."

Her words hung in the air, and I felt a chill run down my spine. This was more than just a ghost story—this was a tale of love and loss, of souls bound by a tragedy that had echoed through the decades.

"I'll help you," I said, my voice steady with conviction. "I'll uncover the truth and find a way to reunite you with your love."

Evelyn's eyes filled with gratitude. "Thank you, Clara," she said softly. "You are my last hope."

I nodded as she shimmered away. I left the room, locked it behind me, and headed down the dark hallway. What had I just agreed to? Helping a ghost solve a century-old mystery was hardly the type of assignment I had envisioned when my editor had tasked me with this story.

Several minutes later, I stepped into the crisp September night, the stars twinkling in the clear night sky. I took a deep breath, knowing I was doing the right thing. This was more than just a story—it was a chance to bring peace to two restless souls, and I was determined to see it through, no matter what it took.

# # #

The following night, I headed back to the library. I waved to the librarian at the desk, who acknowledged me with a nod, but didn’t really pay attention to me. I felt a mix of anticipation and trepidation as I walked through the newer section and headed for the big oak doors leading to the old library. I had until nine to delve into Evelyn’s tragic past. She had haunted my thoughts all day, and I knew that tonight, I would confront her ghostly form and delve deeper into the mystery that had ensnared her soul.

The moment I stepped inside the old library, a chill enveloped me, colder than the night air outside. The ancient library seemed even darker than before, the shadows deeper and more oppressive. I glanced around, half expecting Evelyn to appear before me. The silence was suffocating, broken only by the faint creak of the wooden floorboards under my feet.

"Evelyn?" I called out softly, my voice barely above a whisper.

There was no immediate response, but the air grew colder still, and I felt a presence behind me. I turned slowly, and there she was, her form shimmering in the dim light. Her eyes were filled with a mixture of sorrow and hope as she looked at me.

"You came back," she said, her voice a gentle whisper that seemed to echo through the empty library. "I didn't think you'd come back."

"I promised I would help you," I replied, my voice steady despite the fear that still lingered. "But I need to know more. I need to understand what happened."

Evelyn nodded, her expression somber. "I will tell you everything," she said. "But it is not an easy story to hear."

I took a deep breath, bracing myself for what was to come.

She motioned for me to follow her, and we moved toward the sanctuary, our steps silent on the worn floor. Evelyn gestured for me to sit, but I declined. Perhaps she couldn't see the layers of dust and cobwebs in her spectral world, but I remained standing.

Evelyn stood before me, her translucent form glowing faintly in the darkness. "Jonathan," she began, her voice tinged with sadness, "was the son of a wealthy family, as was I. Although I did not need to work, I wanted to be a librarian. It was my greatest desire." Folding her hands, she continued as she glided past me. "We met by chance one rainy afternoon. He came into the library to escape the rainstorm, and from the moment our eyes met, I knew my life would never be the same." There was a whisper of a smile on her translucent face. "We fell in love," she continued, her eyes distant as if she were reliving those moments. "But our families were enemies, competitors in the shipping business, locked in a bitter feud that had lasted for generations. We knew our love was forbidden, but we couldn't stay away from one another."

Her voice trembled with emotion, and I felt a pang of empathy for her. "We met in secret," she said, "here in this room, where no one would find us. It was our sanctuary, a place where we could be together without fear." Evelyn cast her gaze downward and sighed. "We were…" Evelyn paused and glanced away.

"What happened?" I prompted, sensing she didn't want to share something.

Evelyn's expression darkened. "One night, we were discovered. My father found us in a compromising position and flew into a rage. He forbade me from seeing Jonathan again and threatened to disown me if I disobeyed." Tears shimmered in her eyes. "I didn't care if I was disowned. I loved Jonathan," she whispered, her voice breaking. "We had made plans that night to run away, to escape the town and start a new life together. But before we could leave," Evelyn's form flickered, and she took a deep, shuddering breath. Her pale hands were clasped tightly, trembling. "Jonathan was killed," she said, her voice barely audible. "I was devastated. In my grief, I confronted my father, here, in this room. I wanted the truth. I demanded an explanation."

"And did he give you one?"

She shook her head. "He said, what was done, was done." Her eyes met mine, filled with an unspoken plea. "Something horrible happened to me but I don't remember." She thrust her hands over her face, sobbing. "I need to know the truth. I have been trapped here ever since, my soul bound to this place, unable to move on."

"Evelyn," I said softly, "I will do everything I can to help you find peace. But I need to know more about Jonathan. Where is he now?"

Her eyes filled with sorrow. "His spirit is trapped as well," she said. "Separated from mine, lost in the void between worlds. I can feel his presence, but I cannot reach him. You must help us find each other, Clara. It is the only way we can be free."

I nodded, my resolve strengthening. "I will," I promised. "Are there any clues, anything that can help me piece together what happened?"

Evelyn's form flickered again, and she seemed to gather herself. "There are letters," she said. "Hidden in this room. They contain our correspondence, our plans to escape. They may hold the key to finding Jonathan."

"Where?" I could grab the letters now and bring them home.

"They're hidden beneath the tabletop over there." Evelyn pointed a ghostly finger to the round table. "If you look closely, there is a spring beneath the table that will release a compartment. There you will find the letters and my diary."

I scrambled over to the table and felt beneath the edge. My fingers brushed against a button. I pushed it, and to my surprise and delight, a portion of the tabletop slid open. Peering into the opening, I grinned and looked back at Evelyn. "There's a box in here." I lifted out the metal box, its top engraved with the initials J and E.

"I hope these will help you."

I glanced at my phone. It was time to leave. "I'll read them," I said. "And I'll come back tomorrow."

Evelyn's eyes filled with gratitude. "Thank you, Clara," she said softly. "You are our only hope."

As I left the library that night, I couldn't wait to get home and delve into Evelyn's letters and diary.

# # #

The morning sun filtered through my apartment windows, casting puddles of sunlight over the scattered letters on my desk. I sipped my coffee as I read the pages of Evelyn's diary. Each entry painted a vivid picture of her love for Jonathan and their desperate hope to escape the suffocating grasp of their feuding families.

July 15, 1912

My Dearest Diary,

Today, Jonathan and I spent the afternoon by the river. The summer sun was warm, and the gentle flow of the water made everything feel serene. He looked at me with such love in his eyes, and I knew, without a doubt, that I wanted to spend the rest of my life with him. We spoke of dreams far away from Salem, away from the hatred and bitterness that surrounded our families. How I wish we could leave tonight and never look back.

I could envision them, sitting by the river clasping hands, leaning into one another as young lovers do, their hopes and dreams palpable. There were several other entries as Evelyn wrote about their growing love. The tone had shifted dramatically in the next entry written just a week later.

July 22, 1912

Diary,

Father has been acting strangely. He watches me with suspicion and questions my every move. He's heard rumors, I'm sure of it. Jonathan and I have tried to be so careful, but in this small town, secrets are hard to keep. I'm terrified of what Father will do if he finds out about us. His temper is fierce, and his pride even fiercer. I fear for Jonathan's safety more than my own.

July 30th, 1912

Diary,

Father brings me to the library in his carriage on the days I work and picks me up. I know it's because he wants to make sure I do not meet up with Jonathan after work with an excuse that I am working late. If father only knew that Jonathan and I meet in secret in this sanctuary. No one comes here. No one knows of the place I've created for me and Jonathan.

I read of Evelyn's growing love for Jonathan and the secret visits in the sanctuary when she wasn't working. I also read the fear for her and for Jonathan as the month of August drew into September.

September 4th, 1912

Dear Diary,

Father confronted me today. He demanded to know if the rumors were true, if I was seeing Jonathan Hart. I lied and told him that there was nothing between Jonathan and I. Saying those words cut through my heart as though I was betraying our love. My father must've seen the truth in my eyes. His rage was terrifying, and he swore that if I didn't end things with Jonathan, he would make sure we both regretted it. His threats are not idle. I've heard what he's capable of. I don't know what to do. Jonathan and I have talked about running away, but where would we go? How would we survive?

Evelyn's fear leapt off the page, her anxiety practically tangible. I turned to the next entry, hoping to find some respite for her. The entries grew more desperate, her handwriting shaky, the ink smudged from what I imagined were tears.

September 7, 1912

Diary,

We've decided to leave. Jonathan says we can go to New York, start fresh. He has some money saved, and we'll figure it out together. But Father is watching me like a hawk. I can't leave the house without an excuse, and I'm afraid he'll follow me. We need to act soon, before it's too late.

I felt a knot forming in my stomach as I read on. The urgency in her words was clear, the danger looming ever closer.

September 9, 1912

My Dearest Diary,

Tomorrow is the night. Jonathan and I have everything ready. We will meet by the old oak tree by the river at midnight and take the train to New York. My heart is racing. This is our only chance at happiness. I pray that we make it, that we can finally be together without fear.

I turned the page to find the next entry dated September 11, 1912. The handwriting was barely legible, as though written in a state of utter distress.

September 10, 1912

Diary,

I arrived at the river, but Jonathan never showed. My heart sank as I waited in the dark, the minutes stretching into hours. Father had kept me at a late dinner with friends, and I couldn't leave without raising suspicion. He noticed my distress, my constant peering at the clock, and he smirked at me once or twice. When we finally got home, I had to wait until my parents were asleep before I could sneak out. By then, it was too late. I fear something terrible has happened. I hate Father for what he might have done. I miss Jonathan so much it hurts to breathe.

The words in the next entry were barely decipherable. I traced a teardrop on the page and inhaled.

September 11, 1912

Diary,

Jonathan is dead. They say it was an accident, that he slipped and drowned. But I know in my heart that it wasn't an accident. I suspect Father and his men ambushed him. I have no proof, but the thought haunts me. I need to confront Father, to know the truth. Yet, I hope beyond hope that he had nothing to do with it. I hate him, Diary. I hate him for the possibility that he could have done this. And I miss Jonathan so much it hurts to breathe.

September 15, 1912

Dear Diary,

Mrs. Hart came into the library today asking to speak to me in private. She looked lost and broken. I truly knew how she felt. I was living her heartbreak. I was surprised she came to see me, but despite our families' feud, I couldn't turn her away. Mrs. Hart wiped her tears away as she spoke fondly of Jonathan and knew how much he loved me. She had hoped both sides could've accepted our love and perhaps end the bitterness between the families. I did my best to comfort her although my own grief was unbearable. What surprised me was when she opened a small box saying it was for me from Jonathan. It was a beautiful heart-shaped locket. She also handed me a letter. She told me that she believed the locket held a part of Jonathan's soul and perhaps it was a way for him to be close to me during my darkest days.

September 15, 1912

Dear Diary,

As I write this, my heart is breaking. I'm in the sanctuary where Jonathan and I could truly be together. I am hollow inside. Father is relentless. He found me crying in my room. He said I brought this upon myself, that I should have obeyed him. As I write this, I have vowed to never fall in love again. I've tucked the locket away in this room where I can look at it without fear of Father finding it at home. Without Jonathan, nothing matters. I keep hearing his voice, seeing his face. I'm not sure how much longer I can bear this pain.

Tears blurred my vision as I read the final entry, written just a few days later.

September 18th, 1912

Dear Diary,

I wanted to attend Jonathan's funeral today, but father forbade it. He locked me in my room. I am so angry with him. I've decided to leave on my own, just as Jonathan and I had planned. I will leave Salem behind, never to return. I've packed my belongings where they are safe in the sanctuary and will leave tonight.

I turned the pages to see if she had written anything else, but the pages were blank. I closed the diary, my chest tight with emotion. Evelyn's torment was almost unbearable to read. Her father's cruelty and the hopelessness of her situation had driven her to the edge. The weight of her sorrow pressed heavily on me. I knew that I had to uncover the final pieces of her story, to bring her the peace she so desperately sought.

Their love had been real, their hope genuine, but the forces against them had been too powerful. The diary had given me a window into Evelyn and Jonathan's world, a world filled with love and tragedy. I knew that I had to tell their story, to ensure that their love was not forgotten. And I had an idea of how to reunite Evelyn and Jonathan.

"I have to find that locket," I said, my voice filled with determination.

# # #

I made my way to the sanctuary, my footsteps echoing in the silent hallway. I unlocked the heavy wooden door and stepped inside, the familiar chill enveloping me. "Evelyn?"

She appeared, looking hopeful when she saw me. "Clara," my name came out in a rush. "What did you discover?"

"More than I wanted to, I'm sorry to say." I shook my head. "But the diary ended abruptly. The last thing I read in your diary was that you were planning on leaving Salem, for good, and you would take the locket with you, to have Jonathan with you forever." I brushed my hair back and sighed. "Something happened after that. Something tragic. Do you remember anything? Anything at all?"

Her eyes filled with tears. She bit her pale lip. "I remember now. I had packed my bags that day and kept them at the library. I was going to leave when my parents had fallen asleep. I was going to come here, grab my things along with the locket and then take the train, but…" She inhaled deeply as if to gather her thoughts or the courage to explain more. "When I left my room and started down the stairs, my father came out of his room." She twisted around as her body blinked in and out. "He was furious with me. He demanded to know where I was going. When I refused, he raised his hands into fists. He ordered me back to my room and forget about the whole debacle with Jonathan. How could he ask me to forget about my true love? He was like a madman, Clara! When I refused and took a step down, he lunged for me. He struck me and …" Evelyn cried out, her gaze widening, as she held a hand to her mouth. "I twisted away from him and fell down the stairs."

"That's when you died," I said softly, wanting to reach out and console her sobbing form, but I couldn't. I stood there, helpless. "From the documents I've read, your father told everyone that you had committed suicide." I stepped closer to her. "I'm so sorry."

"My poor mother!" She shrank back against the wall as though trying to sit or kneel in her grief. "My father did this to me. He cursed me to this existence!"

"But you don't need to live this existence anymore, Evelyn." I paused then held out my hands in supplication. "Evelyn, I am so, so sorry for what you had to endure. I…can't imagine knowing your father killed the man you loved and was involved in your death as well."

Evelyn straightened. "Thank you, Clara." Her form grew a bit brighter. "Did you find any answers to help me and Jonathan?"

"I think I may have." I peered at the table. "You believed that the locket held Jonathan's soul, right?"

"Yes, I do." Evelyn smiled. "You think the locket has the power to bring us together?"

"I sure hope so." I looked around the room. "Where is the locket? Where did you hide it?"

She lifted her hand and pointed to the table. "It's in the compartment where you found the box."

I moved quickly to the table and felt beneath the edge of the tabletop until my fingers brushed against the hidden spring. With a gentle push, the compartment slid open. I moved my hand around to the far edge and with a gasp felt a piece of cloth.

"Evelyn," I whispered, "I found it." I pulled it out then unwrapped the faded cloth. Her ghostly form appeared beside me, her eyes wide with wonder.

"The locket," she breathed, reaching out a translucent hand to touch it. "I can feel him."

I opened the locket, my breath catching in my throat. Inside was a tiny portrait of Jonathan and Evelyn, their faces filled with hope and love. I could feel the power of their connection, a tangible presence that seemed to radiate from the locket.

Evelyn's gaze met mine, filled with gratitude and determination. "Thank you." Tears glistened in her eyes.

"Are you ready to see Jonathan again, after all this time?"

Evelyn's translucent face lit up, giving her a silvery hue. "Do you think it will work?"

"I do. We need to go to the river," I said. "Where Jonathan was taken from you. It's the only way."

She nodded. "Let's go."

As the sun began to set over the river, I stood there, wondering if my idea would work. The leaves rustled in the breeze, and the scent of autumn filled the air. The river's edge was quiet, the water flowing gently over the rocks.

Evelyn's form shimmered beside me as we stood at the spot where Jonathan had been found. She glanced around, twisting her hands. "This is where Jonathan died, isn't it?"

I nodded. "I'm so sorry, Evelyn, that this had to happen to the two of you, but I hope my plan works."

Evelyn peered at the river. "This is where we were going to leave and start a new life."

"And this is where you will finally be reunited," I said with a smile of assurance. I held the locket tightly, feeling its weight and significance. I held out the locket and closed my eyes. "Jonathan," I called out softly, "Please show yourself. Evelyn is here."

For a moment, there was only silence. Then, the air grew colder, and a faint light began to glow beside Evelyn. Jonathan's ghostly form appeared, his eyes filled with longing and love.

"Evelyn," he whispered, reaching out to her and clasping her close to him.

Tears streamed down Evelyn's face. "Jonathan, I've missed you so much." She clung to him, sobbing.

I opened the locket and held it between them. "This locket holds a part of your soul, Jonathan. Your mother believed it could bring you together."

Jonathan's eyes filled with understanding. "Thank you, Clara," he said. "You've given us a chance to find peace."

"I love you, Evelyn," Jonathan whispered, leaning into her, his smile brilliant.

"And I love you, Jonathan," she replied, caressing the side of his face, love shining in her eyes.

As I watched, the locket began to glow, a soft light enveloping Evelyn and Jonathan. Their forms shimmered and then merged, becoming one brilliant light that filled the air around us. The light grew brighter, and then, with a final burst of brilliance, it faded, leaving only the peaceful sound of the river.

I stood there for a long moment, the locket still warm in my hand. The weight of their love and their tragedy hung in the air, but I felt a sense of closure and peace.

As I walked back to my apartment, I glanced up at the stars twinkling in the night sky. I knew that Evelyn and Jonathan had finally found the peace they deserved, their souls reunited after a century of being lost in the darkness.

Once I was home, with a cup of tea in hand, I headed to my desk to write; to tell the truth of Evelyn and Jonathan. The words flowed effortlessly. I was determined to share their love and their sacrifice with the world. As I typed, I felt a sense of fulfillment, knowing that I had played a part in bringing them together. This was more than just an article—it was a testament to the enduring power of love, a love that had transcended even death.

THE END

Of Curses and Swans

A Swan Lake Retelling

Part of the Once Upon a Darkened Night Series

Nicole Zoltack

Chapter One

Russick, Liscow Mountains, the first of April 1096

My wings flap as I depart my abode. I am not the owl I appear to be but rather a sorcerer. For some time now, I have spent more and more time as an owl as it is the only way I can come close to the Princess Olesia of Russick. So utterly enchanting with her long blond hair and stunning blue eyes, the princess has captured my heart entirely.

And today is the day. Today is the day I finally reveal to her my love. I have been watching her from afar, never once allowing myself the hope that she might one day come to know me and return my affections, but I am powerful and not altogether terrible looking, even with my yellow eyes, slightly greenish complexion, and black as coal hair. No, I do not look altogether human, my magic perhaps altering my appearance some from the norm, but inside, I still have a heart, and I can love as much as any other.

It does not take me long to reach Chetlas Castle. I fly about the turrets, trying to determine which would be best, for me to enter through the drawbridge as any ordinary person or else to arrive within the princess's chamber. Well, perhaps not her chamber, but the hallway…

Deciding that is the best course of action, I fly through a window into the room next to the princess's chamber. My owl feet touch the window ledge, and I flutter down to the ground, transforming in a puff of smoke to my human form. I pat my hair and adjust my attire—dressed all in black with a cape that matches my skin complexion, the underside as red as anyone's blood, myself included. My belt is black as well, the buckle an oval citrine that nearly matches my eye color.

I blow out a breath and try to steady my nerves as I head out to the hallway. My boots echo with every step, and I pause before forcing aside my nervous anxiety. My knuckles rap against the princess's door, and I glance about, a bit shocked that there are no guards present to protect her from intruders.

Not that I wish her any harm. Not in the slightest.

The door opens, and the object of my desire stands in front of me. Tall and slender, with a long neck, as graceful as any bird, Princess Olesia eyes me. Her gown is all white, and given that I can shape my form into that of a bird, I tend to think that each person has a bird inside of them as well, and Olesia is certainly a swan if I have ever seen one. Majestic. Beautiful. Graceful. Strong. Regal.

"Who are you?" she demands, her voice a bit harsher than I thought it would be.

I bow my head and then bow formally, striving to shower her with respect. "I am but a humble servant, Princess Olesia."

"You do not look humble."

I dare to glance up at her, still bowing. Her chin is lifted, so she appears to be looking down at me as if I am less than.

Which is the truth.

"Who are you?" she repeats. "Why should I not throw you out?"

"I am Rodian."

"Rodian?" Her lips curl into her lilting smile, and she shocks me by grabbing my hand and helping me to rise. "The sorcerer?"

I gape at her. "You have heard of me?"

"Indeed I have!" Her laugh is the most delightful sound in the world. "Come!"

She does not lead me into her chamber, not that that would be proper in the slightest, but the room she rushes me inside is not a tea room or a parlor of sorts. No, there are parchments filled with various maps of other kingdoms all over the world.

"What is all of this?" I ask. "Do you wish to see the world?"

Olesia laughs some more. "See the world? Yes, yes, but not merely just to see. With your help, perhaps I will not have to bother with my father's stuffy advisors any longer."

I furrow my brow. "Your father…"

"I know. It was so tragic when he and my mother died suddenly not even a month ago. Do you know that some think they were poisoned?" Olesia gives me a small smile. "Perhaps if you had been around then, we might know which kingdom to punish, but as we do not… I was thinking perhaps Sigil."

"Sigil? But they are so far away."

"You can turn into an owl, or so they claim. You could go there alone and take over their kingdom in my name. And then, as you fly back to me, you could claim every other kingdom that you fly over to return to Russick."

My mouth falls open. "What has Sigil done to deserve this?"

"They might have killed my parents."

"Princess, why would they do that?" I ask carefully.

I have no doubt that no one from Sigil did anything of the sort. Truthfully, I have not heard anything to suggest the princess's theory concerning her parents' deaths might be accurate. Her parents had been as beloved as herself, and Russick has known peace for over a century. Why would any kingdom make a move against us?

"With your help, Russick can be the largest kingdom of all? Why, we could expand all the way over to Fantasia!" Olesia claps her hands with delight. "What say you, Rodian? Will you help me?"

I swallow hard. "My princess, as much as I would love to assist you in anything that you desire…"

"You will not help me with this?" Her eyes narrow, and she now reminds me of a dark swan, strong and vicious and sharp, ready to attack if provoked.

I fiddle with the citrine on my belt. "Without proof that any kingdom has harmed your parents, I do not feel justified—"

"It is not for you to feel justified or not," she says simply. "You are one of my subjects, and you will do as I say."

"Your father's advisors…"

Her scowl does not mar her delicate beauty. "They do not wish to move against any other kingdoms either. I will not stand for this!"

I lower my head. As much as I love her, I do not know if I can do this. There is nothing inherently wrong or evil about ambition, but for her to want to take over neighboring kingdoms when there is no hint of any wrongdoing…

But what if she has the right of it? What if her parents had been killed?

"I will help you," I say slowly.

"You will?" Her eyes widen, and she claps her hands with delight. "Rodian, I am forever in your debt!"

She presses a kiss to my cheek, and I hate that she is drawing me in to consider something that might be evil.

Chapter Two

Russick, Chetlas Castle, the first of April 1096

"You will fly at one for Sigil, then?" she asks. "How long will it take for you to reach there? Once you are done with Sigil, you could head to— "

"I said I would help you," I say quietly, choosing my words carefully.

"Help me with my plan to make Russick a true power in the world." She embraces me, and it is not easy for me to not return the hug, but I somehow find the power not to and step back. Her arms slowly fall to her side, and she watches me critically.

"I will help you to discover if your parents had died by foul means or not. Poison, magic, anything of the like."

"You can do that?" Her red lips part. "You truly are powerful. Do you need to go to where they were buried or…"

"Merely their chambers. They were found dead in their bed, yes? That is what I heard."

"Yes, in their bed." She briefly shuts her eyes. "The advisors seek for me to take over their chamber, for me to be crowned queen, but I feel I cannot do either. I have not yet found my prince… my king… Perhaps he does not need to be a prince…" Her cheeks turn pink, and she looks away. "If you would follow me…"

"Anywhere, Princess Olesia."

The princess beams at me and directs me out of the room and throughout the castle. Many look at us, some even eyeing me with skeptical looks or even fear, perhaps at my appearance, but I, for one, am most grateful that not only does the princess not seem to mind my coloring but also that she would touch me, embrace me…

Without a word, she opens the double doors that grant us entry to her parents' chamber. There is the grand bed the king and queen slept in until their dying breath caused them to depart from this life.

I step up to the bed and hold out my hands. My magic allows me many great powers, and I can sense the royals' essence, their lives, what they had discussed here, what they felt, their hopes and desires, and much more.

But what I do not sense is much more telling.

Certain I have learned the truth of the matter, I turn to the princess.

"Which kingdom was responsible?" she breathes eagerly. "I will have their heads for this!"

I shake my head. "No, my princess. Your parents were not killed. They were not poisoned."

"Nonsense," she insists. "You are mistaken. For them to have both died the same night, that is too much of a coincidence—"

"Your mother died first," I say. "When your father stirred and woke to find his love had died, his own heart stopped, and he passed as well. I am sorry, but—"

"No," she snaps, stepping away from me. "You are misguided. Your magic has failed you. I am altogether certain—"

"What makes you so certain?" I murmur.

Her eyes widen and then narrow. "You do not presume to believe that I would have done something to my own parents! That is treason!"

"I would not ever dare suggest that," I protest.

Mostly because I know that is not the case. If not for that knowledge…

"You are no better than the other advisors!" she hisses.

"Why? Why must you take over neighboring kingdoms?" I beg.

"You do not understand!"

She is right. I do not understand her quest for powers.

"You love me, do you not?" she asks shrewdly.

I cannot deny the charge.

"Then do this for me!"

Likewise, I cannot do this. That she would try to convince me to use my magic for evil…

"Very well. If you will not help me, nor my father's advisors, well, I do not need you. I can be crowned queen without a husband, and then, I can do as I wish. The army will do my bidding, and…"

She continues to rant about her plans, but I cannot bear to listen, nor can I allow this to happen. I have no choice but to stop her.

"Swan by day," I murmur, "you'll cease your way. Swan by day, on the water you'll lay."

I hesitate before my magic can truly take form. She pays me no mind, but I cannot bring myself to curse her both day and night. Perhaps I am a fool, but my love is far too great for her. Ambition has blinded her, and I truly do get the sense that she believes her parents had been felled not through natural means but from outside forces. She is merely misguided, but if I can show to her one day that she can rise above her grief…

"But by night, your true form will be bright. By night, you'll be your prettiest sight. By night, you will no longer take flight. Princess at night, swan by day, I fear this is the only way. Princess at night, swan by day, the way to save the day."

The princess lets out a shocked whistle that swans can make as the magic sweeps over her, changing her into a swan. Her crown is now much too large for her small swan head, the crown falling down her slender neck.

With a last bit of magic, I have wind lift her crown upon her head and shrink it so that she is both a swan and a princess.

"Forgive me, princess," I murmur.

And she turns her back to me before rushing at me with her wings spread wide. Once more, I call upon my magic, this time banishing her to the lake near the castle where she can be with other swans.

And I? I return to my home in the mountains, hating myself for failing her and wondering how I might ever be able to make things right.

Chapter Three

Russick, Liscow Mountains, the first of May 1096

An entire month has passed since I cursed my love to be a swan. Thus far, I have gone to visit her every night to try to speak with her. She will either try to attack me, causing the other swans to also seek to harm me, or else she will ignore me entirely. If I dare to go near her during the sun-kissed hours, when she remains a swan, the swans will attack me even if she makes no move toward me. They have adopted her as their princess, their queen, and I almost wish I would allow the swans to harm me, even kill me, because what can I do to help her if she will not stand to see reason?

But surely, her hatred toward me grows each day and night, and a week passes when I do not bring myself to visit her, too ashamed of my failure.

On the ninth of May, at night, I think to perhaps go and see her. I will remain my owl and follow her, see what it is that she does at night. Does she speak to anyone? The kingdom has been in much disarray, given the princess's absence, and I had no choice but to tell her father's advisors what I had done. They sought to lock me away until they listened long enough to uncover her battle plans from the room she brought me to. They, like me, do not seek war with any of the neighboring kingdoms, and so they are endeavoring to find someone fit to rule over Russick in the event the princess can never be brought back to her senses. For now, the advisors are acting as a council of sorts to rule.

But Russick has a long history of being ruled by a king or queen, and I long for the princess to return to her seat if at all possible.

Yes, I will go and see her, and one day, perhaps all will be as it should be.

"Rodian!" a sharp, deep voice calls out.

I throw open the door to my house to see a gentleman wearing leggings, an overcoat, a short cape, and tall boots. The sword in his hand completes his look.

“You will release the princess from the curse you have placed upon her!” he shouts.

With a roar, he comes at me, and I chuckle as I snap my fingers. My magic renders his sword a weapon no more but a hundred butterflies that fly off.

“I do not know who you are, but you are not a worthy opponent. Did Olesia put you up to this? Does she seek to have me killed?”

“I will kill you myself,” the man shouts.

“Who even are you?” I ask, still amused.

“My name is Sevastian!”

“Sevastian?” I blink a few times. “Not the Prince of Medora?”

“One and the same,” he bellows, and he dashes forward to remove one of my swords that hangs on the wall.

I grimace. How had Olesia been able to contact the prince of a neighboring kingdom? And for him to have aligned himself with her…

“Do you know what the princess wishes to do?” I demand.

“I do, and I want the same. I will be her prince, and together, we will rule—”

“She loves you?”

“She does,” he says haughtily. “Our love will end this curse, will end you, and all will be as it should have been all along, before you poisoned her life, before you killed her parents!”

I gape at him. “She does not believe that I—”

"You lied to her time and again," he insists. "You do not deserve to live while she still breathes! You have one last chance, Rodian. Release her from the curse, or else I will kill you where you stand! I will strike you down, and it will be as if you had never blighted the world with your foul magic, you vicious, vile sorcerer!"

I do not wish to fight him, so I turn into my owl, but I do not think the prince is as swift as he is, and he slices one of my wings nearly off entirely.

I fall to the ground and barely have time to move out of the way of a swing that would have chopped my head. The blade he wields, one of my own, is magical, so I cannot merely heal myself nor turn it into something else as I had with his, but I have more than one magical blade, and I claim another in time to block and counter strike with my own sword.

"So these weapons are not merely decoration?" Sevastian grunts. "No matter. I will kill you and so save her! Olesia is my one and only love— "

He lies. I can see his heart. All he loves is ambition. I saw that once before in a heart as black and twisted as he. He looks to be about twenty, which would place in about five years the princess's junior, whereas I am five years her senior. For five and twenty years, the princess has lived, and if I can only free her from her own ambition, perhaps she will live five times that amount.

" —and you will die for what you have done to her, you coward!"

Sevastian comes at me, striking my shoulder with his blade. The pain I feel must be nearly equal to that which he feels because I accepted that he would injure me for the sake of myself striking him in near the same spot.

We are both injured, both wounded, both bleeding, and even I have to admit that he is the better swordsman. If we continue, I will be the one to fall, and then, Olesia and this prince will lay waste to kingdoms.

And it is all my fault. If I had only cursed Olesia to be a swan both day and night, she would not have been able to draw this man into the fight.

But I hoped to reach her heart, to turn her back to the light…

Not only have I failed her, but I now have no hope, either.

I will die and soon. I do not know much anymore, but I do know that.

Chapter Four

Russick, the lake near Chetlas Castle, the ninth of May 1096

The next several strikes the prince makes are easy enough to block as he does not have much strength behind the swings, but I lack the power to make any effort in counterattacks, and soon, he has wounded me several times over. I bleed from so many spots on my body, and I feel as if I might fall to my knees soon, and if I do that, it will be all over.

I stagger back, away from him, and I let my hand open. The sword clatters to the ground, and the slow-spreading smile on the handsome prince's face is decidedly chilling.

"Have you decided to stop fighting and accepting your fate?" he asks. "I will make this as painful as possible for you."

I ignore his promise, and despite the pain that fills me as I force my arms wide, I allow my magic to wash over me and transform into an owl for one final time. If I am to die, I will at least seek out Olesia one last time.

It is a struggle to flap my wings, but I manage to soar out of the house. Sevastian gives chase, but I can glide fairly quickly. I highly suspect he reached my house by riding a horse there, so he might be able to give chase, but he is wounded too.

My vision darkens several times during my flight, and it is only because of my owl vision that I can see in the darkness to avoid crashing into trees. Although it takes ages, I finally reach the lake. Is Olesia here? Has she one? She will be herself…

There is a rock on a hill overlooking the lake that I used to perch on, and I do so again now. My magic transforms me back to myself, and I can barely lift my head.

"You are not dead yet," Olesia says from behind me.

If I could, I would stand, bow even, but I can barely even lift my head. My blood drips onto the grass.

"I will be soon," I murmur. "Olesia, it is not too late. Turn back to the light."

"The light?" she crows. "You who doomed me to be myself only at night!"

"The moon is full this night."

"Bah. The sun is far more powerful."

"Who cares about power? Your father did not, nor did your mother."

"They cared only for peace, that is true, but the peace of Russick can be enjoyed elsewhere. We can spread peace—"

"We? You mean you and Sevastian?" I eye her. "He does not wish for peace. Is that what you claim to want now? Do you think me a proper fool?"

"I do not think you a fool at all," she retorts. "You cursed me and perhaps not without reason. I… I do now believe you are right. The other kingdoms… none of them would have sought to kill my parents. To love someone enough to not be able to live without them…I think that is a magic of sorts. Love… peace… They are similar, do you not think?"

"Yes," I say through a gasp of fresh pain. Even the push of the wind against me hurts. "Please, Olesia, leave the other kingdoms be. Release yourself from your ambition. Seek to rule only Russick as your parents had, and I will release you from the magic."

"From the magic. From the curse!"

"Olesia, be reasonable!"

"You cursed me!"

"And you sent a prince to kill me!"

She glances away, her lips twisted, and I allow myself to see to her heart. It is not as black as the prince's, and I realize then that the prince came to kill me of his own volition.

Yet, she could have stopped him and did not.

A horse neighs, and Sevastian glares at me. "You will die, Rodian. Olesia, back away from him! He remains dangerous."

Olesia shakes her head. "He will not harm me. He loves me."

"This foul man knows nothing of love," a clear, bell-like voice says.

I gape as Sevastian jumps down from his horse. He concealed from view that of my daughter, Olenya. Fifteen years of age, half my own age, a decade younger than Olesia, Olenya glares at me with contempt.

"He killed my mother," she says bitterly. "For that, he must die."

Sevastian chuckles and helps my daughter down from the horse. With his other hand, he draws a sword. "Do not worry, Olenya. You will be my bride, and together, we will take over the kingdoms, you and me."

I grit my teeth. "Olenya, please, do not listen to him. He is—"

"Do not speak to me," she shrieks. "Sevastian, do not delay. Kill him now before he can curse us as he had my mother!"

And Sevastian advances on me, evil both in his heart and glinting in his eyes.

Chapter Five

Russick, the lake near Chetlas Castle, the ninth of May 1096

The prince advances on me as I slowly slide to my feet. I have no weapon on me save for my magic. Seeing Olesia reinvigorated me, but to hear Olenya, my own daughter, slander me…

I hold up a hand, and Sevastian halts. He glances back at my daughter, who lifts her chin.

"Your mother sought to steal my magic," I hiss. "She pretended to love me, but she never did. It is because of her that I sought to gain the knowledge and wisdom to see to a person's heart, and—"

"Bah! You still lie!" she screams.

"No. She did steal some of my magic, and you want to know what she did with it? She destroyed all of Rothan."

"Your wife did that?" Olesia's eyes widen. "That town had two hundred persons living there! Everyone thought it was a terrible storm…"

"No. My wife did that. I had no choice. I… I killed her." I briefly shut my eyes before leveling Olesia with a pained look.

It is then that I can see her heart shift some.

"My wife wanted to control the town, but the mayor would not listen to her, and so… She could have killed him, I suppose, which would have been better than two hundred times that number, but no. She destroyed the town because of that one man and because I refused to help her. I did not know why I had fallen ill, not realizing that she stole my magic—"

"How did she do that?" my daughter cries. "You are making up lies—"

"Through a gemstone she was given by a witch," I say calmly. "This gemstone, in fact." I tap the citrine on my belt.

Olenya shakes her head. "You lie. That is all you ever do. Kill him already!"

Olesia moves to stand between myself and the prince. "Do not do this, Sevastian."

"You cannot help me," he hisses. "You are cursed."

"You would betray me like this? After you professed to love me?"

"I never loved you," he says with a snort. "We spoke a few times, and you think that is enough to know that you love me? I am sorry, princess, but if you do not move, I will kill you to reach him."

"Fly away, Rodian," Olesia cries as she rushes toward the prince.

"No!" I bellow.

My hands fall to the rock I sat on moments ago, and I infuse my magic into it, warping its shape to that of a sword. Swiftly, pushing my body to the limits, I bring up the sword in time to block Sevastian's attack. We dance a lethal number, trading blows, Sevastian mocking me all the while. At one point, his attack is so vicious that I stagger back, and he goes to strike Olesia down, her back to him.

"No!" I cry out.

I throw my sword. Before Sevastian can cut the princess, the rock-sword pierces through him. He gasps and falls to his knees. A tear trickles down his face as he grabs the hilt, and he slowly, inch by inch, forces it out of his body.

Olenya rushes over to his side. "Sevastian, hold still. I can heal you."

"She can?" Olesia murmurs to me.

"Perhaps. She is my daughter. She is a sorceress herself. She fled, though, from my side five years ago after—"

"After Rothan."

I nod.

Sevastian stares up at my daughter as blood leaks from the corners of his mouth. "You promised…"

"We will have what we want," she promises.

"You lied!" the prince cries, and he stabs my daughter straight through the chest.

I gasp, starting forward, but Olesia yanks on my arm.

"Do not," she warns.

My daughter slumps down, not moving, but the prince uses his sword and mine to stagger to his feet.

"You," he hisses, but he can barely drag himself forward before he collapses.

He is dead, and I twist free from the princess's grasp to rush to my daughter's side.

"Olenya, I am sorry. I failed—"

My apology is cut short as a sword pierces me from behind. The prince was not dead after all, and I turn my head to see his bitter, bloody smile before he falls down, this time truly dead.

I am dying. I have only seconds left, and I blindly wave my hand. My vision is black.

"Olesia, free from my curse, never fear the worse. Olesia, be free and know only glee. Be free, my love, and feel the warmth of the sun above. Day and night, enjoy the sun and moon bright."

My magic swirls around her just as the morning dawns, and she remains in her human form. I offer her a smile and wonder how many more heartbeats I have.

"I am so sorry," Olesia says, falling to my side. "Please, forgive me. I never… I never wanted any of this to happen. I… I did not think… I was a fool, but know this. I will give my life for yours. I can perhaps go and seek out the witch who aided your wife. I will give her whatever she asks for so that you might be saved."

"Do not," Olenya says through heaving gasps of air. "Do not seek witches. They… They lie. They twist… your mind… trick you…"

"My daughter…"

"You never told me the truth about Mother," she says. She crawls toward me and places her hand on the citrine. "I can feel the remnants of your magic. You spoke the truth."

"Daughter, heal yourself," I beg.

"No. You have strived to make… the world… better… You can… do good…"

My daughter clasps my hand. I squeeze it with the last of my waning strength, but then I feel a strange rush of warmth. Her magic. With her last breath, she gives me a second chance at life.

I weep over Olenya, cradling my daughter close. Olesia weeps too, perhaps for my daughter or the destruction wrought this night, perhaps even for herself.

"You killed your wife, but not me," Olesia murmurs. "Why did you curse me instead of killing me?"

"I know the prince thinks you cannot fall in love with someone without talking much, but I disagree. I saw your heart, and while I did not see your ambition, that was not ever a part of your core. At your center, at your heart, you do not seek power."

"I do not need father's advisors. I need new ones," she murmurs. "I need you, and perhaps… in time… I might come to love you."

She kneels before me, clearly not caring if her white gown becomes dirty, and she wipes away my tears.

"Oh, I should not lie to myself. I do love you. That you would go to such lengths for our kingdom, to keep us all safe, even from myself… You should not be an advisor but my husband, my king. Will you rule alongside me?"

"But you are to be queen. You are to rule," I protest. "I am merely a sorcerer."

"A sorcerer with heart. Rule with me, my love."

"Who am I to deny you anything? You never lost my heart, not even when you were a swan by day."

And we kiss then as we do again by the lake filled with swans three days later when we are wed and she crowned queen and myself king. Each day, we strive to do all we can for Russick, for all of her people, even the least subject, and yes, that includes the swans. Each morning, after we break our fast, the queen and I go to the swan's lake and feed them, a reminder of who we once were and who we lost so that we can recall that we should never allow ambition to rule us but instead our hearts.

On the fifth anniversary of our wedding day, my wife and queen turns to me as she holds our babe in her arms. "Who ever knew that a curse could result in happiness?"

"I do not know, but I could not be happier," I reply before kissing our daughter Svanna on the cheek.

"Nor I," Olesia murmurs, and we kiss, a vow to each other to always strive to be this happy for the rest of our lives.

***

OF CURSES AND SWANS is a part of the twisted fairy tale retelling series Once Upon a Darkened Night. To check out the series, click here.

To check out all of Nicole's books, click here.

To join her newsletter, click here.

About the Author

Nicole Zoltack is a USA Today bestselling author who loves to write romances. Of course. She did marry her first kiss, after all!

When she's not writing about fae, vampires, or monster hunters, she enjoys spending time with her loving husband, three energetic young boys, and three precious little girls. She enjoys riding horses (pretending they're unicorns, of course!) and going to the PA Renaissance Faire dressed in garb. She'll also read anything she can get her hands on. Her favorite TV shows are Supernatural and Stranger Things.

Connect with Author Name

Newsletter

FB group

Instagram

Twitter

Bookbub

Goodreads

* * *

A Descendant's Reckoning

Micca Michaels

Chapter One

Mallory

The Rose family, my family has owned property on the East Coast, since the original Puritan's came to the Americas. Even during the darkest times in my family, we were always able to maintain ownership. Many years of court battles between the city and my family over property control finally resulted in the relocation of my family's second ancestral home to Overseer's Ledge, Salem, Massachusetts. Mallory Manor should never have been built in Washington State.

Since the last nail of construction was hammered into place, Mallory Manor has only allowed blood relations to call her home and any others attempting to make her home usually end up as a form of permanent resident. That's one reason people call her cursed. Personally, I feel the manor chooses who will call her home, and if you're too blind to heed the warnings; you forfeit your life.

Standing outside and looking over the manor's red brick exterior sends chills of excited accomplishment racing across my body. I finally feel at home. Most people know the commercialized stories of Salem. Now, they'll learn about the real cause and effect of dabbling in darkness. My family, along with many others suffered because of the summoned darkness, leading to lies, manipulation, gaslighting and the murders of the innocent. Well, one wasn't innocent in the terms of being a witch.

'Excuse me, Miss Mallory Rose?'

Hearing my name, my full name on my family's land gives me chills all over again. It's a proud feeling and not one of wishing to draw blood. That, well, that will come later. Turning to see who's disturbing my peace, I see a man, darker than the night sky, standing near me, not casting a shadow, because he is a shadow.

"Yes, I'm Mallory Rose; who are you and how long has it been?"

'My name is Joffrey Bayley. My father was once a minister in Salem Village. Everyone believes he left choosing money over anything else. I wish the record to be set straight. I shall not rest until his name is untarnished.'

I wasn't expecting the dead to seek me out so quickly, but with the fresh blood spilling during construction of the manor, I should have known it would wake the dead, so to speak. Not bothering to fake an expression, I motion for Mr. Bayley to enter the manor.

Following him up the drive and into the foyer, I announce our arrival to the house. Now that Mallory Manor is home, she is truly sentient, and it would be insulting to treat her as a mere shelter. Requesting that Mr. Bayley follow me into the main study, I pay no attention to the other spirits currently wandering around.

The main study is in the front of the house and during the day has amazing lighting. However, the opposite can be said for after night fall. Darkness takes over this room that's both comforting and disturbing. I'm still unsure of how those two descriptions can describe the same room, but they really do fit.

"Mr. Bayley -"

'Joffrey, if you will?'

"Alright, Joffrey. How exactly do you believe I'm able to aid in clearing your father's name and is it really that important now?"

'I would expect one, such as yourself, would hold great value in one's family name. I am no different ma'am, and demand the wrong be righted, or the true truth told. However, you wish to put it.'

I meant no foul by my comment. Remembering that tones, words and even facial expressions can and will be construed differently over the decades and centuries, leaves me exhausted. I loathe being in a foul mood and displacing it onto others. Joffrey is obviously from the late sixteen hundreds.

"Joffrey, I do apologize for my curtness. It wasn't my intent to insult your feelings on this matter. I, too, am very protective of my family's honor. I will happily try to help with the clearing of your family name, mainly, your father."

Opening one of the boxes sitting on one side of the room, I pull out a notebook and pencil. Walking over to the side of the black leather sofa closest to the fireplace, and taking a seat, I quickly write the few bits of information I already know. Writing Joffrey Bayley is when the name finally sinks in...

"Wait, is your father John Bayley? My research shows him as living here with his wife, two sons and lone daughter. The young girl, your sister, is said to have died of a mysterious ailment that left her skin red and flaking. Your mother is said to have passed away from a broken heart a short time after your sister was laid to rest. The records show your father demanded all the earning contracted to him, so that he and his boys may escape quote, *'this cursed land'* end quote."

'That is full of half-truths. The part concerning my sister and mother is accurate. The part about my father requesting his pay is incorrect. He requested part of his pay to see us back home to Massachusetts Bay. Heated words were exchanged and the three of us left out on our family wagon, being pulled by our mares. Being out of the Village was not safe. Father thought we would arrive in a prompt manner. My father, brother, and I were looking for a secluded area to camp for the night when father was shot. Men forced us off the trail, pulling him from the wagon and hung him. Those animals grabbed my young brother, tossing him into a pond or some small body of water. I didn't fight, as I wanted to save my brother. They threw me in the water as well, but I was not able to find my brother. I survived by grabbing hold of a fallen tree and staying hidden. Those men from the Village killed my father and brother. They tried to kill me and stole all our belongings.'

My heart aches for the injustice done to him and his family. I'm so glad I took a proper shorthand in college. Examining my notes one last time, I look up to see Joffrey almost invisible. That happens when a spirit either hasn't learned to draw energy from their environment or has used up what they had stored.

"Joffrey, look at me, please? I promise to do what I can to right the wrongs done to your family. I am here to do the same for my own family. I can and will say with a small amount of certainty, you and I share a relative at some point, I'll inquire in my records and see what I'm able to come up with. In the meantime, should you find yourself needing quarters, my home is open to you. I just ask that all spirits stay out of my private chambers."

After he offers a slight bow and walks out of the study, I take a deep breath, place my notepad on the table, and make my way into the kitchen. Mallory Manor is quite large for one person, but after everything is seen too, I'm hoping to fill it with laughter and the pitter patter of little feet, making it a family home once again.

Chapter Two

Ambrose

Who in the holy hell thought that moving that manor to Salem would be a good idea? Salem has enough issues without adding that cursed ancestral house to the mix. Technically, it's the second home, but either way it's still fucking cursed and now it's in a cursed town on fucking cursed land. For the love of all the Gods, whoever had this idea is really wanting to learn what FAFO means.

"Hey Ambrose, is that what I think it is? It's not, right? I mean, there isn't a person alive who would move a cursed manor, especially that one, into a cursed town and place it on the most cursed ground our town has. Well, maybe not the most cursed land, but it's a close runner-up. Damn it Ambrose, what's the story?"

How that man can utter so many words without taking a breath, boggles the mind. If I didn't know him as well as I do, I'd swear he's using the dopy, funny stuff. Eddy has always been the high spirited one.

"Eddy, everything you just said, I literally thought to myself not five minutes prior. All I know is a descendant of the Rose family is responsible for this. She had Mallory Manor deconstructed in Washington, loaded on a train, and brought here to her family's original homestead lands. A ten-foot-high privacy fence was installed blocking the view of what was happening."

What in the hell did this ditzy bitch, that obviously doesn't own a lick of common since, do with the memorial and the hanging tree? The privacy fence has yet to be taken down, so no one can see if the monument has been changed. The community decided to leave the trees as they were and to maintain the property. It completely mind fuck's me that someone used the original charters to reclaim the land.

"Hey brother, I can see the memorial and the pathway to the hanging tree. They don't look disturbed. They look cleaned up and serene. Hell, all the landscaping looks amazing. Come here and look through this slot where the board is missing."

Walking over to where Eddy's got one eye up against the fence, pressing against his shoulder to make him move, I take his place to look at things for myself. Eddy's right; everything looks nice and cleaned up. Some serious landscaping has been done.

"May I help you gentlemen or are you satisfied with what you can see through the small opening in my apparently not so private, privacy fence?"

Jumping back at the sudden appearance of ice-blue eyes, I stumble over Eddy's feet and end up taking him to the ground with me. Her maniacal laughter is not only annoying, but uncalled for. The privacy fence shaking draws my attention and then I see it's being taken down section by section.

"I don't see humor in surprising someone to the point they fall to the ground, taking an innocent bystander to the ground with them. I believe you owe each of us an apology."

"Oh, you do? Well then, I do apologize that you and your friend were inconvenienced by the prominent privacy fence I had installed for my own security, and as mentioned before, my privacy. The fact that I scared the hell out of you while you were breeching my privacy and ended up on your ass must be quite humiliating. Not to mention the embarrassment of taking a friend down with you. I am so, well, not sorry."

'What an entitled little -' "Be careful of your thoughts. You never know when someone's listening."

Well, well, well, I guess she really is a Rose. They say Mary Rose is thought to be the only *'true'* witch that was killed during the trials. Mary Rose is said to have had three daughters. Town historical records only register two births. We all assume that one of the births must have died. Learning a Rose reclaimed the family's ancestral lands, we found out Mary Rose had her oldest daughter before settling in Salem Village. Mallory Rose was supposed to join her family after the winter thaw, but never did. I'd hazard to say she's a case of out of sight, out of mind.

"Well, if you'd ever get off the ground, I'd be happy to quell any suspicions you have concerning the memorial and the tree."

Part of me wants to bristle at her boldness and bluntness, but the other part wants to buy her a drink and thank her for being real. What I'm not going to do is miss the opportunity to see all she's doing to the property.

Standing up and holding out my hand to help Eddy to his feet, we both brush off our pants and then our hands. I don't know her, or her name, and she doesn't know us or our names, and she's too trusting turning her back to us. No street smarts got it.

"Ambrose, just because something is not announced out loud doesn't make it true or false. I know who you are, as well as who Eddy is. Salem's change is physical only. No, we're not related from our shared past. No, we don't know each other from another time. As a descendant I carry the blessing of gifts and one of those shows me images of what you're thinking."

Eddy and I give each other a curt glance and continue to follow her. As she slows down and steps to the side, we see the memorial for those wrongly killed so long ago. Further back and to the side, the hanging tree area is cleaner with a historical metal plate. I see nothing disappointing. Turning my attention to the manor, what I see causes me to stumble backwards.

"Ambrose are you alright? Brother, you look as though you saw a ghost. Excuse the expression ma'am."

"There's no need to apologize, Eddy. Our families lived and worked together at some point. I know who and what I am. I'm neither shy, nor embarrassed by that fact. Would you both like a tour of Mallory Manor? No need to say anything; your expressions speak volumes. Follow me."

I know what I saw in the front window when glancing and the manor. It leaves me feeling as though I was seeing my reflection in a mirror. I need to know who that spirit is and what he wants or needs. Trying to discover the truth of our past, lifting all the curses, and giving our family members their due justice. To truly allow them to rest in peace.

No matter where in the manor we walk, I can feel him, but not see him. I may not know Mallory well, but she must be aware there are several spirits roaming her home. And more still entering as we walk her halls.

Chapter Three

Mallory

Having ESP is both a blessing and a curse. Most people have some form of it. Someone may be clairvoyant, while another is telepathic or even telekinetic, and for a few out there, precognitive abilities. I happen to have all the above and it's draining on the best of days.

"Mr. Ambrose, do you know your name is a combination of two family names? *'Amb'* is a variant of *'Amey'*, which is derived from an old French word *'ami'*, meaning *'friend'*. *'Rose'* has a patronymic root, meaning it's given to someone that is a son or is a descendant of a *'Rose'*."

"Miss Rose, are you trying to say you and I may have some form of distant relation?"

"No, Mr. Ambrose, I am certainly not and can assure you I am the last in my line and the only Rose still alive. What I'm trying to explain is your name comes from the combination of two names. When a family voluntarily does that, it's usually out of guilt, respect, greed, or embarrassment over the original family name. Do you happen to know what your sire family's name was, before the change?"

Well hell, Mal, could you possibly sound more insulting and condescending? Not sure you've added enough insult to injury yet. It takes me a moment to realize the two men are no longer beside me. Stopping on the sixth step from the top of the grand staircase, I glance behind me quickly, only to do a double take.

Following the men's visual path, I'm able to see what has them frozen in place. It's quite interesting too. Joffrey Bayley is standing on the top landing, appearing as much alive as I am. I don't think I can remember a spirit ever displaying that trait before.

"Mr. Joffrey Bayley, son of the slandered and notably murdered John Bayley, allow me to introduce you to John Ambrose, descendant of the Paris family and Edward Charles Hale, another descendant of an original Salem Village family. Gentlemen, Joffrey is here for a similar reason to one of my own. He wants a proper accounting of what actually happened to his father, brother and what was done to him. I've promised to make that happen."

"Who, may I ask, in the hell are you to roll into our town, thinking you can just set history straight? On top of that, the fact that you brought this Manor, of all Manors here to be reconstructed, shows your lack of compassion for people, their feelings—"

"Mr. Ambrose, take this warning very carefully. I am not some stranger from the streets who commercialized one of the saddest events and times in this regions' history. I am a descendant of the only genuine witch who was murdered during the trials. Her crimes were caring about her neighbors and helping in times of need. Like health crisis, child birth and so on. She was placed on a makeshift raft, made of weeds, tied to a cross and told that if she drowns, they know her innocence and will pray for her. Where is the logic in that sentence? Who am I? I am the reckoning your town has been warned about."

Joffrey

Watching the power unleash from the delicate rose before me is breathtaking. Mallory Manor is truly where it belongs. I will even go as far to say that the proper person in now her Mistress. I am one that believes events occur for a set reason, and I am fascinated by the events currently unfolding.

Mallory Rose's posture is straight and rigid. The power she expels is strong enough to move her long dark cherry hair, while sending waves across the fabric that make up her long flowing, cotton skirt. The waves in the fabric make it resemble a waterfall. Her blouse is interesting to me. It has holes in it that form a pattern in the still existing material. I heard her refer to it as a shoulder-less lace V-neck blouse.

'Miss Mallory, I would be doing you a disservice if I did not make you aware of the amount of power you are currently releasing.

I would hate for you to accidentally cause harm to someone. May I suggest the gentlemen leave and return on the morrow? I believe a term of separation will settle tempers and possibly give rise to some understanding.'

The two men, upon hearing my words do not take comfort from them. More appropriately, my words disturb them. The living are fickle, finicky, and emotional beings. The emotional part is understandable.

My words also affect Mallory Rose, as her outlet of power is calming down. She is powerful, but young. She will need to calm down, think things through, and just as important, realize who and what a true enemy is, not just a perceived enemy.

Miss Mallory quietly walks to her suite after she watches the two men leave. I remain silent and will spend the evening in the library. I am able to achieve more feats than before I was invited into the manor. So, I shall put my newly acquired skills to use and assist with the set-up of the library.

Chapter Four

Edward

I don't know what in the fuck-knuckle I just saw, but nope. Ok, well, I do know what I saw, but what I saw doesn't actually exist, so therefore I couldn't have seen what I saw, or I thought I saw. Really? What are we supposed to do with that?

"Ambrose, did you see it and her? Tell me you at least saw it, so I know I've not completely lost all sense of reality. She's really a witch and not one of those in a dark alley, under purple lights, a shiny ball and woo-woo shit. She has real ... real ... I don't know, power? Yeah, power surrounding her, blowing her hair, her clothes, her voice changing and holy fuck, did you notice how fucking hot she is?"

"Eddy, can you please stop talking for a minute and let me collect my thoughts? We were just told to leave by a damn ghost. No, a spirit. Ghosts don't talk, right? It's the spirits and poltergeists who speak and move things. Oh, my fucking Gods, what in hell? Now I'm babbling like you. Just shut up until we can meet with the others and talk about this."

There're a few things I can and will say with absolute certainty: Nothing is going to be the same around here, and that lady means more to me than I care to admit. Whoa. Talk about revelations.

"I was sort of thinking the same thing about her. Being near her was like coming home into the warmth for the first time. The moment her ice-blue eyes locked with mine, I know who she's meant to be, and I'll be damned if someone interferes with that."

Ambrose and I look at each other because somehow, he heard my thoughts. Both of us begin to say something at the same time, which causes us to close our mouths, walk in silence and the darkness to our shared home. Ambrose, Corey, Rory, Peter, and I are the only surviving male descendants. Corey inherited his family's entire estate. So, instead of living all over the place, we all live together and run his ancestral home tour and horse-riding business. Not one of us will talk about the odd happenings around the house or the township itself.

Our families, as a collective, have always said that witchcraft isn't real. It's nothing more than ignorant people rebelling against society and making things up to feel they belong. I used to agree with them. I can't anymore and honestly, I'm not sure they believe that narrative anymore.

We only live a few streets down from Mallory Manor. Walking up the driveway, I see the rest of the guys sitting out back watching the house to see if it does anything. They're not, well, they might believe what happened.

"Hey Peter, is your great aunt still visiting? We met the owner of Mallory Manor today, Miss Mallory Rose. There was, well, there was someone else there and we think your aunt can help us understand who he is."

Watching him slide his cell phone out of his pocket, he types out a message to someone. Once he finishes, he sets his blood red case down to continue what he was originally doing. Ambrose is patient. I, on the other hand, want to know what the hell he's waiting on. Just as I'm about to say something, Peter's phone goes off. Then Corey and Rorey's phones go off. Seeing the pattern, Ambrose and I both take our phones out of our pockets and ready them in our hands. Within seconds, they both go off.

Aunt Nancy: Boys, you all are getting the same text. Stay away from Mallory Manor after dark or overnight. That house is sentient. I'll be there shortly.

We're all looking at each other and we feel the panic and urgency in her words. Nodding at each other, we move inside as a group and wait. Peter, knowing his auntie the best, walks straight to the kitchen and brews some coffee. Walking behind him, Corey grabs coffee cups and sets them on a tray. Aunt Nancy is a Salem Elder and historian, so we know there's a story coming.

Rory is stoking the fire in the Parlor's fireplace when I walk in to set a tray of cucumber finger sandwiches on the coffee table. I have no idea why those sandwiches are even a thing, but whatever. Movement catches my attention from the corner of my eye. Turning toward the large bay window, I swear I see Joffrey.

"Ambrose! Ambrose, come here, it's Joffrey!"

Running into the parlor from the library across the way, he comes to a sliding halt when I raise my hand up to point. "Holy fuck! What the fuck does he want?"

"Mallory Rose, Mallory Manor!"

"What the hell are those two bellowing about? There's no one..."

Ambrose and I look at each other and then run outside, looking up the road in the direction of Mallory Manor, we both take off running.

"The manor's on fire! Mallory's in there!"

I can hear the foot fall behind me as the others chase after us. It only takes a few moments for us to arrive at the manor. Not stopping to look around, Ambrose, Corey and I burst through the front door. Stopping to cover our noses and mouths because of the smoke, "Joffrey! Where's Mallory?"

Joffrey's sudden appearance in front of Corey causes him to scream, which we'll rib him about later, and damn near jump in my arms. Ambrose and I don't hesitate to follow him up the staircase, two steps at a time. We only lost track of Corey and Joffrey for a moment. As Corey catches up to us, Joffrey appears at the end of a long hallway.

'Sirs, Miss Mallory Rose is here, and I fear lost to the living. Please sirs, aid her?'

Running to the end of the hallway feels as though it's ever expanding and takes forever. Arriving at the door, Corey's kick splinters the door before I have a second to think about what to do. Rushing into the room, we can barely see that Mallory is on the floor. Ambrose wastes no time scooping her little frame up and then disappears behind us.

Corey and I are looking for the source of the smoke but find nothing. A flare of light suddenly illuminates a set of double doors I hadn't been able to see. Running over to them, Corey and I see the balcony is on fire. Running to the ensuite, Corey turns the tub on, while I'm grabbing towels and throwing them in the tub. Grabbing the water-soaked towels, we run to the balcony doors, open them and throw the towels over the flames.

On our third trip from the bathroom with more towels, we walk in on her bedroom being saturated by the Salem Fire Department. That fire is out, but from the look of it, her bedroom and balcony are complete losses.

Joffrey materializes in the corner of the room, and he looks overcome with worry and anger. Someone did this and we need to find out who and why. Then they can go to prison for attempted murder and arson.

"Shit, Mallory. We need to go check on her."

"Ambrose raced out of here with her, so breathe, I'm sure she's in capable hands, but you go ahead, and I'll stay here and wait for the fire department."

Running out of the room, down the long spooky ass hallway, I hit the stairs and take them three at a time. Running out the front door, I quickly come to a stop when I don't see the ambulance, I know I heard. What I do see, or rather who I see, is someone I shouldn't.

Walking over to Aunt Nancy, I see a mix of emotions cross her face until she looks directly at me and then it's as if she suddenly slips on a mask with a neutral expression. It's not until I'm a bit closer that I see she's not alone. After looking over the group of familiar faces, my stomach suddenly drops.

"Would you all care to explain why you're here? Why do none of you look shocked at what's happening? Nancy, we were expecting you at the house. My gut tells me you all have some explaining to do and not one of us is going to like it."

Their expressions quickly change from pleased as punch to horror. It's the sudden looks of horror that force me to turn around. On the walkway, in front of the memorial, appears to be all those who were victimized during the Salem witch trials. There are some I've never seen before and know nothing about.

Mallory appears in the corner of my eye, causing me to look at her as she steps out of the ambulance I had yet to see. First looking at her manor, and then turning to the crowd of people, she locks eyes with me before looking past me. When I turn to see who, she's staring at, I see Nancy's eyes full of fear. The rest of the group's expressions quickly match her's.

Gasps from behind me cause me to turn back to where Mallory is standing. Mallory's expressions are changing at an indiscernible pace. I'm seeing love to hate, patience to intolerance, peace to violence. Settling on an expression of peace, she looks at those long dead.

"I am Mallory Rose, the last descendant of the only true witch to be murdered during the trials. I bring the dead love, light, and respect. I promise to end all your suffering so you may finally rest in the ways each of you deserves."

Her words not only silence the gathering crowd of people, the noise of the trucks and those she's addressing, but the very wind itself stills. As her eyes scan the living, a soft purple glow surrounds her. As the wind once again wildly tosses her hair around, I'm reminded of her words: *'I am the reckoning your town has been warned about'*.

Made in the USA
Columbia, SC
31 August 2024